KELLY LINK's stories have won the World Fantasy, James Tiptree, Jr and Nebula Awards. Her first collection, *Stranger Things Happen*, was a Salon.com and *Village Voice* book of the year. She is the editor of the anthology *Trampoline*, and co-editor of the zine *Lady Churchill's Rosebud Wristlet*. With Ellen Datlow and Gavin J. Grant she edits *The Year's Best Fantasy and Horror* (St. Martin's Press).

Link lives in Northampton, Massachusetts and her website is www.kellylink.net

SHELLEY JACKSON has illustrated many children's books including her own, *The Old Woman and the Wave*. She is the author of *The Melancholy of Anatomy*, *Patchwork Girl*, *Skin*, a story told in tattoos, and *Half Life*. She lives in Brooklyn, New York, and her website is www.ineradicablestain.com

Praise for Kelly Link:

'Kelly Link's stories are dazzling, funny, scary, and sexy, but only when they're not all of these at once. Kelly Link has strangeness, charm and spin to spare. Writers better than this don't happen'
KAREN JOY FOWLER

'The dream-logic of *Magic for Beginners* is intoxicating. These stories will come alive, put on zoot suits, and wrestle you to the ground. They want you and you will be theirs' ALICE SEBOLD

'A new short story collection by Kelly Link — and once more, for a little while, the world is worth saving. Kelly Link owns the most darkly playful voice in American fiction since Donald Barthelme. She is pushing the short story into places that it hasn't yet been pushed, while somehow managing to maintain a powerful connection to traditional forms and storytelling values'
MICHAEL CHABON

'Kelly Link is the exact best and strangest and funniest short story writer on earth that you have never heard of at the exact moment you are reading these words and making them slightly inexact. Now pay for the book' JONATHAN LETHEM

'I've not been so moved and affected — and dammit, yes, inspired — by a book for a long time' CHINA MIÉVILLE

'The most impressive writer of her generation' PETER STRAUB

'Link's stories play in a place few writers go, a netherworld between literature and fantasy, Alice Munro and JK Rowling, and Link finds truths there that most authors wouldn't dare touch' *Time* Book of the Year

'I couldn't put these stories out of my mind. That sort of resonance, that lingering, haunting effect, is the product of real magic and Kelly Link is no doubt a sorceress to be reckoned with' *New York Times*

'Kelly Link's exquisite stories mix the aggravations and epiphanies of everyday life with the stuff that myths, dreams and nightmares are made of. Some of them are very scary, others are immensely sad, many are funny and all of them are written in prose so flawless you almost forget how much elemental human chaos they contain'   LAURA MILLER, *Salon* Book of the Year

'Lovers of short fiction should fall over themselves getting out the door to find a copy'   *Washington Post*

'Sly and charming, tart and wise'   *San Francisco Chronicle*

Also by Kelly Link

Stranger Things Happen
Trampoline (editor)
Lady Churchill's Rosebud Wristlet (co-editor)
The Year's Best Fantasy & Horror (co-editor)

Magic for Beginners

KELLY LINK

Magic for Beginners

Illustrated by Shelley Jackson

HARPER PERENNIAL

London, New York, Toronto and Sydney

Harper Perennial
An imprint of HarperCollins*Publishers*
77–85 Fulham Palace Road
Hammersmith
London w6 8jb

www.harperperennial.co.uk

This edition published by Harper Perennial 2007
1

First published in the USA by Small Beer Press in 2005

Cover painting by Shelley Jackson, based on *Lady with an Ermine* by
Leonardo da Vinci, held in The Czartoryskich Museum, Krakow

A catalogue record for this book is available from the British Library

ISBN-13 978-0-00-724200-9
ISBN-10 0-00-724200-X

Printed and bound in Great Britain by Clays Ltd, St Ives plc

Contents

*For Gavin
and the Avenue Victor Hugo Bookshop,
where I met him.*

Before the raiding party arrived, the village packed up all of their belongings and moved into the handbag.

The Faery Handbag

I USED TO GO TO THRIFT STORES WITH MY FRIENDS. We'd take the train into Boston, and go to The Garment District, which is this huge vintage clothing warehouse. Everything is arranged by color, and somehow that makes all of the clothes beautiful. It's kind of like if you went through the wardrobe in the Narnia books, only instead of finding Aslan and the White Witch and horrible Eustace, you found this magic clothing world—instead of talking animals, there were feather boas and wedding dresses and bowling shoes, and paisley shirts and Doc Martens and everything hung up on racks so that first you have black dresses, all together, like the world's largest indoor funeral, and then blue dresses—all the blues you can imagine—and then red dresses and so on. Pink reds and orangey reds and purple reds and exit-light reds and candy reds. Sometimes I would close my eyes and Natasha and Natalie and Jake would drag me over to a rack, and rub a dress against my hand. "Guess what color this is."

We had this theory that you could learn how to tell, just by feeling, what color something was. For example, if you're sitting on a lawn, you can tell what color green the grass is, with your eyes closed, depending on how silky-rubbery it feels. With clothing, stretchy velvet stuff always feels red when your eyes are closed, even if it's not red. Natasha was always best at guessing colors, but Natasha is also best at cheating at games and not getting caught.

One time we were looking through kids' T-shirts and we found a

Muppets T-shirt that had belonged to Natalie in third grade. We knew it belonged to her, because it still had her name inside, where her mother had written it in permanent marker when Natalie went to summer camp. Jake bought it back for her, because he was the only one who had money that weekend. He was the only one who had a job.

Maybe you're wondering what a guy like Jake is doing in The Garment District with a bunch of girls. The thing about Jake is that he always has a good time, no matter what he's doing. He likes everything, and he likes everyone, but he likes me best of all. Wherever he is now, I bet he's having a great time and wondering when I'm going to show up. I'm always running late. But he knows that.

We had this theory that things have life cycles, the way that people do. The life cycle of wedding dresses and feather boas and T-shirts and shoes and handbags involves The Garment District. If clothes are good, or even if they're bad in an interesting way, The Garment District is where they go when they die. You can tell that they're dead, because of the way that they smell. When you buy them, and wash them, and start wearing them again, and they start to smell like you, that's when they reincarnate. But the point is, if you're looking for a particular thing, you just have to keep looking for it. You have to look hard.

Down in the basement at The Garment District they sell clothing and beat-up suitcases and teacups by the pound. You can get eight pounds' worth of prom dresses—a slinky black dress, a poufy lavender dress, a swirly pink dress, a silvery, starry lamé dress so fine you could pass it through a key ring—for eight dollars. I go there every week, hunting for Grandmother Zofia's faery handbag.

The faery handbag: It's huge and black and kind of hairy. Even when your eyes are closed, it feels black. As black as black ever gets, like if you touch it, your hand might get stuck in it, like tar or black quicksand or when you stretch out your hand at night, to turn on a light, but all you feel is darkness.

Fairies live inside it. I know what that sounds like, but it's true.

ᘓ

Grandmother Zofia said it was a family heirloom. She said that it was over two hundred years old. She said that when she died, I had to look after it. Be its guardian. She said that it would be my responsibility.

I said that it didn't look that old, and that they didn't have handbags two hundred years ago, but that just made her cross. She said, "So then tell me, Genevieve, darling, where do you think old ladies used to put their reading glasses and their heart medicine and their knitting needles?"

I know that no one is going to believe any of this. That's okay. If I thought you would, then I couldn't tell you. Promise me that you won't believe a word. That's what Zofia used to say to me when she told me stories. At the funeral, my mother said, half-laughing and half-crying, that her mother was the world's best liar. I think she thought maybe Zofia wasn't really dead. But I went up to Zofia's coffin, and I looked her right in the eyes. They were closed. The funeral parlor had made her up with blue eyeshadow, and blue eyeliner. She looked like she was going to be a news anchor on Fox television, instead of dead. It was creepy and it made me even sadder than I already was. But I didn't let that distract me.

"Okay, Zofia," I whispered. "I know you're dead, but this is important. You know exactly how important this is. Where's the handbag? What did you do with it? How do I find it? What am I supposed to do now?"

Of course, she didn't say a word. She just lay there, this little smile on her face, as if she thought the whole thing—death, blue eyeshadow, Jake, the handbag, faeries, Scrabble, Baldeziwurlekistan, all of it—was a joke. She always did have a weird sense of humor. That's why she and Jake got along so well.

I grew up in a house next door to the house where my mother lived when she was a little girl. Her mother, Zofia Swink, my grandmother, babysat me while my mother and father were at work.

Zofia never looked like a grandmother. She had long black hair, which she plaited up in spiky towers. She had large blue eyes. She was taller than my father. She looked like a spy or ballerina or a lady pirate or a rock star.

She acted like one too. For example, she never drove anywhere. She rode a bike. It drove my mother crazy. "Why can't you act your age?" she'd say, and Zofia would just laugh.

Zofia and I played Scrabble all the time. Zofia always won, even though her English wasn't all that great, because we'd decided that she was allowed to use Baldeziwurleki vocabulary. Baldeziwurlekistan is where Zofia was born, over two hundred years ago. That's what Zofia said. (My grandmother claimed to be over two hundred years old. Or maybe even older. Sometimes she claimed that she'd even met Genghis Khan. He was much shorter than her. I probably don't have time to tell that story.) Baldeziwurlekistan is also an incredibly valuable word in Scrabble points, even though it doesn't exactly fit on the board. Zofia put it down the first time we played. I was feeling pretty good because I'd gotten forty-one points for *zippery* on my turn.

Zofia kept rearranging her letters on her tray. Then she looked over at me, as if daring me to stop her, and put down *eziwurlekistan*, after *bald*. She used *delicious, zippery, wishes, kismet*, and *needle*, and made *to* into *toe*. *Baldeziwurlekistan* went all the way across the board and then trailed off down the righthand side.

I started laughing.

"I used up all my letters," Zofia said. She licked her pencil and started adding up points.

"That's not a word," I said. "*Baldeziwurlekistan* is not a word. Besides, you can't do that. You can't put an eighteen-letter word on a board that's fifteen squares across."

"Why not? It's a country," Zofia said. "It's where I was born, little darling."

"Challenge," I said. I went and got the dictionary and looked it up. "There's no such place."

"Of course there isn't nowadays," Zofia said. "It wasn't a very big place, even when it was a place. But you've heard of Samarkand, and Uzbekistan and the Silk Road and Genghis Khan. Haven't I told you about meeting Genghis Khan?"

I looked up Samarkand. "Okay," I said. "Samarkand is a real place. A real word. But Baldeziwurlekistan isn't."

"They call it something else now," Zofia said. "But I think it's important to remember where we come from. I think it's only fair that I get to use Baldeziwurleki words. Your English is so much better than me. Promise me something, mouthful of dumpling, a small, small thing. You'll remember its real name. Baldeziwurlekistan. Now when I add it up, I get three hundred and sixty-eight points. Could that be right?"

If you called the faery handbag by its right name, it would be something like *orzipanikanikcz*, which means the "bag of skin where the world lives," only Zofia never spelled that word the same way twice. She said you had to spell it a little differently each time. You never wanted to spell it exactly the right way, because that would be dangerous.

I called it the faery handbag because I put *faery* down on the Scrabble board once. Zofia said that you spelled it with an *i*, not an *e*. She looked it up in the dictionary, and lost a turn.

Zofia said that in Baldeziwurlekistan they used a board and tiles for divination, prognostication, and sometimes even just for fun. She said it was a little like playing Scrabble. That's probably why she turned out to be so good at Scrabble. The Baldeziwurlekistanians used their tiles and board to communicate with the people who lived under the hill. The people who lived under the hill knew the future. The Baldeziwurlekistanians gave them fermented milk and honey, and the young women of the village used to go and lie out on the hill and sleep under the stars. Apparently the people under the hill were pretty cute. The important thing was that you never went down into the hill and spent the night there, no matter how cute the guy from under the hill was. If you did, even if you spent only a single night under the hill, when you came out again, a hundred years might have passed. "Remember that," Zofia said to me. "It doesn't matter how cute a guy is. If he wants you to come back to his place, it isn't a good idea. It's okay to fool around, but don't spend the night."

Every once in a while, a woman from under the hill would marry a man from the village, even though it never ended well. The problem was that the women under the hill were terrible cooks. They couldn't get used to the way time worked in the village, which meant that supper always got burnt, or else it wasn't cooked long enough. But they couldn't stand to be criticized. It hurt their feelings. If their village husband complained, or even if he looked like he wanted to complain, that was it. The woman from under the hill went back to her home, and even if her husband went and begged and pleaded and apologized, it might be three years or thirty years or a few generations before she came back out.

Even the best, happiest marriages between the Baldeziwurlekistanians and the people under the hill fell apart when the children got old enough to complain about dinner. But everyone in the village had some hill blood in them.

"It's in you," Zofia said, and kissed me on the nose. "Passed down from my grandmother and her mother. It's why we're so beautiful."

When Zofia was nineteen, the shaman-priestess in her village threw the tiles and discovered that something bad was going to happen. A raiding party was coming. There was no point in fighting them. They would burn down everyone's houses and take the young men and women for slaves. And it was even worse than that. There was going to be an earthquake as well, which was bad news because usually, when raiders showed up, the village went down under the hill for a night and when they came out again, the raiders would have been gone for months or decades or even a hundred years. But this earthquake was going to split the hill right open.

The people under the hill were in trouble. Their home would be destroyed, and they would be doomed to roam the face of the earth, weeping and lamenting their fate until the sun blew out and the sky cracked and the seas boiled and the people dried up and turned to dust and blew away. So the shaman-priestess went and divined some more, and the people under the hill told her to kill a black dog and skin it and use the skin to make a purse big enough to hold a chicken, an egg, and a cooking pot. So she did, and then the people under the hill made the inside of the purse big enough to hold all of the village and all of the people under the hill and mountains and forests and seas and rivers and lakes and orchards and a sky and stars and spirits and fabulous monsters and sirens and dragons and dryads and mermaids and beasties and all the little gods that the Baldeziwurlekistanians and the people under the hill worshipped.

"Your purse is made out of dog skin?" I said. "That's disgusting!"

"Little dear pet," Zofia said, looking wistful, "Dog is delicious. To Baldeziwurlekistanians, dog is a delicacy."

Before the raiding party arrived, the village packed up all of their belongings and moved into the handbag. The clasp was made out of bone. If you opened it one way, then it was just a purse big enough to hold a chicken and an egg and a clay cooking pot, or else a pair of reading glasses and a library book and a pillbox. If you opened the clasp another way, then you found yourself in a little boat floating at the mouth of a river. On either side of you was forest, where the Baldeziwurlekistanian villagers and the people under the hill made their new settlement.

If you opened the handbag the wrong way, though, you found yourself in a dark land that smelled like blood. That's where the guardian of the purse (the dog whose skin had been been sewn into a purse) lived. The guardian had no skin. Its howl made blood come out of your ears and nose. It tore apart anyone who turned the clasp in the opposite direction and opened the purse in the wrong way.

"Here is the wrong way to open the handbag," Zofia said. She twisted the clasp, showing me how she did it. She opened the mouth of the purse, but not very wide, and held it up to me. "Go ahead, darling, and listen for a second."

I put my head near the handbag, but not too near. I didn't hear anything. "I don't hear anything," I said.

"The poor dog is probably asleep," Zofia said. "Even nightmares have to sleep now and then."

After he got expelled, everybody at school called Jake Houdini instead of Jake. Everybody except for me. I'll explain why, but you have to be patient.

It's hard work telling everything in the right order.

Jake is smarter and also taller than most of our teachers. Not quite as tall as me. We've known each other since third grade. Jake has always been in love with me. He says he was in love with me even before third grade, even before we ever met. It took me a while to fall in love with Jake.

In third grade, Jake knew everything already, except how to make friends. He used to follow me around all day long. It made me so mad that I kicked him in the knee. When that didn't work, I threw his backpack out the window of the school bus. That didn't work either, but the next year Jake took some tests and the school decided that he could skip fourth and fifth grade. Even I felt sorry for Jake then. Sixth grade didn't work out. When the sixth graders wouldn't stop flushing his head down the toilet, he went out and caught a skunk and set it loose in the boys' locker room.

The school was going to suspend him for the rest of the year, but instead Jake took two years off while his mother homeschooled him. He learned Latin and Hebrew and Greek, how to write sestinas, how to make sushi, how to play bridge, and even how to knit. He learned fencing and ballroom dancing. He worked in a soup kitchen and made a Super 8 movie about Civil War reenactors who play extreme croquet in full costume instead of firing off cannons. He started learning how to play guitar. He even wrote a novel. I've never read it—he says it was awful.

When he came back two years later, because his mother had cancer for the first time, the school put him back with our year, in seventh grade. He was still way too smart, but he was finally smart enough to figure out how to fit in. Plus he was good at soccer and he was yummy. Did I mention that he played guitar? Every girl in school had a crush on Jake, but he used to come home after school with me and play Scrabble with Zofia and ask her about Baldeziwurlekistan.

Jake's mom was named Cynthia. She collected ceramic frogs and knock-knock jokes. When we were in ninth grade, she had cancer again. When she died, Jake smashed all of her frogs. That was the first funeral I ever went to. A few months later, Jake's father asked Jake's fencing teacher out on a date. They got married right after the school expelled Jake for his AP project on Houdini. That was the first wedding I ever went to. Jake and I stole a bottle of wine and drank it, and I threw up in the swimming pool at the country club. Jake threw up all over my shoes.

So, anyway, the village and the people under the hill lived happily ever after for a few weeks in the handbag, which they had tied around a rock in a dry well that the people under the hill had determined would survive the earthquake. But some of the Baldeziwurlekistanians wanted to come out again and see what was going on in the world. Zofia was one of them. It had been summer when they went into the bag, but when they came out again, and climbed out of the well, snow was falling and their village was ruins and crumbly old rubble. They walked through the snow, Zofia carrying the handbag, until they came to another village, one that they'd never seen before. Everyone in that village was packing up their belongings and leaving, which gave Zofia and her friends a bad feeling. It seemed to be just the same as when they went into the handbag.

They followed the refugees, who seemed to know where they were going, and finally everyone came to a city. Zofia had never seen such a place. There were trains and electric lights and movie theaters, and there were people shooting each other. Bombs were falling. A war going on. Most of the villagers decided to climb right back inside the handbag, but Zofia volunteered to stay in the world and look after the handbag. She had fallen in love with movies and silk stockings and with a young man, a Russian deserter.

Zofia and the Russian deserter married and had many adventures and finally came to America, where my mother was born. Now and then Zofia would consult the tiles and talk to the people who lived in the handbag and they would tell her how best to avoid trouble and how she and her husband could make some money. Every now and then one of the Baldeziwurlek-istanians or one of the people from under the hill came out of the handbag and wanted to go grocery shopping, or to a movie or an amusement park to ride on roller coasters, or to the library.

9

The more advice Zofia gave her husband, the more money they made. Her husband became curious about Zofia's handbag, because he could see that there was something odd about it, but Zofia told him to mind his own business. He began to spy on Zofia, and saw that strange men and women were coming in and out of the house. He became convinced that either Zofia was a spy for the Communists, or maybe that she was having affairs. They fought and he drank more and more, and finally he threw away her divination tiles. "Russians make bad husbands," Zofia told me. Finally, one night while Zofia was sleeping, her husband opened the bone clasp and climbed inside the handbag.

"I thought he'd left me," Zofia said. "For almost twenty years I thought he'd left me and your mother and taken off for California. Not that I minded. I was tired of being married and cooking dinners and cleaning house for someone else. It's better to cook what I want to eat, and clean up when I decide to clean up. It was harder on your mother, not having a father. That was the part that I minded most.

"Then it turned out that he hadn't run away after all. He spent one night in the handbag and came out again twenty years later, exactly as handsome as I remembered, and enough time had passed that I had forgiven him all the quarrels. We made up and it was all very romantic and then when we had another fight the next morning, he went and kissed your mother, who had slept right through his visit, on the cheek, and then he climbed right back inside the handbag. I didn't see him again for another twenty years. The last time he showed up, we went to see *Star Wars* and he liked it so much that he went back inside the handbag to tell everyone else about it. In a couple of years they'll all show up and want to see it on video and all of the sequels too."

"Tell them not to bother with the prequels," I said.

The thing about Zofia and libraries is that she's always losing library books. She says that she hasn't lost them, and in fact that they aren't even overdue, really. It's just that even one week inside the faery handbag is a lot longer in library-world time. So what is she supposed to do about it?

The librarians all hate Zofia. She's banned from using any of the branches in our area. When I was eight, she got me to go to the library for her and check out biographies and science books and Georgette Heyer romance novels. My mother was livid when she found out, but it was too late. Zofia had already misplaced most of them.

It's really hard to write about somebody as if they're really dead. I still think Zofia must be sitting in her living room, in her house, watching some old horror movie, dropping popcorn into her handbag. She's waiting for me to come over and play Scrabble.

Nobody is ever going to return those library books now.

My mother used to come home from work and roll her eyes. "Have you been telling them your fairy stories?" she'd say. "Genevieve, your grandmother is a horrible liar."

Zofia would fold up the Scrabble board and shrug at me and Jake. "I'm a wonderful liar," she'd say. "I'm the best liar in the world. Promise me you won't believe a single word."

But she wouldn't tell the story of the faery handbag to Jake. Only the old Baldeziwurlekistanian folktales and fairy tales about the people under the hill. She told him about how she and her husband made it all the way across Europe, hiding in haystacks and in barns. What she told me was how once, when her husband went off to find food, a farmer found her hiding in his chicken coop and tried to rape her. But she opened up the faery handbag in the way she showed me, and the dog came out and ate the farmer and all his chickens too.

She was teaching Jake and me how to curse in Baldeziwurleki. I also know how to say *I love you*, but I'm not going to ever say it to anyone again, except to Jake, when I find him.

When I was eight, I believed everything Zofia told me. By the time I was thirteen, I didn't believe a single word. When I was fifteen, I saw a man come out of her house and get on Zofia's three-speed bicycle and ride down the street. He wore funny clothes. He was a lot younger than my mother and father, and even though I'd never seen him before, he was familiar. I followed him on my bike, all the way to the grocery store. I waited just past the checkout lanes while he bought peanut butter, Jack Daniel's, half a dozen instant cameras, and at least sixty packs of Reese's peanut butter cups, three bags of Hershey's Kisses, a handful of Milky Way bars and other stuff from the rack of checkout candy. While the checkout clerk was helping him bag up all of that chocolate, he looked up and saw me. "Genevieve?" he said. "That's your name, right?"

I turned and ran out of the store. He grabbed up the bags and ran after me. I don't even think he got his change back. I was still running away, and then one of the straps on my flip-flops popped out of the sole, the way they do, and that made me really angry so I just stopped. I turned around.

"Who are you?" I said.

But I already knew. He looked like he could have been my mom's younger brother. He was really cute. I could see why Zofia had fallen in love with him.

His name was Rustan. Zofia told my parents that he was an expert in Baldeziwurlekistanian folklore who would be staying with her for a few days. She brought him over for dinner. Jake was there too, and I could tell that Jake knew something was up. Everybody except my dad knew something was going on.

"You mean Baldeziwurlekistan is a real place?" my mother asked Rustan. "My mother is telling the truth?"

I could see that Rustan was having a hard time with that one. He obviously wanted to say that his wife was a horrible liar, but then where would he be? Then he couldn't be the person that he was supposed to be.

There were probably a lot of things that he wanted to say. What he said was, "This is really good pizza."

Rustan took a lot of pictures at dinner. The next day I went with him to get the pictures developed. He'd brought back some film with him, with pictures he'd taken inside the faery handbag, but those didn't come out well. Maybe the film was too old. We got doubles of the pictures from dinner so that I could have some too. There's a great picture of Jake, sitting outside on the porch. He's laughing, and he has his hand up to his mouth, like he's going to catch the laugh. I have that picture up on my computer, and also up on my wall over my bed.

I bought a Cadbury Creme Egg for Rustan. Then we shook hands and he kissed me once on each cheek. "Give one of those kisses to your mother," he said, and I thought about how the next time I saw him, I might be Zofia's age, and he would be only a few days older. The next time I saw him, Zofia would be dead. Jake and I might have kids. That was too weird.

I know Rustan tried to get Zofia to go back with him, to live in the handbag, but she wouldn't.

"It makes me dizzy in there," she used to tell me. "And they don't have movie theaters. And I have to look after your mother and you. Maybe when you're old enough to look after the handbag, I'll poke my head inside, just long enough for a little visit."

I didn't fall in love with Jake because he was smart. I'm pretty smart myself. I know that smart doesn't mean nice, or even mean that you have a lot of common sense. Look at all the trouble smart people get themselves into.

I didn't fall in love with Jake because he could make maki rolls and had a black belt in fencing, or whatever it is that you get if you're good in fencing. I didn't fall in love with Jake because he plays guitar. He's a better soccer player than he is a guitar player.

Those were the reasons why I went out on a date with Jake. That, and because he asked me. He asked if I wanted to go see a movie, and I asked if I could bring my grandmother and Natalie and Natasha. He said sure and so all five of us sat and watched *Bring It On* and every once in a while Zofia dropped a couple of Milk Duds or some popcorn into her purse. I don't know if she was feeding the dog, or if she'd opened the purse the right way, and was throwing food at her husband.

I fell in love with Jake because he told stupid knock-knock jokes to Natalie, and told Natasha that he liked her jeans. I fell in love with Jake when he took me and Zofia home. He walked her up to her front door and then he walked me up to mine. I fell in love with Jake when he didn't try to kiss me. The thing is, I was nervous about the whole kissing thing. Most guys think that they're better at it than they really are. Not that I think I'm a real genius at kissing either, but I don't think kissing should be a competitive sport. It isn't tennis.

Natalie and Natasha and I used to practice kissing with each other. Just for practice. We got pretty good at it. We could see why kissing was supposed to be fun.

But Jake didn't try to kiss me. Instead he just gave me this really big hug. He put his face in my hair and he sighed. We stood there like that, and then finally I said, "What are you doing?"

"I just wanted to smell your hair," he said.

"Oh," I said. That made me feel weird, but in a good way. I stuck my nose in his hair, which is brown and curly. I smelled it. We stood there and smelled each other's hair, and I felt so good. I felt so happy.

Jake said into my hair, "Do you know that actor John Cusack?"

I said, "Yeah. One of Zofia's favorite movies is *Better Off Dead*. We watch it all the time."

"So he likes to go up to women and smell their armpits."

"Gross!" I said. "That's such a lie! What are you doing now? That tickles."

"I'm smelling your ear," Jake said.

Jake's hair smelled like iced tea with honey in it, after all the ice has melted.

Kissing Jake is like kissing Natalie or Natasha, except that it isn't just for fun. It feels like something there isn't a word for in Scrabble.

The deal with Houdini is that Jake got interested in him during Advanced Placement American History. He and I were both put in tenth-grade history.

We were doing biography projects. I was studying Joseph McCarthy. My grandmother had all sorts of stories about McCarthy. She hated him for what he did to Hollywood.

Jake didn't turn in his project—instead he told everyone in our AP class except for Mr. Streep (we call him Meryl) to meet him at the gym on Saturday. When we showed up, Jake reenacted one of Houdini's escapes with a laundry bag, handcuffs, a gym locker, bicycle chains, and the school's swimming pool. It took him three and a half minutes to get free, and this guy named Roger took a bunch of photos and then put the photos online. One of the photos ended up in the *Boston Globe*, and Jake got expelled. The really ironic thing was that while his mom was in the hospital, Jake had applied to M.I.T. He did it for his mom. He thought that way she'd have to stay alive. She was so excited about M.I.T. A couple of days after he'd been expelled, right after the wedding, while his dad and the fencing instructor were in Bermuda, he got an acceptance letter in the mail and a phone call from this guy in the admissions office who explained why they had to withdraw the acceptance.

My mother wanted to know why I let Jake wrap himself up in bicycle chains and then watched while Peter and Michael pushed him into the deep end of the school pool. I said that Jake had a backup plan. Ten more seconds and we were all going to jump into the pool and open the locker and get him out of there. I was crying when I said that. Even before he got in the locker, I knew how stupid Jake was being. Afterwards, he promised me that he'd never do anything like that again.

That was when I told him about Zofia's husband, Rustan, and about Zofia's handbag. How stupid am I?

So I guess you can figure out what happened next. The problem is that Jake believed me about the handbag. We spent a lot of time over at Zofia's, playing Scrabble. Zofia never let the faery handbag out of her sight. She even took it with her when she went to the bathroom. I think she even slept with it under her pillow.

I didn't tell her that I'd said anything to Jake. I wouldn't ever have told anybody else about it. Not Natasha. Not even Natalie, who is the most responsible person in all of the world. Now, of course, if the handbag turns up and Jake still hasn't come back, I'll have to tell Natalie. Somebody has to keep an eye on the stupid thing while I go find Jake.

What worries me is that maybe one of the Baldeziwurlekistanians or one of the people under the hill or maybe even Rustan popped out of the handbag to run an errand and got worried when Zofia wasn't there. Maybe they'll come looking for her and bring it back. Maybe they know I'm supposed to look after it now. Or maybe they took it and hid it somewhere. Maybe someone turned it in at the lost-and-found at the library and that stupid librarian called the FBI. Maybe scientists at the Pentagon are examining the handbag right now. Testing it. If Jake comes out, they'll think he's a spy or a superweapon or an alien or something. They're not going to just let him go.

Everyone thinks Jake ran away, except for my mother, who is convinced that he was trying out another Houdini escape and is probably lying at the bottom of a lake somewhere. She hasn't said that to me, but I can see her thinking it. She keeps making cookies for me.

What happened is that Jake said, "Can I see that for just a second?"

He said it so casually that I think he caught Zofia off guard. She was reaching into the purse for her wallet. We were standing in the lobby of the movie theater on a Monday morning. Jake was behind the snack counter. He'd gotten a job there. He was wearing this stupid red paper hat and some kind of apron bib thing. He was supposed to ask us if we wanted to supersize our drinks.

He reached over the counter and took Zofia's handbag right out of her hand. He closed it and then he opened it again. I think he opened it the right way. I don't think he ended up in the dark place. He said to me and Zofia, "I'll be right back." And then he wasn't there anymore. It was just me and Zofia and the handbag, lying there on the counter where he'd dropped it.

If I'd been fast enough, I think I could have followed him. But Zofia had been guardian of the faery handbag for a lot longer. She snatched the bag back and glared at me. "He's a very bad boy," she said. She was absolutely furious. "You're better off without him, Genevieve, I think."

"Give me the handbag," I said. "I have to go get him."

"It isn't a toy, Genevieve," she said. "It isn't a game. This isn't Scrabble. He comes back when he comes back. If he comes back."

"Give me the handbag," I said. "Or I'll take it from you."

She held the handbag up high over her head, so that I couldn't reach it. I hate people who are taller than me. "What are you going to do now?" Zofia said. "Are you going to knock me down? Are you going to steal the handbag? Are you going to go away and leave me here to explain to your parents where you've gone? Are you going to say good-bye to your friends? When you come out again, they will have gone to college. They'll have jobs and babies and houses and they won't even recognize you. Your mother will be an old woman and I will be dead."

"I don't care," I said. I sat down on the sticky red carpet in the lobby and started to cry. Someone wearing a little metal name tag came over and asked if we were okay. His name was MISSY. Or maybe he was wearing someone else's tag.

"We're fine," Zofia said. "My granddaughter has the flu."

She took my hand and pulled me up. She put her arm around me and we walked out of the theater. We never even got to see the stupid movie. We never even got to see another movie together. I don't ever want to go see another movie. The problem is, I don't want to see unhappy endings. And I don't know if I believe in the happy ones.

"I have a plan," Zofia said. "I will go find Jake. You will stay here and look after the handbag."

"You won't come back either," I said. I cried even harder. Or if you do, I'll be like a hundred years old and Jake will still be sixteen."

"Everything will be okay," Zofia said. I wish I could tell you how beautiful she looked right then. It didn't matter if she was lying or if she actually knew that everything was going to be okay. The important thing was how she looked when she said it. She said, with absolute certainty, or maybe with all the skill of a very skillful liar, "My plan will work. First we go to the library, though. One of the people under the hill just brought back an Agatha Christie mystery, and I need to return it."

"We're going to the library?" I said. "Why don't we just go home and play Scrabble for a while." You probably think I was just being sarcastic here, and I was being sarcastic. But Zofia gave me a sharp look. She knew that if I was being sarcastic that my brain was working again. She knew that I knew she was stalling for time. She knew that I was coming up with my own plan, which was a lot like Zofia's plan, except that I was the one who went into the handbag. *How* was the part I was working on.

"We could do that," she said. "Remember, when you don't know what to do, it never hurts to play Scrabble. It's like reading the I Ching or tea leaves."

"Can we please just hurry?" I said.

Zofia just looked at me. "Genevieve, we have plenty of time. If you're going to look after the handbag, you have to remember that. You have to be patient. Can you be patient?"

"I can try," I told her. I'm trying, Zofia. I'm trying really hard. But it isn't fair. Jake is off having adventures and talking to talking animals, and who knows, learning how to fly and some beautiful three-thousand-year-old girl from under the hill is teaching him how to speak fluent Baldeziwurleki. I bet she lives in a house that runs around on chicken legs, and she tells Jake that she'd love to hear him play something on the guitar. Maybe you'll kiss her, Jake, because she's put a spell on you. But whatever you do, don't go up into her house. Don't fall asleep in her bed. Come back soon, Jake, and bring the handbag with you.

I hate those movies, those books, where some guy gets to go off and have adventures and meanwhile the girl has to stay home and wait. I'm a feminist. I subscribe to *Bust* magazine, and I watch *Buffy* reruns. I don't believe in that kind of shit.

❧

We hadn't been in the library for five minutes before Zofia picked up a biography of Carl Sagan and dropped it in her purse. She was definitely stalling for time. She was trying to come up with a plan that would counteract the plan that she knew I was planning. I wondered what she thought I was planning. It was probably much better than anything I'd come up with.

"Don't do that!" I said.

"Don't worry," Zofia said. "Nobody was watching."

"I don't care if nobody saw! What if Jake's sitting there in the boat, or what if he was coming back and you just dropped it on his head!"

"It doesn't work that way," Zofia said. Then she said, "It would serve him right, anyway."

That was when the librarian came up to us. She had a name tag on as well. I was so sick of people and their stupid name tags. I'm not even going to tell you what her name was. "I saw that," the librarian said.

"Saw what?" Zofia said. She smiled down at the librarian, like she was Queen of the Library, and the librarian was a petitioner.

The librarian stared hard at her. "I know you," she said, almost sounding awed, like she was a weekend bird-watcher who had just seen Bigfoot. "We have your picture on the office wall. You're Ms. Swink. You aren't allowed to check out books here."

"That's ridiculous," Zofia said. She was at least two feet taller than the librarian. I felt a bit sorry for the librarian. After all, Zofia had just stolen a seven-day book. She probably wouldn't return it for a hundred years. My mother has always made it clear that it's my job to protect other people from Zofia. I guess I was Zofia's guardian before I became the guardian of the handbag.

The librarian reached up and grabbed Zofia's handbag. She was small but she was strong. She jerked the handbag and Zofia stumbled and fell back against a work desk. I couldn't believe it. Everyone except for me was getting a look at Zofia's handbag. What kind of guardian was I going to be?

"Genevieve," Zofia said. She held my hand very tightly, and I looked at her. She looked wobbly and pale. She said, "I feel very bad about all of this. Tell your mother I said so."

Then she said one last thing, but I think it was in Baldeziwurleki.

The librarian said, "I saw you put a book in here. Right here." She opened the handbag and peered inside. Out of the handbag came a long, lonely, ferocious, utterly hopeless scream of rage. I don't ever want to hear that noise again. Everyone in the library looked up. The librarian made a choking noise and threw Zofia's handbag away from her. A little trickle of blood came out of her nose and a drop fell on the floor. What I thought at first was that it was just plain luck that the handbag was closed when it landed. Later on I was trying to figure out what Zofia said. My Baldeziwurleki isn't very good, but I think she was saying something like "Figures. Stupid librarian. I have to go take care of that damn dog." So maybe that's what happened. Maybe Zofia sent part of herself in there with the skinless dog. Maybe she fought it and won and closed the handbag. Maybe she made friends with it. I mean, she used to feed it popcorn at the movies. Maybe she's still in there.

What happened in the library was Zofia sighed a little and closed her eyes. I helped her sit down in a chair, but I don't think she was really there anymore. I rode with her in the ambulance, when the ambulance finally showed up, and I swear I didn't even think about the handbag until my mother showed up. I didn't say a word. I just left her there in the hospital with Zofia, who was on a respirator, and I ran all the way back to the library. But it was closed. So I ran all the way back again, to the hospital, but you already know what happened, right? Zofia died. I hate writing that. My tall, funny, beautiful, book-stealing, Scrabble-playing, storytelling grandmother died.

But you never met her. You're probably wondering about the handbag. What happened to it. I put up signs all over town, like Zofia's handbag was some kind of lost dog, but nobody ever called.

So that's the story so far. Not that I expect you to believe any of it. Last night Natalie and Natasha came over and we played Scrabble. They don't really like Scrabble, but they feel like it's their job to cheer me up. I won. After they went home, I flipped all the tiles upside-down and then I started picking them up in groups of seven. I tried to ask a question, but it was hard to pick just one. The words I got weren't so great either, so I decided that they weren't English words. They were Baldeziwurleki words.

Once I decided that, everything became perfectly clear. First I put down *kirif* which means "happy news", and then I got a *b*, an *o*, an *l*, an *e*, a *f*, another *i*, an *s*, and a *z*. So then I could make *kirif* into *bolekirifisz*, which could mean "the happy result of a combination of diligent effort and patience."

I would find the faery handbag. The tiles said so. I would work the clasp and go into the handbag and have my own adventures and would rescue Jake. Hardly any time would have gone by before we came back out of the handbag. Maybe I'd even make friends with that poor dog and get to say good-bye, for real, to Zofia. Rustan would show up again and be really sorry that he'd missed Zofia's funeral and this time he would be brave enough to tell my mother the whole story. He would tell her that he was her father. Not that she would believe him. Not that you should believe this story. Promise me that you won't believe a word.

"Hot enough for you?" the man said.

The Hortlak

ERIC WAS NIGHT, AND BATU WAS DAY. The girl, Charley, was the moon. Every night, she drove past the All-Night in her long, noisy, green Chevy, a dog hanging out the passenger window. It wasn't ever the same dog, although they all had the same blissful expression. They were doomed, but they didn't know it.

Bız buradan çok hoşlandık.
We like it here very much.

The All-Night Convenience was a fully stocked, self-sufficient organism, like the *Starship Enterprise*, or the *Kon-Tiki*. Batu went on and on about this. They didn't work retail anymore. They were on a voyage of discovery, one in which they had no need to leave the All-Night, not even to do laundry. Batu washed his pajamas and the extra uniforms in the sink in the back. He even washed Eric's clothes. That was the kind of friend Batu was.

Burada tatil için mi bulunuyorsunuz?
Are you here on holiday?

All during his shift, Eric listened for Charley's car. First she went by on her way to the shelter and then, during her shift, she took the dogs out driving,

25

past the store first in one direction and then back again, two or three times in one night, the lights of her headlights picking out the long, black gap of the Ausible Chasm, a bright slap across the windows of the All-Night. Eric's heart lifted whenever a car went past.

The zombies came in, and he was polite to them, and failed to understand what they wanted, and sometimes real people came in and bought candy or cigarettes or beer. The zombies were never around when the real people were around, and Charley never showed up when the zombies were there.

Charley looked like someone from a Greek play, Electra, or Cassandra. She looked like someone had just set her favorite city on fire. Eric had thought that, even before he knew about the dogs.

Sometimes, when she didn't have a dog in the Chevy, Charley came into the All-Night Convenience to buy a Mountain Dew, and then she and Batu would go outside to sit on the curb. Batu was teaching her Turkish. Sometimes Eric went outside as well, to smoke a cigarette. He didn't really smoke, but it meant he got to look at Charley, the way the moonlight sat on her like a hand. Sometimes she looked back. Wind would rise up, out of the Ausible Chasm, across Ausible Chasm Road, into the parking lot of the All-Night, tugging at Batu's pajama bottoms, pulling away the cigarette smoke that hung out of Eric's mouth. Charley's bangs would float up off her forehead, until she clamped them down with her fingers.

Batu said he was not flirting. He didn't have a thing for Charley. He was interested in her because Eric was interested. Batu wanted to know what Charley's story was: he said he needed to know if she was good enough for Eric, for the All-Night Convenience. There was a lot at stake.

What Eric wanted to know was, why did Batu have so many pajamas? But Eric didn't want to seem nosy. There wasn't a lot of space in the All-Night. If Batu wanted Eric to know about the pajamas, then one day he'd tell him. It was as simple as that.

Erkek arkadaşınız varmı?
Do you have a boyfriend?

Recently Batu had evolved past the need for more than two or three hours' sleep, which was good in some ways and bad in others. Eric had a suspicion he might figure out how to talk to Charley if Batu were tucked away, back in the storage closet, dreaming his own sweet dreams, and not scheming schemes, doing all the flirting on Eric's behalf, so that Eric never had to say a thing.

Eric had even rehearsed the start of a conversation. Charley would say, "Where's Batu?" and Eric would say, "Asleep." Or even, "Sleeping in the closet."

Charley's story: she worked night shifts at the animal shelter. Every night, when Charley got to work, she checked the list to see which dogs were on the schedule. She took the dogs—any that weren't too ill, or too mean—out for one last drive around town. Then she drove them back and she put them to sleep. She did this with an injection. She sat on the floor and petted them until they weren't breathing anymore.

When she was telling Batu this, Batu sitting far too close to her, Eric not close enough, Eric had this thought, which was what it would be like to lie down and put his head on Charley's leg. But the longest conversation that he'd ever managed with Charley was with Charley on one side of the counter, him on the other, when he'd explained that they weren't taking money anymore, at least not unless people wanted to give them money.

"I want a Mountain Dew," Charley had said, making sure Eric understood that part.

"I know," Eric said. He tried to show with his eyes how much he knew, and how much he didn't know, but wanted to know.

"But you don't want me to pay you for it."

"I'm supposed to give you what you want," Eric said, "and then you give me what you want to give me. It doesn't have to be about money. It doesn't even have to be something, you know, tangible. Sometimes people tell Batu their dreams if they don't have anything interesting in their wallets."

"All I want is a Mountain Dew," Charley said. But she must have seen the panic on Eric's face, and she dug in her pocket. Instead of change, she pulled out a set of dog tags and plunked it down on the counter.

"This dog is no longer alive," she said. "It wasn't a very big dog, and I think it was part Chihuahua and part collie, and how pitiful is that. You should have seen it. Its owner brought it in because it would jump up on her bed in the morning, lick her face, and get so excited that it would pee. I don't know, maybe she thought someone else would want to adopt an ugly little bedwetting dog, but nobody did, and so now it's not alive anymore. I killed it."

"I'm sorry," Eric said. Charley leaned her elbows against the counter. She was so close, he could smell her smell: chemical, burnt, doggy. There were dog hairs on her clothes.

"I killed it," Charley said. She sounded angry at him. "Not you."

When Eric looked at her, he saw that that city was still on fire. It was still burning down, and Charley was watching it burn. She was still holding the dog tags. She let go and they lay there on the counter until Eric picked them up and put them in the register.

"This is all Batu's idea," Charley said. "Right?" She went outside and sat on the curb, and in a while Batu came out of the storage closet and went outside as well. Batu's pajama bottoms were silk. There were smiling hydrocephalic cartoon cats on them, and the cats carried children in their mouths. Either the children were mouse-sized, or the cats were bear-sized. The children were either screaming or laughing. Batu's pajama top was red flannel, faded, with guillotines, and heads in baskets.

Eric stayed inside. He leaned his face against the window every once in a while, as if he could hear what they were saying. But even if he could have heard them, he guessed he wouldn't have understood. The shapes their mouths made were shaped like Turkish words. Eric hoped they were talking about retail.

Kar yağacak.
It's going to snow.

The way the All-Night worked at the moment was Batu's idea. They sized up the customers before they got to the counter—that had always been part of retail. If the customer was the right sort, then Batu or Eric gave the customer what they said they needed, and the customer paid with money sometimes, and sometimes with other things: pot, books on tape, souvenir maple syrup tins. They were near the border. They got a lot of Canadians. Eric suspected someone, maybe a traveling Canadian pajama salesman, was supplying Batu with novelty pajamas.

Siz de mi bekliyorsunuz?
Are you waiting too?

What Batu thought Eric should say to Charley, if he really liked her: "Come live with me. Come live at the All-Night."

What Eric thought about saying to Charley: "If you're going away, take me with you. I'm about to be twenty years old, and I've never been to college. I sleep days in a storage closet, wearing someone else's pajamas. I've worked retail jobs since I was sixteen. I know people are hateful. If you need to bite someone, you can bite me."

Başka bir yere gidelim mi?
Shall we go somewhere else?

Charley drives by. There is a little black dog in the passenger window, leaning out to swallow the fast air. There is a yellow dog. An Irish setter. A Doberman. Akitas. Charley has rolled the window so far down that these dogs could jump out, if they wanted, when she stops the car at a light. But the dogs don't jump. So Charley drives them back again.

Batu said it was clear Charley had a great capacity for hating, and also a great capacity for love. Charley's hatred was seasonal: in the months after Christmas, Christmas puppies started growing up. People got tired of trying to house-train them. All February, all March, Charley hated people. She hated people in December too, just for practice.

Being in love, Batu said, like working retail, meant that you had to settle for being hated, at least part of the year. That was what the months after Christmas were all about. Neither system—not love, not retail—was perfect. When you looked at dogs, you saw this, that love didn't work.

Batu said it was likely that Charley, both her person and her Chevy, were infested with dog ghosts. These ghosts were different from the zombies. Nonhuman ghosts, he said, were the most difficult of all ghosts to dislodge, and dogs were worst of all. There is nothing as persistent, as loyal, as *clingy* as a dog.

"So can you see these ghosts?" Eric said.

"Don't be ridiculous," Batu said. "You can't see that kind of ghost. You smell them."

Civarda turistik yerler var mı, acaba?
Are there any tourist attractions around here, I wonder?

Eric woke up and found it was dark. It was always dark when he woke up, and this was always a surprise. There was a little window on the back wall of the storage closet, which framed the dark like a picture. You could feel the cold night air propping up the walls of the All-Night, thick and wet as glue.

Batu had let him sleep in. Batu was considerate of other people's sleep.

All day long, in Eric's dreams, store managers had arrived, one after another, announced themselves, expressed dismay at the way Batu had reinvented—*compromised*—convenience retail. In Eric's dream, Batu had put his large, handsome arm over the shoulder of the store managers, promised to explain everything in a satisfactory manner, if they would only come and see. The store managers had all gone, in a docile, trusting way, trotting after Batu, across the road, looking both ways, to the edge of the Ausible Chasm. They stood there, in Eric's dream, peering down into the Chasm, and then Batu had given them a little push, a small push, and that was the end of that store manager, and Batu walked back across the road to wait for the next store manager.

Eric bathed standing up at the sink and put on his uniform. He brushed his teeth. The closet smelled like sleep.

It was the middle of February, and there was snow in the All-Night parking lot. Batu was clearing the parking lot, carrying shovelfuls of snow across the road, dumping the snow into the Ausible Chasm. Eric went outside for a smoke and watched. He didn't offer to help. He was still upset about the way Batu had behaved in his dream.

There was no moon, but the snow was lit by its own whiteness. There was the shadowy figure of Batu, carrying in front of him the shadowy scoop of the shovel, full of snow, like an enormous spoon full of falling light, which was still falling all around them. The snow came down, and Eric's smoke went up and up.

He walked across the road to where Batu stood, peering down into the Ausible Chasm. Down in the Chasm, it was no darker than the kind of dark the rest of the world, including Eric, especially Eric, was used to. Snow fell into the Chasm, the way snow fell on the rest of the world. And yet there was a wind coming out of the Chasm that worried Eric.

"What do you think is down there?" Batu said.

"Zombie Land," Eric said. He could almost taste it. "Zomburbia. They have everything down there. There's even supposed to be a drive-in movie theater down there, somewhere, that shows old black-and-white horror movies, all night long. Zombie churches with AA meetings for zombies, down in the basements, every Thursday night."

"Yeah?" Batu said. "Zombie bars too? Where they serve zombies Zombies?"

Eric said, "My friend Dave went down once, when we were in high school, on a dare. He used to tell us all kinds of stories."

"You ever go?" Batu said, pointing with his empty shovel at the narrow, crumbly path that went down into the Chasm.

"I never went to college. I've never even been to Canada," Eric said. "Not even when I was in high school, to buy beer."

All night the zombies came out of the Chasm, holding handfuls of snow. They carried the snow across the road, and into the parking lot, and left it there. Batu was back in the closet, sending off faxes, and Eric was glad about this, that Batu couldn't see what the zombies were up to.

Zombies came into the store, tracking in salt and melting snow. Eric hated mopping up after the zombies.

He sat on the counter, facing the road, hoping Charley would drive by soon. Two weeks ago, Charley had bitten a man who'd brought his dog to the animal shelter to be put down.

The man was bringing his dog because it had bit him, he said, but Charley said you knew when you saw this guy, and when you saw the dog, that the dog had had a very good reason.

This man had a tattoo of a mermaid coiled around his meaty forearm, and even this mermaid had an unpleasant look to her: scaly, corseted bottom; tiny black dot eyes; a sour, fangy smile. Charley said it was as if even the mermaid were telling her to bite the arm, and so she did. When she did, the dog went nuts. The guy dropped its leash. He was trying to get Charley off his arm. The dog, misunderstanding the situation, or rather, understanding the situation, but not the larger situation, had grabbed Charley by her leg, sticking its teeth into her calf.

Both Charley and the dog's owner had needed stitches. But it was the dog who was doomed. Nothing had changed that.

Charley's boss at the shelter was going to fire her, anytime soon—in fact, he had fired her. But they hadn't found someone to take her shift yet, and so she was working there, for a few more days, under a different name. Everyone at the shelter understood why she'd had to bite the man.

Charley said she was going to drive all the way across Canada. Maybe keep on going, up into Alaska. Go watch bears pick through garbage.

"When a bear hibernates," she told Batu and Eric, "it sleeps all winter and never goes to the bathroom. So when she wakes up in spring, she's really constipated. The first thing she does is take this really painful shit. And then she goes and jumps in a river. She's really pissed off now, about everything. When she comes out of the river, she's covered in ice. It's like armor. She goes on a rampage and she's wearing armor. Isn't that great? That bear can take a bite out of anything it wants."

*

Uykum geldi.
My sleep has come.

The snow kept falling. Sometimes it stopped. Charley came by. Eric had bad dreams. Batu did not go to bed. When the zombies came in, he followed them around the store, taking notes. The zombies didn't care at all. They were done with all that.

Batu was wearing Eric's favorite pajamas. These were blue, and had towering Hokusai-style white-blue waves, and up on the waves, there were boats with owls looking owlish. If you looked closely, you could see that the owls were gripping newspapers in their wings, and if you looked even closer, you could read the date and the headline:

"Tsunami Tsweeps Pussy
Overboard, All is Lots."

Batu had spent a lot of time reorganizing the candy aisle according to chewiness and meltiness. The week before, he had arranged it so that if you took the first letter of every candy, reading across from left to right, and then down, it had spelled out the first sentence of *To Kill a Mockingbird*, and then also a line of Turkish poetry. Something about the moon.

The zombies came and went, and Batu put his notebook away. He said, "I'm going to go ahead and put jerky with Sugar Daddies. It's almost a candy. It's very chewy. About as chewy as you can get. Chewy Meat gum."

"Frothy Meat Drink," Eric said automatically. They were always thinking of products that no one would ever want to buy, and that no one would ever try to sell.

"Squeezable Pork. *It's on your mind, it's in your mouth, it's pork.* Remember that ad campaign? She can come live with us," Batu said. It was the same old speech, only a little more urgent each time he gave it. "The All-Night needs women, especially women like Charley. She falls in love with you, I don't mind one bit."

"What about you?" Eric said.

"What about me?" Batu said. "Charley and I have the Turkish language. That's enough. Tell me something I need. I don't even need sleep!"

"What are you talking about?" Eric said. He hated when Batu talked about Charley, except that he loved hearing her name.

Batu said, "The All-Night is a great place to raise a family. Everything you need, right here. Diapers, Vienna sausages, grape-scented Magic Markers, Moon Pies—kids like Moon Pies—and then one day, when they're tall enough, we teach them how to operate the register."

"There are laws against that," Eric said. "Mars needs women. Not the All-Night. And we're running out of Moon Pies." He turned his back on Batu.

Some of Batu's pajamas worry Eric. He won't wear these, although Batu has told him that he may wear any pajamas he likes.

For example, ocean liners navigating icebergs on a pair of pajama bottoms. A man with an enormous pair of scissors, running after women whose long hair whips out behind them like red and yellow flags, they are moving so fast. Spiderwebs with houses stuck to them.

A few nights ago, about two or three in the morning, a woman came into the store. Batu was over by the magazines, and the woman went and stood next to Batu.

Batu's eyes were closed, although that doesn't necessarily mean he was asleep. The woman stood and flicked through magazines, and then at some point she realized that the man standing there with his eyes closed was wearing pajamas. She stopped reading through *People* magazine and started reading Batu's pajamas instead. Then she gasped, and poked Batu with a skinny finger.

"Where did you get those?" she said. "How on earth did you get those?"

Batu opened his eyes. "Excuse me," he said. "May I help you find something?"

"You're wearing my diary," the woman said. Her voice went up and up in a wail. "That's my handwriting! That's the diary that I kept when I was fourteen! But it had a lock on it, and I hid it under my mattress, and I never let anyone read it. Nobody ever read it!"

Batu held out his arm. "That's not true," he said. "I've read it. You have very nice handwriting. Very distinctive. My favorite part is when—"

The woman screamed. She put her hands over her ears and walked backwards, down the aisle, and still screaming, turned around and ran out of the store.

"What was that about?" Eric said. "What was up with her?"

"I don't know," Batu said. "The thing is, I thought she looked familiar! And I was right. Hah! What are the odds, you think, the woman who kept that diary coming in the store like that?"

"Maybe you shouldn't wear those anymore," Eric said. "Just in case she comes back."

Gelebilirmiyim?
Can I come?

Batu had originally worked Tuesday through Saturday, second shift. Now he was all day, every day. Eric worked all night, all nights. They didn't need anyone else, except maybe Charley.

What had happened was this. One of the managers had left, supposedly to have a baby, although she had not looked in the least bit pregnant, Batu said, and besides, it was clearly not Batu's kid, because of the vasectomy. Then, shortly after the incident with the man in the trench coat, the other manager had quit, claiming to be sick of that kind of shit. No one was sent to replace him, so Batu had stepped in.

The door rang and a customer came into the store. Canadian. Not a zombie. Eric turned around in time to see Batu duck down, slipping around the corner of the candy aisle, and heading towards the storage closet.

The customer bought a Mountain Dew, Eric too disheartened to explain that cash was no longer necessary. He could feel Batu, fretting, in the storage closet, listening to this old-style retail transaction. When the customer was gone, Batu came out again.

"Do you ever wonder," Eric said, "if the company will ever send another manager?" He saw again the dream-Batu, the dream-managers, the cartoonish, unbridgeable gape of the Ausible Chasm.

"They won't," Batu said.

"They might," Eric said.

"They won't," Batu said.

"How do you know for sure?" Eric said. "What if they do?"

"It was a bad idea in the first place," Batu said. He gestured towards the parking lot and the Ausible Chasm. "Not enough steady business."

"So why do we stay here?" Eric said. "How do we change the face of retail if nobody ever comes in here except joggers and truckers and zombies and Canadians? I mean, I tried to explain about how new-style retail worked, the other night—to this woman—and she told me to fuck off. She acted like I was insane."

"The customer isn't always right. Sometimes the customer is an asshole. That's the first rule of retail," Batu said. "But it's not like anywhere else is better. I used to work for the CIA. Believe me, this is better."

"Were you really in the CIA?" Eric said.

"We used to go to this bar, sometimes, me and the people I worked with," Batu said. "Only we have to pretend that we don't know each other. No fraternizing. So we all sit there, along the bar, and don't say a word to each other. All these guys, all of us, we could speak maybe five hundred languages, dialects, whatever, between us. But we don't talk in this bar. Just sit and drink and sit and drink. Used to drive the bartender crazy. We used to leave nice tips. Didn't matter to him."

"So did you ever kill people?" Eric said. He never knew whether or not Batu was joking about the CIA thing.

"Do I look like a killer?" Batu said, standing there in his pajamas, rumpled and red-eyed. When Eric burst out laughing, he smiled and yawned and scratched his head.

When other employees had quit the All-Night, for various reasons of their own, Batu had not replaced them.

Around this same time, Batu's girlfriend had kicked him out, and with Eric's permission, he had moved into the storage closet. That had been just *before* Christmas, and it was a few days *after* Christmas when Eric's mother lost her job as a security guard at the mall and decided she was going to go find Eric's father. She'd gone hunting online, and made a list of names she thought he might be going under. She had addresses as well.

Eric wasn't sure what she was going to do if she found his father, and he didn't think she knew, either. She said she just wanted to talk, but Eric knew she kept a gun in the glove compartment of her car. Before she left, Eric had copied down her list of names and addresses, and sent out Christmas cards to all of them. It was the first time he'd ever had a reason to send out Christmas cards, and it had been difficult, finding the right things to say in them, especially since they probably weren't his father, no matter what his mother thought. Not all of them, anyway.

Before she left, Eric's mother had put most of the furniture in storage. She'd sold everything else, including Eric's guitar and his books, at a yard sale one Saturday morning while Eric was working an extra shift at the All-Night.

The rent was still paid through the end of January, but after his mother left, Eric had worked longer and longer hours at the store, and then, one morning, he didn't bother going home. The All-Night, and Batu, they needed him. Batu said this attitude showed Eric was destined for great things at the All-Night.

Every night Batu sent off faxes to the *World Weekly News*, and to the *National Enquirer*, and to the *New York Times*. These faxes concerned the Ausible Chasm and the zombies. Someday someone would send reporters. It was all part of the plan, which was going to change the way retail worked. It was going to be a whole different world, and Eric and Batu were going to be right there at the beginning. They were going to be famous heroes. Revolutionaries. Heroes of the revolution. Batu said that Eric didn't need to understand that part of the plan yet. It was essential to the plan that Eric didn't ask questions.

Ne zaman geri geleceksiniz?
When will you come back?

The zombies were like Canadians, in that they looked enough like real people at first, to fool you. But when you looked closer, you saw they were from some other place, where things were different: where even the same things, the things that went on everywhere, were just a little bit different.

The zombies didn't talk at all, or they said things that didn't make sense. "Wooden hat," one zombie said to Eric, "Glass leg. Drove around all day in my wife. Did you ever hear me on the radio?" They tried to pay Eric for things that the All-Night didn't sell.

Real people, the ones who weren't heading towards Canada or away from Canada, mostly had better things to do than drive out to the All-Night at 3 A.M. So real people, in a way, were even weirder, when they came in. Eric kept a close eye on the real people. Once a guy had pulled a gun on him—there was no way to understand that, but, on the other hand, you knew exactly what was going on. With the zombies, who knew?

Not even Batu knew what the zombies were up to. Sometimes he said that they were just another thing you had to deal with in retail. They were the kind of customer that you couldn't ever satisfy, the kind of customer who wanted something you couldn't give them, who had no other currency, except currency that was sinister, unwholesome, confusing, and probably dangerous.

Meanwhile, the things that the zombies tried to purchase were plainly things that they had brought with them into the store—things that had fallen, or been thrown into the Ausible Chasm, like pieces of safety glass. Rocks from the bottom of Ausible Chasm. Beetles. The zombies liked shiny things, broken things, trash like empty soda bottles, handfuls of leaves, sticky dirt, dirty sticks.

Eric thought maybe Batu had it wrong. Maybe it wasn't supposed to be a transaction. Maybe the zombies just wanted to give Eric something. But what was he going to do with their leaves? Why him? What was he supposed to give them in return?

Eventually, when it was clear Eric didn't understand, the zombies drifted off, away from the counter and around the aisles again, or out the doors, making their way like raccoons, scuttling back across the road, still clutching their leaves. Batu would put away his notebook, go into the storage closet, and send off his faxes.

The zombie customers made Eric feel guilty. He hadn't been trying hard enough. The zombies were never rude, or impatient, or tried to shoplift things. He hoped that they found what they were looking for. After all, he would be dead someday too, and on the other side of the counter.

Maybe his friend Dave had been telling the truth and there was a country down there that you could visit, just like Canada. Maybe when the zombies got all the way to the bottom, they got into zippy zombie cars and drove off to their zombie jobs, or back home again, to their sexy zombie wives, or maybe they went off to the zombie bank to make their deposits of stones, leaves, linty, birdsnesty tangles, all the other debris real people didn't know the value of.

It wasn't just the zombies. Weird stuff happened in the middle of the day too. When there were still managers and other employers, once, on Batu's shift, a guy had come in wearing a trench coat and a hat. Outside, it must have been ninety degrees, and Batu admitted he had felt a little spooked about the trench coat thing, but there was another customer, a jogger, poking at the bottled waters to see which were coldest. Trench-coat guy walked around the store, putting candy bars and safety razors in his pockets, like he was getting ready for Halloween. Batu had thought about punching the alarm. "Sir?" he said. "Excuse me, sir?"

The man walked up and stood in front of the counter. Batu couldn't take his eyes off the trench coat. It was like the guy was wearing an electric fan strapped to his chest, under the trench coat, and the fan was blowing things around underneath. You could hear the fan buzzing. It made sense, Batu had thought: this guy had his own air-conditioning unit under there. Pretty neat, although you still wouldn't want to go trick-or-treating at this guy's house.

"Hot enough for you?" the man said, and Batu saw that this guy was sweating. He twitched, and a bee flew out of the gray trench coat sleeve. Batu and the man both watched it fly away. Then the man opened his trench coat, flapped his arms, gently, gently, and the bees inside his trench coat began to leave the man in long, clotted, furious trails, until the whole store was vibrating with clouds of bees. Batu ducked under the counter. Trench-coat man, bee guy, reached over the counter, dinged the register in a calm and experienced way so that the drawer popped open, and scooped all the bills out of the till.

Then he walked back out again and left all his bees. He got in his car and drove away. That's the way that all All-Night stories end, with someone driving away.

But they had to get a beekeeper to come in, to smoke the bees out. Batu got stung three times, once on the lip, once on his stomach, and once when he put his hand into the register and found no money, only a bee. The jogger sued the All-Night parent company for a lot of money, and Batu and Eric didn't know what had happened with that.

Karanlık ne zaman basar?
When does it get dark?

Eric has been having this dream recently. In the dream, he's up behind the counter in the All-Night, and then his father is walking down the aisle of the All-Night, past the racks of magazines and towards the counter, his father's hands full of stones from the Ausible Chasm. Which is ridiculous: his father is alive, and not only that, but living in another state, maybe in a different time zone, probably under a different name.

When he told Batu about it, Batu said, "Oh, that dream. I've had it too."

"About your father?" Eric said.

"About your father," Batu said. "Who do you think I meant, *my* father?"

"You haven't ever met my father," Eric said.

"I'm sorry if it upsets you, but it was definitely your father," Batu said. "You look just like him. If I dream about him again, what do you want me to do? Ignore him? Pretend he isn't there?"

Eric never knew when Batu was pulling his leg. Dreams could be a touchy subject. Eric thought maybe Batu was nostalgic about sleeping, maybe Batu collected pajamas in the way that people nostalgic about their childhoods collected toys.

Another dream, one that Eric hasn't told Batu about. In this dream, Charley comes in. She wants to buy a Mountain Dew, but then Eric realizes that all the Mountain Dews have little drowned dogs floating in them. You can win a prize if you drink one of the dog sodas. When Charley gets up to the counter with an armful of doggy Mountain Dews, Eric realizes that he's got one of Batu's pajama tops on, one of the inside-out ones. Things are rubbing against his arms, his back, his stomach, transferring themselves like tattoos to his skin.

And he hasn't got any pants on.

Batık gemilerle ilgileniyorum.
I'm interested in sunken ships.

"You need to make your move," Batu said. He said it over and over, day after day, until Eric was sick of hearing it. "Any day now, the shelter is going to find someone to replace her, and Charley will split. Tell you what you should do, you tell her you want to adopt a dog. Give it a home. We've got room here. Dogs are good practice for when you and Charley are parents."

"How do you know?" Eric said. He knew he sounded exasperated. He couldn't help it. "That makes no sense at all. If dogs are good practice, then what kind of mother is Charley going to be? What are you saying? So say Charley has a kid, you're saying she's going to put it down if it cries at night or wets the bed?"

"That's not what I'm saying at all," Batu said. "The only thing I'm worried about, Eric, really, is whether or not Charley may be too old. It takes longer to have kids when you're her age. Things can go wrong."

"What are you talking about?" Eric said. "Charley's not old."

"How old do you think she is?" Batu said. "So what do you think? Should the toothpaste and the condiments go next to the Elmer's glue and the hair gel and lubricants? Make a shelf of sticky things? Or should I put it with the chewing tobacco and the mouthwash, and make a little display of things that you spit?"

"Sure," Eric said. "Make a little display. I don't know how old Charley is, maybe she's my age? Nineteen? A little older?"

Batu laughed. "A little older? So how old do you think I am?"

"I don't know," Eric said. He squinted at Batu. "Thirty-five? Forty?"

Batu looked pleased. "You know, since I started sleeping less, I think I've stopped getting older. I may be getting younger. You keep on getting a good night's sleep, and we're going to be the same age pretty soon. Come take a look at this and tell me what you think."

"Not bad," Eric said. "We could put watermelons with this stuff too, if we had watermelons. The kind with seeds. What's the point of seedless watermelons?"

"It's not such a big deal," Batu said. He knelt down in the aisle, marking off inventory on his clipboard. "No big thing if Charley's older than you think. Nothing wrong with older women. And it's good you're not bothered about the ghost dogs or the biting thing. Everyone's got problems. The only real concern I have is about her car."

"What about her car?" Eric said.

"Well," Batu said. "It isn't a problem if she's going to live here. She can park it here for as long as she wants. That's what the parking lot is for. But whatever you do: if she invites you to go for a ride, don't go for a ride."

"Why not?" Eric said. "What are you talking about?"

"Think about it," Batu said. "All those dog ghosts." He scooted down the aisle on his butt. Eric followed. "Every time she drives by here with some poor dog, that dog is doomed. That car is bad luck. The passenger side especially. You want to stay out of that car. I'd rather climb down into the Ausible Chasm."

Something cleared its throat; a zombie had come into the store. It stood behind Batu, looking down at him. Batu looked up. Eric retreated down the aisle, towards the counter.

"Stay out of her car," Batu said, ignoring the zombie.

"And who will be fired out of the cannon?" the zombie said. It was wearing a suit and tie. "My brother will be fired out of the cannon."

"Why can't you talk like sensible people?" Batu said, turning around and looking up. Sitting on the floor, he sounded as if he were about to cry. He swatted at the zombie.

The zombie coughed again, yawning. It grimaced at them. Something was snagged on its gray lips now, and the zombie put up its hand. It tugged, dragging at the thing in its mouth, coughing out a black, glistening, wadded rope. The zombie's mouth stayed open, as if to show that there was nothing else in there, even as it held the wet black rope out to Batu. The wet thing hung down from its hands and became pajamas. Batu looked back at Eric. "I don't want them," he said. He looked shy.

"What should I do?" Eric said. He hovered by the magazines. Charlize Theron was grinning at him, as if she knew something he didn't.

"You shouldn't be here." It wasn't clear to Eric whether Batu was speaking to the zombie. "I have all the pajamas I need."

The zombie said nothing. It dropped the pajamas into Batu's lap.

"Stay out of Charley's car!" Batu said to Eric. He closed his eyes and began to snore.

"Shit," Eric said to the zombie. "How did you do that?"

There was another zombie in the store now. The first zombie took Batu's arms and the second zombie took Batu's feet. They dragged him down the aisle and toward the storage closet. Eric came out from behind the counter.

"What are you doing?" he said. "You're not going to eat him, are you?"

But the zombies had Batu in the closet. They put the black pajamas on him, yanking them over the other pair of pajamas. They lifted Batu up onto the mattress, and pulled the blanket over him, up to his chin.

Eric followed the zombies out of the storage closet. He shut the door behind him. "So I guess he's going to sleep for a while," he said. "That's a good thing, right? He needed to get some sleep. So how did you do that with the pajamas? Is there some kind of freaky pajama factory down there?"

The zombies ignored Eric. They held hands and went down the aisles, stopping to consider candy bars and Tampax and toilet paper and all the things that you spit. They wouldn't buy anything. They never did.

Eric went back to the counter. He wished, very badly, that his mother still lived in their apartment. He would have liked to call someone. He sat behind the register for a while, looking through the phone book, just in case he came across someone's name and it seemed like a good idea to call them. Then he went back to the storage closet and looked at Batu. Batu was snoring. His eyelids twitched, and there was a tiny, knowing smile on his face, as if he were dreaming, and everything was being explained to him, at last, in this dream. It was hard to feel worried about someone who looked like that. Eric would have been jealous, except he knew that no one ever managed to hold on to those explanations, once you woke up. Not even Batu.

Hangi yol daha kısa?
Which is the shorter route?

Hangi yol daha kolay?
Which is the easier route?

Charley came by at the beginning of her shift. She didn't come inside the All-Night. Instead she stood out in the parking lot, beside her car, looking out across the road, at the Ausible Chasm. The car hung low to the ground, as if the trunk were full of things. When Eric went outside, he saw that there was a suitcase in the backseat. If there were ghost dogs, Eric couldn't see them, but there were doggy smudges on the windows.

"Where's Batu?" Charley said.

"Asleep," Eric said. He realized that he'd never figured out how the conversation would go, after that.

He said, "Are you going someplace?"

"I'm going to work," Charley said. "Like normal."

"Good," Eric said. "Normal is good." He stood and looked at his feet.

A zombie wandered into the parking lot. It nodded at them, and went into the All-Night.

"Aren't you going to go back inside?" Charley said.

"In a bit," Eric said. "It's not like they ever buy anything." But he kept an eye on the All-Night, and the zombie, in case it headed towards the storage closet.

"So how old are you?" Eric said. "I mean, can I ask you that? How old you are?"

"How old are you?" Charley said right back.

"I'm almost twenty," Eric said. "I know I look older."

"No you don't," Charley said. "You look exactly like you're almost twenty."

"So how old are you?" Eric said again.

"How old do you think I am?" Charley said.

"About my age?" Eric said.

"Are you flirting with me?" Charley said. "Yes? No? How about in dog years? How old would you say I am in dog years?"

The zombie finished looking for whatever it was looking for inside the All-Night. It came outside and nodded to Charley and Eric. "Beautiful people," it said. "Why won't you ever visit my hand?"

"I'm sorry," Eric said.

The zombie turned its back on them. It tottered across the road, looking neither to the left, nor to the right, and went down the footpath into the Ausible Chasm.

"Have you?" Charley said. She pointed at the path.

"No," Eric said. "I mean, someday I will, I guess."

"Do you think they have pets down there? Dogs?" Charley said.

"I don't know," Eric said. "Regular dogs?"

"The thing I think about sometimes," Charley said, "is whether or not they have animal shelters, and if someone has to look after the dogs. If someone has to have a job where they put down dogs down there. And if you do put dogs to sleep, down there, then where do they wake up?"

"Batu says that if you need another job, you can come live with us at the

All-Night," Eric said. His lips felt so cold that it was hard to talk.

"Is *that* what Batu says?" Charley said. She started to laugh.

"Batu likes you," Eric said.

"I like him too," Charley said. "But I don't want to live in a convenience store. No offense. I'm sure it's nice."

"It's okay," Eric said. "I don't want to work retail my whole life."

"There are worse jobs," Charley said. She leaned against her Chevy. "Maybe I'll stop by later tonight. We could always go for a long ride, go somewhere else, and talk about retail."

"Like where? Where are you going?" Eric said. "Are you thinking about going to Turkey? Is that why Batu is teaching you Turkish?" He wanted to stand there and ask Charley questions all night long.

"I want to learn Turkish so that when I go somewhere else I can pretend to be Turkish. I can pretend I *only* speak Turkish. That way no one will bother me," Charley said.

"Oh," Eric said. "Good plan. We could always go somewhere and not talk, if you want to practice. Or I could talk to you, and you could pretend you don't understand what I'm saying. We don't have to go for a ride. We could just go across the road, go down into the Chasm. I've never been down there."

"It's not a big deal," Charley said. "We can do it some other time." Suddenly she looked much older.

"No, wait," Eric said. "I do want to come with you. We can go for a ride. It's just that Batu's asleep. Someone has to look after him. Someone has to be awake to sell stuff."

"So re you going to work there your whole life?" Charley said. "Take care of Batu? Figure out how to rip off dead people?"

"What do you mean?" Eric said.

"Batu says the All-Night is thinking about opening up another store, down there," Charley said, waving across the road. "You and he are this big experiment in retail, according to him. Once the All-Night figures out what dead people want to buy, it's going to be like the discovery of America all over again."

"It's not like that," Eric said. He could feel his voice going up at the end, as if it were a question. He could almost smell what Batu meant about Charley's car. The ghosts, those dogs, were getting impatient. You could tell that. They were tired of the parking lot, they wanted to be going for a ride. "You don't understand. I don't think you understand?"

"Batu said that you have a real way with dead people," Charley said. "Most retail clerks flip out. Of course, you're from around here. Plus you're young. You probably don't even understand about death yet. You're just like my dogs."

"I don't know what they want," Eric said. "The zombies."

"Nobody ever really knows what they want," Charley said. "Why should that change after you die?"

"Good point," Eric said.

"You shouldn't let Batu mess you around so much," Charley said. "I shouldn't be saying all this, I know. Batu and I are friends. But we could be friends too, you and me. You're sweet. It's okay that you don't talk much, although this is okay too, us talking. Why don't you come for a drive with me?" If there had been dogs inside her car, or the ghosts of dogs, then Eric would have heard them howling. Eric heard them howling. The dogs were telling him to get lost. They were telling him to fuck off. Charley belonged to them. She was *their* murderer.

"I can't," Eric said, longing for Charley to ask again. "Not right now."

"Well, that's okay. I'll stop by later," Charley said. She smiled at him and for a moment he was standing in that city where no one ever figured out how to put out that fire, and all the dead dogs howled again, and scratched at the smeary windows. "For a Mountain Dew. So you can think about it for a while."

She reached out and took Eric's hand in her hand. "Your hands are cold," she said. Her hands were hot. "You should go back inside."

Rengi beğenmiyorum.
I don't like the color.

It was already 4 A.M. and there still wasn't any sign of Charley when Batu came out of the back room. He was rubbing his eyes. The black pajamas were gone. Now Batu was wearing pajama bottoms with foxes running across a field towards a tree with a circle of foxes sitting on their haunches around it. The outstretched tails of the running foxes were fat as zeppelins, with commas of flame hovering over them. Each little flame had a Hindenburg inside it, with a second littler flame above it, and so on. Some fires you just can't put out.

The pajama top was a color that Eric could not name. Dreary, creeping shapes lay upon it. Eric had read Lovecraft. He felt queasy when he looked at the pajama top.

"I just had the best dream," Batu said.

"You've been asleep for almost six hours," Eric said. When Charley came, he would go with her. He would stay with Batu. Batu needed him. He would go with Charley. He would go and come back. He wouldn't ever come back. He would send Batu postcards with bears on them. "So what was all that about? With the zombies."

"I don't know what you're talking about," Batu said. He took an apple from the fruit display and polished it on his non-Euclidean pajama top. The apple took on a horrid, whispery sheen. "Has Charley come by?"

"Yeah," Eric said. He and Charley would go to Las Vegas. They would buy Batu gold lamé pajamas. "I think you're right. I think she's about to leave town."

"Well, she can't!" Batu said. "That's not the plan. Here, I tell you what we'll do. You go outside and wait for her. Make sure she doesn't get away."

"She's not wanted by the police, Batu," Eric said. "She doesn't belong to us. She can leave town if she wants to."

"And you're okay with that?" Batu said. He yawned ferociously, and yawned again, and stretched, so that the pajama top heaved up in an eldritch manner. Eric closed his eyes.

"Not really," Eric said. He had already picked out a toothbrush, some toothpaste, and some novelty teeth, left over from Halloween, which he could give to Charley, maybe. "Are you okay? Are you going to fall asleep again? Can I ask you some questions?"

"What kind of questions?" Batu said, lowering his eyelids in a way that seemed both sleepy and cunning.

"Questions about our mission," Eric said. "About the All-Night and what we're doing here next to the Ausible Chasm. I need to understand what just happened with the zombies and the pajamas, and whether or not what happened is part of the plan, and whether or not the plan belongs to us, or whether the plan was planned by someone else, and we're just somebody else's big experiment in retail. Are we brand-new, or are we just the same old thing?"

"This isn't a good time for questions," Batu said. "In all the time that we've worked here, have I lied to you? Have I led you astray?"

"Well," Eric said. "That's what I need to know."

"Perhaps I haven't told you everything," Batu said. "But that's part of the plan. When I said that we were going to make everything new again, that we were going to reinvent retail, I was telling the truth. The plan is still the plan, and you are still part of that plan, and so is Charley."

"What about the pajamas?" Eric said. "What about the Canadians and the maple syrup and the people who come in to buy Mountain Dew?"

"You need to know this?" Batu said.

"Yes," Eric said. "Absolutely."

"Okay, then. My pajamas are *experimental CIA pajamas*," Batu said. "Like batteries. You've been charging them for me when you sleep. That's all I can say right now. Forget about the Canadians. These pajamas the zombies just gave me—do you have any idea what this means?"

Eric shook his head no.

Batu said, "Never mind. Do you know what we need now?"

"What do we need?" Eric said.

"We need you to go outside and wait for Charley," Batu said. "We don't have time for this. It's getting early. Charley gets off work any time now."

"Explain all of that again," Eric said. "What you just said. Explain the plan to me one more time."

"Look," Batu said. "Listen. Everybody is alive at first, right?"

"Right," Eric said.

"And everybody dies," Batu said. "Right?"

"Right," Eric said. A car drove by, but it still wasn't Charley.

"So everybody starts here," Batu said. "Not here, in the All-Night, but somewhere *here*, where we are. Where we live now. Where we live is here. The world. Right?"

"Right," Eric said. "Okay."

"And where we go is there," Batu said, flicking a finger towards the road. "Out there, down into the Ausible Chasm. Everybody goes there. And here we are, *here*, the All-Night, which is on the way to *there*."

"Right," Eric said.

"So it's like the Canadians," Batu said. "People are going someplace, and if they need something, they can stop here, to get it. But we need to know what they need. This is a whole new unexplored demographic. So they stuck the All-Night right here, lit it up like a Christmas tree, and waited to see who stopped in and what they bought. I shouldn't be telling you this. This is all need-to-know information only."

"You mean the All-Night or the CIA or whoever needs us to figure out how to sell things to zombies," Eric said.

"Forget about the CIA," Batu said. "Now will you go outside?"

"But is it our plan? Or are we just following someone else's plan?"

"Why does that matter to you?" Batu said. He put his hands on his head and tugged at his hair until it stood straight up, but Eric refused to be intimidated.

"I thought we were on a mission," Eric said, "to help mankind. Womankind too. Like the *Starship Enterprise*. But how are we helping anybody? What's new-style retail about this?"

"*Eric*," Batu said. "Did you see those pajamas? Look. On second thought, forget about the pajamas. You never saw them. Like I said, this is bigger than the All-Night. There are bigger fish that are fishing, if you know what I mean."

"No," Eric said. "I don't."

"Excellent," Batu said. His experimental CIA pajama top writhed and boiled. "Your job is to be helpful and polite. Be patient. Be *careful*. Wait for the zombies to make the next move. I send off some faxes. Meanwhile, we still need Charley. Charley is a natural-born saleswoman. She's been selling death for years. And she's got a real gift for languages—she'll be speaking zombie in no time. Think what kind of work she could do here! Go outside. When she drives by, you flag her down. Talk to her. Explain why she needs to come live here. But whatever you do, don't get in the car with her. That car is full of ghosts. The wrong kind of ghosts. The kind who are never going to understand the least little thing about meaningful transactions."

"I know," Eric said. "I could smell them."

"So are we clear on all this?" Batu said. "Or maybe you think I'm still lying to you?"

"I don't think you'd lie to me, exactly," Eric said. He put on his jacket.

"You better put on a hat too," Batu said. "It's cold out there. You know you're like a son to me, which is why I tell you to put on your hat. And if I lied to you, it would be for your own good, because I love you like a son. One day, Eric, all of this will be yours. Just trust me and do what I tell you. Trust the plan."

Eric said nothing. Batu patted him on the shoulder, pulled an All-Night shirt over his pajama top, and grabbed a banana and a Snapple. He settled in behind the counter. His hair was still standing straight up, but at 4 A.M., who was going to complain? Not Eric, not the zombies. Eric put on his hat, gave a little wave to Batu, which was either, Glad we cleared all *that* up at last, or else, So long!, he wasn't sure which, and walked out of the All-Night. This is the last time, he thought, I will ever walk through this door. He didn't know how he felt about that.

Eric stood outside in the parking lot for a long time. Out in the bushes, on the other side of the road, he could hear the zombies hunting for the things that were valuable to other zombies.

Some woman, a real person, but not Charley, drove into the parking lot. She went inside, and Eric thought he knew what Batu would say to her when she went to the counter. Batu would explain when she tried to make her purchase that he didn't want money. That wasn't what retail was really about. What Batu would want to know was what this woman really wanted. It was that simple, that complicated. Batu might try to recruit this woman, if she didn't seem litigious, and maybe that was a good thing. Maybe the All-Night really did need women.

Eric walked backwards, away and then even farther away from the All-Night. The farther he got, the more beautiful he saw it all was—it was all lit up like the moon. Was this what the zombies saw? What Charley saw, when she drove by? He couldn't imagine how anyone could leave it behind and never come back.

Maybe Batu had a pair of pajamas in his collection with All-Night Convenience Stores and light spilling out; the Ausible Chasm; a road with zombies, and Charleys in Chevys, a different dog hanging out of every passenger window, driving down that road. Down on one leg of those pajamas, down the road a long ways, there would be bears dressed up in ice; Canadians; CIA operatives and tabloid reporters and All-Night executives. Las Vegas showgirls. G-men and bee men in trench coats. His mother's car, always getting farther and farther away. He wondered if zombies wore zombie pajamas, or if they'd just invented them for Batu. He tried to picture Charley wearing silk pajamas and a flannel bathrobe, but she didn't look comfortable in them. She still looked miserable and angry and hopeless, much older than Eric had ever realized.

He jumped up and down in the parking lot, trying to keep warm. The woman, when she came out of the store, gave him a funny look. He couldn't see Batu behind the counter. Maybe he'd fallen asleep again, or maybe he was sending off more faxes. But Eric didn't go back inside the store. He was afraid of Batu's pajamas.

He was afraid of Batu.

He stayed outside, waiting for Charley.

But a few hours later, when Charley drove by—he was standing on the curb, keeping an eye out for her, she wasn't going to just slip away, he was determined to see her, not to miss her, to make sure that she saw him, to make her take him with her, wherever she was going—there was a Labrador in the passenger seat. The backseat of her car was full of dogs, real dogs and ghost dogs, and all of the dogs poking their doggy noses out of the windows at him. There wouldn't have been room for him, even if he'd been able to make her stop. But he ran out in the road anyway, like a damn dog, chasing after her car for as long as he could.

He tickled her with his funis ignarii.

The Cannon

Q: AND WHO WILL BE FIRED OUT OF THE CANNON?
A: My brother will be fired out of the cannon.

Q: And what is the name of the cannon?
A: Mons Meg. Dulle Greite. Malik-i-Mydan, Tzar Pooska, Dhool Dhanee, Zufr Bukh. Her nickname is Inevitable. She is also called Sweet Mouth and The Up, Up, And Away. She is known as The Widow for her coloring and because she has had congress with many men. She is also called The Mermaid by her husbands—the men who oil her parts and polish the O of her mouth, and harness her and pull her along from town to town—they say we should release her into the harbor, to see if she swims away. It is their little joke. She is called The Conversation, because she will speak courteously if you address her with a match. She is called The Only Answer, because she only ever gives the same answer, no matter your question.

Q: And what is your brother's name?
A: I have already forgotten it.

Q: How far will he travel?
A: He will travel so far, he will never come home again. His feet will never

touch the ground, not for the rest of his life. He will never see his family again. He will never see the cannon again, but for the rest of his life, he will dream of her round, fixed, roaring black mouth.

Q: Who are these women?
A: They are his wives. After my brother is fired from the cannon, his two youngest wives will take his place in the cannon. They are wearing his luggage on their backs, filled with his belongings, his books, his golf clubs, his correspondences, his record collection, his toiletries, his identification. His wives will climb into the cannon and leave the cannon in much the same way that my brother will leave it, but they won't go to the same place he is going. Men and women don't travel to the same place.

Q: Why not?
A: No one knows why.

Q: Will he never come home again?
A: He will never come home again.

Q: Why must the cannon be fired?
A: The cannon must be fired because that is the reason for cannons. Ordnance must be placed in the cannon. Ordnance must be fired out of the cannon. The cannon serves no other purpose. A man may accidentally fall asleep in a cannon, or take shelter from a rainstorm, or hide from his enemies inside a cannon, but in the end, the cannon must be fired.

I once fornicated with a married woman inside the Sweet Mouth. She was agoraphobic. I said I was agnostic.

I said, "Yes, like that, don't wriggle so much," and she said, "How do you like this?" and "Watch your head," and while we were fucking, her husband came up and lit a match, and then we were flying. We sailed out like grappling shot. My lover yelled back at her husband, "Cock her up a bit, master gunner!" and we watched him get smaller and smaller.

I held on to her hips and the tails of her hair and fucked her as we passed over the countryside, and she wrapped her legs around my waist and fucked me back. When we were finished, we flew along side by side, and she remarked that she was grateful to me and the cannon and her husband. The affair had cured her of her agoraphobia. We fucked some more, to celebrate, and then we came to a town and I grabbed on to the steeple of an Episcopal church. She kept on going along. She wasn't ready to go back down again. I had a long walk home. I haven't seen her since.

Q: Did your brother have a happy childhood?
A: Why don't you ask him? He used to sit on my head. Once he set off fire-crackers in my closet. He substituted toothpaste-and-cucumber sandwiches for my lunch. He ripped out the last pages of his comics before he gave them to me to read. He saved up his allowance and paid Josepha Howley and her four sisters to chase me around the neighborhood. When they caught me, they took off my shorts and tied them to a tree branch.

Q. Did the cannon have a happy childhood?
A. A long time ago, before all the wars were over and done with, when large artillery still had other uses, there was a master gunner who loved the cannon. Wherever he traveled he took her with him. She was his mascot, his victory, his confidante, his clock. For love of the master gunner she took Odruik. She took Prague, Famagusta, Seringapatam, Bajadoz. She took Cairo, she took dancing lessons, she took Beethoven's hearing and Napoléon's arm. She took and took and the master gunner gave and gave. He tickled her with his *funis ignarii* and his wands and his wormers, he wooed her with Valturio's patented incendiary shells, with fireworks and grapeshot, lead, granite, and bronze; he anointed her with costly scents—saltpetre, serpentine, sulfur, charcoal, antimony. When the master gunner was old and rich and tired of going to war, he retired to the Riviera and built a castle. He married the cannon and he tied up her muzzle in a bonnet of white silk so that she would look like a lady. On Sundays the master gunner harnessed his wife to four ex-cavalry horses and rode her down the road to the chapel.

His wife was too stout to fit through the doors, though, and when the priest turned down the master gunner's offer to pay for a new set of doors, the gunner left her tied up next door in the cemetery. The horses cropped the grass and the gunner paid a small boy to watch and make sure that no one took his wife to melt down for scrap. After services, the younger members of the congregation used to go pick through the cemetery for rocks and small bits of masonry, for the master gunner to fire off.

Inside his castle the master gunner built a ramp so that when he went up to bed, the cannon went with him, and when he came down in the mornings for his breakfast, the cannon went too. To their great sorrow, they never had children and when at last the master gunner died, the undertakers dressed him in his traveling clothes and placed him inside his wife, the cannon. This was consummation. But the charge was inadequate, and when the master gunner left his wife at last, he got only as far as the next town over. They found his boots in an irrigation ditch, his johnnie in a lemon tree, his body tumbled over a sheep wall, his head in the shepherd girl's lap.

His heirs sold his widow to a circus impresario.

Q: Is there such a thing as a happy marriage?
A: Let me answer that question. My name is Venus Shebby. When I was a young girl, they fired me from the cannon one day and when I came down, I was in a different place. A beautiful place, full of beautiful people! The people who live in that beautiful place are hairy in winter and in spring they shed their hair and go naked.

In winter, they catch fish by setting fires on the frozen lakes, but in summer they don't eat fish. In summer they eat fruit and grains which they ferment in bladders, and those people stay drunk the whole summer long. Summer is the time of ghosts. In winter, ghosts are easy to spot. There are stories about winter ghosts found tangled like lice in their lovers' hair. Dead people have no hair themselves, which is how they can be recognized in winter. But in summer, the living and dead may pass each other on the street, and no one knows the difference. There are epic comedies, famous tragedies about the misunderstandings that ensue.

Those beautiful people collect their hair as they shed it, and keep it in pouches which they wear around their waists. The people wash the hair and perfume it and card it and comb it. In summer, the living wear woven hair belts and their pouches of hair around their waist, to show they are living people. But there are always fashionable people, who pretend to be dead, and there are cunning dead people, who steal hair from living people. For this reason, it is a deadly insult to pick off a strand of someone else's hair and put it in your own pouch, unless you have been invited to do so.

The people form societies to weave enormous carpets from their shed hair, and these carpets are soft and warm and heavy. The people sleep under these carpets in winter, once they are married, and they marry as many wives and husbands as can sleep together comfortably under one carpet. There is one word, which means all three of these things: *marriage, carpet, society.* There is no word for *war* or for *travel.* The people do not have a word for *cannon.* There are no cannons. All of the people's artifacts are made of hair and bone and skin. (Can you imagine a cannon made out of hair?) Even their histories are told on tapestries woven out of hair. But there is nothing as beautiful as the marriage carpets.

I have a collection of photographs of married people, lying together, all piled together beneath their marriage carpets, red and brown and black and amber and gray, looking as if particularly thick and hairy circus tents have collapsed. Heads and feet poke out at the edges, and some of the people are sneaking looks out of the embroidered, unfastened holes which are for breathing. The fastening buttons are carved of bone. If you have money, I'll show you these photographs. Industrious people sometimes weave carpets so large that they can marry several hundred other people all at once.

Other carpets the beautiful people keep in houses which are only for this kind of carpet, and not for living in. The carpets kept in these houses are the carpets in which the people are buried.

In summer, I might have been born in that place. The first winter, I was a novelty. I had my pick of husbands and wives. At the end of the second winter, when the ice was thawing, they sent me away. They said it was like sleeping with a dead person. I gave them bad dreams, and finally they couldn't sleep at all if I was near them. They use the same word for *dead* and for *summer* and for *hairless*, and after a while that word became my name. I left when they divorced me. They have no word for *divorce*.

I built a cannon out of ice, and wrapped myself in the funeral carpet which my husbands and wives had woven for me out of their own hair, and one of my wives was my gunner. I came back here, after many adventures, and once, when I'd been drinking, donated the funeral carpet to the national museum. When I was sober again, I asked for it back, but they claimed not to know what I was talking about. I live by myself and this old, bald, shabby thing I wear is a horsehair throw I found in a thrift store.

When I wake up, sometimes, before I open my eyes, I imagine that I am still lying under a marriage carpet with my husbands and wives. My hands are full of their sweet, perfumed hair. My name is Venus Shebby and once I was very beautiful, as beautiful as a cannon carved out of ice.

Q: Who was that woman?
A: Venus Shebby.

Q: How is a cannon like a marriage?
A: I don't know.

Q: Who was the first person to be fired from a cannon? Was it a man or a woman?
A: The first person to be fired from a cannon was a young man dressed as a woman. His name was Lulu. Sometimes, when someone is fired from a cannon, they say they are demonstrating "the Lulu leap."

Q: Do you love your brother?
A: I love my brother like a brother.

Q: Do you think I'm beautiful?
A: You are beautiful, but not as beautiful as Venus Shebby was, when she was young. You're not as beautiful as the cannon.

Q: Thank you for being honest. Why does your brother have so many wives, when you have no wives at all?
A: I don't know.

Q: Will you say yes when I ask you to marry me?
A: I don't know.

Q: What noise will the cannon make? Why can't you love me, just for a little while? Why must the cannon be fired? How long will your brother be gone? Why won't your brother come back? Will he never come back? What are you putting in your ears? Is it time for the cannon to be fired? May I ask the cannon these questions? What will she say?
A: A noise as loud as God, but only my brother and his wives will hear it. Everyone else is putting beeswax in their ears. I don't know. I don't know. A long time. He won't come back again. No. Beeswax and cotton. Soon. I don't know. No. Not now. Be patient. Listen. Listen.

"I always thought they were rabbits," the real estate agent said.

Stone Animals

HENRY ASKED A QUESTION. He was joking.

"As a matter of fact," the real estate agent snapped, "it is."

It was not a question she had expected to be asked. She gave Henry a goofy, appeasing smile and yanked at the hem of the skirt of her pink linen suit, which seemed as if it might, at any moment, go rolling up her knees like a window shade. She was younger than Henry, and sold houses that she couldn't afford to buy.

"It's reflected in the asking price, of course," she said. "Like you said."

Henry stared at her. She blushed.

"I've never seen anything," she said. "But there are stories. Not stories that I know. I just know there are stories. If you believe that sort of thing."

"I don't," Henry said. When he looked over to see if Catherine had heard, she had her head up the tiled fireplace, as if she were trying it on, to see whether it fit. Catherine was six months pregnant. Nothing fit her except for Henry's baseball caps, his sweatpants, his T-shirts. But she liked the fireplace.

Carleton was running up and down the staircase, slapping his heels down hard, keeping his head down and his hands folded around the banister. Carleton was serious about how he played. Tilly sat on the landing, reading a book, legs poking out through the railings. Whenever Carleton ran past, he thumped her on the head, but Tilly never said a word.

Carleton would be sorry later, and never even know why.

Catherine took her head out of the fireplace. "Guys," she said. "Carleton, Tilly. Slow down a minute and tell me what you think. Think King Spanky will be okay out here?"

"King Spanky is a cat, Mom," Tilly said. "Maybe we should get a dog, you know, to help protect us." She could tell by looking at her mother that they were going to move. She didn't know how she felt about this, except she had plans for the yard. A yard like that needed a dog.

"I don't like big dogs," said Carleton, six years old and small for his age. "I don't like this staircase. It's too big."

"Carleton," Henry said. "Come here. I need a hug."

Carleton came down the stairs. He lay down on his stomach on the floor and rolled, noisily, floppily, slowly, over to where Henry stood with the real estate agent. He curled like a dead snake around Henry's ankles. "I don't like those dogs outside," he said.

"I know it looks like we're out in the middle of nothing, but if you go down through the backyard, cut through that stand of trees, there's this little path. It takes you straight down to the train station. Ten-minute bike ride," the agent said. Nobody ever remembered her name, which was why she had to wear too-tight skirts. She was, as it happened, writing a romance novel, and she spent a lot of time making up pseudonyms, just in case she ever finished it. Ophelia Pink. Matilde Hightower. LaLa Treeble. Or maybe she'd write gothics. Ghost stories. But not about people like these. "Another ten minutes on that path and you're in town."

"What dogs, Carleton?" Henry said.

"I think they're lions, Carleton," said Catherine. "You mean the stone ones beside the door? Just like the lions at the library. You love those lions, Carleton. Patience and Fortitude?"

"I've always thought they were rabbits," the real estate agent said. "You know, because of the ears. They have big ears." She flopped her hands and then tugged at her skirt, which would not stay down. "I think they're pretty valuable. The guy who built the house had a gallery in New York. He knew a lot of sculptors."

Henry was struck by that. He didn't think he knew a single sculptor.

"I don't like the rabbits," Carleton said. "I don't like the staircase. I don't like this room. It's too big. I don't like *her*."

"Carleton," Henry said. He smiled at the real estate agent.

"I don't like the house," Carleton said, clinging to Henry's ankles. "I don't like houses. I don't want to live in a house."

"Then we'll build you a teepee out on the lawn," Catherine said. She sat on the stairs beside Tilly, who shifted her weight, almost imperceptibly, towards Catherine. Catherine sat as still as possible. Tilly was in fourth grade and difficult in a way that girls weren't supposed to be. Mostly she refused to be cuddled or babied. But she sat there, leaning on Catherine's arm, emanating saintly fragrances: peacefulness, placidness, goodness. *I want this house*, Catherine said, moving her lips like a silent movie heroine, to Henry, so that neither Carleton nor the agent, who had bent over to inspect a piece of dust on the floor, could see. "You can live in your teepee, and we'll invite you to come over for lunch. You like lunch, don't you? Peanut butter sandwiches?"

"I don't," Carleton said, and sobbed once.

But they bought the house anyway. The real estate agent got her commission. Tilly rubbed the waxy, stone ears of the rabbits on the way out, pretending that they already belonged to her. They were as tall as she was, but that wouldn't always be true. Carleton had a peanut butter sandwich.

The rabbits sat on either side of the front door. Two stone animals sitting on cracked, mossy haunches. They were shapeless, lumpish, patient in a way that seemed not worn down, but perhaps never really finished in the first place. There was something about them that reminded Henry of Stonehenge. Catherine thought of topiary shapes; *The Velveteen Rabbit*; soldiers who stand guard in front of palaces and never even twitch their noses. Maybe they could be donated to a museum. Or broken up with jackhammers. They didn't suit the house at all.

"So what's the house like?" said Henry's boss. She was carefully stretching rubber bands around her rubber band ball. By now the rubber band ball was so big, she had to get special extra-large rubber bands from the art department. She claimed it helped her think. She had tried knitting for a while, but it turned out that knitting was too utilitarian, too feminine. Making an enormous ball out of rubber bands struck the right note. It was something a man might do.

It took up half of her desk. Under the fluorescent office lights it had a peeled red liveliness. You almost expected it to shoot forward and out the door. The larger it got, the more it looked like some kind of eyeless, hairless, legless animal. Maybe a dog. A Carleton-sized dog, Henry thought, although not a Carleton-sized rubber band ball.

Catherine joked sometimes about using the carleton as a measure of unit.

"Big," Henry said. "Haunted."

"Really?" his boss said. "So's this rubber band." She aimed a rubber band at Henry and shot him in the elbow. This was meant to suggest that she and Henry were good friends, and just goofing around, the way good friends did. But what it really meant was that she was angry at him. "Don't leave me," she said.

"I'm only two hours away." Henry put up his hand to ward off rubber bands. "Quit it. We talk on the phone, we use email. I come back to town when you need me in the office."

"You're sure this is a good idea?" his boss said. She fixed her reptilian, watery gaze on him. She had problematical tear ducts. Though she could have had a minor surgical procedure to fix this, she'd chosen not to. It was a tactical advantage, the way it spooked people.

It didn't really matter that Henry remained immune to rubber bands and crocodile tears. She had backup strategies. She thought about which would be most effective while Henry pitched his stupid idea all over again.

Henry had the movers' phone number in his pocket, like a talisman. He wanted to take it out, wave it at The Crocodile, say, Look at this! Instead he said, "For nine years, we've lived in an apartment next door to a building that smells like urine. Like someone built an entire building out of bricks made of compressed red pee. Someone spit on Catherine in the street last week. This old Russian lady in a fur coat. A kid rang our doorbell the other day and tried to sell us gas masks. Door-to-door gas-mask salesmen. Catherine bought one. When she told me about it, she burst into tears. She said she couldn't figure out if she was feeling guilty because she'd bought a gas mask, or if it was because she hadn't bought enough for everyone."

"Good Chinese food," his boss said. "Good movies. Good bookstores. Good dry cleaners. Good conversation."

"Treehouses," Henry said. "I had a treehouse when I was a kid."

"You were never a kid," his boss said.

"Three bathrooms. Crown moldings. We can't even see our nearest neighbor's house. I get up in the morning, have coffee, put Carleton and Tilly on the bus, and go to work in my pajamas."

"What about Catherine?" The Crocodile put her head down on her rubber band ball. Possibly this was a gesture of defeat.

"There was that thing. Catherine's whole department is leaving. Like rats deserting a sinking ship. Anyway, Catherine needs a change. And so do I," Henry said. "We've got another kid on the way. We're going to garden. Catherine'll teach ESOL, find a book group, write her book. Teach the kids how to play bridge. You've got to start them early."

He picked a rubber band off the floor and offered it to his boss. "You should come out and visit some weekend."

"I never go upstate," The Crocodile said. She held on to her rubber band ball. "Too many ghosts."

"Are you going to miss this? Living here?" Catherine said. She couldn't stand the way her stomach poked out. She couldn't see past it. She held up her left foot to make sure it was still there, and pulled the sheet off Henry.

"I love the house," Henry said.

"Me too," Catherine said. She was biting her fingernails. Henry could hear her teeth going *click, click*. Now she had both feet up in the air. She wiggled them around. Hello, feet.

"What are you doing?"

She put them down again. On the street outside, cars came and went, pushing smears of light along the ceiling, slow and fast at the same time. The baby was wriggling around inside her, kicking out with both feet like it was swimming across the English Channel, the Pacific. Kicking all the way to China. "Did you buy that story about the former owners moving to France?"

"I don't believe in France," Henry said. "*Je ne crois pas en France.*"

"Neither do I," Catherine said. "Henry?"

"What?"

"Do you love the house?"

"I love the house."

"I love it more than you do," Catherine said, although Henry hated it when she said things like that. "What do you love best?"

"That room in the front," Henry said. "With the windows. Our bedroom. Those weird rabbit statues."

"Me too," Catherine said, although she didn't. "I love those rabbits."

Then she said, "Do you ever worry about Carleton and Tilly?"

"What do you mean?" Henry said. He looked at the alarm clock: it was 4 A.M. "Why are we awake right now?"

"Sometimes I worry that I love one of them better," Catherine said. "Like I might love Tilly better. Because she used to wet the bed. Because she's always so angry. Or Carleton, because he was so sick when he was little."

"I love them both the same," Henry said.

He didn't even know he was lying. Catherine knew, though. She knew he was lying, and she knew he didn't even know it. Most of the time she thought that it was okay. As long as he thought he loved them both the same, and acted as if he did, that was good enough.

"Well, do you ever worry that you love them more than me?" she said. "Or that I love them more than I love you?"

"Do you?" Henry said.

"Of course," Catherine said. "I have to. It's my job."

She found the gas mask in a box of wineglasses, and also six recent issues of *The New Yorker*, which she still might get a chance to read someday. She put the gas mask under the sink and *The New Yorker*s in the sink. Why not? It was her sink. She could put anything she wanted into it. She took the magazines out again and put them into the refrigerator, just for fun.

Henry came into the kitchen, holding silver candlesticks and a stuffed armadillo, which someone had made into a purse. It had a shoulder strap made out of its own skin. You opened its mouth and put things inside it, lipstick and subway tokens. It had pink gimlet eyes and smelled strongly of vinegar. It belonged to Tilly, although how it had come into her possession was unclear. Tilly claimed she'd won it at school in a contest involving donuts. Catherine thought it more likely Tilly had either stolen it or (slightly preferable) found it in someone's trash. Now Tilly kept her most valuable belongings inside the purse, to keep them safe from Carleton, who was covetous of the precious things—because they were small, and because they belonged to Tilly—but afraid of the armadillo.

"I've already told her she can't take it to school for at least the first two weeks. Then we'll see." She took the purse from Henry and put it with the gas mask under the sink.

"What are they doing?" Henry said. Framed in the kitchen window, Carleton and Tilly hunched over the lawn. They had a pair of scissors and a notebook and a stapler.

"They're collecting grass," Catherine took dishes out of a box, put the Bubble Wrap aside for Tilly to stomp, and stowed the dishes in a cabinet. The baby kicked like it knew all about Bubble Wrap. "Woah, Fireplace," she said. "We don't have a dancing license in there."

Henry put out his hand, rapped on Catherine's stomach. *Knock, knock.* It was Tilly's joke. Catherine would say, "Who's there?" and Tilly would say, Candlestick's here. Fat Man's here. Box. Hammer. Milkshake. Clarinet. Mousetrap. Fiddlestick. Tilly had a whole list of names for the baby. The real estate agent would have approved.

"Where's King Spanky?" Henry said.

"Under our bed," Catherine said. "He's up in the box frame."

"Have we unpacked the alarm clock?" Henry said.

"Poor King Spanky," Catherine said. "Nobody to love except an alarm clock. Come upstairs and let's see if we can shake him out of the bed. I've got a present for you."

The present was in a U-Haul box exactly like all the other boxes in the bedroom, except that Catherine had written HENRY'S PRESENT on it instead of LARGE FRONT BEDROOM. Inside the box were Styrofoam peanuts and then a smaller box from Takashimaya. The Takashimaya box was fastened with a silver ribbon. The tissue paper inside was dull gold, and inside the tissue paper was a green silk robe with orange sleeves and heraldic animals in orange and gold thread. "Lions," Henry said.

"Rabbits," Catherine said.

"I didn't get you anything," Henry said.

Catherine smiled nobly. She liked giving presents better than getting presents. She'd never told Henry, because it seemed to her that it must be selfish in some way she'd never bothered to figure out. Catherine was grateful to be married to Henry, who accepted all presents as his due; who looked good in the clothes that she bought him; who was vain, in an easy-going way, about his good looks. Buying clothes for Henry was especially satisfying now, while she was pregnant and couldn't buy them for herself.

She said, "If you don't like it, then I'll keep it. Look at you, look at those sleeves. You look like the emperor of Japan."

They had already colonized the bedroom, making it full of things that belonged to them. There was Catherine's mirror on the wall, and their mahogany wardrobe, their first real piece of furniture, a wedding present from Catherine's great-aunt. There was their serviceable, queen-sized bed with King Spanky lodged up inside it, and there was Henry, spinning his arms in the wide orange sleeves, like an embroidered windmill. Henry could see all of these things in the mirror, and behind him, their lawn and Tilly and Carleton, stapling grass into their notebook. He saw all of these things and he found them good. But he couldn't see Catherine. When he turned around, she stood in the doorway, frowning at him. She had the alarm clock in her hand.

"Look at you," she said again. It worried her, the way something, some-one, *Henry*, could suddenly look like a place she'd never been before. The alarm began to ring and King Spanky came out from under the bed, trotting over to Catherine. She bent over, awkwardly—ungraceful, ungainly, so clumsy, so fucking awkward, being pregnant was like wearing a fucking suitcase strapped across your middle—put the alarm clock down on the ground, and King Spanky hunkered down in front of it, his nose against the ringing glass face.

And that made her laugh again. Henry loved Catherine's laugh. Downstairs, their children slammed a door open, ran through the house, carrying scissors, both Catherine and Henry knew, and slammed another door open and were outside again, leaving behind the smell of grass. There was a store in New York where you could buy a perfume that smelled like that.

Catherine and Carleton and Tilly came back from the grocery store with a tire, a rope to hang it from, and a box of pancake mix for dinner. Henry was online, looking at a jpeg of a rubber band ball. There was a message too. The Crocodile needed him to come into the office. It would be just a few days. Someone was setting fires and there was no one smart enough to see how to put them out except for him. They were his accounts. He had to come in and save them. She knew Catherine and Henry's apartment hadn't sold; she'd checked with their listing agent. So surely it wouldn't be impossible, not impossible, only inconvenient.

He went downstairs to tell Catherine. "That *witch*," she said, and then bit her lip. "She called the listing agent? I'm sorry. We talked about this. Never mind. Just give me a moment."

Catherine inhaled. Exhaled. Inhaled. If she were Carleton, she would hold her breath until her face turned red and Henry agreed to stay home, but then again, it never worked for Carleton. "We ran into our new neighbors in the grocery store. She's about the same age as me. Liz and Marcus. One kid, older, a girl, um, I think her name was Alison, maybe from a first marriage—potential babysitter, which is really good news. Liz is a lawyer. Gorgeous. Reads Oprah books. He likes to cook."

"So do I," Henry said.

"You're better looking," Catherine said. "So do you have to go back tonight, or can you take the train in the morning?"

"The morning is fine," Henry said, wanting to seem agreeable.

Carleton appeared in the kitchen, his arms pinned around King Spanky's middle. The cat's front legs stuck straight out, as if Carleton were dowsing. King Spanky's eyes were closed. His whiskers twitched Morse code. "What are you wearing?" Carleton said.

"My new uniform," Henry said. "I wear it to work."

"Where do you work?" Carleton said, testing.

"I work at home," Henry said. Catherine snorted.

"He looks like the king of rabbits, doesn't he? The plenipotentiary of Rabbitaly," she said, no longer sounding particularly pleased about this.

"He looks like a princess," Carleton said, now pointing King Spanky at Henry like a gun.

"Where's your grass collection?" Henry said. "Can I see it?"

"No," Carleton said. He put King Spanky on the floor, and the cat slunk out of the kitchen, heading for the staircase, the bedroom, the safety of the bedsprings, the beloved alarm clock, the beloved. The beloved may be treacherous, greasy-headed and given to evil habits, or else it can be a man in his late forties who works too much, or it can be an alarm clock.

"After dinner," Henry said, trying again, "we could go out and find a tree for your tire swing."

"No," Carleton said, regretfully. He lingered in the kitchen, hoping to be asked a question to which he could say yes.

"Where's your sister?" Henry said.

"Watching television," Carleton said. "I don't like the television here."

"It's too big," Henry said, but Catherine didn't laugh.

Henry dreams he is the king of the real estate agents. Henry loves his job. He tries to sell a house to a young couple with twitchy noses and big dark eyes. Why does he always dream that he's trying to sell things?

The couple stare at him nervously. He leans towards them as if he's going to whisper something in their silly, expectant ears. It's a secret he's never told anyone before. It's a secret he didn't even know that he knew.

"Let's stop fooling," he says. "You can't afford to buy this house. You don't have any money. You're rabbits."

"Where do you work?" Carleton said, in the morning, when Henry called from Grand Central.

"I work at home," Henry said. "Home where we live now, where you are. Eventually. Just not today. Are you getting ready for school?"

Carleton put the phone down. Henry could hear him saying something to Catherine. "He says he's not nervous about school," she said. "He's a brave kid."

"I kissed you this morning," Henry said, "but you didn't wake up. There were all these rabbits on the lawn. They were huge. King Spanky—sized. They were just sitting there like they were waiting for the sun to come up. It was funny, like some kind of art installation. But it was kind of creepy too. Think they'd been there all night?"

"Rabbits? Can they have rabies? I saw them this morning when I got up," Catherine said. "Carleton didn't want to brush his teeth this morning. He says something's wrong with his toothbrush."

"Maybe he dropped it in the toilet, and he doesn't want to tell you," Henry said.

"Maybe you could buy a new toothbrush and bring it home," Catherine said. "He doesn't want one from the drugstore here. He wants one from New York."

"Where's Tilly?" Henry said.

"She says she's trying to figure out what's wrong with Carleton's toothbrush. She's still in the bathroom." Catherine said.

"Can I talk to her for a second?" Henry said.

"Tell her she needs to get dressed and eat her Cheerios," Catherine said. "After I drive them to school, Liz is coming over for coffee. Then we're going to go out for lunch. I'm not unpacking another box until you get home. Here's Tilly."

"Hi," Tilly said. She sounded as if she were asking a question.

Tilly never liked talking to people on the telephone. How were you supposed to know if they were really who they said they were? And even if they were who they claimed to be, they didn't know whether you were who you said you were. You could be someone else. They might give away information about you, and not even know it. There were no protocols. No precautions.

She said, "Did you brush your teeth this morning?"

"Good morning, Tilly," her father (if it was her father) said. "My toothbrush was fine. Perfectly normal."

"That's good," Tilly said. "I let Carleton use mine."

"That was very generous," Henry said.

"No problem," Tilly said. Sharing things with Carleton wasn't like having to share things with other people. It wasn't really like sharing things at all. Carleton belonged to her, like the toothbrush. "Mom says that when we get home today, we can draw on the walls in our rooms if we want to, while we decide what color we want to paint them."

"Sounds like fun," Henry said. "Can I draw on them too?"

"Maybe," Tilly said. She had already said too much. "Gotta go. Gotta eat breakfast."

"Don't be worried about school," Henry said.

"I'm not worried about school," Tilly said.

"I love you," Henry said.

"I'm real concerned about this toothbrush," Tilly said.

He closed his eyes only for a minute. Just for a minute. When he woke up, it was dark and he didn't know where he was. He stood up and went over to the door, almost tripping over something. It sailed away from him in an exuberant, rollicking sweep. According to the clock on his desk, it was 4 A.M. Why was it always 4 A.M.? There were four messages on his cell phone, all from Catherine.

He checked train schedules online. Then he sent Catherine a fast email.

Fell asleep @ midnight? Mssed trains. Awake now, going to

keep on working. Pttng out fires. Take the train home early
afternoon? Still lv me?

Before he went back to work, he kicked the rubber band ball back down
the hall towards The Crocodile's door.

Catherine called him at 8:45.

"I'm sorry," Henry said.

"I bet you are," Catherine said.

"I can't find my razor. I think The Crocodile had some kind of tantrum
and tossed my stuff."

"Carleton will love that," Catherine said. "Maybe you should sneak
in the house and shave before dinner. He had a hard day at school yes-
terday."

"Maybe I should grow a beard," Henry said. "He can't be afraid of
everything, all the time. Tell me about the first day of school."

"We'll talk about it later," Catherine said. "Liz just drove up. I'm going
to be her guest at the gym. Just make it home for dinner."

At 6 A.M. Henry emailed Catherine again. "Srry. Accidentally startd ava-
lanche while puttng out fires. Wait up for me? How ws 2nd day of school?"
She didn't write him back. He called and no one picked up the phone. She
didn't call.

He took the last train home. By the time it reached the station, he was
the only one left in his car. He unchained his bicycle and rode it home in
the dark. Rabbits pelted across the footpath in front of his bike. There
were rabbits foraging on his lawn. They froze as he dismounted and pushed
the bicycle across the grass. The lawn was rumpled; the bike went up and
down over invisible depressions that he supposed were rabbit holes. There
were two short fat men standing in the dark on either side of the front
door, waiting for him, but when he came closer, he remembered that they
were stone rabbits. "Knock, knock," he said.

The real rabbits on the lawn tipped their ears at him. The stone rabbits waited for the punch line, but they were just stone rabbits. They had nothing better to do.

The front door wasn't locked. He walked through the downstairs rooms, putting his hands on the backs and tops of furniture. In the kitchen, cut-down boxes leaned in stacks against the wall, waiting to be recycled or remade into cardboard houses and spaceships and tunnels for Carleton and Tilly.

Catherine had unpacked Carleton's room. Night-lights in the shape of bears and geese and cats were plugged into every floor outlet. There were little low-watt table lamps as well—hippo, robot, gorilla, pirate ship. Everything was soaked in a tender, peaceable light, translating Carleton's room into something more than a bedroom: something luminous, numinous, Carleton's cartoony Midnight Church of Sleep.

Tilly was sleeping in the other bed.

Tilly would never admit that she sleepwalked, the same way that she would never admit that she sometimes still wet the bed. But she refused to make friends. Making friends would have meant spending the night in strange houses. Tomorrow morning she would insist that Henry or Catherine must have carried her from her room, put her to bed in Carleton's room for reasons of their own.

Henry knelt down between the two beds and kissed Carleton on the forehead. He kissed Tilly, smoothed her hair. How could he not love Tilly better? He'd known her longer. She was so brave, so angry.

On the walls of Carleton's bedroom, Henry's children had drawn a house. A cat nearly as big as the house. There was a crown on the cat's head. Trees or flowers with pairs of leaves that pointed straight up, still bigger, and a stick figure on a stick bicycle, riding past the trees. When he looked closer, he thought that maybe the trees were actually rabbits. The wall smelled like Fruit Loops. Someone had written *Henry Is A Rat Fink! Ha Ha!* He recognized his wife's handwriting.

"Scented markers," Catherine said. She stood in the door, holding a pillow against her stomach. "I was sleeping downstairs on the sofa. You walked right past and didn't see me."

"The front door was unlocked," Henry said.

"Liz says nobody ever locks their doors out here," Catherine said. "Are you coming to bed, or were you just stopping by to see how we were?"

"I have to go back in tomorrow." Henry said. He pulled a toothbrush out of his pocket and showed it to her. "There's a box of Krispy Kreme donuts on the kitchen counter."

"Delete the donuts," Catherine said. "I'm not that easy." She took a step towards him and accidentally kicked King Spanky. The cat yowled. Carleton woke up. He said, "Who's there? Who's there?"

"It's me," Henry said. He knelt beside Carleton's bed in the light of the Winnie the Pooh lamp. "I brought you a new toothbrush."

Carleton whimpered.

"What's wrong, spaceman?" Henry said. "It's just a toothbrush." He leaned towards Carleton and Carleton scooted back. He began to scream.

In the other bed, Tilly was dreaming about rabbits. When she'd come home from school, she and Carleton had seen rabbits, sitting on the lawn as if they had kept watch over the house all the time that Tilly had been gone. In her dream they were still there. She dreamed she was creeping up on them. They opened their mouths, wide enough to reach inside like she was some kind of rabbit dentist, and so she did. She put her hand around something small and cold and hard. Maybe it was a ring, a diamond ring. Or a. Or. It was a. She couldn't wait to show Carleton. Her arm was inside the rabbit all the way to her shoulder. Someone put their little cold hand around her wrist and yanked. Somewhere her mother was talking. She said—

"It's the beard."

Catherine couldn't decide whether to laugh or cry or scream like Carleton. That would surprise Carleton, if she started screaming too. "Shoo! Shoo, Henry—go shave and come back as quick as you can, or else he'll never go back to sleep."

"Carleton, honey," she was saying as Henry left the room. "It's your dad. It's not Santa Claus. It's not the big bad wolf. It's your dad. Your dad just forgot. Why don't you tell me a story? Or do you want to go watch your daddy shave?"

Catherine's hot water bottle was draped over the tub. Towels were heaped on the floor. Henry's things had been put away behind the mirror. It made him feel tired, thinking of all the other things that still had to be put away. He washed his hands, then looked at the bar of soap. It didn't feel right. He put it back on the sink, bent over and sniffed it and then tore off a piece of toilet paper, used the toilet paper to pick up the soap. He threw it in the trash and unwrapped a new bar of soap. There was nothing wrong with the new soap. There was nothing wrong with the old soap either. He was just tired. He washed his hands and lathered up his face, shaved off his beard and watched the little bristles of hair wash down the sink. When he went to show Carleton his brand-new face, Catherine was curled up in bed beside Carleton. They were both asleep. They were still asleep when he left the house at 5:30 the next morning.

"Where are you?" Catherine said.

"I'm on my way home. I'm on the train." The train was still in the station. They would be leaving any minute. They had been leaving any minute for the last hour or so, and before that, they had had to get off the train twice, and then back on again. They had been assured there was nothing to worry about. There was no bomb threat. There was no bomb. The delay was only temporary. The people on the train looked at each other, trying to seem as if they were not looking. Everyone had their cell phones out.

"The rabbits are out on the lawn again," Catherine said. "There must be at least fifty or sixty. I've never counted rabbits before. Tilly keeps trying to go outside to make friends with them, but as soon as she's outside, they all go bouncing away like beach balls. I talked to a lawn specialist today. He says we need to do something about it, which is what Liz was saying. Rabbits can be a big problem out here. They've probably got tunnels and warrens all through the yard. It could be a problem. Like living on top of a sinkhole. But Tilly is never going to forgive us. She knows something's up. She says she doesn't want a dog anymore. It would scare away the rabbits. Do you think we should get a dog?"

"So what do they do? Put out poison? Dig up the yard?" Henry said.

The man in the seat in front of him got up. He took his bags out of the luggage rack and left the train. Everyone watched him go, pretending they were not.

"He was telling me they have these devices, kind of like ultrasound equipment. They plot out the tunnels, close them up, and then gas the rabbits. It sounds gruesome," Catherine said. "And this kid, this baby has been kicking the daylights out of me. All day long it's kick, kick, jump, kick, like some kind of martial artist. He's going to be an angry kid, Henry. Just like his sister. Her sister. Or maybe I'm going to give birth to rabbits."

"As long as they have your eyes and my chin," Henry said.

"I've gotta go," Catherine said. "I have to pee again. All day long it's the kid jumping, me peeing, Tilly getting her heart broken because she can't make friends with the rabbits, me worrying because she doesn't want to make friends with other kids, just with rabbits, Carleton asking if today he has to go to school, does he have to go to school tomorrow, why am I making him go to school when everybody there is bigger than him, why is my stomach so big and fat, why does his teacher tell him to act like a big boy? Henry, why are we doing this again? Why am I pregnant? And where are you? Why aren't you here? What about our deal? Don't you want to be here?"

"I'm sorry," Henry said. "I'll talk to The Crocodile. We'll work something out."

"I thought you wanted this too, Henry. Don't you?"

"Of course," Henry said. "Of course I want this."

"I've gotta go," Catherine said again. "Liz is bringing some women over. We're finally starting that book club. We're going to read *Fight Club*. Her stepdaughter Alison is going to look after Tilly and Carleton for me. I've already talked to Tilly. She promises she won't bite or hit or make Alison cry."

"What's the trade? A few hours of bonus TV?"

"No," Catherine said. "Something's up with the TV."

"What's wrong with the TV?"

"I don't know," Catherine said. "It's working fine. But the kids won't go near it. Isn't that great? It's the same thing as the toothbrush. You'll see when you get home. I mean, it's not just the kids. I was watching the news earlier, and then I had to turn it off. It wasn't the news. It was the TV."

"So it's the downstairs bathroom and the coffeemaker and Carleton's toothbrush and now the TV?"

"There's some other stuff as well, since this morning. Your office, apparently. Everything in it—your desk, your bookshelves, your chair, even the paper clips."

"That's probably a good thing, right? I mean, that way they'll stay out of there."

"I guess," Catherine said. "The thing is, I went and stood in there for a while and it gave me the creeps too. So now I can't pick up email. And I had to throw out more soap. And King Spanky doesn't love the alarm clock anymore. He won't come out from under the bed when I set it off."

"The alarm clock too?"

"It does sound different," Catherine said. "Just a little bit different. Or maybe I'm insane. This morning, Carleton told me that he knew where our house was. He said we were living in a secret part of Central Park. He said he recognizes the trees. He thinks that if he walks down that little path, he'll get mugged. I've really got to go, Henry, or I'm going to wet my pants, and I don't have time to change again before everyone gets here."

"I love you," Henry said.

"Then why aren't you here?" Catherine said victoriously. She hung up and ran down the hallway towards the downstairs bathroom. But when she got there, she turned around. She went racing up the stairs, pulling down her pants as she went, and barely got to the master bedroom bathroom in time. All day long she'd gone up and down the stairs, feeling extremely silly. There was nothing wrong with the downstairs bathroom. It's just the fixtures. When you flush the toilet or run water in the sink. She doesn't like the sound the water makes.

Several times now, Henry had come home and found Catherine painting rooms, which was a problem. The problem was that Henry kept going away. If he didn't keep going away, he wouldn't have to keep coming home.

That was Catherine's point. Henry's point was that Catherine wasn't supposed to be painting rooms while she was pregnant. Pregnant women weren't supposed to breathe around paint fumes.

Catherine solved this problem by wearing the gas mask while she painted. She had known the gas mask would come in handy. She told Henry she promised to stop painting as soon as he started working at home, which was the plan. Meanwhile, she couldn't decide on colors. She and Carleton and Tilly spent hours looking at paint strips with colors that had names like Sangria, Peat Bog, Tulip, Tantrum, Planetarium, Galactica, Tea Leaf, Egg Yolk, Tinker Toy, Gauguin, Susan, Envy, Aztec, Utopia, Wax Apple, Rice Bowl, Cry Baby, Fat Lip, Green Banana, Trampoline, Finger Nail. It was a wonderful way to spend time. They went off to school, and when they got home, the living room would be Harp Seal instead of Full Moon. They'd spend some time with that color, getting to know it, ignoring the television, which was haunted (*haunted* wasn't the right word, of course, but Catherine couldn't think what the right word was) and then a couple of days later, Catherine would go buy some more primer and start again. Carleton and Tilly loved this. They begged her to repaint their bedrooms. She did.

She wished she could eat paint. Whenever she opened a can of paint, her mouth watered. When she'd been pregnant with Carleton, she hadn't been able to eat anything except for olives and hearts of palm and dry toast. When she'd been pregnant with Tilly, she'd eaten dirt, once, in Central Park. Tilly thought they should name the baby after a paint color, Chalk, or Dilly Dilly, or Keelhauled. Lapis Lazulily. Knock Knock.

Catherine kept meaning to ask Henry to take the television and put it in the garage. Nobody ever watched it now. They'd had to stop using the microwave as well, and a colander, some of the flatware, and she was keeping an eye on the toaster. She had a premonition, or an intuition. It didn't feel wrong, not yet, but she had a feeling about it. There was a gorgeous pair of earrings that Henry had given her—how was it possible to be spooked by a pair of diamond earrings?—and yet. Carleton wouldn't play with his Lincoln Logs, and so they were going to the Salvation Army, and Tilly's armadillo purse had disappeared. Tilly hadn't said anything about it, and Catherine hadn't wanted to ask.

Sometimes, if Henry wasn't coming home, Catherine painted after Carleton and Tilly went to bed. Sometimes Tilly would walk into the room where Catherine was working, Tilly's eyes closed, her mouth open, a tourist-somnambulist. She'd stand there, with her head cocked towards Catherine. If Catherine spoke to her, she never answered, and if Catherine took her hand, she would follow Catherine back to her own bed and lie down again. But sometimes Catherine let Tilly stand there and keep her company. Tilly was never so attentive, so *present*, when she was awake. Eventually she would turn and leave the room and Catherine would listen to her climb back up the stairs. Then she would be alone again.

Catherine dreams about colors. It turns out her marriage was the same color she had just painted the foyer. Velveteen Fade. Leonard Felter, who had had an ongoing affair with two of his graduate students, several adjuncts, two tenured faculty members, brought down Catherine's entire department, and saved Catherine's marriage, would make a good lipstick or nail polish. Peach Nooky. There's The Crocodile, a particularly bilious Eau De Vil, a color that tastes bad when you say it. Her mother, who had always been disappointed by Catherine's choices, turned out to have been a beautiful, rich, deep chocolate. Why hadn't Catherine ever seen that before? Too late, too late. It made her want to cry.

Liz and she are drinking paint. "Have some more paint," Catherine says. "Do you want sugar?"

"Yes, lots," Liz says. "What color are you going to paint the rabbits?"

Catherine passes her the sugar. She hasn't even thought about the rabbits, except which rabbits does Liz mean, the stone rabbits or the real rabbits? How do you make them hold still?

"I got something for you," Liz says. She's got Tilly's armadillo purse. It's full of paint strips. Catherine's mouth fills with saliva.

Henry dreams he has an appointment with the exterminator. "You've got to take care of this," he says. "We have two small children. These things could be rabid. They might carry plague."

"See what I can do," the exterminator says, sounding glum. He stands next to Henry. He's an odd-looking, twitchy guy. He has big ears. They contemplate the skyscrapers that poke out of the grass like obelisks. The lawn is teeming with skyscrapers. "Never seen anything like this before. Never wanted to see anything like this. But if you want my opinion, it's the house that's the real problem—"

"Never mind about my wife," Henry says. He squats down beside a knee-high art-deco skyscraper, and peers into a window. A little man looks back at him and shakes his fists, screaming something obscene. Henry flicks a finger at the window, almost hard enough to break it. He feels hot all over. He's never felt this angry before in his life, not even when Catherine told him that she'd accidentally slept with Leonard Felter. The little bastard is going to regret what he just said, whatever it was. He lifts his foot.

The exterminator says, "I wouldn't do that if I were you. You have to dig them up, get the roots. Otherwise, they just grow back. Like your house. Which is really just the tip of the iceberg lettuce, so to speak. You've probably got seventy, eighty stories underground. You gone down on the elevator yet? Talked to the people living down there? It's your house, and you're just going to let them live there rent-free? Mess with your things like that?"

"What?" Henry says, and then he hears helicopters, fighter planes the size of hummingbirds. "Is this really necessary?" he says to the exterminator.

The exterminator nods. "You have to catch them off guard."

"Maybe we're being hasty," Henry says. He has to yell to be heard above the noise of the tiny, tinny, furious planes. "Maybe we can settle this peacefully."

"Hemree," the interrogator says, shaking his head. "You called me in, because I'm the expert, and you knew you needed help."

Henry wants to say "You're saying my name wrong." But he doesn't want to hurt the undertaker's feelings.

The alligator keeps on talking. "Listen up, Hemreeee, and shut up about negotiations and such, because if we don't take care of this right away, it may be too late. This isn't about homeownership, or lawn care, Hemreeeeee, this is war. The lives of your children are at stake. The happiness of your family. Be brave. Be strong. Just hang on to your rabbit and fire when you see delight in their eyes."

He woke up. "Catherine," he whispered. "Are you awake? I was having this dream."

Catherine laughed. "That's the phone, Liz," she said. "It's probably Henry, saying he'll be late."

"Catherine," Henry said. "Who are you talking to?"

"Are you mad at me, Henry?" Catherine said. "Is that why you won't come home?"

"I'm right here," Henry said.

"You take your rabbits and your crocodiles and get out of here," Catherine said. "And then come straight home again."

She sat up in bed and pointed her finger. "I am sick and tired of being spied on by rabbits!"

When Henry looked, something stood beside the bed, rocking back and forth on its heels. He fumbled for the light, got it on, and saw Tilly, her mouth open, her eyes closed. She looked larger than she ever did when she was awake. "It's just Tilly," he said to Catherine, but Catherine lay back down again. She put her pillow over her head. When he picked Tilly up, to carry her back to bed, she was warm and sweaty, her heart racing as if she had been running through all the rooms of the house.

He walked through the house. He rapped on walls, testing. He put his ear against the floor. No elevator. No secret rooms, no hidden passageways.

There isn't even a basement.

Tilly has divided the yard in half. Carleton is not allowed in her half, unless she gives permission.

From the bottom of her half of the yard, where the trees run beside the driveway, Tilly can barely see the house. She's decided to name the yard Matilda's Rabbit Kingdom. Tilly loves naming things. When the new baby is born, her mother has promised that she can help pick out the real names, although there will only be two real names, a first one and a middle. Tilly doesn't understand why there can only be two. *Oishi* means "delicious" in Japanese. That would make a good name, either for the baby or for the yard, because of the grass. She knows the yard isn't as big as Central Park, but it's just as good, even if there aren't any pagodas or castles or carriages or people on roller skates. There's plenty of grass. There are hundreds of rabbits. They live in an enormous underground city, maybe a city just like New York. Maybe her dad can stop working in New York, and come work under the lawn instead. She could help him, go to work with him. She could be a biologist, like Jane Goodall, and go and live underground with the rabbits. Last year her ambition had been to go and live secretly in the Metropolitan Museum of Art, but someone has already done that, even if it's only in a book. Tilly feels sorry for Carleton. Everything he ever does, she'll have already been there. She'll already have done that.

Tilly has left her armadillo purse sticking out of a rabbit hole. First she made the hole bigger; then she packed the dirt back in around the armadillo so that only the shiny, peeled snout poked out. Carleton digs it out again with his stick. Maybe Tilly meant him to find it. Maybe it was a present for the rabbits, except what is it doing here, in his half of the yard? When he lived in the apartment, he was afraid of the armadillo purse, but there are better things to be afraid of out here. But be careful, Carleton. Might as well be careful. The armadillo purse says Don't touch me. So he doesn't. He uses his stick to pry open the snap-mouth, dumps out Tilly's most valuable things, and with his stick pushes them one by one down the hole. Then he puts his ear to the rabbit hole so that he can hear the rabbits say thank you. Saying thank you is polite. But the rabbits say nothing. They're holding their breath, waiting for him to go away. Carleton waits too. Tilly's armadillo, empty and smelly and haunted, makes his eyes water.

Someone comes up and stands behind him. "I didn't do it," he says. "They fell."

But when he turns around, it's the girl who lives next door. Alison. The sun is behind her and makes her shine. He squints. "You can come over to my house if you want to," she says. "Your mom says. She's going to pay me fifteen bucks an hour, which is way too much. Are your parents really rich or something? What's that?"

"It's Tilly's," he says. "But I don't think she wants it anymore."

She picks up Tilly's armadillo. "Pretty cool," she says. "Maybe I'll keep it for her."

Deep underground, the rabbits stamp their feet in rage.

Catherine loves the house. She loves her new life. She's never understood people who get stuck, become unhappy, can't change, can't adapt. So she's out of a job. So what? She'll find something else to do. So Henry can't leave his job yet, won't leave his job yet. So the house is haunted. That's okay. They'll work through it. She buys some books on gardening. She plants a rosebush and a climbing vine in a pot. Tilly helps. The rabbits eat off all the leaves. They bite through the vine.

"Shit," Catherine says when she sees what they've done. She shakes her fists at the rabbits on the lawn. The rabbits flick their ears at her. They're laughing, she knows it. She's too big to chase after them.

"Henry, wake up. Wake up."

"I'm awake," he said, and then he was. Catherine was crying: noisy, wet, ugly sobs. He put his hand out and touched her face. Her nose was running.

"Stop crying," he said. "I'm awake. Why are you crying?"

"Because you weren't here," she said. "And then I woke up and you were here, but when I wake up tomorrow morning you'll be gone again. I miss you. Don't you miss me?"

"I'm sorry," he said. "I'm sorry I'm not here. I'm here now. Come here."

"No," she said. She stopped crying, but her nose still leaked. "And now the dishwasher is haunted. We have to get a new dishwasher before I have this baby. You can't have a baby and not have a dishwasher. And you have to live here with us. Because I'm going to need some help this time. Remember Carleton, how fucking hard that was."

"He was one cranky baby," Henry said. When Carleton was three months old, Henry had realized that they'd misunderstood something. Babies weren't babies—they were land mines; bear traps; wasp nests. They were a noise, which was sometimes even not a noise, but merely a listening for a noise; they were a damp, chalky smell; they were the heaving, jerky, sticky manifestation of not-sleep. Once Henry had stood and watched Carleton in his crib, sleeping peacefully. He had not done what he wanted to do. He had not bent over and yelled in Carleton's ear. Henry still hadn't forgiven Carleton, not yet, not entirely, not for making him feel that way.

"Why do you have to love your job so much?" Catherine said.

"I don't know," Henry said. "I don't love it."

"Don't lie to me," Catherine said.

"I love you better," Henry said. He does, he does, he does loves Catherine better. He's already made that decision. But she isn't even listening.

"Remember when Carleton was little and you would get up in the morning and go to work and leave me all alone with them?" Catherine poked him in the side. "I used to hate you. You'd come home with takeout, and I'd forget I hated you, but then I'd remember again, and I'd hate you even more because it was so easy for you to trick me, to make things okay again, just because for an hour I could sit in the bathtub and eat Chinese food and wash my hair."

"You used to carry an extra shirt with you, when you went out," Henry said. He put his hand down inside her T-shirt, on her fat, full breast. "In case you leaked."

"You can't touch that breast," Catherine said. "It's haunted." She blew her nose on the sheets.

Catherine's friend Lucy owns an online boutique, Nice Clothes for Fat People. There's a woman in Tarrytown who knits stretchy, sexy Argyle sweaters exclusively for NCFP, and Lucy has an appointment with her. She wants to stop off and see Catherine afterwards, before she has to drive back to the city again. Catherine gives her directions, and then begins to clean house, feeling out of sorts. She's not sure she wants to see Lucy right now. Carleton has always been afraid of Lucy, which is embarrassing. And Catherine doesn't want to talk about Henry. She doesn't want to explain about the downstairs bathroom. She had planned to spend the day painting the wood trim in the dining room, but now she'll have to wait.

The doorbell rings, but when Catherine goes to answer it, no one is there. Later on, after Tilly and Carleton have come home, it rings again, but no one is there. It rings and rings, as if Lucy is standing outside, pressing the bell over and over again. Finally Catherine pulls out the wire. She tries calling Lucy's cell phone, but can't get through. Then Henry calls. He says that he's going to be late.

Liz opens the front door, yells, "Hello, anyone home! You've got to see your rabbits, there must be thousands of them. Catherine, is something wrong with your doorbell?"

Henry's bike, so far, was okay. He wondered what they'd do if the Toyota suddenly became haunted. Would Catherine want to sell it? Would resale value be affected? The car and Catherine and the kids were gone when he got home, so he put on a pair of work gloves and went through the house with a cardboard box, collecting all the things that felt haunted. A hairbrush in Tilly's room, an old pair of Catherine's tennis shoes. A pair of Catherine's underwear that he finds at the foot of the bed. When he picked them up he felt a sudden shock of longing for Catherine, like he'd been hit by some kind of spooky lightning. It hit him in the pit of the stomach, like a cramp. He dropped them in the box.

The silk kimono from Takashimaya. Two of Carleton's night-lights. He opened the door to his office, put the box inside. All the hair on his arms stood up. He closed the door.

Then he went downstairs and cleaned paintbrushes. If the paintbrushes were becoming haunted, if Catherine was throwing them out and buying new ones, she wasn't saying. Maybe he should check the Visa bill. How much were they spending on paint, anyway?

Catherine came into the kitchen and gave him a hug. "I'm glad you're home," she said. He pressed his nose into her neck and inhaled. "I left the car running—I've got to pee. Would you go pick up the kids for me?"

"Where are they?" Henry said.

"They're over at Liz's. Alison is babysitting them. Do you have money on you?"

"You mean I'll meet some neighbors?"

"Wow, sure," Catherine said. "If you think you're ready. Are you ready? Do you know where they live?"

"They're our neighbors, right?"

"Take a left out of the driveway, go about a quarter of a mile, and they're the red house with all the trees in front."

But when he drove up to the red house and went and rang the doorbell, no one answered. He heard a child come running down a flight of stairs and then stop and stand in front of the door. "Carleton? Alison?" he said. "Excuse me, this is Catherine's husband, Henry. Carleton and Tilly's dad." The whispering stopped. He waited for a bit. When he crouched down and lifted the mail slot, he thought he saw someone's feet, the hem of a coat, something furry? A dog? Someone standing very still, just to the right of the door? Carleton, playing games. "I see you," he said, and wiggled his fingers through the mail slot. Then he thought maybe it wasn't Carleton after all. He got up quickly and went back to the car. He drove into town and bought more soap.

Tilly was standing in the driveway when he got home, her hands on her hips. "Hi, Dad," she said. "I'm looking for King Spanky. He got outside. Look what Alison found."

She held out a tiny toy bow strung with what looked like dental floss, an arrow as small as a needle.

"Be careful with that," Henry said. "It looks sharp. Archery Barbie, right? So did you guys have a good time with Alison?"

"Alison's okay," Tilly said. She belched. "'Scuse me. I don't feel very good."

"What's wrong?" Henry said.

"My stomach is funny," Tilly said. She looked up at him, frowned, and then vomited all over his shirt, his pants.

"Tilly!" he said. He yanked off his shirt, used a sleeve to wipe her mouth. The vomit was foamy and green.

"It tastes horrible," she said. She sounded surprised. "Why does it always taste so bad when you throw up?"

"So that you won't go around doing it for fun," he said. "Are you going to do it again?"

"I don't think so," she said, making a face.

"Then I'm going to go wash up and change clothes. What were you eating, anyway?"

"Grass," Tilly said.

"Well, no wonder," Henry said. "I thought you were smarter than that, Tilly. Don't do that anymore."

"I wasn't planning to," Tilly said. She spat in the grass.

When Henry opened the front door, he could hear Catherine talking in the kitchen. "The funny thing is," she said, "none of it was true. It was just made up, just like something Carleton would do. Just to get attention."

"Dad," Carleton said. He was jumping up and down on one foot. "Want to hear a song?"

"I was looking for you," Henry said. "Did Alison bring you home? Do you need to go to the bathroom?"

"Why aren't you wearing any clothes?" Carleton said.

Someone in the kitchen laughed, as if they had heard this.

"I had an accident," Henry said, whispering. "But you're right, Carleton, I should go change." He took a shower, rinsed and wrung out his shirt, put on clean clothes, but by the time he got downstairs, Catherine and Carleton and Tilly were eating Cheerios for dinner. They were using paper bowls, plastic spoons, as if it were a picnic. "Liz was here, and Alison, but they were going to a movie," she said. "They said they'd meet you some other day. It was awful—when they came in the door, King Spanky went rushing outside. He's been watching the rabbits all day. If he catches one, Tilly is going to be so upset."

"Tilly's been eating grass," Henry said.

Tilly rolled her eyes. As if.

"Not again!" Catherine said. "Tilly, real people don't eat grass. Oh, look, fantastic, there's King Spanky. Who let him in? What's he got in his mouth?"

King Spanky sits with his back to them. He coughs and something drops to the floor, maybe a frog, or a baby rabbit. It goes scrabbling across the floor, half-leaping, dragging one leg. King Spanky just sits there, watching as it disappears under the sofa. Carleton freaks out. Tilly is shouting "Bad King Spanky! Bad cat!" When Henry and Catherine push the sofa back, it's too late, there's just King Spanky and a little blob of sticky blood on the floor.

Catherine would like to write a novel. She'd like to write a novel with no children in it. The problem with novels with children in them is that bad things will happen either to the children or else to the parents. She wants to write something funny, something romantic.

It isn't very comfortable to sit down now that she's so big. She's started writing on the walls. She writes in pencil. She names her characters after paint colors. She imagines them leading beautiful, happy, useful lives. No haunted toasters. No mothers no children no crocodiles no photocopy machines no Leonard Felters. She writes for two or three hours, and then she paints the walls again before anyone gets home. That's always the best part.

"I need you next weekend," The Crocodile said. Her rubber band ball sat on the floor beside her desk. She had her feet up on it, in an attempt to show it who was boss. The rubber band ball was getting too big for its britches. Someone was going to have to teach it a lesson, send it a memo.

She looked tired. Henry said, "You don't need me."

"I do," The Crocodile said, yawning. "I do. The clients want to take you out to dinner at Four Seasons when they come in to town. They want to go see musicals with you. *Rent. Phantom of the Cabaret Lion.* They want to go to Coney Island with you and eat hot dogs. They want to go out to trendy bars and clubs and pick up strippers and publicists and performance artists. They want to talk about poetry, philosophy, sports, politics, their lousy relationships with their fathers. They want to ask you for advice about their love lives. They want you to come to the weddings of their children and make toasts. You're indispensable, honey. I hope you know that."

"Catherine and I are having some problems with rabbits," Henry said. The rabbits were easier to explain than the other thing. "They've taken over the yard. Things are a little crazy."

"I don't know anything about rabbits," The Crocodile said, digging her pointy heels into the flesh of the rubber band ball until she could feel the red rubber blood come running out. She pinned Henry with her beautiful, watery eyes.

"Henry." She said his name so gently that he had to lean forward to hear what she was saying.

She said, "You have the best of both worlds. A wife and children who adore you, a beautiful house in the country, a secure job at a company that depends on you, a boss who appreciates your talents, clients who think you're the shit. You *are* the shit, Henry, and the thing is, you're probably thinking that no one deserves to have all this. You think you have to make a choice. You think you have to give up something. But you don't have to give up anything, Henry, and anyone who tells you otherwise is a fucking rabbit. Don't listen to them. You can have it all. You *deserve* to have it all. You love your job. Do you love your job?"

"I love my job," Henry says. The Crocodile smiles at him tearily.

It's true. He loves his job.

When Henry came home, it must have been after midnight, because he never got home before midnight. He found Catherine standing on a ladder in the kitchen, one foot resting on the sink. She was wearing her gas mask, a black cotton sports bra, and a pair of black sweatpants rolled down so he could see she wasn't wearing any underwear. Her stomach stuck out so far, she had to hold her arms at a funny angle to run the roller up and down the wall in front of her. Up and down in a V. Then fill the V in. She had painted the kitchen ceiling a shade of purple so dark, it almost looked black. Midnight Eggplant.

Catherine has been buying paints from a specialty catalog. All the colors are named after famous books, *Madame Bovary, Forever Amber, Fahrenheit 451, Tin Drum, A Curtain of Green, Twenty Thousand Leagues Beneath the Sea.* She was painting the walls *Catch-22*, a novel she'd taught over and over again to undergraduates. It always went over well. The paint color was nice too. She couldn't decide if she missed teaching. The thing about teaching and having children is that you always ended up treating your children like undergraduates, and your undergraduates like children. There was a particular tone of voice. She'd even used it on Henry a few times, just to see if it worked.

All the cabinets were fenced around with masking tape, like a crime scene. The room stank of new paint.

Catherine took off the gas mask and said, "Tilly picked it out. What do you think?" Her hands were on her hips. Her stomach poked out at Henry. The gas mask had left a ring of white and red around her eyes and chin.

Henry said, "How was the dinner party?"

"We had fettuccine. Liz and Marcus stayed and helped me do the dishes."

("Is something wrong with your dishwasher?" "No. I mean, yes. We're getting a new one.")

She had had a feeling. It had been a feeling like déjà vu, or being drunk, or falling in love. Like teaching. She had imagined an audience of rabbits out on the lawn, watching her dinner party. A classroom of rabbits, watching a documentary. Rabbit television. Her skin had felt electric.

"So she's a lawyer?" Henry said.

"You haven't even met them yet," Catherine said, suddenly feeling possessive. "But I like them. I really, really like them. They wanted to know all about us. You. I think they think that either we're having marriage problems or that you're imaginary. Finally I took Liz upstairs and showed her your stuff in the closet. I pulled out the wedding album and showed them photos."

"Maybe we could invite them over on Sunday? For a cookout?" Henry said.

"They're away next weekend," Catherine said. "They're going up to the mountains on Friday. They have a house up there. They've invited us. To come along."

"I can't," Henry said. "I have to take care of some clients next weekend. Some big shots. We're having some cash flow problems. Besides, are you allowed to go away? Did you check with your doctor, what's his name again, Dr. Marks?"

"You mean, did I get my permission slip signed?" Catherine said. Henry put his hand on her leg and held on. "Dr. Marks said I'm shipshape. Those were his exact words. Or maybe he said tip-top. It was something alliterative."

"Well, I guess you ought to go, then," Henry said. He rested his head against her stomach. She let him. He looked so tired. "Before Golf Cart shows up. Or what is Tilly calling the baby now?"

"She's around here somewhere," Catherine said. "I keep putting her back in her bed and she keeps getting out again. Maybe she's looking for you."

"Did you get my email?" Henry said. He was listening to Catherine's stomach. He wasn't going to stop touching her unless she told him to.

"You know I can't check email on your computer anymore," Catherine said.

"This is so stupid," Henry said. "This house isn't haunted. There isn't any such thing as a haunted house."

"It isn't the house," Catherine said. "It's the stuff we brought with us. Except for the downstairs bathroom, and that might just be a draft, or an electrical problem. The house is fine. I love the house."

"Our stuff is fine," Henry said. "I love our stuff."

"If you really think our stuff is fine," Catherine said, "then why did you buy a new alarm clock? Why do you keep throwing out the soap?"

"It's the move," Henry said. "It was a hard move."

"King Spanky hasn't eaten his food in three days," Catherine said. "At first I thought it was the food, and I bought new food and he came down and ate it and I realized it wasn't the food, it was King Spanky. I couldn't sleep all night, knowing he was up under the bed. Poor spooky guy. I don't know what to do. Take him to the vet? What do I say? Excuse me, but I think my cat is haunted? Anyway, I can't get him out of the bed. Not even with the old alarm clock, the haunted one."

"I'll try," Henry said. "Let me try and see if I can get him out." But he didn't move. Catherine tugged at a piece of his hair and he put up his hand. She gave him her roller. He popped off the cylinder and bagged it and put it in the freezer, which was full of paintbrushes and other rollers. He helped Catherine down from the ladder. "I wish you would stop painting."

"I can't," she said. "It has to be perfect. If I can just get it right, then everything will go back to normal and stop being haunted and the rabbits won't tunnel under the house and make it fall down, and you'll come home and stay home, and our neighbors will finally get to meet you and they'll like you and you'll like them, and Carleton will stop being afraid of everything, and Tilly will fall asleep in her own bed, and stay there, and—"

"Hey," Henry said. "It's all going to work out. It's all good. I really like this color."

"I don't know," Catherine said. She yawned. "You don't think it looks too old-fashioned?"

They went upstairs and Catherine took a bath while Henry tried to coax King Spanky out of the bed. But King Spanky wouldn't come out. When Henry got down on his hands and knees, and stuck the flashlight under the bed, he could see King Spanky's eyes, his tail hanging down from the box frame.

Out on the lawn the rabbits were perfectly still. Then they sprang up in the air, turning and dropping and landing and then freezing again. Catherine stood at the window of the bathroom, toweling her hair. She turned the bathroom light off, so that she could see them better. The moonlight picked out their shining eyes, the moon-colored fur, each hair tipped in paint. They were playing some rabbit game like leapfrog. Or they were dancing the quadrille. Fighting a rabbit war. Did rabbits fight wars? Catherine didn't know. They ran at each other and then turned and darted back, jumping and crouching and rising up on their back legs. A pair of rabbits took off like racehorses, sailing through the air and over a long curled shape in the grass. Then back over again. She put her face against the window. It was Tilly, stretched out against the grass, Tilly's legs and feet bare and white.

"Tilly," she said, and ran out of the bathroom, wearing only the towel around her hair.

"What is it?" Henry said as Catherine darted past him, and down the stairs. He ran after her, and by the time she had opened the front door, was kneeling beside Tilly, the wet grass tickling her thighs and her belly, Henry was there, too, and he picked up Tilly and was carrying her back into the house. They wrapped her in a blanket and put her in her bed, and because neither of them wanted to sleep in the bed where King Spanky was hiding, they lay down on the sofa in the family room, curled up against each other. When they woke up in the morning, Tilly was asleep in a ball at their feet.

For a whole minute or two, last year, Catherine thought she had it figured out. She was married to a man whose specialty was solving problems, salvaging bad situations. If she did something dramatic enough, if she fucked up badly enough, it would save her marriage. And it did, except that once the problem was solved and the marriage was saved and the baby was conceived and the house was bought, then Henry went back to work.

She stands at the window in the bedroom and looks out at all the trees. For a minute she imagines that Carleton is right, and they are living in Central Park and Fifth Avenue is just right over there. Henry's office is just a few blocks away. All those rabbits are just tourists.

Henry wakes up in the middle of the night. There are people downstairs. He can hear women talking, laughing, and he realizes Catherine's book club must have come over. He gets out of bed. It's dark. What time is it anyway? But the alarm clock is haunted again. He unplugs it. As he comes down the stairs, a voice says, "Well, will you look at that!" and then, "Right under his nose the whole time!"

Henry walks through the house, turning on lights. Tilly stands in the middle of the kitchen. "May I ask who's calling?" she says. She's got Henry's cell phone tucked between her shoulder and her face. She's holding it upside down. Her eyes are open, but she's asleep.

"Who are you talking to?" Henry says.

"The rabbits," Tilly says. She tilts her head, listening. Then she laughs. "Call back later," she says. "He doesn't want to talk to you. Yeah. Okay." She hands Henry his phone. "They said it's no one you know."

"Are you awake?" Henry says.

"Yes," Tilly says, still asleep. He carries her back upstairs. He makes a bed out of pillows in the hall closet and lays her down across them. He tucks a blanket around her. If she refuses to wake up in the same bed that she goes to sleep in, then maybe they should make it a game. If you can't beat them, join them.

Catherine hadn't had an affair with Leonard Felter. She hadn't even slept with him. She had just said she had, because she was so mad at Henry. She could have slept with Leonard Felter. The opportunity had been there. And he had been magical, somehow: the only member of the department who could make the photocopier make copies, and he was nice to all of the secretaries. Too nice, as it turned out. And then, when it turned out that Leonard Felter had been fucking everyone, Catherine had felt she couldn't take it back. So she and Henry had gone to therapy together. Henry had taken some time off work. They'd taken the kids to Yosemite. They'd gotten pregnant. She'd been remorseful for something she hadn't done. Henry had forgiven her. Really, she'd saved their marriage. But it had been the sort of thing you could do only once.

If someone has to save the marriage a second time, it will have to be Henry.

CR

Henry went looking for King Spanky. They were going to see the vet: he had the cat cage in the car, but no King Spanky. It was early afternoon, and the rabbits were out on the lawn. Up above, a bird hung, motionless, on a hook of air. Henry craned his head, looking up. It was a big bird, a hawk maybe. It circled, once, twice, again, and then dropped like a stone, towards the rabbits. The rabbits didn't move. There was something about the way they waited, as if this were all a game. The bird dropped through the air, folded like a knife, and then it jerked, tumbled, fell. The wings loose. The bird smashed into the grass and feathers flew up. The rabbits moved closer, as if investigating.

Henry went to see for himself. The rabbits scattered, and the lawn was empty. No rabbits, no bird. But there, down in the trees, beside the bike path, Henry saw something move. King Spanky swung his tail angrily, slunk into the woods.

When Henry came out of the woods, the rabbits were back, guarding the lawn again and Catherine was calling his name. "Where were you?" she said. She was wearing her gas mask around her neck, and there was a smear of paint on her arm. Whiskey Horse. She'd been painting the linen closet.

"King Spanky took off," Henry said. "I couldn't catch him. I saw the weirdest thing—this bird was going after the rabbits, and then it fell—"

"Marcus came by," Catherine said. Her cheeks were flushed. He knew that if he touched her, her skin would be hot. "He stopped by to see if you wanted to go play golf."

"Who wants to play golf?" Henry said. "I want to go upstairs with you. Where are the kids?"

"Alison took them into town, to see a movie," Catherine said. "I'm going to pick them up at three."

Henry lifted the gas mask off her neck, fitted it around her face. He unbuttoned her shirt, undid the clasp of her bra. "Better take this off," he said. "Better take all your clothes off. I think they're haunted."

"You know what would make a great paint color? Can't believe no one has done this yet. Yellow Sticky. What about King Spanky?" Catherine said.

She sounded like Darth Vader, maybe on purpose, and Henry thought it was sexy: Darth Vader, pregnant, with his child. She put her hand against his chest and shoved. Not too hard, but harder than she meant to. It turned out that painting had given her some serious muscle. That will be a good thing when she has another kid to haul around.

"Yellow Sticky. That's great. Forget King Spanky," Henry said. "King Spanky is a terrible name for a paint color."

Catherine was painting Tilly's room Lavender Fist. It was going to be a surprise. But when Tilly saw it, she burst into tears. "Why can't you just leave it alone?" she said. "I liked it the way it was."

"I thought you liked purple," Catherine said, astounded. She took off her gas mask.

"I hate purple," Tilly said. "And I hate you. You're so fat. Even Carleton thinks so."

"Tilly!" Catherine said. She laughed. "I'm pregnant, remember?"

"That's what you think," Tilly said. She ran out of the room and across the hall. There were crashing noises, the sounds of things breaking.

"Tilly!" Catherine said.

Tilly stood in the middle of Carleton's room. All around her lay broken night-lights, lamps, broken lightbulbs. The carpet was dusted in glass. Tilly's feet were bare and Catherine looked down, realized that she wasn't wearing shoes either. "Don't move, Tilly," she said.

"They were haunted," Tilly said, and began to cry.

"So how come your dad's never home?" Alison said.

"I don't know," Carleton said. "Guess what? Tilly broke all my night-lights?"

"Yeah," Alison said. "You must be pretty mad."

"No, it's good that she did," Carleton said, explaining. "They were haunted. Tilly didn't want me to be afraid."

"But aren't you afraid of the dark?" Alison said.

"Tilly said I shouldn't be," Carleton said. "She said the rabbits stay awake all night, that they make sure everything is okay, even when it's dark. Tilly slept outside once, and the rabbits protected her."

"So you're going to stay with us this weekend," Alison said.

"Yes," Carleton said.

"But your dad isn't coming," Alison said.

"No," Carleton said. "I don't know."

"Want to go higher?" Alison said. She pushed the swing and sent him soaring.

When Henry puts his hand against the wall in the living room, it gives a little, as if the wall is pregnant. The paint under the paint is wet. He walks around the house, running his hands along the walls. Catherine has been painting a mural in the foyer. She's painted trees and trees and trees. Golden trees with brown leaves and green leaves and red leaves, and reddish trees with purple leaves and yellow leaves and pink leaves. She's even painted some leaves on the wooden floor, as if the trees are dropping them. "Catherine," he says. "You have got to stop painting the damn walls. The rooms are getting smaller."

Nobody says anything back. Catherine and Tilly and Carleton aren't home. It's the first time Henry has spent the night alone in his house. He can't sleep. There's no television to watch. Henry throws out all of Catherine's paintbrushes. But when Catherine gets home, she'll just buy new ones.

He sleeps on the couch, and during the night someone comes and stands and watches him sleep. Tilly. Then he wakes up and remembers that Tilly isn't there.

The rabbits watch the house all night long. It's their job.

Tilly is talking to the rabbits. It's cold outside, and she's lost her gloves. "What's your name?" she says. "Oh, you beauty. You beauty." She's on her hands and knees. Carleton watches from his side of the yard.

"Can I come over?" he says. "Can I please come over?"

Tilly ignores him. She gets down on her hands and knees, moving even closer to the rabbits. There are three of them, one of them almost close enough to touch. If she moved her hand, slowly, maybe she could grab it by the ears. Maybe she can catch it and train it to live inside. They need a pet rabbit. King Spanky is haunted. He spends most of his time outside. Her parents keep their bedroom door shut so that King Spanky can't get in.

"Good rabbit," Tilly says. "Just stay still. Stay still."

The rabbits flick their ears. Carleton begins to sing a song Alison has taught them, a skipping song. Carleton is such a girl. Tilly puts out her hand. There's something tangled around the rabbit's neck, like a piece of string or a leash. She wiggles closer, holding out her hand. She stares and stares and can hardly believe her eyes. There's a person, a little man sitting behind the rabbit's ears, holding on to the rabbit's fur and the piece of knotted string, with one hand. His other hand is cocked back, like he's going to throw something. He's looking right at her—his hand flies forward and something hits her hand. She pulls her hand back, astounded. "Hey!" she says, and she falls over on her side and watches the rabbits go springing away. "Hey, you! Come back!"

"What?" Carleton yells. He's frantic. "What are you doing? Why won't you let me come over?"

She closes her eyes, just for a second. Shut up, Carleton. Just shut up. Her hand is throbbing and she lies down, holds her hand up to her face. Shut. Up.

When she wakes up, Carleton is sitting beside her. "What are you doing on my side?" she says, and he shrugs.

"What are you doing?" he says. He rocks back and forth on his knees. "Why did you fall over?"

"None of your business," she says. She can't remember what she was doing. Everything looks funny. Especially Carleton. "What's wrong with you?"

"Nothing's wrong with me," Carleton says, but something is wrong. She studies his face and begins to feel sick, as if she's been eating grass. Those sneaky rabbits! They've been distracting her, and now, while she wasn't paying attention, Carleton's become haunted.

"Oh yes it is," Tilly says, forgetting to be afraid, forgetting her hand hurts, getting angry instead. She's not the one to blame. This is her mother's fault, her father's fault, and it's Carleton's fault too. How could he have let this happen? "You just don't know it's wrong. I'm going to tell Mom."

Haunted Carleton is still a Carleton who can be bossed around. "Don't tell," he begs.

Tilly pretends to think about this, although she's already made up her mind. Because what can she say? Either her mother will notice that something's wrong or else she won't. Better to wait and see. "Just stay away from me," she tells Carleton. "You give me the creeps."

Carleton begins to cry, but Tilly is firm. He turns around, walks slowly back to his half of the yard, still crying. For the rest of the afternoon, he sits beneath the azalea bush at the edge of his side of the yard, and cries. It gives Tilly the creeps. Her hand throbs where something has stung it. The rabbits are all hiding underground. King Spanky has gone hunting.

"What's up with Carleton?" Henry said, coming downstairs. He couldn't stop yawning. It wasn't that he was tired, although he was tired. He hadn't given Carleton a good-night kiss, just in case it turned out he was coming down with a cold. He didn't want Carleton to catch it. But it looked like Carleton, too, was already coming down with something.

Catherine shrugged. Paint samples were balanced across her stomach like she'd been playing solitaire. All weekend long, away from the house, she'd thought about repainting Henry's office. She'd never painted a haunted room before. Maybe if you mixed the paint with a little bit of holy water? She wasn't sure: What was holy water, anyway? Could you buy it? "Tilly's being mean to him," she said. "I wish they would make some friends out here. He keeps talking about the new baby, about how he'll take care of it. He says it can sleep in his room. I've been trying to explain babies to him, about how all they do is sleep and eat and cry."

"And get bigger," Henry said.

"That too," Catherine said. "So did he go to sleep okay?"

"Eventually," Henry said. "He's just acting really weird."

"How is that different from usual?" Catherine said. She yawned. "Is

Tilly finished with her homework?"

"I don't know," Henry said. "You know, just weird. Different weird. Maybe he's going through a weird spell. Tilly wanted me to help her with her math, but I couldn't get it to come out right. So what's up with my office?"

"I cleared it out," Catherine said. "Alison and Liz came over and helped. I told them we were going to redecorate. Why is it that we're the only ones who notice everything is fucking haunted around here?"

"So where'd you put my stuff?" Henry said. "What's up?"

"You're not working here now," Catherine pointed out. She didn't sound angry, just tired. "Besides, it's all haunted, right? So I took your computer into the shop, so they could have a look at it. I don't know, maybe they can unhaunt it."

"Well," Henry said. "Okay. Is that what you told them? It's haunted?"

"Don't be ridiculous," Catherine said. She discarded a paint strip. Too lemony. "So I heard about the bomb scare on the radio."

"Yeah," Henry said. "The subways were full of kids with crew cuts and machine guns. And they evacuated our building for about an hour. We all went and stood outside, holding on to our laptops like idiots, just in case. The Crocodile carried out her rubber band ball, which must weigh about thirty pounds. It kind of freaked people out, even the firemen. I thought the bomb squad was going to blow it up. So tell me about your weekend."

"Tell me about yours," Catherine said.

"You know," Henry said. "Those clients are assholes. But they don't know they're assholes, so it's almost okay. You just have to feel sorry for them. They don't get it. You have to explain how to have fun, and then they get anxious, so they drink a lot and so you have to drink too. Even The Crocodile got drunk. She did this weird wriggly dance to a Pete Seeger song. So what's their place like?"

"It's nice," Catherine said. "You know, really nice."

"So you had a good weekend? Carleton and Tilly had a good time?"

"It was really nice," Catherine said. "No, really, it was great. I had a fucking great time. So you're sure you can make it home for dinner on Thursday."

It wasn't a question.

"Carleton looks like he might be coming down with something," Henry said. "Here. Do you think I feel hot? Or is it cold in here?"

Catherine said, "You're fine. It's going to be Liz and Marcus and some of the women from the book group and their husbands, and what's her name, the real estate agent. I invited her too. Did you know she's written a book? I was going to do that! I'm getting the new dishwasher tomorrow. No more paper plates. And the lawn care specialist is coming on Monday to take care of the rabbits. I thought I'd drop off King Spanky at the vet, take Tilly and Carleton back to the city, stay with Lucy for two or three days—did you know she tried to find this place and got lost? She's supposed to come up for dinner too—just in case the poison doesn't go away right away, you know, or in case we end up with piles of dead rabbits on the lawn. Your job is to make sure there are no dead rabbits when I bring Tilly and Carleton back."

"I guess I can do that," Henry said.

"You'd better," Catherine said. She stood up with some difficulty, came and leaned over his chair. Her stomach bumped into his shoulder. Her breath was hot. Her hands were full of strips of color. "Sometimes I wish that instead of working for The Crocodile, you were having an affair with her. I mean, that way you'd come home when you're supposed to. You wouldn't want me to be suspicious."

"I don't have any time to have affairs," Henry said. He sounded put out. Maybe he was thinking about Leonard Felter. Or maybe he was picturing The Crocodile naked. The Crocodile wearing stretchy red rubber sex gear. Catherine imagined telling Henry the truth about Leonard Felter. I didn't have an affair. Did not. I made it up. Is that a problem?

"That's exactly what I mean," Catherine said. "You'd better be here for dinner. You live here, Henry. You're my husband. I want you to meet our friends. I want you to be here when I have this baby. I want you to fix what's wrong with the downstairs bathroom. I want you to talk to Tilly. She's having a rough time. She won't talk to me about it."

"Tilly's fine," Henry said. "We had a long talk tonight. She said she's sorry she broke all of Carleton's night-lights. I like the trees, by the way. You're not going to paint over them, are you?"

"I had all this leftover paint," Catherine said. "I was getting tired of just slapping paint on with the rollers. I wanted to do something fancier."

"You could paint some trees in my office, when you paint my office."

"Maybe," Catherine said. "Ooof, this baby won't stop kicking me." She lay down on the floor in front of Henry, and lifted her feet into his lap. "Rub my feet. I've still got so much fucking paint. But once your office is done, I'm done with the painting. Tilly told me to stop it or else. She keeps hiding my gas mask. Will you be here for dinner?"

"I'll be here for dinner," Henry said, rubbing her feet. He really meant it. He was thinking about the exterminator, about rabbit corpses scattered all across the lawn, like a war zone. Poor rabbits. What a mess.

After they went to see the therapist, after they went to Yosemite and came home again, Henry said to Catherine, "I don't want to talk about it anymore. I don't want to talk about it ever again. Can we not talk about it?"

"Talk about what?" Catherine said. But she had almost been sorry. It had been so much work. She'd had to invent so many details that eventually it began to seem as if she hadn't made it up after all. It was too strange, too confusing, to pretend it had never happened, when, after all, it *had* never happened.

Catherine is dressing for dinner. When she looks in the mirror, she's as big as a cruise ship. A water tower. She doesn't look like herself at all. The baby kicks her right under the ribs.

"Stop that," she says. She's sure the baby is going to be a girl. Tilly won't be pleased. Tilly has been extra good all day. She helped make the salad. She set the table. She put on a nice dress.

Tilly is hiding from Carleton under a table in the foyer. If Carleton finds her, Tilly will scream. Carleton is haunted, and nobody has noticed. Nobody cares except Tilly. Tilly says names for the baby, under her breath.

Dollop. Shampool. Custard. Knock, knock. The rabbits are out on the lawn, and King Spanky has gotten into the bed again, and he won't come out, not for a million haunted alarm clocks.

Her mother has painted trees all along the wall under the staircase. They don't look like real trees. They aren't real colors. It doesn't look like Central Park at all. In among the trees, her mother has painted a little door. It isn't a real door, except that when Tilly goes over to look at it, it is real. There's a doorknob, and when Tilly turns it, the door opens. Underneath the stairs, there's another set of stairs, little dirt stairs, going down. On the third stair, there's a rabbit sitting there, looking up at Tilly. It hops down, one step, and then another. Then another.

"Rumpled Stiltskin!" Tilly says to the rabbit. "Lipstick!"

Catherine goes to the closet to get out Henry's pink shirt. What's the name of that real estate agent? Why can't she ever remember? She lays the shirt on the bed and then stands there for a moment, stunned. It's too much. The pink shirt is haunted. She pulls out all of Henry's suits, his shirts, his ties. All haunted. Every fucking thing is haunted. Even the fucking shoes. When she pulls out the drawers, socks, underwear, handkerchiefs, everything, it's all spoiled. All haunted. Henry doesn't have a thing to wear. She goes downstairs, gets trash bags, and goes back upstairs again. She begins to dump clothes into the trash bags.

She can see Carleton framed in the bedroom window. He's chasing the rabbits with a stick. She hoists open the window, leans out, yells, "Stay away from those fucking rabbits, Carleton! Do you hear me?"

She doesn't recognize her own voice.

Tilly is running around downstairs somewhere. She's yelling too, but her voice gets farther and farther away, fainter and fainter. She's yelling, "Hairbrush! Zeppelin! Torpedo! Marmalade!"

The doorbell rings.

The Crocodile started laughing. "Okay, Henry. Calm down."

He fired off another rubber band. "I mean it," he said. "I'm late. I'll be late. She's going to kill me."

"Tell her it's my fault," The Crocodile said. "So they started dinner without you. Big deal."

"I tried calling," Henry said. "Nobody answered." He had an idea that the phone was haunted now. That's why Catherine wasn't answering. They'd have to get a new phone. Maybe the lawn specialist would know a house specialist. Maybe somebody could do something about this. "I should go home," he said. "I should go home right now." But he didn't get up. "I think we've gotten ourselves into a mess, me and Catherine. I don't think things are good right now."

"Tell someone who cares," The Crocodile suggested. She wiped at her eyes. "Get out of here. Go catch your train. Have a great weekend. See you on Monday."

So Henry goes home, he has to go home, but of course he's late, it's too late. The train is haunted. The closer they get to his station, the more haunted the train gets. None of the other passengers seem to notice. And of course, his bike turns out to be haunted, too. He leaves it at the station and he walks home in the dark, down the bike path. Something follows him home. Maybe it's King Spanky.

Here's the yard, and here's his house. He loves his house, how it's all lit up. You can see right through the windows, you can see the living room, which Catherine has painted Ghost Crab. The trim is Rat Fink. Catherine has worked so hard. The driveway is full of cars, and inside, people are eating dinner. They're admiring Catherine's trees. They haven't waited for him, and that's fine. His neighbors: he loves his neighbors. He's going to love them as soon as he meets them. His wife is going to have a baby any day now. His daughter will stop walking in her sleep. His son isn't haunted. The moon shines down and paints the world a color he's never seen before. Oh, Catherine, wait till you see this. Shining lawn, shining rabbits, shining world. The rabbits are out on the lawn. They've been waiting for him, all this time, they've been waiting. Here's his rabbit, his very own rabbit. Who needs a bike? He sits on his rabbit, legs pressed against the warm, silky, shining flanks, one hand holding on to the rabbit's fur, the knotted string around its neck. He has something in his other hand, and when he looks, he sees it's a spear. All around him, the others are sitting on their rabbits, waiting patiently, quietly. They've been waiting for a long time, but the waiting is almost over. In a little while, the dinner party will be over and the war will begin.

The cats are beginning to look a little shabby.

Catskin

CATS WENT IN AND OUT OF THE WITCH'S house all day long. The windows stayed open, and the doors, and there were other doors, cat-sized and private, in the walls and up in the attic. The cats were large and sleek and silent. No one knew their names, or even if they had names, except for the witch.

Some of the cats were cream-colored and some were brindled. Some were black as beetles. They were about the witch's business. Some came into the witch's bedroom with live things in their mouths. When they came out again, their mouths were empty.

The cats trotted and slunk and leapt and crouched. They were busy. Their movements were catlike, or perhaps clockwork. Their tails twitched like hairy pendulums. They paid no attention to the witch's children.

The witch had three living children at this time, although at one time she had had dozens, maybe more. No one, certainly not the witch, had ever bothered to tally them up. But at one time the house had bulged with cats and babies.

Now, since witches cannot have children in the usual way—their wombs are full of straw or bricks or stones, and when they give birth, they give birth to rabbits, kittens, tadpoles, houses, silk dresses, and yet even witches must have heirs, even witches wish to be mothers—the witch had acquired her children by other means: she had stolen or bought them.

She'd had a passion for children with a certain color of red hair. Twins she had never been able to abide (they were the wrong kind of magic), although she'd sometimes attempted to match up sets of children, as though she had been putting together a chess set, and not a family. If you were to say *a witch's chess set*, instead of *a witch's family*, there would be some truth in that. Perhaps this is true of other families as well.

One girl she had grown like a cyst, upon her thigh. Other children she had made out of things in her garden, or bits of trash that the cats brought her: aluminum foil with strings of chicken fat still crusted to it, broken television sets, cardboard boxes that the neighbors had thrown out. She had always been a thrifty witch.

Some of these children had run away and others had died. Some of them she had simply misplaced, or accidentally left behind on buses. It is to be hoped that these children were later adopted into good homes, or reunited with their natural parents. If you are looking for a happy ending in this story, then perhaps you should stop reading here and picture these children, these parents, their reunions.

Are you still reading? The witch, up in her bedroom, was dying. She had been poisoned by an enemy, a witch, a man named Lack. The child Finn, who had been her food taster, was dead already and so were three cats who'd licked her dish clean. The witch knew who had killed her and she snatched pieces of time, here and there, from the business of dying, to make her revenge. Once the question of this revenge had been settled to her satisfaction, the shape of it like a black ball of twine in her head, she began to divide up her estate between her three remaining children.

Flecks of vomit stuck to the corners of her mouth, and there was a basin beside the foot of the bed, which was full of black liquid. The room smelled like cats' piss and wet matches. The witch panted as if she were giving birth to her own death.

"Flora shall have my automobile," she said, "and also my purse, which will never be empty, so long as you always leave a coin at the bottom, my darling, my spendthrift, my profligate, my drop of poison, my pretty, pretty Flora. And when I am dead, take the road outside the house and go west. There's one last piece of advice."

Flora, who was the oldest of the witch's living children, was redheaded and stylish. She had been waiting for the witch's death for a long time now, although she had been patient. She kissed the witch's cheek and said, "Thank you, Mother."

The witch looked up at her, panting. She could see Flora's life, already laid out, flat as a map. Perhaps all mothers can see as far.

"Jack, my love, my birdsnest, my bite, my scrap of porridge," the witch said, "you shall have my books. I won't have any need of books where I am going. And when you leave my house, strike out in an an easterly direction and you won't be any sorrier than you are now."

Jack, who had once been a little bundle of feathers and twigs and eggshell all tied up with a tatty piece of string, was a sturdy lad, almost full grown. If he knew how to read, only the cats knew it. But he nodded and kissed his mother's gray lips.

"And what shall I leave to my boy Small?" the witch said, convulsing. She threw up again in the basin. Cats came running, leaning on the lip of the basin to inspect her vomitus. The witch's hand dug into Small's leg.

"Oh it is hard, hard, so very hard, for a mother to leave her children (though I have done harder things). Children need a mother, even such a mother as I have been." She wiped at her eyes, and yet it is a fact that witches cannot cry.

Small, who still slept in the witch's bed, was the youngest of the witch's children. (Perhaps not as young as you think.) He sat upon the bed, and although he didn't cry, it was only because witch's children have no one to teach them the use of crying. His heart was breaking.

Small could juggle and sing and every morning he brushed and plaited the witch's long, silky hair. Surely every mother must wish for a boy like Small, a curly-headed, sweet-breathed, tenderhearted boy like Small, who can cook a fine omelet, and who has a good strong singing voice as well as a gentle hand with a hairbrush.

"Mother," he said, "if you must die, then you must die. And if I can't come along with you, then I'll do my best to live and make you proud. Give me your hairbrush to remember you by, and I'll go make my own way in the world."

"You shall have my hairbrush, then," said the witch to Small, looking, and panting, panting. "And I love you best of all. You shall have my tinderbox and my matches, and also my revenge, and you will make me proud, or I don't know my own children."

"What shall we do with the house, Mother?" said Jack. He said it as if he didn't care.

"When I am dead," the witch said, "this house will be of no use to anyone. I gave birth to it—that was a very long time ago—and raised it from just a dollhouse. Oh, it was the most dear, most darling dollhouse ever. It had eight rooms and a tin roof, and a staircase that went nowhere at all. But I nursed it and rocked it to sleep in a cradle, and it grew up to be a real house, and see how it has taken care of me, its parent, how it knows a child's duty to its mother. And perhaps you can see how it is now, how it pines, how it grows sick to see me dying like this. Leave it to the cats. They'll know what to do with it."

All this time the cats have been running in and out of the room, bringing things and taking things away. It seems as if they will never slow down, never come to rest, never nap, never have the time to sleep, or to die, or even to mourn. They have a certain proprietary look about them, as if the house is already theirs.

The witch vomits up mud, fur, glass buttons, tin soldiers, trowels, hat pins, thumbtacks, love letters (mislabeled or sent without the appropriate amount of postage and never read), and a dozen regiments of red ants, each ant as long and wide as a kidney bean. The ants swim across the perilous stinking basin, clamber up the sides of the basin, and go marching across the floor in a shiny ribbon. They are carrying pieces of Time in their mandibles. Time is heavy, even in such small pieces, but the ants have strong jaws, strong legs. Across the floor they go, and up the wall, and out the window. The cats watch, but don't interfere. The witch gasps and coughs and then lies still. Her hands beat against the bed once and then are still. Still the children wait, to make sure that she is dead, and that she has nothing else to say.

In the witch's house, the dead are sometimes quite talkative.

But the witch has nothing else to say at this time.

The house groans and all the cats begin to mew piteously, trotting in and out of the room as if they have dropped something and must go and hunt for it—they will never find it—and the children, at last, find they know how to cry, but the witch is perfectly still and quiet. There is a tiny smile on her face, as if everything has happened exactly to her satisfaction. Or maybe she is looking forward to the next part of the story.

The children buried the witch in one of her half-grown dollhouses. They crammed her into the downstairs parlor, and knocked out the inner walls so that her head rested on the kitchen table in the breakfast nook, and her ankles threaded through a bedroom door. Small brushed out her hair, and, because he wasn't sure what she should wear now that she was dead, he put all her dresses on her, one over the other over the other, until he could hardly see her white limbs at all beneath the stack of petticoats and coats and dresses. It didn't matter: once they'd nailed the dollhouse shut again, all they could see was the red crown of her head in the kitchen window, and the worn-down heels of her dancing shoes knocking against the shutters of the bedroom window.

Jack, who was handy, rigged a set of wheels for the dollhouse, and a harness so that it could be pulled. They put the harness on Small, and Small pulled and Flora pushed, and Jack talked and coaxed the house along, over the hill, down to the cemetery, and the cats ran along beside them.

○8

The cats are beginning to look a bit shabby, as if they are molting. Their mouths look very empty. The ants have marched away, through the woods, and down into town, and they have built a nest on your yard, out of the bits of Time. And if you hold a magnifying glass over their nest, to see the ants dance and burn, Time will catch fire and you will be sorry.

Outside the cemetery gates, the cats had been digging a grave for the witch. The children tipped the dollhouse into the grave, kitchen window first. But then they saw that the grave wasn't deep enough, and the house sat there on its end, looking uncomfortable. Small began to cry (now that he'd learned how, it seemed he would spend all his time practicing), thinking how horrible it would be to spend one's death, all of eternity, upside down and not even properly buried, not even able to feel the rain when it beat down on the exposed shingles of the house, and seeped down into the house and filled your mouth and drowned you, so that you had to die all over again, every time it rained.

The dollhouse chimney had broken off and fallen on the ground. One of the cats picked it up and carried it away, like a souvenir. That cat carried the chimney into the woods and ate it, a mouthful at a time, and passed out of this story and into another one. It's no concern of ours.

The other cats began to carry up mouthfuls of dirt, dropping it and mounding it around the house with their paws. The children helped, and when they'd finished, they'd managed to bury the witch properly, so that only the bedroom window was visible, a little pane of glass like an eye at the top of a small dirt hill.

On the way home, Flora began to flirt with Jack. Perhaps she liked the way he looked in his funeral black. They talked about what they planned to be, now that they were grown up. Flora wanted to find her parents. She was a pretty girl: someone would want to look after her. Jack said he would like to marry someone rich. They began to make plans.

Small walked a little behind, slippery cats twining around his ankles. He had the witch's hairbrush in his pocket, and his fingers slipped around the figured horn handle for comfort.

The house, when they reached it, had a dangerous, grief-stricken look to it, as if it was beginning to pull away from itself. Flora and Jack wouldn't go back inside. They squeezed Small lovingly, and asked if he wouldn't want to come along with them. He would have liked to, but who would have looked after the witch's cats, the witch's revenge? So he watched as they drove off together. They went north. What child has ever heeded a mother's advice?

Jack hasn't even bothered to bring along the witch's library: he says there isn't space in the trunk for everything. He'll rely on Flora and her magic purse.

Small sat in the garden, and ate stalks of grass when he was hungry, and pretended that the grass was bread and milk and chocolate cake. He drank out of the garden hose. When it began to grow dark, he was lonelier than he had ever been in his life. The witch's cats were not good company. He said nothing to them and they had nothing to tell him, about the house, or the future, or the witch's revenge, or about where he was supposed to sleep. He had never slept anywhere except in the witch's bed, so at last he went back over the hill and down to the cemetery.

Some of the cats were still going up and down the grave, covering the base of the mound with leaves and grass and feathers, their own loose fur. It was a soft sort of nest to lie down on. The cats were still busy when Small fell asleep—cats are always busy—cheek pressed against the cool glass of the bedroom window, hand curled in his pocket around the hair-brush, but in the middle of the night, when he woke up, he was swaddled, head to foot, in warm, grass-scented cat bodies.

A tail is curled around his chin like a rope, and all the bodies are soughing breath in and out, whiskers and paws twitching, silky bellies rising and falling. All the cats are sleeping a frantic, exhausted, busy sleep, except for one, a white cat who sits near his head, looking down at him. Small has never seen this cat before, and yet he knows her, the way that you know the people who visit you in dreams: she's white everywhere, except for reddish tufts and frills at her ears and tail and paws, as if someone has embroidered her with fire around the edges.

"What's your name?" Small says. He's never talked to the witch's cats before.

The cat lifts a leg and licks herself in a private place. Then she looks at him. "You may call me Mother," she says.

But Small shakes his head. He can't call the cat that. Down under the blanket of cats, under the windowpane, the witch's Spanish heel is drinking in moonlight.

"Very well, then, you may call me The Witch's Revenge," the cat says. Her mouth doesn't move, but he hears her speak inside his head. Her voice is furry and sharp, like a blanket made of needles. "And you may comb my fur."

Small sits up, displacing sleeping cats, and lifts the brush out of his pocket. The bristles have left rows of little holes indented in the pink palm of his hand, like some sort of code. If he could read the code, it would say: Comb my fur.

Small combs the fur of The Witch's Revenge. There's grave dirt in the cat's fur, and one or two red ants, who drop and scurry away. The Witch's Revenge bends her head down to the ground, snaps them up in her jaws. The heap of cats around them is yawning and stretching. There are things to do.

"You must burn her house down," The Witch's Revenge says. "That's the first thing."

Small's comb catches a knot, and The Witch's Revenge turns and nips him on the wrist. Then she licks him in the tender place between his thumb and his first finger. "That's enough," she says. "There's work to do."

So they all go back to the house, Small stumbling in the dark, moving farther and farther away from the witch's grave, the cats trotting along, their eyes lit like torches, twigs and branches in their mouths, as if they plan to build a nest, a canoe, a fence to keep the world out. The house, when they reach it, is full of lights, and more cats, and piles of tinder. The house is making a noise, like an instrument that someone is breathing into. Small realizes that all the cats are mewing, endlessly, as they run in and out the doors, looking for more kindling. The Witch's Revenge says, "First we must latch all the doors."

So Small shuts all the doors and windows on the first floor, leaving open only the kitchen door, and The Witch's Revenge shuts the catches on the secret doors, the cat doors, the doors in the attic, and up on the roof, and the cellar doors. Not a single secret door is left open. Now all the noise is on the inside, and Small and The Witch's Revenge are on the outside.

All the cats have slipped into the house through the kitchen door. There isn't a single cat in the garden. Small can see the witch's cats through the windows, arranging their piles of twigs. The Witch's Revenge sits beside him, watching. "Now light a match and throw it in," says The Witch's Revenge.

Small lights a match. He throws it in. What boy doesn't love to start a fire?

"Now shut the kitchen door," says The Witch's Revenge, but Small can't do that. All the cats are inside. The Witch's Revenge stands on her hindpaws and pushes the kitchen door shut. Inside, the lit match catches something on fire. Fire runs along the floor and up the kitchen walls. Cats catch fire, and run into the other rooms of the house. Small can see all this through the windows. He stands with his face against the glass, which is cold, and then warm, and then hot. Burning cats with burning twigs in their mouths press up against the kitchen door, and the other doors of the house, but all the doors are locked. Small and The Witch's Revenge stand in the garden and watch the witch's house and the witch's books and the witch's sofas and the witch's cooking pots and the witch's cats, her cats, too, all her cats burn.

You should never burn down a house. You should never set a cat on fire. You should never watch and do nothing while a house is burning. You should never listen to a cat who says to do any of these things. You should listen to your mother when she tells you to come away from watching, to go to bed, to go to sleep. You should listen to your mother's revenge.

You should never poison a witch.

In the morning, Small woke up in the garden. Soot covered him in a greasy blanket. The Witch's Revenge was curled up asleep on his chest. The witch's house was still standing, but the windows had melted and run down the walls.

The Witch's Revenge woke and stretched and licked Small clean with her small sharkskin tongue. She demanded to be combed. Then she went into the house and came out, carrying a little bundle. It dangled, boneless, from her mouth, like a kitten.

It is a catskin, Small sees, only there is no longer a cat inside it. The Witch's Revenge drops it in his lap.

He picked it up and something shiny fell out of the loose light skin. It was a piece of gold, sloppy, slippery with fat. The Witch's Revenge brought out dozens and dozens of catskins, and there was a gold piece in every skin. While Small counted his fortune, The Witch's Revenge bit off one of her own claws, and pulled one long witch hair out of the witch's comb. She sat up, like a tailor, cross-legged in the grass, and began to stitch up a bag, out of the many catskins.

Small shivered. There was nothing to eat for breakfast but grass, and the grass was black and cooked.

"Are you cold?" said The Witch's Revenge. She put the bag aside and picked up another catskin, a fine black one. She slit a sharp claw down the middle. "We'll make you a warm suit."

She used the coat of a black cat, and the coat of a calico cat, and she put a trim around the paws, of grey-and-white-striped fur.

While she did this, she said to Small, "Did you know that there was once a battle, fought on this very patch of ground?"

Small shook his head no.

"Wherever there's a garden," The Witch's Revenge said, scratching with one paw at the ground, "I promise you there are people buried somewhere beneath it. Look here." She plucked up a little brown clot, put it in her mouth, and cleaned it with her tongue.

When she spat the little circle out again, Small saw it was an ivory regimental button. The Witch's Revenge dug more buttons out of the ground—as if buttons of ivory grew in the ground—and sewed them onto the catskin. She fashioned a hood with two eyeholes and a set of fine whiskers, and sewed four fine cat tails to the back of the suit, as if the single tail that grew there wasn't good enough for Small. She threaded a bell on each one. "Put this on," she said to Small.

Small put on the suit and the bells chime. The Witch's Revenge laughs. "You make a fine-looking cat," she says. "Any mother would be proud."

The inside of the cat suit is soft and a little sticky against Small's skin. When he puts the hood over his head, the world disappears. He can see only the vivid corners of it through the eyeholes—grass, gold, the cat who sits cross-legged, stitching up her sack of skins—and air seeps in, down at the loosely sewn seam, where the skin droops and sags over his chest and around the gaping buttons. Small holds his tails in his clumsy fingerless paw, like a handful of eels, and swings them back and forth to hear them ring. The sound of the bells and the sooty, cooked smell of the air, the warm stickiness of the suit, the feel of his new fur against the ground: he falls asleep and dreams that hundreds of ants come and lift him and gently carry him off to bed.

When Small tipped his hood back again, he saw that The Witch's Revenge had finished with her needle and thread. Small helped her fill the bag with gold. The Witch's Revenge stood up on her hind legs, took the bag, and swung it over her shoulders. The gold coins went sliding against each other, mewling and hissing. The bag dragged along the grass, picking up ash, leaving a trail of green behind it. The Witch's Revenge strutted along as if she were carrying a sack of air.

Small put the hood on again, and he got down on his hands and knees. And then he trotted after The Witch's Revenge. They left the garden gate wide open and went into the forest, towards the house where the witch Lack lived.

The forest is smaller than it used to be. Small is growing, but the forest is shrinking. Trees have been cut down. Houses have been built. Lawns rolled, roads laid. The Witch's Revenge and Small walked alongside one of the roads. A school bus rolled by: The children inside looked out their windows and laughed when they saw The Witch's Revenge walking on her hind legs, and at her heels, Small, in his cat suit. Small lifted his head and peered out of his eyeholes after the school bus.

"Who lives in these houses?" he asked The Witch's Revenge.

"That's the wrong question, Small," said The Witch's Revenge, looking down at him and striding along.

Miaow, the catskin bag says. *Clink.*

"What's the right question, then?" Small said.

"Ask me who lives under the houses," The Witch's Revenge said.

Obediently, Small said, "Who lives under the houses?"

"What a good question!" said The Witch's Revenge. "You see, not everyone can give birth to their own house. Most people give birth to children instead. And when you have children, you need houses to put them in. So children and houses: most people give birth to the first and have to build the second. The houses, that is. A long time ago, when men and women were going to build a house, they would dig a hole first. And they'd make a little room—a little, wooden, one-room house—in the hole. And they'd steal or buy a child to put in the house in the hole, to live there. And then they built their house over that first little house."

"Did they make a door in the lid of the little house?" Small said.

"They did not make a door," said The Witch's Revenge.

"But then how did the girl or the boy climb out?" Small said.

"The boy or the girl stayed in that little house," said The Witch's Revenge. "They lived there all their life, and they are living in those houses still, under the other houses where the people live, and the people who live in the houses above may come and go as they please, and they don't ever think about how there are little houses with little children, sitting in little rooms, under their feet."

"But what about the mothers and fathers?" Small asked. "Didn't they ever go looking for their boys and girls?"

"Ah," said The Witch's Revenge. "Sometimes they did and sometimes they didn't. And after all, who was living under *their* houses? But that was a long time ago. Now people mostly bury a cat when they build their house, instead of a child. That's why we call cats house-cats. Which is why we must walk along smartly. As you can see, there are houses under construction here."

And so there are. They walk by clearings where men are digging little holes. First Small puts his hood back and walks on two legs, and then he puts on his hood again, and goes on all fours: He makes himself as small and slinky as possible, just like a cat. But the bells on his tails jounce and the coins in the bag that The Witch's Revenge carries go *clink, miaow,* and the men stop their work and watch them go by.

How many witches are there in the world? Have you ever seen one? Would you know a witch if you saw one? And what would you do if you saw one? For that matter, do you know a cat when you see one? Are you sure?

Small followed The Witch's Revenge. Small grew calluses on his knees and the pads of his fingers. He would have liked to carry the bag sometimes, but it was too heavy. How heavy? You would not have been able to carry it, either.

They drank out of streams. At night they opened the catskin bag and climbed inside to sleep, and when they were hungry they licked the coins, which seemed to sweat golden fat, and always more fat. As they went, The Witch's Revenge sang a song:

> I had no mother
> and my mother had no mother
> and her mother had no mother
> and her mother had no mother
> and her mother had no mother
> and you have no mother
> to sing you
> this song

The coins in the bag sang too, *miaow, miaow,* and the bells on Small's tails kept the rhythm.

Every night Small combs The Witch's Revenge's fur. And every morning The Witch's Revenge licks him all over, not neglecting the places behind his ears, and at the backs of his knees. And then he puts the catsuit back on, and she grooms him all over again.

Sometimes they were in the forest, and sometimes the forest became a town, and then The Witch's Revenge would tell Small stories about the people who lived in the houses, and the children who lived in the houses under the houses. Once, in the forest, The Witch's Revenge showed Small where there had once been a house. Now there were only the stones of the foundation, upholstered in moss, and the chimney stack, propped up with fat ropes and coils of ivy.

The Witch's Revenge rapped on the grassy ground, moving clockwise around the foundation, until both she and Small could hear a hollow sound; The Witch's Revenge dropped to all fours and clawed at the ground, tearing it up with her paws and biting at it, until they could see a little wooden roof. The Witch's Revenge knocked on the roof, and Small lashed his tails.

"Well, Small," said The Witch's Revenge, "shall we take off the roof and let the poor child go?"

Small crept up close to the hole she had made. He put his ear to it and listened, but he heard nothing at all. "There's no one in there," he said.

"Maybe they're shy," said The Witch's Revenge. "Shall we let them out, or shall we leave them be?"

"Let them out!" said Small, but what he meant to say was, "Leave them alone!" Or maybe he said *Leave them be!* although he meant the opposite. The Witch's Revenge looked at him, and Small thought he heard something then—beneath him where he crouched, frozen—very faint: a scrabbling at the dirty, sunken roof.

Small sprang away. The Witch's Revenge picked up a stone and brought it down hard, caving the roof in. When they peered inside, there was nothing except blackness and a faint smell. They waited, sitting on the ground, to see what might come out, but nothing came out. After a while, The Witch's Revenge picked up her catskin bag, and they set off again.

For several nights after that, Small dreamed that someone, something, was following them. It was small and thin and bleached and cold and dirty and afraid. One night it crept away again, and Small never knew where it went. But if you come to that part of the forest, where they sat and waited by the stone foundation, perhaps you will meet the thing that they set free.

No one knew the reason for the quarrel between the witch Small's mother and the witch Lack, although the witch Small's mother had died for it. The witch Lack was a handsome man and he loved his children dearly. He had stolen them out of the cribs and beds of palaces and manors and harems. He dressed his children in silks, as befitted their station, and they wore gold crowns and ate off gold plates. They drank from cups of gold. Lack's children, it was said, lacked nothing.

Perhaps the witch Lack had made some remark about the way the witch Small's mother was raising her children, or perhaps the witch Small's mother had boasted of her children's red hair. But it might have been something else. Witches are proud and they like to quarrel.

When Small and The Witch's Revenge came at last to the house of the witch Lack, The Witch's Revenge said to Small, "Look at this monstrosity! I've produced finer turds and buried them under leaves. And the smell, like an open sewer! How can his neighbors stand the stink?"

Male witches have no wombs, and must come by their houses in other ways, or else buy them from female witches. But Small thought it was a very fine house. There was a prince or a princess at each window staring down at him, as he sat on his haunches in the driveway, beside The Witch's Revenge. He said nothing, but he missed his brothers and sisters.

"Come along," said The Witch's Revenge. "We'll go a little ways off and wait for the witch Lack to come home."

Small followed The Witch's Revenge back into the forest, and in a while, two of the witch Lack's children came out of the house, carrying baskets made of gold. They went into the forest as well and began to pick blackberries.

The Witch's Revenge and Small sat in the briar and watched.

There was a wind in the briar. Small was thinking of his brothers and sisters. He thought of the taste of blackberries, the feel of them in his mouth, which was not at all like the taste of fat.

The Witch's Revenge nestled against the small of Small's back. She was licking down a lump of knotted fur at the base of his spine. The princesses were singing.

Small decided that he would live in the briar with The Witch's Revenge. They would live on berries and spy on the children who came to pick them, and The Witch's Revenge would change her name. The word *Mother* was in his mouth, along with the sweet taste of the blackberries.

"Now you must go out," said The Witch's Revenge, "and be kittenish. Be playful. Chase your tail. Be shy, but don't be too shy. Don't talk too much. Let them pet you. Don't bite."

She pushed at Small's rump, and Small tumbled out of the briar and sprawled at the feet of the witch Lack's children.

The Princess Georgia said, "Look! It's a dear little cat!"

Her sister Margaret said doubtfully, "But it has five tails. I've never seen a cat that needed so many tails. And its skin is done up with buttons and it's almost as large as you are."

Small, however, began to caper and prance. He swung his tails back and forth so that the bells rang out and then he pretended to be alarmed by this. First he ran away from his tails and then he chased his tails. The two princesses put down their baskets, half-full of blackberries, and spoke to him, calling him a silly puss.

At first he wouldn't go near them. But, slowly, he pretended to be won over. He allowed himself to be petted and fed blackberries. He chased a hair ribbon and he stretched out to let them admire the buttons up and down his belly. Princess Margaret's fingers tugged at his skin; then she slid one hand in between the loose catskin and Small's boy skin. He batted her hand away with a paw, and Margaret's sister Georgia said knowingly that cat's didn't like to be petted on their bellies.

They were all good friends by the time The Witch's Revenge came out of the briar, standing on her hind legs and singing

> I have no children
> and my children have no children
> and their children
> have no children
> and their children
> have no whiskers
> and no tails

At this sight, the Princesses Margaret and Georgia began to laugh and point. They had never heard a cat sing, or seen a cat walk on its hind legs. Small lashed his five tails furiously, and all the fur of the catskin stood up on his arched back, and they laughed at that too.

When they came back from the forest, with their baskets piled with berries, Small was stalking close at their heels, and The Witch's Revenge came walking just behind. But she left the bag of gold hidden in the briar.

That night, when the witch Lack came home, his hands were full of gifts for his children. One of his sons ran to meet him at the door and said, "Come and see what followed Margaret and Georgia home from the forest! Can we keep them?"

And the table had not been set for dinner, and the children of the witch Lack had not sat down to do their homework, and in the witch Lack's throne room, there was a cat with five tails, spinning in circles, while a second cat sat impudently upon his throne, and sang

> Yes!
> your father's house
> is the shiniest
> brownest largest
> the most expensive
> the sweetest-smelling
> house
> that has ever
> come out of
> anyone's
> ass!

The witch Lack's children began to laugh at this, until they saw the witch, their father, standing there. Then they fell silent. Small stopped spinning.

"You!" said the witch Lack.

"Me!" said The Witch's Revenge, and sprang from the throne. Before anyone knew what she was about, her jaws were fastened about the witch Lack's neck, and then she ripped out his throat. Lack opened his mouth to speak and his blood fell out, making The Witch's Revenge's fur more red now than white. The witch Lack fell down dead, and red ants went marching out of the hole in his neck and the hole of his mouth, and they held pieces of Time in their jaws as tightly as The Witch's Revenge had held Lack's throat in hers. But she let Lack go and left him lying in his blood on the floor, and she snatched up the ants and ate them, quickly, as if she had been hungry for a very long time.

While this was happening, the witch Lack's children stood and watched and did nothing. Small sat on the floor, his tails curled about his paws. Children, all of them, they did nothing. They were too surprised. The Witch's Revenge, her belly full of ants, her mouth stained with blood, stood up and surveyed them.

"Go and fetch me my catskin bag," she said to Small.

Small found that he could move. Around him, the princes and princesses stayed absolutely still. The Witch's Revenge was holding them in her gaze.

"I'll need help," Small said. "The bag is too heavy for me to carry."

The Witch's Revenge yawned. She licked a paw and began to pat at her mouth. Small stood still.

"Very well," she said. "Take those big strong girls the Princesses Margaret and Georgia with you. They know the way."

The Princesses Margaret and Georgia, finding that they could move again, began to tremble. They gathered their courage and they went with Small, the two girls holding each other's hands, out of the throne room, not looking down at the body of their father, the witch Lack, and back into the forest.

Georgia began to weep, but the Princess Margaret said to Small: "Let us go!"

"Where will you go?" said Small. "The world is a dangerous place. There are people in it who mean you no good." He threw back his hood, and the Princess Georgia began to weep harder.

"Let us go," said the Princess Margaret. "My parents are the King and Queen of a country not three days' walk from here. They will be glad to see us again."

Small said nothing. They came to the briar and he sent the Princess Georgia in to hunt for the catskin bag. She came out scratched and bleeding, the bag in her hand. It had caught on the briars and torn open. Gold coins rolled out, like glossy drops of fat, falling on the ground.

"Your father killed my mother," said Small.

"And that cat, your mother's devil, will kill us, or worse," said Princess Margaret. "Let us go!"

Small lifted the catskin bag. There were no coins in it now. The Princess Georgia was on her hands and knees, scooping up coins and putting them into her pockets.

"Was he a good father?" Small asked.

"He thought he was," Princess Margaret said. "But I'm not sorry he's dead. When I grow up, I will be Queen. I'll make a law to put all the witches in the kingdom to death, and all their cats as well."

Small became afraid. He took up the catskin bag and ran back to the house of the witch Lack, leaving the two princesses in the forest. And whether they made their way home to the Princess Margaret's parents, or whether they fell into the hands of thieves, or whether they lived in the briar, or whether the Princess Margaret grew up and kept her promise and rid her kingdom of witches and cats, Small never knew, and neither do I, and neither shall you.

When he came back into the witch Lack's house, The Witch's Revenge saw at once what had happened. "Never mind," she said.

There were no children, no princes and princesses, in the throne room. The witch Lack's body still lay on the floor, but The Witch's Revenge had skinned it like a coney, and sewn up the skin into a bag. The bag wriggled and jerked, the sides heaving as if the witch Lack were still alive somewhere inside. The Witch's Revenge held the witchskin bag in one hand, and with the other, she was stuffing a cat into the neck of the skin. The cat wailed as it went into the bag. The bag was full of wailing. But the discarded flesh of the witch Lack lolled, slack.

There was a little pile of gold crowns on the floor beside the flayed corpse, and transparent, papery things that blew about the room, on a current of air, surprised looks on the thin, shed faces.

Cats were hiding in the corners of the room, and under the throne. "Go catch them," said The Witch's Revenge. "But leave the three prettiest alone."

"Where are the witch Lack's children?" Small said.

The Witch's Revenge nodded around the room. "As you see," she said. "I've slipped off their skins, and they were all cats underneath. They're cats now, but if we were to wait a year or two, they would shed these skins as well and become something new. Children are always growing."

Small chased the cats around the room. They were fast, but he was faster. They were nimble, but he was nimbler. He had worn his cat suit longer. He drove the cats down the length of the room, and The Witch's Revenge caught them and dropped them into her bag. At the end there were only three cats left in the throne room and they were as pretty a trio of cats as anyone could ask for. All the other cats were inside the bag.

"Well done and quickly done, too," said The Witch's Revenge, and she took her needle and stitched shut the neck of the bag. The skin of the witch Lack smiled up at Small, and a cat put its head through Lack's stained mouth, wailing. But The Witch's Revenge sewed Lack's mouth shut too, and the hole on the other end, where a house had come out. She left only his earholes and his eyeholes and his nostrils, which were full of fur, rolled open so that the cats could breathe.

The Witch's Revenge slung the skin full of cats over her shoulder and stood up.

"Where are you going?" Small said.

"These cats have mothers and fathers," The Witch's Revenge said. "They have mothers and fathers who miss them very much."

She gazed at Small. He decided not to ask again. So he waited in the house with the two princesses and the prince in their new cat suits, while The Witch's Revenge went down to the river. Or perhaps she took them down to the market and sold them. Or maybe she took each cat home, to its own mother and father, back to the kingdom where it had been born. Maybe she wasn't so careful to make sure that each child was returned to the right mother and father. After all, she was in a hurry, and cats look very much alike at night.

No one saw where she went—but the market is closer than the palaces of the Kings and Queens whose children had been stolen by the witch Lack, and the river is closer still.

When The Witch's Revenge came back to Lack's house, she looked around her. The house was beginning to stink very badly. Even Small could smell it now.

"I suppose the Princess Margaret let you fuck her," said The Witch's Revenge, as if she had been thinking about this while she ran her errands. "And that is why you let them go. I don't mind. She was a pretty puss. I might have let her go myself."

She looked at Small's face and saw that he was confused. "Never mind," she said.

She had a length of string in her paw, and a cork, which she greased with a piece of fat she had cut from the witch Lack. She threaded the cork on the string, calling it a good, quick, little mouse, and greased the string as well, and she fed the wriggling cork to the tabby who had been curled up in Small's lap. And when she had the cork back again, she greased it again and fed it to the little black cat, and then she fed it to the cat with two white forepaws, so that she had all three cats upon her string.

She sewed up the rip in the catskin bag, and Small put the gold crowns in the bag, and it was nearly as heavy as it had been before. The Witch's Revenge carried the bag, and Small took the greased string, holding it in his teeth, so the three cats were forced to run along behind him as they left the house of the witch Lack.

Small strikes a match, and he lights the house of the dead witch, Lack, on fire, as they leave. But shit burns slowly, if at all, and that house might be burning still, if someone hasn't gone and put it out. And maybe, someday, someone will go fishing in the river near that house, and hook their line on a bag full of princes and princesses, wet and sorry and wriggling in their catsuit skins—that's one way to catch a husband or a wife.

Small and The Witch's Revenge walked without stopping and the three cats came behind them. They walked until they reached a little village very near where the witch Small's mother had lived and there they settled down in a room The Witch's Revenge rented from a butcher. They cut the greased string, and bought a cage and hung it from a hook in the kitchen. They kept the three cats in it, but Small bought collars and leashes, and sometimes he put one of the cats on a leash and took it for a walk around the town.

Sometimes he wore his own catsuit and went out prowling, but The Witch's Revenge used to scold him if she caught him dressed like that. There are country manners and there are town manners and Small was a boy about town now.

The Witch's Revenge kept house. She cleaned and she cooked and she made Small's bed in the morning. Like all of the witch's cats, she was always busy. She melted down the gold crowns in a stewpot, and minted them into coins.

The Witch's Revenge wore a silk dress and gloves and a heavy veil, and ran her errands in a fine carriage, Small at her side. She opened an account in a bank, and she enrolled Small in a private academy. She bought a piece of land to build a house on, and she sent Small off to school every morning, no matter how he cried. But at night she took off her clothes and slept on his pillow and he combed her red and white fur.

Sometimes at night she twitched and moaned, and when he asked her what she was dreaming, she said, "There are ants! Can't you comb them out? Be quick and catch them, if you love me."

But there were never any ants.

One day when Small came home, the little cat with the white front paws was gone. When he asked The Witch's Revenge, she said that the little cat had fallen out of the cage and through the open window and into the garden and before The Witch's Revenge could think what to do, a crow had swooped down and carried the little cat off.

They moved into their new house a few months later, and Small was always very careful when he went in and out the doorway, imagining the little cat, down there in the dark, under the doorstep, under his foot.

Small got bigger. He didn't make any friends in the village, or at his school, but when you're big enough, you don't need friends.

One day while he and The Witch's Revenge were eating their dinner, there was a knock at the door. When Small opened the door, there stood Flora and Jack. Flora was wearing a drab, thrift-store coat, and Jack looked more than ever like a bundle of sticks.

"Small!" said Flora. "How tall you've become!" She burst into tears, and wrung her beautiful hands. Jack said, looking at The Witch's Revenge, "And who are you?"

The Witch's Revenge said to Jack, "Who am I? I'm your mother's cat, and you're a handful of dry sticks in a suit two sizes too large. But I won't tell anyone if you won't tell, either."

Jack snorted at this, and Flora stopped crying. She began to look around the house, which was sunny and large and well appointed.

"There's room enough for both of you," said The Witch's Revenge, "if Small doesn't mind."

Small thought his heart would burst with happiness to have his family back again. He showed Flora to one bedroom and Jack to another. Then they went downstairs and had a second dinner, and Small and The Witch's Revenge listened, and the cats in their hanging cage listened, while Flora and Jack recounted their adventures.

A pickpocket had taken Flora's purse, and they'd sold the witch's automobile, and lost the money in a game of cards. Flora found her parents, but they were a pair of old scoundrels who had no use for her. (She was too old to sell again. She would have realized what they were up to.) She'd gone to work in a department store, and Jack had sold tickets in a movie theater. They'd quarreled and made up, and then fallen in love with other people, and had many disappointments. At last they had decided to go home to the witch's house and see if it would do for a squat, or if there was anything left, to carry away and sell.

But the house, of course, had burned down. As they argued about what to do next, Jack had smelled Small, his brother, down in the village. So here they were.

"You'll live here, with us," Small said.

Jack and Flora said they could not do that. They had ambitions, they said. They had plans. They would stay for a week, or two weeks, and then they would be off again. The Witch's Revenge nodded and said that this was sensible.

Every day Small came home from school and went out again, with Flora, on a bicycle built for two. Or he stayed home and Jack taught him how to hold a coin between two fingers, and how to follow the egg, as it moved from cup to cup. The Witch's Revenge taught them to play bridge, although Flora and Jack couldn't be partners. They quarreled with each other as if they were husband and wife.

"What do you want?" Small asked Flora one day. He was leaning against her, wishing he were still a cat, and could sit in her lap. She smelled of secrets. "Why do you have to go away again?"

Flora patted Small on the head. She said, "What do I want? That's easy enough! To never have to worry about money. I want to marry a man and know that he'll never cheat on me, or leave me." She looked at Jack as she said this.

Jack said, "I want a rich wife who won't talk back, who doesn't lie in bed all day, with the covers pulled up over her head, weeping and calling me a bundle of twigs." And he looked at Flora when he said this.

The Witch's Revenge put down the sweater that she was knitting for Small. She looked at Flora and she looked at Jack and then she looked at Small.

Small went into the kitchen and opened the door of the hanging cage. He lifted out the two cats and brought them to Flora and Jack. "Here," he said. "A husband for you, Flora, and a wife for Jack. A prince and a princess, and both of them beautiful, and well brought up, and wealthy, no doubt."

Flora picked up the little tomcat and said, "Don't tease at me, Small! Who ever heard of marrying a cat!"

The Witch's Revenge said, "The trick is to keep their catskins in a safe hiding place. And if they sulk, or treat you badly, sew them back into their catskin and put them into a bag and throw them in the river."

Then she took her claw and slit the skin of the tabby-colored cat suit, and Flora was holding a naked man. Flora shrieked and dropped him on the ground. He was a handsome man, well made, and he had a princely manner. He was not a man that anyone would ever mistake for a cat. He stood up and made a bow, very elegant, for all that he was naked. Flora blushed, but she looked pleased.

"Go fetch some clothes for the Prince and the Princess," The Witch's Revenge said to Small. When he got back, there was a naked princess hiding behind the sofa, and Jack was leering at her.

A few weeks after that, there were two weddings, and then Flora left with her new husband, and Jack went off with his new princess. Perhaps they lived happily ever after.

The Witch's Revenge said to Small, "We have no wife for you."

Small shrugged. "I'm still too young," he said.

But try as hard as he can, Small is getting older now. The catskin barely fits across his shoulders. The buttons strain when he fastens them. His grown-up fur—his people fur—is coming in. At night he dreams.

The witch his mother's Spanish heel beats against the pane of glass. The princess hangs in the briar. She's holding up her dress, so he can see the catfur down there. Now she's under the house. She wants to marry him, but the house will fall down if he kisses her. He and Flora are children again, in the witch's house. Flora lifts up her skirt and says, see my pussy? There's a cat down there, peeking out at him, but it doesn't look like any cat he's ever seen. He says to Flora, I have a pussy too. But his isn't the same.

At last he knows what happened to the little, starving, naked thing in the forest, where it went. It crawled into his catskin, while he was asleep, and then it climbed right inside him, his Small skin, and now it is huddled in his chest, still cold and sad and hungry. It is eating him from the inside, and getting bigger, and one day there will be no Small left at all, only that nameless, hungry child, wearing a Small skin.

Small moans in his sleep.

There are ants in The Witch's Revenge's skin, leaking out of her seams, and they march down into the sheets and pinch at him, down under his arms, and between his legs where his fur is growing in, and it hurts, it aches and aches. He dreams that The Witch's Revenge wakes now, and comes and licks him all over, until the pain melts. The pane of glass melts. The ants march away again on their long, greased thread.

"What do you want?" says The Witch's Revenge.

Small is no longer dreaming. He says, "I want my mother!"

Light from the moon comes down through the window over their bed. The Witch's Revenge is very beautiful—she looks like a Queen, like a knife, like a burning house, a cat—in the moonlight. Her fur shines. Her whiskers stand out like pulled stitches, wax and thread. The Witch's Revenge says, "Your mother is dead."

"Take off your skin," Small says. He's crying and The Witch's Revenge licks his tears away. Small's skin pricks all over, and down under the house, something small wails and wails. "Give me back my mother," he says.

"Oh, my darling," says his mother, the witch, The Witch's Revenge, "I can't do that. I'm full of ants. Take off my skin, and all the ants will spill out, and there will be nothing left of me."

Small says, "Why have you left me all alone?"

His mother the witch says, "I've never left you alone, not even for a minute. I sewed up my death in a catskin so I could stay with you."

"Take it off! Let me see you!" Small says. He pulls at the sheet on the bed, as if it were his mother's catskin.

The Witch's Revenge shakes her head. She trembles and beats her tail back and forth. She says, "How can you ask me for such a thing, and how can I say no to you? Do you know what you're asking me for? Tomorrow night. Ask me again, tomorrow night."

And Small has to be satisfied with that. All night long, Small combs his mother's fur. His fingers are looking for the seams in her catskin. When The Witch's Revenge yawns, he peers inside her mouth, hoping to catch a glimpse of his mother's face. He can feel himself becoming smaller and smaller. In the morning he will be so small that when he tries to put his catskin on, he can barely do up the buttons. He'll be so small, so sharp, you might mistake him for an ant, and when The Witch's Revenge yawns, he'll creep inside her mouth, he'll go down into her belly, he'll go find his mother. If he can, he'll help his mother cut her catskin open so that she can get out again and come and live in the world with him, and if she won't come out, then he won't, either. He'll live there, the way that sailors learn to live, inside the belly of fish who have eaten them, and keep house for his mother inside the house of her skin.

This is the end of the story. The Princess Margaret grows up to kill witches and cats. If she doesn't, then someone else will have to do it. There is no such thing as witches, and there is no such thing as cats, either, only people dressed up in catskin suits. They have their reasons, and who is to say that they might not live that way, happily ever after, until the ants have carried away all of the time that there is, to build something new and better out of it?

Mike said it was a painting of an iceberg.

Some Zombie Contingency Plans

THIS IS A STORY ABOUT being lost in the woods.

This guy Soap is at a party out in the suburbs. The thing you need to know about Soap is that he keeps a small framed oil painting in the trunk of his car. The painting is about the size of a paperback novel. Wherever Soap goes, this oil painting goes with him. But he leaves the painting in the trunk of his car, because you don't walk around a party carrying a painting. People will think you're weird.

Soap doesn't know anyone here. He's crashed the party, which is what he does now, when he feels lonely. On weekends, he just drives around the suburbs until he finds one of those summer twilight parties that are so big that they spill out onto the yard.

Kids are out on the lawn of a two-story house, lying on the damp grass and drinking beer out of plastic cups. Soap has brought along a six-pack. It's the least he can do. He walks through the house, past four black guys sitting all over a couch. They're watching a football game and there's some music on the stereo. The television is on mute. Over by the TV, a white girl is dancing by herself. When she gets too close to it, the guys on the couch start complaining.

Soap finds the kitchen. There's one of those big professional ovens and a lot of expensive-looking knives stuck to a magnetic strip on the wall.

It's funny, Soap thinks, how expensive stuff always looks more dangerous, and also safer, both of these things at the same time. He pokes around in the fridge and finds some pre-sliced cheese and English muffins. He grabs three slices of cheese, the muffins, and puts the beer in the fridge. There's also a couple of steaks, and so he takes one out, heats up the broiler.

A girl wanders into the kitchen. She's black and her hair goes up and up and on top are these sturdy, springy curls like little waves. Toe to top of her architectural haircut, she's as tall as Soap. She has eyes the color of iceberg lettuce. There's a heart-shaped rhinestone under one green eye. The rhinestone winks at Soap like it knows him. She's gorgeous, but Soap knows better than to fool around with girls who aren't out of high school yet, maybe. "What are you doing?" she says.

"Cooking a steak," Soap says. "Want one?"

"No," she says. "I already ate."

She sits up on the counter beside the sink and swings her legs. She's wearing a bikini top, pink shorts, and no shoes. "Who are you?" she says.

"Will," Soap says, although Will isn't his name. Soap isn't his real name, either.

"I'm Carly," she says. "You want a beer?"

"There's beer in the fridge," Will says, and Carly says, "I know there is."

Will opens and closes drawers and cabinet doors until he's found a plate, a fork and a knife, and garlic salt. He takes his steak out of the oven.

"You go to State?" Carly says. She pops off the beer top against the lip of the kitchen counter, and Will knows she's showing off.

"No," Will says. He sits down at the kitchen table and cuts off a piece of steak. He's been lonely ever since he and his friend Mike got out of prison and Mike went out to Seattle. It's nice to sit in a kitchen and talk to a girl.

"So what do you do?" Carly says. She sits down at the table, across from him. She lifts her arms up and stretches until her back cracks. She's got nice tits.

"Telemarketing," Will says, and Carly makes a face.

"That sucks," she says.

"Yeah," Will says. "No, it isn't too bad. I like talking to people. I just got out of prison." He takes another big bite of steak.

"No way," Carly says. "What did you do?"

Will chews. He swallows. "I don't want to talk about it right now."

"Okay," Carly says.

"Do you like museums?" Will says. She looks like a girl who goes to museums.

Some drunk white kid wanders into the kitchen. He says hey to Will and then he lies down on the floor with his head under Carly's chair. "Carly, Carly, Carly," he says. "I am so in love with you right now. You're the most beautiful girl in the world. And you don't even know my name. That's hurtful."

"Museums are okay," Carly says. "I like concerts. Jazz. Improvisational comedy. I like stuff that isn't the same every time you look at it."

"How about zombies?" Will says. No more steak. He mops up meat juice with one of the muffins. Maybe he could eat another one of those steaks. The kid with his head under Carly's chair says, "Carly? Carly? Carly? I like it when you sit on my face, Carly."

"You mean like horror movies?" Carly says.

"The living dead," says the kid under the chair. "The walking dead. Why do the dead walk everywhere? Why don't they just catch the bus?"

"You still hungry?" Carly says to Will. "I could make you some cinnamon toast. Or some soup."

"They could carpool," the kid under the chair says. "Hey y'all, I don't know why they call carpools *carpools*. It's not like there are cars with swimming pools in them. Because people might drown on their way to school. What a weird word. Carpool. Carpool. Carly's pool. There are naked people in Carly's pool, but Carly isn't naked in Carly's pool."

"Is there a phone around here?" Will says. "I was thinking I should call my dad. He's having open-heart surgery tomorrow."

It's not his name, but let's call him Soap. That's what they called him in prison, although not for the reasons you're thinking. When he was a kid, he'd read a book about a boy named Soap. So he didn't mind the nickname. It was better than Oatmeal, which is what one guy ended up getting called. You don't want to know why Oatmeal got called Oatmeal. It would put you off oatmeal.

Soap was in prison for six months. In some ways, six months isn't a long time. You spend longer inside your mother. But six months in prison is enough time to think about things and all around you, everyone else is thinking too. It can make you go crazy, wondering what other people are thinking about. Some guys thought about their families, and other guys thought about revenge, or how they were going to get rich. Some guys took correspondence courses or fell in love because of what one of the volunteer art instructors said about one of their watercolors. Soap didn't take an art course, but he thought about art. Art was why Soap was in prison. This sounded romantic, but really, it was just stupid.

Even before Soap and his friend Mike went to prison, Soap was sure that he'd had opinions about art, even though he hadn't known much about art. It was the same with prison. Art and prison were the kind of things that you had opinions about, even if you didn't know anything about them. Soap still didn't know much about art. These were some of the things that he had known about art before prison:

He knew what he liked when he saw it. As it had turned out, he knew what he liked, even when he couldn't see it.

Museums gave him hiccups. He had hiccups a lot of the time while he was in prison too.

These were some of the things Soap figured out about art while he was in prison.

Great art came out of great suffering. Soap had gone through a lot of shit because of art.

There was a difference between art, which you just looked at, and things like soap, which you used. Even if the soap smelled so good that you didn't want to use it, only smell it. This was why people got so pissed off about art. Because you didn't eat it, and you didn't sleep on it, and you couldn't put it up your nose. A lot of people said things like "That's not art" when whatever they were talking about could clearly not have been anything else, except art.

When Soap got tired of thinking about art, he thought about zombies. He worked on his zombie contingency plan. Thinking about zombies was less tiring than thinking about art. Here's what Soap knew about zombies:

Zombies were not about sex.

Zombies were not interested in art.

Zombies weren't complicated. It wasn't like werewolves or ghosts or vampires. Vampires, for example, were the middle/upper-middle management of the supernatural world. Some people thought of vampires as rock stars, but really they were more like Martha Stewart. Vampires were prissy. They had to follow rules. They had to look good. Zombies weren't like that. You couldn't exorcise zombies. You didn't need luxury items like silver bullets or crucifixes or holy water. You just shot zombies in the head, or set fire to them, or hit them over the head really hard. There were some guys in the prison who knew about that. There were guys in the prison who knew about anything you might want to know about. There were guys who knew things that you didn't want to know. It was like a library, except it wasn't.

Zombies didn't discriminate. Everyone tasted equally good as far as zombies were concerned. And anyone could *be* a zombie. You didn't have to be special, or good at sports, or good-looking. You didn't have to smell good, or wear the right kind of clothes, or listen to the right kind of music. You just had to be slow.

Soap liked this about zombies.

There is never just one zombie.

There was something about clowns that was worse than zombies. (Or maybe something that was the same. When you see a zombie, you want to laugh at first. When you see a clown, most people get a little nervous. There's the pallor and the cakey mortician-style makeup, the shuffling and the untidy hair. But clowns were probably malicious, and they moved fast on those little bicycles and in those little, crammed cars. Zombies weren't much of anything. They didn't carry musical instruments and they didn't care whether or not you laughed at them. You always knew what zombies wanted.) Given a choice, Soap would take zombies over clowns any day. There was a white guy in the prison who had been a clown. Nobody was sure why he was in prison.

It turned out that everyone in the prison had a zombie contingency plan, once you asked them, just like everyone in prison had a prison escape plan, only nobody talked about those. Soap tried not to dwell on escape plans, although sometimes he dreamed that he was escaping. Then the zombies would show up. They always showed up in his escape dreams. You could escape prison, but you couldn't escape zombies. This was true in Soap's dreams, just the way it was true in the movies. You couldn't get any more true than that.

According to Soap's friend Mike, who was also in prison, people worried too much about zombies and not enough about icebergs. Even though icebergs were real. Mike pointed out that icebergs were slow, like zombies. Maybe you could adapt zombie contingency plans to cope with icebergs.

Mike asked Soap to start thinking about icebergs. No one else was. Somebody had to plan for icebergs, according to Mike.

Even after Soap got out of prison, when it was much too late, he still dreamed about escaping from prison.

"So whose house is this, anyway?" Will asks Carly. She's walking up the stairs in front of him. If he reached out just one hand, he could untie her bikini top. It would just fall off.

"This girl," Carly says, and proceeds to relate a long, sad story. "A friend of mine. Her parents took her to France for this bicycle tour. They're into Amway. This trip is some kind of bonus. Like, her father sold a bunch of water filters and so now everyone has to go to France and build their own bicycles. In Marseilles. Isn't that lame? She can't even speak French. She's a Francophilophobe. She's a klutz. Her parents don't even like her. If they could have, they would have left her at home. Or maybe they'll leave her somewhere in France. Shit, would I love to see her try and ride a bike in France. She'll probably fall right over the Alps. I hate her. We were going to have this party and then she said I should go ahead and have it without her. She's really pissed off at her parents."

"Is this a bathroom?" Will says. "Hold on a minute."

He goes in and takes a piss. He flushes and when he goes to wash his hands, he sees that the people who own this house have put some chunk of fancy soap beside the sink. He sniffs the soap. Then he opens up the door. Carly is standing there talking to some Asian girl wearing a strapless dress with little shiny fake plastic flowers all over it. It's too big for her in the bust, so she's holding the front out like she's waiting for someone to come along and drop a weasel in it. Will wonders who the dress belongs to, and why this girl would want to wear an ugly dress like that, anyway.

He holds out the soap. "Smell this," he says to Carly and she does. "What does it smell like?"

"I don't know," she says. "Marmalade?"

"Lemongrass," Will says. He marches back into the bathroom and opens up the window. There's a swimming pool down there with people in it. He throws the soap out the window and some guy in the pool yells, "Hey!"

"Why'd he do that?" the girl in the hall says. Carly starts laughing.

Soap's friend Mike had a girlfriend named Jenny. Jenny never came to see Mike in prison. Soap felt bad about this.

Soap's dad was living in New Zealand and every once in a while Soap got a postcard.

Soap's mom, who lived in California out near Manhattan Beach, was too busy and too pissed off with Soap to visit him in prison. Soap's mom didn't tolerate stupidity or bad luck.

Soap's older sister, Becka, was the only family member who ever came to visit him in prison. Becka was an actress-waitress who had once been in a low-budget zombie movie. Soap had watched it once and wasn't sure which was stranger: seeing your sister naked, or seeing your naked sister get eaten by zombies. Becka was almost good looking enough to be on a reality dating show, but not funny looking or sad enough to be on one of the makeover shows. Becka was always giving notice. So then their mom would buy Becka a round-trip ticket to go visit Soap. Soap figured he was supposed to be an example to Becka: find a good job and keep it, or you'll end up in prison like your brother.

Becka might have been average in L.A., but average in L.A. is Queen of Mars in the visiting room of a federal penitentiary in North Carolina. Guys kept asking Soap when they were going to see his sister on TV.

Soap's mom owned a boutique right on Manhattan Beach. It was called Float. Becka and Soap called it Wash Your Mouth. The boutique sold soaps and shampoos, nothing else. The soaps and shampoos were supposed to smell like food. What the soaps really smelled like were those candles that were supposed to smell like food, but which smelled instead like those air fresheners which hang from the rearview mirrors in taxis or stolen cars. Like looking behind you smells like strawberries. Like making a clean get-away smells the same as the room freshener Soap and Becka used to spray when they'd been smoking their mother's pot, before she got home.

Once when they were in high school, Soap and Becka had bought a urinal cake. It smelled like peppermint. They'd taken the urinal cake out of its packaging and put it in a fancy box with some tissue paper and a ribbon. Soap had wrapped it up and given it to their mother for Mother's Day. Told her it was a pumice soap for exfoliating feet. Soap liked soap that smelled like soap. His mom was always sending care packages of soaps that smelled like olive oil and neroli and peppermint and brown sugar and cucumber and martinis and toasted marshmallow.

You weren't supposed to have bars of soap in prison. If you put a bar of soap in a sock, you could hit somebody over the head with it. You could clobber somebody. But Becka made an arrangement with the guards in the visiting room, and the guards in the visiting room made an arrangement with the guards in charge of the mailroom. Soap gave out his mother's soaps to everyone in prison. Whoever wanted them. It turned out everyone wanted soap that smelled like food: social workers and prison guards and drug dealers and murderers and even people who hadn't been able to afford good lawyers. No wonder his mom's boutique did so well.

While Soap was in prison, Becka kept Soap's painting for him. Sometimes he asked and she brought it with her when she came to visit. He made her promise not to give it to their mother, not to pawn it for rent money, to keep it under her bed where it would be safe as long as her roommate's cat didn't sneak in. Becka promised that if there were a fire or an earthquake, she'd rescue the painting first. Even before she rescued her roommate or her roommate's cat.

Carly takes Will into a bedroom. There's a big painting of a flower garden, and under the painting is a king-sized bed with dresses lying all over it. There are dresses on the floor. "Go ahead and call your dad," Carly says. "I'll come back in a while with some more beer. You want another beer?"

"Why not?" Will says. He waits until she leaves the room and then he calls his dad. When his dad picks up the phone, he says, "Hey, Dad, how's it going?"

"Junior!" his dad says. "How's it going?"

"Did I wake you up? What time is it there?" Junior says.

"Doesn't matter," his dad says. "I was working on a jigsaw puzzle. No picture on the box. I think it's lemurs. Or maybe binturongs."

"Not much," Junior says. "Staying out of trouble."

"Super," his dad says. "That's super."

"I was thinking about that thing we talked about. About how I could come visit you sometime?" Junior says.

"Sure," his dad says. His dad is always enthusiastic about Junior's ideas. "Hey, that would be great. Get out of that fucking country while you still can. Come visit your old dad. We could do father-son stuff. Go bungee jumping."

The girl in the plastic flower dress marches into the bedroom. She takes the dress off and drops it on the bed. She goes into the closet and comes out again holding a dress made out of black and purple feathers. It looks like something a dancer in Las Vegas might wear when she got off work.

"Some girl just came in and took off all her clothes," Junior says to his dad.

"Well you give her my best," his dad says, and hangs up.

"My dad says hello," Junior says to the naked girl. Then he says, "My dad and I have a question for you. Do you ever worry about zombies? Do you have a zombie contingency plan?"

The girl just smiles like she thinks that's a good question. She puts the new dress on. She walks out. Will calls his sister, but Becka isn't answering her cell phone. So Will picks up all the dresses and goes into the closet. He hangs them up. People clean up after themselves. Zombies don't.

In Will's opinion, zombies are attracted to suburbs the way that tornadoes are attracted to trailer parks. Maybe it's all the windows. Maybe houses in suburbs have too many windows and that's what drives zombies nuts.

If the zombies showed up tonight, Will would barricade the bedroom door with the heavy oak dresser. Will will let the naked girl come in first. Carly too. The three of them will make a rope by tying all those dresses together and escape through the window. Maybe they could make wings out of that feather dress and fly away. Will could be the Bird Man of Suburbitraz.

Will looks under the bed, just to make sure there are no zombies or suitcases or that drunk guy from downstairs under there.

There's a little black kid in Superman pajamas curled up asleep under the bed.

When Becka was a kid, she kept a suitcase under the bed. The suitcase was full of things that were to be rescued in case of an earthquake or a fire or murderers. The suitcase's secondary function was using up some of the dangerous, dark space under the bed which might otherwise have been inhabited by monsters or dead people. Here be suitcases. In the suitcase, Becka kept a candle shaped like a dragon, which she'd bought at the mall with some birthday money and then couldn't bear to use as a candle; a little ceramic dog; some favorite stuffed animals; their mother's charm bracelet; a photo album; *Black Beauty* and a whole lot of other horse books. Every once in a while Becka and her little brother would drag the suitcase back out from under the bed and sort through it. Becka would take things out and put other things in. Her little brother always felt happy and safe when he helped Becka do this. When things got bad, you would rescue what you could.

Modern art is a waste of time. When the zombies show up, you can't worry about art. Art is for people who aren't worried about zombies. Besides zombies and icebergs, there are other things that Soap has been thinking about. Tsunamis, earthquakes, Nazi dentists, killer bees, army ants, black plague, old people, divorce lawyers, sorority girls, Jimmy Carter, giant squids, rabid foxes, strange dogs, news anchors, child actors, fascists, narcissists, psychologists, ax murderers, unrequited love, footnotes, zeppelins, the Holy Ghost, Catholic priests, John Lennon, chemistry teachers, redheaded men with British accents, librarians, spiders, nature books with photographs of spiders in them, darkness, teachers, swimmming pools, smart girls, pretty girls, rich girls, angry girls, tall girls, nice girls, girls with superpowers, giant lizards, blind dates who turn out to have narcolepsy, angry monkeys, feminine hygiene commercials, sitcoms about aliens, things under the bed, contact lenses, ninjas, performance artists, mummies, spontaneous combustion. Soap has been afraid of all of these things at one time or another. Ever since he went to prison, he's realized that he doesn't have to be afraid. All he has to do is come up with a plan. Be prepared. It's just like the Boy Scouts, except you have to be even more prepared. You have to prepare for everything that the Boy Scouts didn't prepare you for, which is pretty much everything.

Soap is a waste of time too. What good is soap in a zombie situation? Soap sometimes imagines himself trapped in his mother's soap boutique. Zombies are coming out of the surf, dripping wet, hellishly hungry, always so fucking slow, shuffling hopelessly up through the sand of Manhattan Beach. Soap has barricaded himself in Float with his mother and some blond Japanese tourists with surfboards. "Do something, sweetheart!" his mother implores. So Sweetheart throws water all over the floor. There's the surfboards, a baseball bat under the counter, some rolls of quarters, and a swordfish mounted up on the wall, but Sweetheart decides the cash register is best for bashing. He tells the Japanese tourists to get down on their hands and knees and rub soap all over the floor. When the zombies finally find a way into Float, his mother and the tourists can hide behind the counter. The zombies will slip all over the floor and Sweetheart will bash them in the head with the cash register. It will be just like a Busby Berkeley zombie musical.

"What's going on?" Carly says. "How's your father doing?"

"He's fine," Will says. "Except for the open-heart surgery thing. Except for that, he's good. I was just looking under the bed. There's a little kid under there."

"Oh," Carly says. "Him. That's the little brother. Of my friend. *Le bro de mon ami.* I'm taking care of him. He likes to sleep under the bed."

"What's his name?" Will says.

"Leo," Carly says. She hands Will a beer and sits down on the bed beside him. "So tell me about this prison thing. What did you do? Should I be afraid of you?"

"Probably not," Will says. "It doesn't do much good to be afraid of things."

"So tell me what you did," Carly says. She burps so loud that Will is amazed that the kid under the bed doesn't wake up. Leo.

"This is a great party," Will says. "Thanks for hanging out with me."

"Somebody just puked out of a window in the living room. Someone else almost threw up in the swimming pool, but I got them out in time. If someone throws up on the piano, I'm in big trouble. You can't get puke out from between piano keys."

Will thinks Carly says this like she knows what she's talking about. There are girls who have had years of piano lessons, and then there are girls who have taken piano lessons who also know how to throw a party and how to clean throw-up out of a piano. There's something sexy about a girl who knows how to play the piano, and keys that stick for no apparent reason. Will doesn't have any zombie contingency plans that involve pianos, and it makes him sick. How could he have forgotten pianos?

"I'll help you clean up," Will says. "If you want."

"You don't have to try so hard, you know," Carly says. She stares right at him, like there's a spider on his face or an interesting tattoo, some word spelled upside down in a foreign language that she wants to understand. Will doesn't have any tattoos. As far as he's concerned, tattoos are like art, only worse.

Will stares right back. He says, "When I was at this party outside Kansas City, I heard this story about a kid who threw a lot of parties while his parents were on vacation. Right before they got home, he realized how fucked up the house was, and so he burned it down." This story always makes Will laugh. What a dumb kid.

"You want to help me burn down my friend's house?" Carly says. She smiles, like, what a good joke. What a nice guy he is. "What time is it?

Two? If it's two in the morning, then you have to tell me why you went to prison. It's like a rule. We've known each other for at least an hour, and it's late at night and I still don't know why you were in prison, even though I can tell you want to tell me or otherwise you wouldn't have told me you were in prison in the first place. Was what you did that bad?"

"No," Will says. "It was just really stupid."

"Stupid is good," Carly says. "Come on. Pretty please."

She pulls back the cover on the bed and crawls under it, pulls the sheets up to her chin. Good night, Carly. Good night, Carly's gorgeous tits.

It was so small and it was so far away, even when you looked at it up close. Soap said it was trees. A wood. Mike said it was a painting of an iceberg.

When Soap thinks about the zombies, he thinks about how there's nowhere you can go that the zombies won't find you. Even the fairy tales that Becka used to read to him. Ali Baba and the Forty Zombies. Open Zombie. Snow White and the Seven Tiny Zombies.

Any place Will thinks of, the zombies will eventually get there too. He pictures all of these places as paintings in a gallery, because as long as a place is just a painting, it's a safe place. Landscapes with frames around them, to keep the landscapes from leaking out. To keep the zombies from getting in. A ski resort in summer, all those lonely gondolas. An oil rig on a sea at night. The Museum of Natural History. The Playboy mansion. The Eiffel Tower. The Matterhorn. David Letterman's house. Buckingham Palace. A bowling alley. A Laundromat. He puts himself in the painting of the flower garden that's hanging above the bed where he and Carly are sitting, and it's sunny and warm and safe and beautiful. But once he puts himself into the painting, the zombies show up just like they always do. The space station. New Zealand. He bets his dad thinks he's safe from zombies in New Zealand, because it's an island. His dad is an idiot.

People paint trees all the time. All kinds of trees. Art is supposed to be about things like trees. Or icebergs, although there are more paintings of trees than there are paintings of icebergs, so Mike doesn't know what he's talking about.

"I wasn't in prison for very long," Soap says. "What Mike and I did wasn't really that bad. We didn't hurt anybody."

"You don't look like a bad guy," Carly says. And when Soap looks at Carly, she looks like a nice kid. A nice girl with nice tits. But Soap knows you can't tell by looking.

Soap and Mike were going to be rich once they got out of college. The two of them had it all figured out. They were going to have an excellent website, just as soon as they figured out what it was going to be about, and what to call it. While they were in prison, they decided this website would have been about zombies. That would have been fucking awesome.

Hungryzombie.com, lonelyzombie.com, nakedzombie.com, soyoumarriedazombie.com, zombiecontingencyplan.com, dotcomofthewalkingdead.com were just a few of the names they came up with. In Will's opinion, people will go anywhere if there's a zombie involved.

Cool people would have gone to the site and hooked up. People would have talked about old horror movies, or about their horrible temp jobs. There would have been comics and concerts. There would have been advertising, sponsors, movie deals. Soap would have been able to afford art. He would have bought Picassos and Vermeers and original comic book art. He would have bought drinks for women. Beautiful, bisexual, bionic women with unpronounceable names and weird habits in bed.

Only by the time Soap and Mike and the rest of their friends got out of school, all of that was already over. Nobody cared if you had a website. Everybody already had websites. No one was going to give you money.

There were lots of guys who knew how to do what Soap and Mike knew how to do. It turned out that Mike's and Soap's parents had paid a lot of money for them to learn how to do things that everyone could already do.

Mike had a girlfriend named Jenny. Soap liked Jenny because she teased him, but Jenny really isn't important to this story. She wasn't ever going to fall in love with Soap, and Soap knew it. What matters is that Jenny worked in a museum, and so Soap and Mike started going to museum events, because you got Brie on crackers and wine and martinis. Free food. All you had to do was wear a suit and listen to people talk about art and mortgages and their children. There would be a lot of older women who reminded Soap of his mother, and it was clear that Soap reminded these women of their sons. What was never clear was whether these women were flirting with him, or whether they wanted his advice about something that even they couldn't put their finger on.

One morning, in prison, Soap woke up and realized that the opportunity had been there and he'd never even seen it. He and Mike, they could have started a website for older upper-middle-class women with strong work ethics and confused, resentful grown-up children with bachelor degrees and no jobs. That was better than zombies. They could even have done some good.

"Okay," Will says. "I'll tell you why I went to prison. But first you have to tell me what you'd do if zombies showed up at your party. Tonight. I ask everyone this. Everyone has a zombie contingency plan."

"You mean like with colleges, just in case you don't get into your first choice?" Carly says. She holds an eyelid open, puts her finger to her eyeball, and pops out a contact lens. She puts it on the table beside the bed. She doesn't take the other lens out. Maybe that eye isn't scratchy. "So my eyes aren't actually green. The breasts are real, by the way. I don't watch a lot of horror movies. They give me nightmares. Leo likes that stuff."

Will sits on the other side of the bed and watches her. She's thinking about it. Maybe she likes how the world looks through one green contact lens. "My parents keep a gun in the fridge. I guess I'd go get it and shoot the zombies? Or maybe I'd hide in my mom's closet? Behind all her shoes and stuff? I'd cry a lot. I'd scream for help. I'd call the police."

"Okay," Will says. "I was just wondering. What about your brother? How would you protect him?"

Carly yawns like she isn't impressed at all, but Will can see she's impressed. It's just that she's sleepy, too. "Smart Will. You knew this was my house all along. You knew Leo was my brother. Am I such a bad liar?"

"Yeah," Will says. "There's a picture of you and Leo over on your parents' dresser."

"Okay," Carly says. "This is my parents' bedroom. They're in France building bicycles, and they left me and they left Leo here. So I threw a party. Serves them right if someone burns their house down."

"I feel like we've known each other for a long time," Will says. "Even though we just met. For example, I knew your eyes weren't really green."

"We don't really know each other very well," Carly says. But she says it in a friendly way. "I keep trying to get to know you better. I bet you didn't know that I want to be president someday."

"I bet you didn't know that I think about icebergs a lot, although not as much as I think about zombies," Will says.

"I'd like to go live on an iceberg," Carly says. "And I'd like to be president too. Maybe I could do both. I could be the first black woman president who lives on an iceberg."

"I'd vote for you," Will says.

"Will," Carly says. "Don't you want to get under the covers with me? Are you intimidated by the fact that I'm going to be president someday? Are you intimidated by competent, sucessful women?"

Will says, "Do you want to fool around or do you want me to tell how I ended up in prison? Door A or Door B. I'm a really good kisser, but Leo is asleep under the bed. Your brother." Jenny and Mike used to go off and kiss in the museum where Jenny worked, but Soap never kissed Jenny. Once, in college, Soap kissed Mike. They were both drunk. Men kissed men in prison. White men made out with black men. Becka used to make out with her boyfriends out on the beach while her brother hid in the dunes and watched. In the zombie movie, a zombie ate Becka's lips. You don't ever want to kiss a zombie.

"He's a heavy sleeper," Carly says. "Maybe you should just tell me what you did and we can go from there."

Soap and Mike and a couple of their friends were at one of the parties at the little private museum where Jenny worked. They drank a lot of wine and they didn't eat much except some olives. Jenny was busy and so Soap and Mike and their friends left the gallery where the wine and cheese were laid out, where the docents and the rich people were getting to know each other, and wandered out into the rest of the museum. They got farther and farther away from Jenny's event, but nobody told them to come back and nobody showed up and asked them what they were doing. The other galleries were dark and so somebody dared Mike to go in one of them. They wanted to see if an alarm would go off. Mike did and the alarm didn't.

Next Soap went into the gallery. His name wasn't Soap then. His name was Arthur, but everybody called him Art. Ha ha. You couldn't see anything in the gallery. Art felt stupid just standing there, so he put his hands straight out in front of him in the darkness and walked forward until his fingers touched a wall. He kept his fingers on the wall and walked around the room. Every now and then his fingers would touch a frame and he'd move his hand up and down and along the frame to see how big the painting was. He walked all the way around the room until he was at the door again.

Then somebody else went in, it was Markson who went in, and when Markson came out, he was holding a painting in his arms. It was about three feet by three feet. A painting of a ship with a lot of masts and sails. Lots of little dabs of blue. Little people on the deck of the ship, looking busy.

"Holy shit," Mike said. "Markson, what did you just do?"

You have to understand that Markson was an idiot. Everyone knew that. Right then he was a drunk idiot, but everyone else was drunk too.

"I just wanted to see what it looked like," Markson said. "I didn't think it would be so heavy." He put the painting down against the wall.

No alarms were going off. The gallery on the other side of the hall was dark too. So they made it a game. Everyone went into one of the galleries and walked around and chose a painting. Then you came out again and saw what you had. Someone got a Seurat. Someone had a Mary Cassatt. Someone else had a Winslow Homer. There were a lot of paintings by artists whom none of them knew. So those didn't count. Art went back into the first gallery. This time he was slow. There were already some gaps on the gallery wall. He put his ear up against some of the paintings. He felt that he was listening for something, only he didn't know what.

He chose a very small painting. When he got it out into the hall, he saw it was an oil painting. A blobby blue-green mass that might have been water or a person or it might have been trees. Woods from very far away. Something slow and far away. He couldn't read the artist's signature.

Mike was in the other gallery. When he came out with a painting, the painting turned out to be a Picasso. Some sad-looking freaky woman and her sad-looking freaky dog. Everyone agreed that Mike had won. Then that idiot Markson said, "I bet you can't walk out of here with that Picasso."

Sometimes when he's in houses that don't belong to him, Soap feels bad. He shouldn't be where he is. He doesn't belong anywhere. Nobody really knows him. If they did, they wouldn't like him. Everyone always seems happier than Soap, and as if they know something that Soap doesn't. He tells himself that things will be different when the zombies show up.

"You guys stole a Picasso?" Carly says.

"It was a minor Picasso. Hardly a Picasso at all. We weren't really stealing it," Will says. "We just thought it would be funny to smuggle it out of Jenny's museum and see how far we got with it. We just walked out of the museum and nobody stopped us. We put the Picasso in the car and drove back to our apartment. I took that little painting too, just so the Picasso would have company. And because I wanted to spend some more time looking at it. I put it under my coat, under one arm, while the other guys were helping Mike get past the party without being seen. We hung the Picasso in the living room when we got back and I put the little painting in my bedroom. We were still drunk when the police showed up.

Jenny lost her job. We went to prison. Markson and the other guys had to do community service."

He stops talking. Carly takes his hand. She squeezes it. She says, "That's the weirdest story I've ever heard. Why is it that everything is so much sadder and funnier and so much more true when you're drunk?"

"I haven't told you the weird part yet," Will says. He can't tell her the weirdest part of the story, although maybe he can try to show her.

"Did I tell you that I used to be on my school's debate team?" Carly says. "That's the weirdest thing about me. I like getting in arguments. The boy with his head under my chair, I kicked his ass in a debate about marijuana. I humiliated him all over the map."

Will doesn't use drugs anymore. It's too much like being in a museum. It makes everything look like art, and makes everything feel like just before the zombies show up. He says, "The museum said that I hadn't stolen the little painting from them. They said it wasn't theirs, even when I explained the whole thing. I told the truth and everyone thought I was lying. The police asked around, just in case Mike and I had done the same thing somewhere else, at some other museum, and nobody came forward. Nobody knew the artist's name. So finally they just gave the painting back to me. They thought I was trying to pull some scam."

"So what happened to it?" Carly says.

"I've still got it. My sister kept it for me while I was in prison," Will says. "For two years. Since I got out, I've been trying to find a place to ditch it. I've left it a couple of places, but then it turns out that I haven't. I can't leave it behind. No matter how hard I try. It doesn't belong to me, but I can't get rid of it."

"My friend Jessica does this thing she calls shopleaving," Carly says. "When someone gives her a hideous shirt for her birthday or if she buys a book and it's not any good, she goes into a store and leaves the shirt on a hanger. She leaves the book on the shelf. Once she took this crazy, mean parakeet to a shoe store and put him in a shoebox. What happened to your friend? Mike?"

"He went to Seattle. He started up a website for ex-cons. He got a lot of funding. There are a lot of people out there who have been in prison. They need websites."

"That's nice," Carly says. "That's like a happy ending."

"I've got the painting in the car," Will says. "Do you want it?"

"I like Van Gogh," Carly says. "And Georgia O'Keeffe."

"Let me go get it," Will says. He goes downstairs before she can stop him. The guys on the couch are watching somebody's wedding video now. He wonders what they would think if they knew Carly was upstairs in bed, waiting for him. The dancing girl is in the kitchen with the boy under the table. The girl in the dress is out on the lawn. She isn't doing anything except maybe looking at stars. She watches Will go to his car, open the trunk, and take out the little painting. Out behind the house, Will can hear people in the pool. Will hasn't felt this peaceful in a long time. It's like that first slow part in a horror movie, before the bad thing happens. Will knows that sometimes you shouldn't try to anticipate the bad thing. Sometimes you are supposed to just listen to swimmers fooling around in a pool. People you can't see. The night and the moon and the girl in the dress. Will stands on the lawn for a while, holding the painting, wishing that Becka was here with him. Or Mike.

Will takes the painting back upstairs and into the master bedroom. He turns the lights off and wakes Carly up. She's been crying in her sleep. "Here it is," he says.

"Will?" Carly says. "You turned off the light. Is it the ocean? It looks like the ocean. I can't really see anything."

"Sure you can," Will says. "There's moonlight."

"I only have one contact lens in," Carly says.

Will stands on the bed and lifts the painting of the garden off its picture hook. How can a painting of some flowers be so heavy? He leans it against the bed and hangs up the painting from the car. Iceberg, zombie, a bunch of trees. Some obscured and unknowable thing. How are you supposed to tell what it is? It makes him want to die, sometimes. "There you go," he says. "It's yours."

"It's beautiful," Carly says. Will thinks maybe she's crying again. She says, "Will? Will you just lie down with me? For a little while?"

Sometimes Soap has this dream. He isn't sure whether it's a prison dream or a dream about art or a dream about zombies. Maybe it isn't about any of those things. He dreams that he's in a dark room. Sometimes it's an enormous room, very long and narrow. Sometimes there are people in it, leaning silently up against the walls. He can only figure out if there are people or how big the room is when he stretches out his arms and walks forward. He has no idea what they're doing in the room with him. He has no idea what he's supposed to do, either. Sometimes it's a very small room. It's dark. It's dark.

"Hey, kid. Hey, Leo. Wake up, Leo. We gotta go." Soap is lying on the floor beside the bed, holding up the dust ruffle. He has to whisper. Carly is asleep on the too-big bed, under the covers.

Leo uncurls. He wriggles forward, towards Will. Then he wriggles back again, away from Will. He's maybe six or seven years old. "Who are you?" Leo says. "Where's Carly?"

"Carly sent me to get you, Leo," Soap says. "You have to be very, very quiet and do exactly what I say. There are zombies in the house. There are brain-eating zombies in the house. We have to get to a safe place. We have to go get Carly. She needs us." Leo stretches out his hand. Soap takes it and pulls him out from under the bed. He picks Leo up. Leo holds on to Will tightly. He doesn't weigh a lot, but he's so warm. Little kids have fast metabolisms.

"The zombies are chasing Carly?" Leo says.

"That's right," Soap says. "We have to go save her."

"Can I bring my robot?" Leo says.

"I've already put your robot in the car," Will says. "And your dinosaur T-shirt and your basketball."

"Are you Wolverine?" Leo says.

"That's right," Wolverine says. "I'm Wolverine. Let's get out of here."

Leo says, "Can I see your claws?"

"Not now," Wolverine says.

"I have to go to the bathroom before we go," Leo says.

"Okay," Wolverine says. "That's a great idea. I'm proud of you for telling me that."

Some things that you could try with zombies, but which won't work:

Panic.

Don't panic. Remain calm.

Call the police.

Take them out to dinner. Get them drunk.

Ask them to come back later.

Ignore them.

Take them home.

Tell them jokes. Play board games with them.

Tell them you love them.

Rescue them.

Wolverine and Leo have a backpack. They put a box of Cheerios and some bananas and Leo and Carly's parents' gun and a Game Boy and some batteries and a Ziploc bag full of twenty-dollar bills from the closet in the master bedroom in the backpack. There's a late-night horror movie on TV, but no one is there to watch it. The girl in the dress on the lawn is gone. If there's someone in the pool, they're keeping quiet.

Wolverine and Leo get in Wolverine's car and drive away.

Carly is dreaming that she's the President of the United States of America. She's living in the White House—it turns out that the White House is built out of ice. It's more like the Whitish Greenish Bluish House. Everybody wears big fur coats and when President Carly gives presidential addresses, she can see her breath. All her words hanging there. She's hanging out with rock stars and Nobel Prize winners. It's a wonderful dream. Carly's going to save the world. Everyone loves her, even her parents. Her parents are so proud of her. When she wakes up, the first thing she sees—before she sees all the other things that are missing besides the oil painting of the woods that nobody lives in, nobody painted, and nobody stole—is the empty space on the wall in the bedroom above her parents' bed.

The medium had always loved watching amusement park
visitors wait in long, orderly lines.

The Great Divorce

THERE ONCE WAS A MAN WHOSE WIFE WAS DEAD. She was dead when he fell in love with her, and she was dead for the twelve years they lived together, during which time she bore him three children, all of them dead as well, and at the time of which I am speaking, the time during which her husband began to suspect that she was having an affair, she was still dead.

It has been only in the last two decades that the living have been in the habit of marrying the dead, and it is still not common practice. Divorcing the dead is still less common. More usual is that the living husband—or wife—who regrets a marriage no longer acknowledges the admittedly tenuous presence of his spouse. Bigamy is easily accomplished when one's first wife is dead. It may not even be bigamy. And yet, where there are children concerned, the dissolution of a mixed marriage becomes stickier. Thirteen years after they first met at a cocktail party in the home of a celebrated medium and matchmaker who had been both profiled in *The New Yorker* and picketed by conservative religious groups, it was clear to both Alan Robley (living) and Lavvie Tyler (deceased), that there were worse fates than death. Their marriage was as dead as a doorknob.

At least, that was what Alan Robley said.

Alan and Lavvie Robley-Tyler's children had communicated to their father, via the household planchette and Ouija board, a desire to be taken to Disneyland; because divorce is always hardest on the children, and because Disneyland offered, at that time, an extraordinary discount to the dead, their medium had agreed to meet Alan Robley and his wife at Disneyland, which was only a fifteen-minute commute from her home, provided Alan Robley pay her admission as well as the usual fee. Besides, the medium had always loved watching amusement park visitors wait in long, orderly lines. She found it comforting.

The medium's name was Sarah Parminter. Her movements were economical: abbreviated and curiously ungraceful. Alan Robley imagined that this was so because she could see, at all times, the dead crowding around her. He himself had grown accustomed to moving slowly when he came home from work, in order to avoid unexpectedly stepping on or passing through his wife, or one of his three children. It takes great effort for the dead to make the living see them and therefore mixed marriages rely on dedicated dead-spaces: areas of floor and furniture that have been marked out with special red tape, red tile, squares of red fabric. (The children of the living and the dead most often take after their dead parents. Life, like red hair or blue eyes, is a recessive gene.)

Alan Robley longed for a better, less complicated relationship with his children. He wanted to know them better. Who doesn't?

Sarah Parminter and Alan sat on an uncomfortable bench beneath a pink bougainvillea. The three Robley-Tyler children were ignoring a YOU MUST BE THIS TALL sign. There are advantages to being the child of a mixed marriage. The usual rules don't apply. Their mother, Lavvie, was sitting in the crown of the bougainvillea above the bench, shaking down the papery flowers. He loves me not. He loves me not. The bougainvillea hung like tiny lanterns in Alan Robley's longish hair and in the curl of his collar. He ignored them. Lavvie got up to worse things. At one time, he'd found her behavior endearing.

Lavvie Tyler had stopped living sometime around the turn of the century. She'd been twenty-two and unmarried. She'd died of tuberculosis. Even in death, she still trembled and coughed, silently, so that the bougainvillea shook too. She was both older and younger than her husband. Marriage and the birth of three children had only made this more true.

"Explain this to me again, Alan," Sarah Parminter said. "You say that you and Lavvie have talked about this a great deal. You agree that there are irreconcilable differences. You say you both want this. This divorce."

"Yes," Alan said. He looked away. He wore an expensive shirt, in a shade of red that the dead were supposed to find attractive. He wore lipstick in the same shade of red, and there were greasy little flecks of it on his front teeth. Red fingernail polish. No doubt the soles of his shoes were red as well. Was it for Lavvie, despite their difficulties, or for his children? To draw them near? Sarah wondered why the living, who were so very much more solid, after all, than the dead, so often looked shifty and deceitful to her. She tried not to be prejudiced. But the dead were so beautiful, so fixed and so fluid, like sheets of calligraphy. They belonged to her, although she told herself that she was wrong to feel this way.

"Lavvie says that this is your idea, not hers," Sarah said. "That's what she's telling me. She says that there have been difficulties. She admits that. She says that the children take up a great deal of her time. She says your romantic life has suffered. She says that there have been arguments. Smashed dishes, icy silences, bouts of unearthly weeping. She knows that she has a temper. But she says she still loves you. You don't understand her, but she still loves you. She says she wonders if you've met someone else."

"I don't believe this!" Alan said. He laughed. He looked around, as if Lavvie might suddenly, finally, at last, materialize. But he never once looked up at the top of the bougainvillea. "Why is she saying this? I sat up all Tuesday night with the Ouija board, helping Carson and Allie and Essie with their homework, and she never said one single word to me. Carson said that Lavvie was down in the basement folding laundry, but I think it was one of the kids who was folding laundry, covering up for their mother. I think Lavvie has a boyfriend. A dead boyfriend. Some days I don't even feel like the kids are mine. I love them to pieces, but it's hard for me, thinking that they don't really belong to me. They already spend so much time with their mother. Who knows what she says to them about me?"

"Lavvie says you're jealous of her friends," Sarah said. "She says she's the one who should be jealous. She says that you only married a dead woman because you like the people at your work to think you're trendy. She says she can see the way you look at living women. You're always flirting with women at the grocery store. She knows you spend hours looking at porn online, and you don't even think about whether the children are there, too."

Silence. Sarah could hear Alan Robley's teeth, grinding together like pieces of chalk. Lavvie trembled in her tree.

"Where are the kids?" Alan said. "Do me a favor, Sarah, tell the kids not to get too far away. Last time we came, Essie got lost. Apparently she just kept getting on different boats at It's a Small World. She was singing "It's a Small World After All" in people's ears, only she kept changing the lyrics. All these kids were getting off the ride in tears. If Carson wants to go to Frontierland, he should come ask us. We can all walk over."

"They're still in line for Space Mountain," Sarah said. "They're beautiful kids, Alan. And even though this must be difficult for them, they're handling it so well. You and Lavvie must be very proud. Lavvie says she falls in love with you again each time she looks at them. They look so much like you, Alan."

Alan's red lower lip was trembling now, too. Tremble, tremble: Lavvie in the bougainvillea. Tremble, tremble: Alan's lip. Sarah Parminter realized that she had begun to tap one foot in sympathy. She stopped her foot and made herself look at the faces of the people waiting in line. Dead people hung in the air, their heels resting on the shoulders of living people, and living people walked right through two dead people who were making out, well, having sex right there in line, practically, but nobody got upset. It was astonishing how well the dead and living got along under normal circumstances, just so long as they could ignore each other.

Alan said, "I only look at other women because—because when a woman walks by, I think maybe that's how Lavvie looks. Maybe Lavvie walks fast like that. Maybe Lavvie's ass moves like that when she's walking. And when some woman laughs, I think maybe that's how Lavvie sounds when she laughs. I know Lavvie's hair is blonde. I find her hairs on the sheets sometimes, and in the drain. She's told me that she has brown eyes. I know how tall she is. Sex. Ah, sex isn't very good right now, but sometimes I wake up in the middle of the night and I can feel her lying on top of me. She's so heavy! She's cold and she's real curvy and she doesn't breathe, but sometimes she coughs and coughs and can't stop. She just lies there on top of me, with her cheek on my cheek. And I think she's smiling, but I don't know why she's smiling. I don't know what she's smiling about. She won't tell me. She writes stuff on my skin with her finger, but I don't know what she's writing. Sometimes the kids get in bed too, and do you know what that's like, rolling over and there are a couple of dead kids in bed with you? And Lavvie, I don't know if Lavvie bounces when she walks, or if she trips over things, or if she still thinks my jokes are funny, or if she even listens when I'm talking. If she's even there. Or if she just laughs at me when I'm yelling at her. I don't know when she's being sarcastic or when I've really hurt her feelings or when she's teasing me. I know she's there, but she seems so far away. Sometimes when I come up to bed, I think maybe somebody else has been up there. Not one of the kids, or Lavvie, but somebody else. Some other dead person. He goes through my drawers and he throws stuff around. If it isn't Lavvie's boyfriend, then it's Lavvie or one of the kids. But they swear up and down it isn't them, they say I'm imagining things. And then I think, so okay, even if you're really my kids, you're her kids, really. Because they're like her. They're just like her. They're dead too. So what I keep thinking is that this was a mistake right from the beginning. Like people say. Maybe the living shouldn't fall in love with the dead."

Now Lavvie had come down out of the bougainvillea. She was curled up in her husband's lap, gazing up at him. Alan didn't seem to know she was there. Lavvie didn't say anything, she just winked at Sarah Parminter. It was a furious wink. Isn't he a card? Isn't he a blabbermouth? He never shuts up, she said to Sarah. Talk, talk, talk. Let me tell you what I did today, Lavvie. Let me tell you what this guy said at work. Blah, blah, blah. Don't you just want to eat him up? If he leaves me, I'll make him wish he were dead, too.

"What's she saying?" Alan said. "She's saying something to you, isn't she? Where is she? You can't believe a word she says. You think that just because you can hear her talking, just because you can see her, you think you know what she's thinking. You think you can tell if she's telling the truth. But I've lived with her for the last twelve years and she's a liar and a bitch and she's a whore. Every time she opens that cold little mouth of hers, it's because she's thought up some new lie. Every time she says she loves me. If she could lie about death, if she could make people believe she was a living woman, she'd lie about that, too. Just because."

The bougainvillea was getting thick with dead people. They hung down from the branches and listened to Alan. Lavvie listened hardest of all. Her face shone with wifely approval.

"Alan," Sarah said. "Let's try to talk about this in a calm and reasonable manner."

Recently, Sarah Parminter's clients had been coming to her, wanting her to fix their love lives. If you read horoscopes, you'd think it was something in the air. Perhaps someday soon the alignment of the stars would change, all recent unhappinesses and catastrophes would be reversed and people would fall in love all over again and life would be good and death would be good too. Perhaps Sarah Parminter's own horoscope had advised her not to meddle in other people's affairs at this time. But Sarah didn't believe in astrology. Her cousin Fred was also a medium, and his clients were just as difficult, just as unhappy. Sarah and Fred sometimes sat out on her balcony in the airless, dirty yellow afternoons, watching cars go up and down the ramps of the I-5. They talked about work. Opposite the apartment building, there was a DEAD END sign across the street which someone had turned into DEAD ED. Every time she saw it, Sarah Parminter thought about going down and adding an FR. But Fred didn't have a great sense of humor. He claimed it had been eroded away by contact with the other world. But Sarah remembered him as a child, and even then he'd never enjoyed the sort of practical jokes that the dead liked to play.

Fred had a new client, a man named Sam Callahan whose wife was also dead, just like Lavvie Tyler. Only the Callahans had been married for decades while both were still living, and the problem was now that she was dead, his wife didn't want to have anything to do with Sam Callahan.

As far as she was concerned, the marriage was over. But Callahan couldn't let go.

Fred didn't approve of the way that Sarah coddled her clients. When Callahan came in, what he'd said straightaway was, "I know who you want to talk to. But she doesn't want to talk to you."

Callahan was a big man with small hands. He said, "I was just hoping that I could talk to her one more time. I fucked up. I'm sorry. I wanted to explain. I need to tell her how much I loved her. Please make her talk to me."

Fred said, "You do know she's dead, right?"

There had been a boy at Callahan's school. Paul. That had been his name. After he did what he did, he still wasn't very popular, but he became more distinct. He came into focus.

The name of the girl he'd done it for: Popsicle. A nickname, because she was so cool.

Everyone at school followed Popsicle around. Even the girls had crushes on Popsicle. People gave her things. Sometimes at recess there was an ice-cream truck parked across the street. Somebody bought Popsicle a cherry popsicle. Paul came back with six ice creams—a screwball, a popsicle, two creamsicles, a fudge pop, an ice-cream sandwich. He spent all his lunch money. His hands were full of ice cream. He went and stood in front of Popsicle. She said something like, I can't eat all those.

Paul said, "I'll eat them for you. To prove how much I love you." As if they'd been arguing about it. Nobody even knew if he'd ever said anything to Popsicle before.

All the other kids stood around and watched. Those who weren't there, who weren't watching, were pretty sure later on that they had been there: they'd heard the story so many times. Callahan thought he'd been there, although really he hadn't. When he fell in love for the first time, he remembered Paul's hands, Popsicle's polite, confused smile.

Later on, everybody watched Paul eat stuff, except for Popsicle, who hid in the girl's bathroom every single time. Nobody had crushes on her after a while. Nobody else loved her as much as Paul.

In his locker, Callahan had kept a list of everything Paul ate. It was a love poem, a grocery list, secret evidence: Paul loves Popsicle. Paul ate a few ants. He drank someone's milk, which had gone off. Everyone smelled it. Paul ate a little glue booger that someone brought him. He ate dead leaves, and a ball of hair that someone took from Popsicle's comb. He ate a piece of raw meat a girl stole from her mother's refrigerator. He ate other things, all year long. The teachers never saw what was going on.

The next year Paul didn't come back. Neither did Popsicle. Someone made a joke about it. Perhaps Paul had eaten Popsicle.

Callahan didn't know what had happened to Paul or to Popsicle. Fred, on the other hand, knew what happens to everyone eventually. He could see the map that Paul and Popsicle had left on Callahan's face, just like Callahan's wife could see it now that she was dead. The dead can afford to see more than the living. Fred said, "She says you didn't really love her. And that she's better off without you. She hopes you grow old and die alone."

Callahan said, "I'm paying you so you can say these things to me? This is bullshit! And how do I even know if she's really here? Why should I believe what some guy says? Why would she talk to you and not to me?"

Fred said, "Remember you're talking to a medium. Not a therapist." (He tried to sound reasonable; detached rather than snappish. He knew as he said it that he sounded like Callahan's therapist.) "Laura says you have more money than you know how to spend, and she says she hopes you spend it all on charlatans and quacks. Don't get angry at me. I'm just saying this because you want me to tell you what she's saying."

Callahan said, "Laura, if you're here, talk to me—why are you talking to him, and not to me?" Like Fred, he was trying his best to talk reasonably. Soon he'd be throwing furniture around. "Don't you know how much I love you?"

She knew. Even Fred knew. But what did how much matter to a dead woman?

Fred said, "She says you ought to take better care of yourself. Your refrigerator is empty. She wants you to go out and buy some groceries. She doesn't want you to starve to death. She doesn't want to see you anytime soon. She's got her own afterlife to live, her own things to deal with. This is an important time for her. She has things to do."

"So is that it?" Callahan said. "Is that all you can do for me?"

Fred shrugged. "Do you want me to produce some ectoplasm? A souvenir of the spirit world? Would you like to talk to somebody famous? Marilyn Monroe?"

"You are one real son of a bitch," Callahan said. "So how do you like the way this asshole talks to me, Laura? You approve?"

Fred said nothing. Laura said nothing, either. She indicated, however, that she'd like to write something down.

The table where they were sitting was solid oak. Round. No sharp edges. It was good to have a nice heavy piece of furniture to sit behind. Both the living and the dead liked to throw stuff around, as if it proved something. Fred kept a pad of paper and a ballpoint pen on the table. He picked the pen up so that Laura could write down exactly what she wanted to say. He didn't watch as Laura wrote. It was uncomfortable, watching someone else use your hand. The fingers always looked too wriggly. Stretched. Laura dragged the pen across the page as if Fred's fingers were bags of dirt.

Callahan kept on talking to Laura. He had this feeling that Laura was hiding somewhere in the room, maybe under the medium's floppy toupee, or under the oak table. Laura had never been good at keeping still. She liked to swim laps until she could barely climb out of the pool. He couldn't help it. He said, "Do they have swimming pools? For dead people? Does Laura still swim every day?"

Fred tried to keep a straight face. Swimming pools? He couldn't wait to tell that one to Sarah. "Yeah, sure," he said. "They have swimming pools. Laura's learning to play bridge. And she's thinking about getting a dog. You know, for companionship."

Callahan thought about that. He could learn how to play bridge, if that was what Laura wanted. He was sure he could feel Laura moving around the room, brushing her fingers against the walls, sliding behind the curtains at the window, touching the backs of the chair where he sat, but Laura never touched him. What if she touched him and he couldn't feel anything? How was all this supposed to work, if they tried to make it work? They'd been married for almost thirty years.

Fred read what Laura had written. Terrible handwriting, even for a dead person. "So she wants you to throw a dinner party. But she doesn't want you to invite anyone else. This is the menu she's giving me. She says, you want to prove you love her, then prove it. Make her dinner."

Callahan said, "I used to make dinner for her all the time."

Fred said, "You'll notice I haven't asked you why she's so mad at you. I'm not going to ask you, either. I don't like to pry." He looked down at the list Laura was making, and then back up at Callahan. "But yeah, she's pretty pissed. This is one weird-ass menu. She says ants, a piece of churt—sorry, chalk, her handwriting is execrable—old milk, vinegar, popsicles, erasers, grass, sawdust, sand, dirt. She says if you really love her, you'll show her how much you love her."

"So what did he do?" Sarah Parminter said, after a while. "Is he going to do it?"

"I don't know," Fred said. "I just thought it was kind of funny. He wrote me a check and it bounced. And she said he had lots of money too, so maybe it wasn't really his wife, even. Maybe it was just somebody who wanted to fuck with him. I wouldn't eat grass just for a dead girl. Not unless she was paying me."

"You haven't mentioned your mother yet," Sarah Parminter said to Alan Robley.

"Why?" Alan said. "Is she here? Does she want to talk to me?"

"She's over there with the kids," Sarah said. "They're teasing a Goofy."

"She's good with the kids," Alan said. But he didn't look over to where a crowd was gathering around the Goofy. He wasn't going to tell his kids to leave the Goofy alone. Living parents had a hard time disciplining dead children. You had to indulge them, even when their fun got a little vicious. You had to pretend that they didn't belong to you. "I mean, even when she was alive, she was good with them. She was so excited to have grandchildren. She read to them all the time."

"She didn't like Lavvie much," Sarah said.

"No," Alan said. "They didn't get along."

"Your mother still doesn't approve," Sarah said. "She still thinks Lavvie's too old for you."

Lavvie said something.

"Lavvie says your mother is a real, ah, bitch."

"Fuck Lavvie," Alan said, but he didn't really mean it. And now he was watching the Goofy stumble around, and he was feeling an odd jealousy. Here he was, all dressed up in red, and the kids still preferred a guy in a fur suit to their own father. Dead people had favorite characters at Disneyland. Goofy, for example. The costume was so baggy. That silly hat. You could poke him in the ass, really jab him good, and he never moved fast enough. Minnie Mouses were also popular with dead people. They liked hiding her pocketbook. Or putting things in it.

The Goofy was shouting obscenities now. Living children were crying. Dead ones were laughing. Alan said, "She never made any effort. She always made fun of my mother, the way she put on lipstick, and why are the dead so obsessed with makeup, anyway? The way my mother cut up her food real small."

Lavvie said something else.

"Lavvie wants to know if you ever loved her," Sarah said. It delighted her, how the line for Space Mountain never got any shorter, no matter how long you sat and watched. She'd never waited, herself. It was enough to watch the tourists shuffle into line, disappear and come back out again, and wander over to join the line once again.

"Could I talk to my mom?" Alan said.

Sarah tried waving Alan's mother over, but Mrs. Robley only gave her a black, murderous glare. Her lips were pressed together so tightly that her entire mouth had disappeared. One hand was clamped around the Goofy's long ear. The other hand was burrowing into the Goofy's costume, as if she were going to disembowel him right through the fake fur. Lavvie was still sitting weightlessly in Alan's lap. The little slut. She gave Mrs. Robley the finger when the kids weren't looking.

"She's, ah, she's busy," Sarah said. "And our time's up, Alan. I have another appointment at four. But Lavvie has one last thing to say to you."

Lavvie didn't really have anything to say to Alan, but Sarah knew she wouldn't mind that Sarah was making something up. The stranger the better: it would only amuse her. All of it was true, after all. I love you. I don't love you. Don't leave me. Fuck off. I fuck the ghost of Eleanor Roosevelt with a dildo all day long while you're at work.

If Alan divorced Lavvie, he'd still need Sarah. There would be issues of child custody. And there was Mrs. Robley, too. There would be things Alan needed to ask his mother about his childhood.

A divorce would mean more trips to amusement parks for the kids and for Sarah. She could always say the kids wanted to go to Six Flags next week. There were always good lines for the Psyclone.

Alan was still waiting, his hands in his lap. Let him wait a minute longer. It was strange, the way his arms just disappeared right through Lavvie's body. And it was unkind of Lavvie, Sarah thought, to sit like that. It was indecent and unkind. Someday she might write an etiquette book for the dead, although it would be the living that ended up reading it, no doubt, and one ought to draw a veil over certain things. Or at least not pull the veil back too far. Sarah had talked to a historian once—had he been a living man or had he already been dead? He was certainly dead now—about the past. The past was, of course, a different country. A different amusement park and the lines were much longer. The dead didn't know the way back any better than the living did.

Sarah's historian said that one way you went about figuring out what the past had been like was to read contemporary books of etiquette. When one of these etiquette books suggested that it was not well-bred behavior to pick up a human turd from the gutter to remark upon its color or size, you knew then that people had needed to be told not to do such things because they'd once done such things. Sarah hadn't batted an eye when he'd said that. Better not to let on about the habits of the dead, she knew. Sarah knew this, and Lavvie Tyler and the Robley-Tyler children and Mrs. Robley know this, and me, I know, too. Even as I've been telling you this story, I haven't described things exactly as they went on. I haven't been honest about the dead people in this story, about how the dead carry on.

There were living people waiting in line at Disneyland, and there was a dead woman sitting on the park bench with Sarah Parminter and Alan Robley and there were lots of other dead people, too, hundreds of them, and what they got up to isn't any of your business. It's just as well that only people like Sarah Parminter and her cousin Fred ever see what the dead are really like. But the dead, of course, see everything that you do. Next time you and your new wife take your kids to Disneyland and you're waiting in line, you think about me. You think about that.

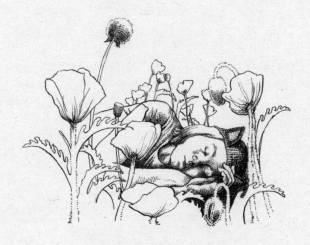

Euphoria: The Librarian's Tonic—When
Watchfulness Is Not Enough.

Magic for Beginners

FOX IS A TELEVISION CHARACTER, and she isn't dead yet. But she will be, soon. She's a character on a television show called *The Library*. You've never seen *The Library* on TV, but I bet you wish you had.

In one episode of *The Library*, a boy named Jeremy Mars, fifteen years old, sits on the roof of his house in Plantagenet, Vermont. It's eight o'clock at night, a school night, and he and his friend Elizabeth should be studying for the math quiz which their teacher, Mr. Cliff, has been hinting at all week long. Instead, they've sneaked out onto the roof. It's cold. They don't know everything they should know about X, when X is the square root of Y. They don't even know Y. They ought to go in.

But there's nothing good on TV and the sky is very beautiful. They have jackets on, and up in the corners where the sky begins are patches of white in the darkness, still, where there's snow, up on the mountains. Down in the trees around the house, some animal is making a small, anxious sound: "Why cry? Why cry?"

"What's that one?" Elizabeth says, pointing at a squarish configuration of stars.

"That's The Parking Structure," Jeremy says. "And right next to that is The Big Shopping Mall and The Lesser Shopping Mall."

"And that's Orion, right? Orion the Bargain Hunter?"

Jeremy squints up. "No, Orion is over there. That's The Austrian Bodybuilder. That thing that's sort of wrapped around his lower leg is The Amorous Cephalopod. The Hungry, Hungry Octopus. It can't make up its mind whether it should eat him or make crazy, eight-legged love to him. You know that myth, right?"

"Of course," Elizabeth says. "Is Karl going to be pissed off that we didn't invite him over to study?"

"Karl's always pissed off about something," Jeremy says. Jeremy is resolutely resisting a notion about Elizabeth. Why are they sitting up here? Was it his idea or was it hers? Are they friends, are they just two friends sitting on the roof and talking? Or is Jeremy supposed to try to kiss her? He thinks maybe he's supposed to kiss her. If he kisses her, will they still be friends? He can't ask Karl about this. Karl doesn't believe in being helpful. Karl believes in mocking.

Jeremy doesn't even know if he wants to kiss Elizabeth. He's never thought about it until right now.

"I should go home," Elizabeth says. "There could be a new episode on right now, and we wouldn't even know."

"Someone would call and tell us," Jeremy says. "My mom would come up and yell for us." His mother is something else Jeremy doesn't want to worry about, but he does, he does.

Jeremy Mars knows a lot about the planet Mars, although he's never been there. He knows some girls, and yet he doesn't know much about them. He wishes there were books about girls, the way there are books about Mars, that you could observe the orbits and brightness of girls through telescopes without appearing to be perverted. Once Jeremy read a book about Mars out loud to Karl, except he kept replacing the word Mars with the word "girls." ("It was in the seventeenth century that girls at last came under serious scrutiny." "Girls have virtually no surface liquid water: their temperatures are too cold and the air is too thin." And so on.) Karl cracked up every time.

Jeremy's mother is a librarian. His father writes books. Jeremy reads biographies. He plays trombone in a marching band. He jumps hurdles while wearing a school tracksuit. Jeremy is also passionately addicted to a television show in which a renegade librarian and magician named Fox is trying to save her world from thieves, murderers, cabalists, and pirates. Jeremy is a geek, although he's a telegenic geek. Somebody should make a TV show about him.

Jeremy's friends call him Germ, although he would rather be called Mars. His parents haven't spoken to each other in a week.

Jeremy doesn't kiss Elizabeth. The stars don't fall out of the sky, and Jeremy and Elizabeth don't fall off the roof either. They go inside and finish their homework.

Someone that Jeremy has never met, never even heard of—a woman named Cleo Baldrick—has died. Lots of people, so far, have managed to live and die without making the acquaintance of Jeremy Mars, but Cleo Baldrick has left Jeremy Mars and his mother something strange in her will: a phone booth on a state highway, some forty miles outside of Las Vegas, and a Las Vegas wedding chapel. The wedding chapel is called Hell's Bells. Jeremy isn't sure what kind of people get married there. Bikers, maybe. Supervillains, freaks, and Satanists.

Jeremy's mother wants to tell him something. It's probably something about Las Vegas and about Cleo Baldrick, who—it turns out—was his mother's great-aunt. (Jeremy never knew his mother had a great-aunt. His mother is a mysterious person.) But it may be, on the other hand, something concerning Jeremy's father. For a week and a half now, Jeremy has managed to avoid finding out what his mother is worrying about. It's easy not to find out things, if you try hard enough. There's band practice. He has overslept on weekdays in order to rule out conversations at breakfast, and at night he climbs up on the roof with his telescope to look at stars, to look at Mars. His mother is afraid of heights. She grew up in L.A.

It's clear that whatever it is she has to tell Jeremy is not something she wants to tell him. As long as he avoids being alone with her, he's safe.

But it's hard to keep your guard up at all times. Jeremy comes home from school, feeling as if he has passed the math test, after all. Jeremy is an optimist. Maybe there's something good on TV. He settles down with the remote control on one of his father's pet couches: oversized and re-upholstered in an orange-juice-colored corduroy that makes it appear as if the couch has just escaped from a maximum security prison for criminally insane furniture. This couch looks as if its hobby is devouring interior decorators. Jeremy's father is a horror writer, so no one should be surprised if some of the couches he reupholsters are hideous and eldritch.

Jeremy's mother comes into the room and stands above the couch, look-ing down at him. "Germ?" she says. She looks absolutely miserable, which is more or less how she has looked all week.

The phone rings and Jeremy jumps up.

As soon as he hears Elizabeth's voice, he knows. She says, "Germ, it's on. Channel forty-two. I'm taping it." She hangs up.

"It's on!" Jeremy says. "Channel forty-two! Now!"

His mother has the television on by the time he sits down. Being a librarian, she has a particular fondness for *The Library.* "I should go tell your dad," she says, but instead she sits down beside Jeremy. And of course it's now all the more clear something is wrong between Jeremy's parents. But *The Library* is on and Fox is about to rescue Prince Wing.

When the episode ends, he can tell without looking over that his mother is crying. "Don't mind me," she says and wipes her nose on her sleeve. "Do you think she's really dead?"

But Jeremy can't stay around and talk.

Jeremy has wondered about what kind of television shows the characters *in* television shows watch. Television characters almost always have better haircuts, funnier friends, simpler attitudes toward sex. They marry magi-cians, win lotteries, have affairs with women who carry guns in their purses. Curious things happen to them on an hourly basis. Jeremy and I can forgive their haircuts. We just want to ask them about their television shows.

Just like always, it's Elizabeth who worked out in the nick of time that the new episode was on. Everyone will show up at Elizabeth's house afterwards, for the postmortem. This time, it really is a postmortem. Why did Prince Wing kill Fox? How could Fox let him do it? Fox is ten times stronger.

Jeremy runs all the way, slapping his old track shoes against the sidewalk for the pleasure of the jar, for the sweetness of the sting. He likes the rough, cottony ache in his lungs. His coach says you have to be part-masochist to enjoy something like running. It's nothing to be ashamed of. It's something to exploit.

Talis opens the door. She grins at him, although he can tell that she's been crying, too. She's wearing a T-shirt that says I'M SO GOTH I SHIT TINY VAMPIRES.

"Hey," Jeremy says. Talis nods. Talis isn't so Goth, at least not as far as Jeremy or anyone else knows. Talis just has a lot of T-shirts. She's an enigma wrapped in a mysterious T-shirt. A woman once said to Calvin Coolidge, "Mr. President, I bet my husband that I could get you to say more than two words." Coolidge said, "You lose." Jeremy can imagine Talis as Calvin Coolidge in a former life. Or maybe she was one of those dogs that don't bark. A basenji. Or a rock. A dolmen. There was an episode of *The Library*, once, with some sinister dancing dolmens in it.

Elizabeth comes up behind Talis. If Talis is unGoth, then Elizabeth is Ballerina Goth. She likes hearts and skulls and black pen-ink tattoos, pink tulle and Hello Kitty. When the woman who invented Hello Kitty was asked why Hello Kitty was so popular, she said, "Because she has no mouth." Elizabeth's mouth is small. Her lips are chapped.

"That was the most horrible episode ever! I cried and cried," she says. "Hey, Germ, so I was telling Talis about how you inherited a gas station."

"A phone booth," Jeremy says. "In Las Vegas. This great-great aunt died. And there's a wedding chapel, too."

"Hey! Germ!" Karl says, yelling from the living room. "Shut up and get in here! The commercial with the talking cats is on—"

"Shut it, Karl," Jeremy says. He goes in and sits on Karl's head. You have to show Karl who's boss once in a while.

Amy turns up last. She was in the next town over, buying comics. She hasn't seen the new episode and so they all shut it (except for Talis, who has not been saying anything at all) and Elizabeth puts on the tape.

In the previous episode of *The Library*, masked pirate-magicians said they would sell Prince Wing a cure for the spell which infested Faithful Margaret's hair with miniature, wicked, fire-breathing golems. (Faithful Margaret's hair keeps catching fire, but she refuses to shave it off. Her hair is the source of all her magic.)

The pirate-magicians lured Prince Wing into a trap so obvious that it seemed impossible it could really be a trap, on the one-hundred-and-fortieth floor of The Free People's World-Tree Library. The pirate-magicians used finger magic to turn Prince Wing into a porcelain teapot, put two Earl Grey tea bags into the teapot, and poured in boiling water, toasted the Eternally Postponed and Overdue Reign of the Forbidden Books, drained their tea in one gulp, belched, hurled their souvenir pirate mugs to the ground, and then shattered the teapot which had been Prince Wing into hundreds of pieces. Then the wicked pirate-magicians swept the pieces of both Prince Wing and collectable mugs carelessly into a wooden cigar box, buried the box in the Angela Carter Memorial Park on the seventeenth floor of The World-Tree Library, and erected a statue of George Washington above it.

So then Fox had to go looking for Prince Wing. When she finally discovered the park on the seventeenth floor of The Library, the George Washington statue stepped down off his plinth and fought her tooth and nail. Literally tooth and nail, and they'd all agreed that there was something especially nightmarish about a biting, scratching, life-sized statue of George Washington with long, pointed metal fangs that threw off sparks when he gnashed them. The statue of George Washington bit Fox's pinky finger right off, just like Gollum biting Frodo's finger off on the top of Mount Doom. But of course, once the statue tasted Fox's magical blood, it fell in love with Fox. It would be her ally from now on.

In the new episode, the actor playing Fox is a young Latina actress whom Jeremy Mars thinks he recognizes. She has been a snotty but well-intentioned fourth-floor librarian in an episode about an epidemic of food-poisoning that triggered bouts of invisibility and/or levitation, and she was also a lovelorn, suicidal Bear Cult priestess in the episode where Prince Wing discovered his mother was one of the Forbidden Books.

This is one of the best things about *The Library*, the way the cast swaps parts, all except for Faithful Margaret and Prince Wing, who are only ever themselves. Faithful Margaret and Prince Wing are the love interests and the main characters, and therefore, inevitably, the most boring characters, although Amy has a crush on Prince Wing.

Fox and the dashing-but-treacherous pirate-magician Two Devils are never played by the same actor twice, although in the twenty-third episode of *The Library*, the same woman played them both. Jeremy supposes that the casting could be perpetually confusing, but instead it makes your brain catch on fire. It's magical.

You always know Fox by her costume (the too-small green T-shirt, the long, full skirts she wears to hide her tail), by her dramatic hand gestures and body language, by the soft, breathy-squeaky voice the actors use when they are Fox. Fox is funny, dangerous, bad-tempered, flirtatious, greedy, untidy, accident-prone, graceful, and has a mysterious past. In some episodes, Fox is played by male actors, but she always sounds like Fox. And she's always beautiful. Every episode you think that this Fox, surely, is the most beautiful Fox there could ever be, and yet the Fox of the next episode will be even more heartbreakingly beautiful.

On television, it's night in The Free People's World-Tree Library. All the librarians are asleep, tucked into their coffins, their scabbards, priest-holes, button holes, pockets, hidden cupboards, between the pages of their enchanted novels. Moonlight pours through the high, arched windows of the Library and between the aisles of shelves, into the park. Fox is on her knees, clawing at the muddy ground with her bare hands. The statue of George Washington kneels beside her, helping.

"So that's Fox, right?" Amy says. Nobody tells her to shut up. It would be pointless. Amy has a large heart and an even larger mouth. When it rains, Amy rescues worms off the sidewalk. When you get tired of having a secret, you tell Amy.

Understand: Amy isn't that much stupider than anyone else in this story. It's just that she thinks out loud.

Elizabeth's mother comes into the living room. "Hey guys," she says. "Hi, Jeremy. Did I hear something about your mother inheriting a wedding chapel?"

"Yes, ma'am," Jeremy says. "In Las Vegas."

"Las Vegas," Elizabeth's mom says. "I won three hundred bucks once in Las Vegas. Spent it on a helicopter ride over the Grand Canyon. So how many times can you guys watch the same episode in one day?" But she sits down to watch, too. "Do you think she's really dead?"

"Who's dead?" Amy says. Nobody says anything.

Jeremy isn't sure he's ready to see this episode again so soon, anyway, especially not with Amy. He goes upstairs and takes a shower. Elizabeth's family have a large and distracting selection of shampoos. They don't mind when Jeremy uses their bathroom.

Jeremy and Karl and Elizabeth have known each other since the first day of kindergarten. Amy and Talis are a year younger. The five have not always been friends, except for Jeremy and Karl, who have. Talis is, famously, a loner. She doesn't listen to music as far as anyone knows, she doesn't wear significant amounts of black, she isn't particularly good (or bad) at math or English, and she doesn't drink, debate, knit or refuse to eat meat. If she keeps a blog, she's never admitted it to anyone.

The Library made Jeremy and Karl and Talis and Elizabeth and Amy friends. No one else in school is as passionately devoted. Besides, they are all the children of former hippies, and the town is small. They all live within a few blocks of each other, in run-down Victorians with high ceilings and ranch houses with sunken living rooms. And although they have not always been friends, growing up, they've gone skinny-dipping in lakes on summer nights, and broken bones on each others' trampolines. Once, during an argument about dog names, Elizabeth, who is hot-tempered, tried to run Jeremy over with her ten-speed bicycle, and once, a year ago, Karl got drunk on green-apple schnapps at a party and tried to kiss Talis, and once, for five months in the seventh grade, Karl and Jeremy communicated only through angry emails written in all caps. I'm not allowed to tell you what they fought about.

Now the five are inseparable; invincible. They imagine that life will always be like this—like a television show in eternal syndication—that they will always have each other. They use the same vocabulary. They borrow each other's books and music. They share lunches, and they never say anything when Jeremy comes over and takes a shower. They all know Jeremy's father is eccentric. He's supposed to be eccentric. He's a novelist.

When Jeremy comes back downstairs, Amy is saying, "I've always thought there was something wicked about Prince Wing. He's a dork and he looks like he has bad breath. I never really liked him."

Karl says, "We don't know the whole story yet. Maybe he found out something about Fox while he was a teapot." Elizabeth's mom says, "He's under a spell. I bet you anything." They'll be talking about it all week.

Talis is in the kitchen, making a Velveeta-and-pickle sandwich.

"So what did you think?" Jeremy says. It's like having a hobby, only more pointless, trying to get Talis to talk. "Is Fox really dead?"

"Don't know," Talis says. Then she says, "I had a dream."

Jeremy waits. Talis seems to be waiting, too. She says, "About you." Then she's silent again. There is something dreamlike about the way that she makes a sandwich. As if she is really making something that isn't a sandwich at all; as if she's making something far more meaningful and mysterious. Or as if soon he will wake up and realize that there are no such thing as sandwiches.

"You and Fox," Talis says. "The dream was about the two of you. She told me. To tell you. To call her. She gave me a phone number. She was in trouble. She said you were in trouble. She said *to keep in touch.*"

"Weird," Jeremy says, mulling this over. He's never had a dream about *The Library.* He wonders who was playing Fox in Talis's dream. He had a dream about Talis, once, but it isn't the kind of dream that you'd ever tell anybody about. They were just sitting together, not saying anything. Even Talis's T-shirt hadn't said anything. Talis was holding his hand.

"It didn't feel like a dream," Talis says.

"So what was the phone number?" Jeremy says.

"I forgot," Talis says. "When I woke up, I forgot."

Kurt's mother works in a bank. Talis's father has a karaoke machine in his basement, and he knows all the lyrics to "Like a Virgin" and "Holiday" as well as the lyrics to all the songs from *Godspell* and *Cabaret.* Talis's mother is a licensed therapist who composes multiple-choice personality tests for women's magazines. "Discover Which Television Character You Resemble Most." Etc. Amy's parents met in a commune in Ithaca: her name was Galadriel Moon Shuyler before her parents came to their senses and had it changed legally. Everyone is sworn to secrecy about this, which is ironic, considering that this is Amy.

But Jeremy's father is Gordon Strangle Mars. He writes novels about giant spiders, giant leeches, giant moths, and once, notably, a giant carnivorous rosebush who lives in a mansion in upstate New York, and falls in love with a plucky, teenaged girl with a heart murmur. Saint Bernard–sized spiders chase his character's cars down dark, bumpy country roads. They fight the spiders off with badminton rackets, lawn tools, and fireworks. The novels with spiders are all bestsellers.

Once a Gordon Strangle Mars fan broke into the Mars's house. The fan stole several German first editions of Gordon Strangle's novels, a hairbrush, and a used mug in which there were two ancient, dehydrated tea bags. The fan left behind a betrayed and abusive letter on a series of Post-It Notes, and the manuscript of his own novel, told from the point of view of the iceberg that sank the *Titanic.* Jeremy and his mother read the manuscript out loud to each other. It begins: "The iceberg knew it had a destiny." Jeremy's favorite bit happens when the iceberg sees the doomed ship drawing nearer, and remarks plaintively, "Oh my, does not the Captain know about my large and impenetrable bottom?"

Jeremy discovered, later, that the novel-writing fan had put Gordon

Strangle Mars's used tea bags and hairbrush up for sale on eBay, where someone paid forty-two dollars and sixty-eight cents, which was not only deeply creepy, but, Jeremy still feels, somewhat cheap. But of course this is appropriate, as Jeremy's father is famously stingy and just plain weird about money.

Gordon Strangle Mars once spent eight thousand dollars on a Japanese singing toilet. Jeremy's friends love that toilet. Jeremy's mother has a painting of a woman wearing a red dress by some artist, Jeremy can never remember who. Jeremy's father gave her that painting. The woman is beautiful, and she looks right at you as if you're the painting, not her. As if *you're* beautiful. The woman has an apple in one hand and a knife in the other. When Jeremy was little, he used to dream about eating that apple. Apparently it's worth more than the whole house and everything else in the house, including the singing toilet. But art and toilets aside, the Mars buy most of their clothes at thrift stores.

Jeremy's father clips coupons.

On the other hand, when Jeremy was twelve and begged his parents to send him to baseball camp in Florida, his father ponied up. And on Jeremy's last birthday, his father gave him a couch reupholstered in several dozen yards of heavy-duty *Star Wars*-themed fabric. That was a good birthday.

When his writing is going well, Gordon Strangle Mars likes to wake up at 6 A.M. and go out driving. He works out new plot lines about giant spiders and keeps an eye out for abandoned couches, which he wrestles into the back of his pickup truck. Then he writes for the rest of the day. On weekends he reupholsters the thrown-away couches in remaindered, discount fabrics. A few years ago, Jeremy went through his house, counting up fourteen couches, eight love seats, and one rickety chaise lounge. That was a few years ago. Once Jeremy had a dream that his father combined his two careers and began reupholstering giant spiders.

All lights in all rooms of the Mars house are on fifteen-minute timers, in case Jeremy or his mother leave a room and forget to turn off a lamp. This has caused confusion—and sometimes panic—on the rare occasions that the Marses throw dinner parties.

Everyone thinks that writers are rich, but it seems to Jeremy that his family is only rich some of the time. Some of the time they aren't.

Whenever Gordon Mars gets stuck in a Gordon Strangle Mars novel, he worries about money. He worries that he won't, in fact, manage to finish the current novel. He worries that it will be terrible. He worries that no one will buy it and no one will read it, and that the readers who do read it will demand to be refunded the cost of the book. He's told Jeremy that he imagines these angry readers marching on the Mars house, carrying torches and crowbars.

It would be easier on Jeremy and his mother if Gordon Mars did not work at home. It's difficult to shower when you know your father is timing you, and thinking dark thoughts about the water bill, instead of concentrating on the scene in the current Gordon Strangle Mars novel, in which the giant spiders have returned to their old haunts in the trees surrounding the ninth hole of the accursed golf course, where they sullenly feast on the pulped entrail-juices of a brace of unlucky poodles and their owner.

During these periods, Jeremy showers at school, after gym, or at his friends' houses, even though it makes his mother unhappy. She says that sometimes you just need to ignore Jeremy's father. She takes especially long showers, lots of baths. She claims that baths are even nicer when you know that Jeremy's father is worried about the water bill. Jeremy's mother has a cruel streak.

What Jeremy likes about showers is the way you can stand there, surrounded by water and yet in absolutely no danger of drowning, and not think about things like whether you fucked up on the Spanish assignment, or why your mother is looking so worried. Instead you can think about things like if there's water on Mars, and whether or not Karl is shaving, and if so, who is he trying to fool, and what the statue of George Washington meant when it said to Fox, during their desperate, bloody fight, "You have a long journey ahead of you," and, "Everything depends on this." And is Fox really dead?

After she dug up the cigar box, and after George Washington helped her carefully separate out the pieces of tea mug from the pieces of teapot, after they glued back together the hundreds of pieces of porcelain, when

Fox turned the ramshackle teapot back into Prince Wing, Prince Wing looked about a hundred years old, and as if maybe there were still a few pieces missing. He looked pale. When he saw Fox, he turned even paler, as if he hadn't expected her to be standing there in front of him. He picked up his leviathan sword, which Fox had been keeping safe for him—the one which faithful viewers know was carved out of the tooth of a giant, ancient sea creature that lived happily and peacefully (before Prince Wing was tricked into killing it) in the enchanted underground sea on the third floor—and skewered the statue of George Washington like a kebab, pinning it to a tree. He kicked Fox in the head, knocked her down, and tied her to a card catalog. He stuffed a handful of moss and dirt into her mouth so she couldn't say anything, and then he accused her of plotting to murder Faithful Margaret by magic. He said Fox was more deceitful than a Forbidden Book. He cut off Fox's tail and her ears and he ran her through with the poison-edged, dog-headed knife that he and Fox had stolen from his mother's secret house. Then he left Fox there, tied to the card catalog, limp and bloody, her beautiful head hanging down. He sneezed (Prince Wing is allergic to swordplay) and walked off into the stacks. The librarians crept out of their hiding places. They untied Fox and cleaned off her face. They held a mirror to her mouth, but the mirror stayed clear and unclouded.

When the librarians pulled Prince Wing's leviathan sword out of the tree, the statue of George Washington staggered over and picked up Fox in his arms. He tucked her ears and tail into the capacious pockets of his bird-shit-stained, verdigris riding coat. He carried Fox down seventeen flights of stairs, past the enchanted-and-disagreeable Sphinx on the eighth floor, past the enchanted-and-stormy underground sea on the third floor, past the even-more-enchanted checkout desk on the first floor, and through the hammered-brass doors of the Free People's World-Tree Library. Nobody in *The Library*, not in one single episode, has ever gone outside. *The Library* is full of all the sorts of things that one usually has to go outside to enjoy: trees and lakes and grottoes and fields and mountains and precipices (and full of indoors things as well, like books, of course). Outside The Library, everything is dusty and red and alien, as if George Washington has carried Fox out of The Library and onto the surface of Mars.

○8

"I could really go for a nice cold Euphoria right now," Jeremy says. He and Karl are walking home.

Euphoria is: *The Librarian's Tonic—When Watchfulness Is Not Enough*. There are frequently commercials for Euphoria on *The Library*. Although no one is exactly sure what Euphoria is for, whether it is alcoholic or caffeinated, what it tastes like, if it is poisonous or delightful, or even whether or not it's carbonated, everyone, including Jeremy, pines for a glass of Euphoria once in a while.

"Can I ask you a question?" Karl says.

"Why do you always say that?" Jeremy says. "What am I going to say? 'No, you can't ask me a question?'"

"What's up with you and Talis?" Karl says. "What were you talking about in the kitchen?" Jeremy sees that Karl has been Watchful.

"She had this dream about me," he says, uneasily.

"So do you like her?" Karl says. His chin looks raw. Jeremy is sure now that Karl has tried to shave. "Because, remember how I liked her first?"

"We were just talking," Jeremy says. "So did you shave? Because I didn't know you had facial hair. The idea of you shaving is pathetic, Karl. It's like voting Republican if we were old enough to vote. Or farting in Music Appreciation."

"Don't try to change the subject," Karl says. "When have you and Talis ever had a conversation before?"

"One time we talked about a Diana Wynne Jones book that she'd checked out from the library. She dropped it in the bath accidentally. She wanted to know if I could tell my mother," Jeremy says. "Once we talked about recycling."

"Shut up, Germ," Karl says. "Besides, what about Elizabeth? I thought you liked Elizabeth!"

"Who said that?" Jeremy says. Karl is glaring at him.

"Amy told me," Karl says.

"I never told Amy I liked Elizabeth," Jeremy says. So now Amy is a mind-reader as well as a blabbermouth? What a terrible, deadly combination!

"No," Karl says, grudgingly. "Elizabeth told Amy that she likes you. So I just figured you liked her back."

"Elizabeth likes me?" Jeremy says.

"Apparently everybody likes you," Karl says. He sounds sorry for himself. "What is it about you? It's not like you're all that special. Your nose is funny looking and you have stupid hair."

"Thanks, Karl." Jeremy changes the subject. "Do you think Fox is really dead?" he says. "For good?" He walks faster, so that Karl has to almost-jog to keep up. Presently Jeremy is much taller than Karl, and he intends to enjoy this as long as it lasts. Knowing Karl, he'll either get tall, too, or else chop Jeremy off at the knees.

"They'll use magic," Karl says. "Or maybe it was all a dream. They'll make her alive again. I'll never forgive them if they've killed Fox. And if you like Talis, I'll never forgive you, either. And I know what you're thinking. You're thinking that I think I mean what I say, but if push came to shove, eventually I'd forgive you, and we'd be friends again, like in seventh grade. But I wouldn't, and you're wrong, and we wouldn't be. We wouldn't ever be friends again."

Jeremy doesn't say anything. Of course he likes Talis. He just hasn't realized how much he likes her, until recently. Until today. Until Karl opened his mouth. Jeremy likes Elizabeth too, but how can you compare Elizabeth and Talis? You can't. Elizabeth is Elizabeth and Talis is Talis.

"When you tried to kiss Talis, she hit you with a boa constrictor," he says. It had been Amy's boa constrictor. It had probably been an accident. Karl shouldn't have tried to kiss someone while they were holding a boa constrictor.

"Just try to remember what I just said," Karl says. "You're free to like anyone you want to. Anyone except for Talis."

The Library has been on television for two years now. It isn't a regularly scheduled program. Sometimes it's on two times in the same week, and then not on again for another couple of weeks. Often new episodes debut in the middle of the night. There is a large online community who spend hours scanning channels; sending out alarms and false alarms; fans swap theories, tapes, files; write fanfic. Elizabeth has rigged up her computer to shout "Wake up, Elizabeth! The television is on fire!" when reliable *Library* watch-sites discover a new episode.

The Library is a pirate TV show. It's shown up once or twice on most network channels, but usually it's on the kind of channels that Jeremy thinks of as ghost channels. The ones that are just static, unless you're paying for several hundred channels of cable. There are commercial breaks, but the products being advertised are like Euphoria. They never seem to be real brands, or things that you can actually buy. Often the commercials aren't even in English, or in any other identifiable language, although the jingles are catchy, nonsense or not. They get stuck in your head.

Episodes of *The Library* have no regular schedule, no credits, and sometimes not even dialogue. One episode of *The Library* takes place inside the top drawer of a card catalog, in pitch dark, and it's all in Morse code with subtitles. Nothing else. No one has ever claimed responsibility for inventing *The Library*. No one has ever interviewed one of the actors, or stumbled across a set, film crew, or script, although in one documentary-style episode, the actors filmed the crew, who all wore paper bags on their heads.

When Jeremy gets home, his father is making upside-down pizza in a casserole dish for dinner.

Meeting writers is usually disappointing, at best. Writers who write sexy thrillers aren't necessarily sexy or thrilling in person. Children's book writers might look more like accountants, or ax murderers for that matter. Horror writers are very rarely scary looking, although they are frequently good cooks.

Though Gordon Strangle Mars *is* scary looking. He has long, thin fingers—currently slimy with pizza sauce—which is why he chose 'Strangle' for his fake middle name. He has white-blond hair that he tugs on while he writes until it stands straight up. He has a bad habit of suddenly appearing beside you, when you haven't even realized he was in the same part of the house. His eyes are deep-set and he doesn't blink very often. Karl says that when you meet Jeremy's father, he looks at you as if he were imagining you bundled up and stuck away in some giant spider's larder. Which is probably true.

People who read books probably never bother to wonder if their favorite writers are also good parents. Why would they?

Gordon Strangle Mars is a recreational shoplifter. He has a special, complicated, and unspoken arrangement with the local bookstore, where, in exchange for autographing as many Gordon Strangle Mars novels as they can possibly sell, the store allows Jeremy's father to shoplift books without comment. Jeremy's mother shows up sooner or later and writes a check.

Jeremy's feelings about his father are complicated. His father is a cheap-skate and a petty thief, and yet Jeremy likes his father. His father hardly ever loses his temper with Jeremy, he is always interested in Jeremy's life, and he gives interesting (if confusing) advice when Jeremy asks for it. For example, if Jeremy asked his father about kissing Elizabeth, his father might suggest that Jeremy not worry about giant spiders when he kisses Elizabeth. Jeremy's father's advice usually has something to do with giant spiders.

When Jeremy and Karl weren't speaking to each other, it was Jeremy's father who straightened them out. He lured Karl over, and then locked them both into his study. He didn't let them out again until they were on speaking terms.

"I thought of a great idea for your book," Jeremy says. "What if one of the spiders builds a web on a soccer field, across a goal? And what if the goalie doesn't notice until the middle of the game? Could somebody kill one of the spiders with a soccer ball, if they kicked it hard enough? Would it explode? Or even better, the spider could puncture the soccer ball with its massive fangs. That would be cool, too."

"Your mother's out in the garage," Gordon Strangle Mars says to Jeremy. "She wants to talk to you."

"Oh," Jeremy says. All of a sudden, he thinks of Fox in Talis's dream, trying to phone him. Trying to warn him. Unreasonably, he feels that it's his parents' fault that Fox is dead now, as if they have killed her. "Is it about you? Are you getting divorced?"

"I don't know," his father says. He hunches his shoulders. He makes a face. It's a face that Jeremy's father makes frequently, and yet this face is even more pitiful and guilty than usual.

"What did you do?" Jeremy says. "Did you get caught shoplifting at Wal-Mart?"

"No," his father says.

"Did you have an affair?"

"No!" his father says, again. Now he looks disgusted, either with himself or with Jeremy for asking such a horrible question. "I screwed up. Let's leave it at that."

"How's the book coming?" Jeremy says. There is something in his father's voice that makes him feel like kicking something, but there are never giant spiders around when you need them.

"I don't want to talk about that, either," his father says, looking, if possible, even more ashamed. "Go tell your mother dinner will be ready in five minutes. Maybe you and I can watch the new episode of *The Library* after dinner, if you haven't already seen it a thousand times."

"Do you know the end? Did Mom tell you that Fox is—"

"Oh shit," his father interrupts. "They killed Fox?"

That's the problem with being a writer, Jeremy knows. Even the biggest and most startling twists are rarely twists for you. You know how every story goes.

Jeremy's mother is an orphan. Jeremy's father claims that she was raised by feral silent-film stars, and it's true, she looks like a heroine out of a Harold Lloyd movie. She has an appealingly disheveled look to her, as if someone has either just tied or untied her from a set of train tracks. She met Gordon Mars (before he added the Strangle and sold his first novel) in the food court of a mall in New Jersey, and fell in love with him before realizing that he was a writer and a recreational shoplifter. She didn't read anything he'd written until after they were married, which was a typically cunning move on Jeremy's father's part.

Jeremy's mother doesn't read horror novels. She doesn't like ghost stories or unexplained phenomena or even the kind of phenomena that requires excessively technical explanations. For example: microwaves, airplanes. She doesn't like Halloween, not even Halloween candy. Jeremy's father gives her special editions of his novels, where the scary pages have been glued together.

Jeremy's mother is quiet more often than not. Her name is Alice and sometimes Jeremy thinks about how the two quietest people he knows are named Alice and Talis. But his mother and Talis are quiet in different ways. Jeremy's mother is the kind of person who seems to be keeping something hidden, something secret. Whereas Talis just *is* a secret. Jeremy's mother could easily turn out to be a secret agent. But Talis is the death ray or the key to immortality or whatever it is that secret agents have to keep secret. Hanging out with Talis is like hanging out with a teenaged black hole.

Jeremy's mother is sitting on the floor of the garage, beside a large cardboard box. She has a photo album in her hands. Jeremy sits down beside her.

There are photographs of a cat on a wall, and something blurry that looks like a whale or a zeppelin or a loaf of bread. There's a photograph of a small girl sitting beside a woman. The woman wears a fur collar with a sharp little muzzle, four legs, a tail, and Jeremy feels a sudden pang. Fox is the first dead person that he's ever cared about, but she's not real. The little girl in the photograph looks utterly blank, as if someone has just hit her with a hammer. Like the person behind the camera has just said, "Smile! Your parents are dead!"

"Cleo," Jeremy's mother says, pointing to the woman. "That's Cleo. She was my mother's aunt. She lived in Los Angeles. I went to live with her when my parents died. I was four. I know I've never talked about her. I've never really known what to say about her."

Jeremy says, "Was she nice?"

His mother says, "She tried to be nice. She didn't expect to be saddled with a little girl. What an odd word. Saddled. As if she were a horse. As if somebody put me on her back and I never got off again. She liked to buy clothes for me. She liked clothes. She hadn't had a happy life. She drank a lot. She liked to go to movies in the afternoon and to séances in the evenings. She had boyfriends. Some of them were jerks. The love of her life was a small-time gangster. He died and she never married. She always said marriage was a joke and that life was a bigger joke, and it was just her bad luck that she didn't have a sense of humor. So it's strange to think that all these years she was running a wedding chapel."

Jeremy looks at his mother. She's half-smiling, half-grimacing, as if her stomach hurts. "I ran away when I was sixteen. And I never saw her again. Once she sent me a letter, care of your father's publishers. She said she'd read all his books, and that was how she found me, I guess, because he kept dedicating them to me. She said she hoped I was happy and that she thought about me. I wrote back. I sent a photograph of you. But she never wrote again. Sounds like an episode of *The Library*, doesn't it?"

Jeremy says, "Is that what you wanted to tell me? Dad said you wanted to tell me something."

"That's part of it," his mother says. "I have to go out to Las Vegas, to check out some things about this wedding chapel. Hell's Bells. I want you to come with me."

"Is that what you wanted to ask me?" Jeremy says, although he knows there's something else. His mother still has that sad half-smile on her face.

"Germ," his mother says. "You know I love your father, right?"

"Why?" Jeremy says. "What did he do?"

His mother flips through the photo album. "Look," she says. "This was when you were born." In the picture, his father holds Jeremy as if someone has just handed him an enchanted porcelain teapot. Jeremy's father grins, but he looks terrified, too. He looks like a kid. A scary, scared kid.

"He wouldn't tell me either," Jeremy says. "So it has to be pretty bad. If you're getting divorced, I think you should go ahead and tell me."

"We're not getting divorced," his mother says, "but it might be a good thing if you and I went out to Las Vegas. We could stay there for a few months while I sort out this inheritance. Take care of Cleo's estate. I'm going to talk to your teachers. I've given notice at the library. Think of it as an adventure."

She sees the look on Jeremy's face. "No, I'm sorry. That was a stupid, stupid thing to say. I know this isn't an adventure."

"I don't want to go," Jeremy says. "All my friends are here! I can't just go away and leave them. That would be terrible!" All this time, he's been preparing himself for the most terrible thing he can imagine. He's imagined a conversation with his mother, in which his mother reveals her terrible secret, and in his imagination, he's been calm and reasonable. His imaginary parents have wept and asked for his understanding. The imaginary Jeremy has understood. He has imagined himself understanding everything. But now, as his mother talks, Jeremy's heartbeat speeds up, and his lungs fill with air, as if he is running. He starts to sweat, although the floor of the garage is cold. He wishes he were sitting up on top of the roof with his telescope. There could be meteors, invisible to the naked eye, careening through the sky, hurtling towards Earth. Fox is dead. Everyone he knows is doomed. Even as he thinks this, he knows he's overreacting. But it doesn't help to know this.

"I know it's terrible," his mother says. His mother knows something about terrible.

"So why can't I stay here?" Jeremy says. "You go sort things out in Las Vegas, and I'll stay here with Dad. Why can't I stay here?"

"Because he put you in a book!" his mother says. She spits the words out. He has never heard her sound so angry. His mother never gets angry. "He put you in one of his books! I was in his office, and the manuscript was on his desk. I saw your name, and so I picked it up and started reading."

"So what?" Jeremy says. "He's put me in his books before. Like, stuff I've said. Like when I was eight and I was running a fever and told him the trees were full of dead people wearing party hats. Like when I accidentally set fire to his office."

"It isn't like that," his mother says. "It's you. It's *you*. He hasn't even changed your name. The boy in the book, he jumps hurdles and he wants to be a rocket scientist and go to Mars, and he's cute and funny and sweet and his best friend Elizabeth is in love with him and he talks like you and he looks like you and then he dies, Jeremy. He has a brain tumor and he dies. He dies. There aren't any giant spiders. There's just you, and you die."

Jeremy is silent. He imagines his father writing the scene in his book where the kid named Jeremy dies, and crying, just a little. He imagines this Jeremy kid, Jeremy the character who dies. Poor messed-up kid. Now Jeremy and Fox have something in common. They're both made-up people. They're both dead.

"Elizabeth is in love with me?" he says. Just on principle, he never believes anything that Karl says. But if it's in a book, maybe it's true.

"Oh shit," his mother says. "I really didn't want to say that. I'm just so angry at him. We've been married for seventeen years. I was just four years older than you when I met him, Jeremy. I was nineteen. He was only twenty. We were babies. Can you imagine that? I can put up with the singing toilet and the shoplifting and the couches and I can put up with him being so weird about money. But he killed you, Jeremy. He wrote you into a book and he killed you off. And he knows it was wrong, too. He's ashamed of himself. He didn't want me to tell you. I didn't mean to tell you."

Jeremy sits and thinks. "I still don't want to go to Las Vegas," he says to his mother. "Maybe we could send Dad there instead."

His mother says, "Not a bad idea." But he can tell she's already planning their itinerary.

In one episode of *The Library*, everyone was invisible. You couldn't see the actors: you could only see the books and the bookshelves and the study carrels on the fifth floor where the coin-operated wizards come to flirt and practice their spells. Invisible Forbidden Books were fighting invisible pirate-magicians and the pirate-magicians were fighting Fox and her friends, who were also invisible. The fight was clumsy and full of deadly accidents. You could hear them fighting. Shelves were overturned. Books were thrown. Invisible people tripped over invisible dead bodies, but you didn't find out who'd died until the next episode. Several of the characters—The Accidental Sword, Hairy Pete, and Ptolemy Krill, who (much like the

Vogons in Douglas Adams's *The Hitchhiker's Guide to the Galaxy*) wrote poetry so bad it killed anyone who read it—disappeared for good, and nobody is sure whether they're dead or not.

In another episode, Fox stole a magical drug from The Norns, a prophetic girl band who headline at a cabaret on the mezzanine of The Free People's World-Tree Library. She accidentally injected it, became pregnant, and gave birth to a bunch of snakes who led her to the exact shelf where renegade librarians had misshelved an ancient and terrible book of magic which had never been translated, until Fox asked the snakes for help. The snakes writhed and curled on the ground, spelling out words, letter by letter, with their bodies. As they translated the book for Fox, they hissed and steamed. They became fiery lines on the ground, and then they burnt away entirely. Fox cried. That's the only time anyone has ever seen Fox cry, ever. She isn't like Prince Wing. Prince Wing is a crybaby.

The thing about *The Library* is that characters don't come back when they die. It's as if death is for real. So maybe Fox really is dead and she really isn't coming back. There are a couple of ghosts who hang around The Library looking for blood libations, but they've always been ghosts, all the way back to the beginning of the show. There aren't any evil twins or vampires, either. Although someday, hopefully, there will be evil twins. Who doesn't love evil twins?

"Mom told me about how you wrote about me," Jeremy says. His mother is still in the garage. He feels like a tennis ball in a game where the tennis players love him very, very much, even while they lob and smash and send him back and forth, back and forth.

His father says, "She said she wasn't going to tell you, but I guess I'm glad she did. I'm sorry, Germ. Are you hungry?"

"She's going out to Las Vegas next week. She wants me to go with her," Jeremy says.

"I know," his father says, still holding out a bowl of upside-down pizza. "Try not to worry about all of this, if you can. Think of it as an adventure."

"Mom says that's a stupid thing to say. Are you going to let me read the book with me in it?" Jeremy says.

"No," his father says, looking straight at Jeremy. "I burned it."

"Really?" Jeremy says. "Did you set fire to your computer too?"

"Well, no," his father says. "But you can't read it. It wasn't any good, anyway. Want to watch *The Library* with me? And will you eat some damn pizza, please? I may be a lousy father, but I'm a good cook. And if you love me, you'll eat the damn pizza and be grateful."

So they go sit on the orange couch and Jeremy eats pizza and watches *The Library* for the second-and-a-half time with his father. The lights on the timer in the living room go off, and Prince Wing kills Fox again. And then Jeremy goes to bed. His father goes away to write or to burn stuff. Whatever. His mother is still out in the garage.

On Jeremy's desk is a scrap of paper with a phone number on it. If he wanted to, he could call his phone booth. When he dials the number, it rings for a long time. Jeremy sits on his bed in the dark and listens to it ringing and ringing. When someone picks it up, he almost hangs up. Someone doesn't say anything, so Jeremy says, "Hello? Hello?"

Someone breathes into the phone on the other end of the line. Someone says in a soft, musical, squeaky voice, "Can't talk now, kid. Call back later." Then someone hangs up.

Jeremy dreams that he's sitting beside Fox on a sofa that his father has reupholstered in spider silk. His father has been stealing spider webs from the giant-spider superstores. From his own books. Is that shoplifting or is it self-plagiarism? The sofa is soft and gray and a little bit sticky. Fox sits on either side of him. The right-hand-side Fox is being played by Talis. Elizabeth plays the Fox on his left. Both Foxes look at him with enormous compassion.

"Are you dead?" Jeremy says.

"Are you?" the Fox who is being played by Elizabeth says, in that unmistakable Fox voice which, Jeremy's father once said, sounds like a sexy and demented helium balloon. It makes Jeremy's brain hurt, to hear Fox's voice coming out of Elizabeth's mouth.

The Fox who looks like Talis doesn't say anything at all. The writing on her T-shirt is so small and so foreign that Jeremy can't read it without feeling as if he's staring at Fox-Talis's breasts. It's probably something he needs to know, but he'll never be able to read it. He's too polite, and besides he's terrible at foreign languages.

"Hey look," Jeremy says. "We're on TV!" There he is on television, sitting between two Foxes on a sticky gray couch in a field of red poppies. "Are we in Las Vegas?"

"We're not in Kansas," Fox-Elizabeth says. "There's something I need you to do for me."

"What's that?" Jeremy says.

"If I tell you in the dream," Fox-Elizabeth says, "you won't remember. You have to remember to call me when you're awake. Keep on calling until you get me."

"How will I remember to call you," Jeremy says, "if I don't remember what you tell me in this dream? Why do you need me to help you? Why is Talis here? What does her T-shirt say? Why are you both Fox? Is this Mars?"

Fox-Talis goes on watching TV. Fox-Elizabeth opens her kind and beautiful un-Hello-Kitty-like mouth again. She tells Jeremy the whole story. She explains everything. She translates Fox-Talis's T-shirt, which turns out to explain everything about Talis that Jeremy has ever wondered about. It answers every single question that Jeremy has ever had about girls. And then Jeremy wakes up—

It's dark. Jeremy flips on the light. The dream is moving away from him. There was something about Mars. Elizabeth was asking who he thought was prettier, Talis or Elizabeth. They were laughing. They both had pointy fox ears. They wanted him to do something. There was a telephone number he was supposed to call. There was something he was supposed to do.

In two weeks, on the fifteenth of April, Jeremy and his mother will get in her van and start driving out to Las Vegas. Every morning before school,

Jeremy takes long showers and his father doesn't say anything at all. One day it's as if nothing is wrong between his parents. The next day they won't even look at each other. Jeremy's father won't come out of his study. And then the day after that, Jeremy comes home and finds his mother sitting on his father's lap. They're smiling as if they know something stupid and secret. They don't even notice Jeremy when he walks through the room. Even this is preferable, though, to the way they behave when they do notice him. They act guilty and strange and as if they are about to ruin his life. Gordon Mars makes pancakes every morning, and Jeremy's favorite dinner, macaroni and cheese, every night. Jeremy's mother plans out an itinerary for their trip. They will be stopping at libraries across the country, because his mother loves libraries. But she's also bought a new two-man tent and two sleeping bags and a portable stove, so that they can camp, if Jeremy wants to camp. Even though Jeremy's mother hates the outdoors.

Right after she does this, Gordon Mars spends all weekend in the garage. He won't let either of them see what he's doing, and when he does let them in, it turns out that he's removed the seating in the back of the van and bolted down two of his couches, one on each side, both upholstered in electric-blue fake fur.

They have to climb in through the cargo door at the back because one of the couches is blocking the sliding door. Jeremy's father says, looking very pleased with himself, "So now you don't have to camp outside, unless you want to. You can sleep inside. There's space underneath for suitcases. The sofas even have seat belts."

Over the sofas, Jeremy's father has rigged up small wooden shelves that fold down on chains from the walls of the van and become table tops. There's a travel-sized disco ball dangling from the ceiling, and a wooden panel—with Velcro straps and a black, quilted pad—behind the driver's seat, where Jeremy's father explains they can hang up the painting of the woman with the apple and the knife.

The van looks like something out of an episode of *The Library*. Jeremy's mother bursts into tears. She runs back inside the house. Jeremy's father says, helplessly, "I just wanted to make her laugh."

Jeremy wants to say, "I hate both of you." But he doesn't say it, and he doesn't. It would be easier if he did.

◌

When Jeremy told Karl about Las Vegas, Karl punched him in the stomach. Then he said, "Have you told Talis?"

Jeremy said, "You're supposed to be nice to me! You're supposed to tell me not to go and that this sucks and you're not supposed to punch me. Why did you punch me? Is Talis all you ever think about?"

"Kind of," Karl said. "Most of the time. Sorry, Germ, of course I wish you weren't going and yeah, it also pisses me off. We're supposed to be best friends, but you do stuff all the time and I never get to. I've never driven across the country or been to Las Vegas, even though I'd really, really like to. I can't feel sorry for you when I bet you anything that while you're there, you'll sneak into some casino and play slot machines and win like a million bucks. You should feel sorry for me. I'm the one that has to stay here. Can I borrow your dirt bike while you're gone?"

"Sure," Jeremy said.

"How about your telescope?" Karl said.

"I'm taking it with me," Jeremy said.

"Fine. You have to call me every day," Karl said. "You have to email. You have to tell me about Las Vegas show girls. I want to know how tall they really are. Whose phone number is this?"

Karl was holding the scrap of paper with the number of Jeremy's phone booth.

"Mine," Jeremy said. "That's my phone booth. The one I inherited."

"Have you called it?" Karl said.

"No," Jeremy said. He'd called the phone booth a few times. But it wasn't a game. Karl would think it was a game.

"Cool," Karl said and he went ahead and dialed the number. "Hello?" Karl said, "I'd like to speak to the person in charge of Jeremy's life. This is Jeremy's best friend Karl."

"Not funny," Jeremy said.

"My life is boring," Karl said, into the phone. "I've never inherited anything. This girl I like won't talk to me. So is someone there? Does anybody want to talk to me? Does anyone want to talk to my friend, the Lord of the Phone Booth? Jeremy, they're demanding that you liberate the phone booth from yourself."

"Still not funny," Jeremy said and Karl hung up the phone.

Jeremy told Elizabeth. They were up on the roof of Jeremy's house and he told her the whole thing. Not just the part about Las Vegas, but also the part about his father and how he put Jeremy in a book with no giant spiders in it.

"Have you read it?" Elizabeth said.

"No," Jeremy said. "He won't let me. Don't tell Karl. All I told him is that my mom and I have to go out for a few months to check out the wedding chapel."

"I won't tell Karl," Elizabeth said. She leaned forward and kissed Jeremy and then she wasn't kissing him. It was all very fast and surprising, but they didn't fall off the roof. Nobody falls off the roof in this story. "Talis likes you," Elizabeth said. "That's what Amy says. Maybe you like her back. I don't know. But I thought I should go ahead and kiss you now. Just in case I don't get to kiss you again."

"You can kiss me again," Jeremy said. "Talis probably doesn't like me."

"No," Elizabeth said. "I mean, let's not. I want to stay friends and it's hard enough to be friends, Germ. Look at you and Karl."

"I would never kiss Karl," Jeremy said.

"Funny, Germ. We should have a surprise party for you before you go," Elizabeth said.

"It won't be a surprise party now," Jeremy said. Maybe kissing him once was enough.

"Well, once I tell Amy it can't really be a surprise party," Elizabeth said. "She would explode into a million pieces and all the little pieces would start yelling, 'Guess what? Guess what? We're having a surprise party for you, Jeremy!' But just because I'm letting you in on the surprise doesn't mean there won't be surprises."

"I don't actually like surprises," Jeremy said.

"Who does?" Elizabeth said. "Only the people who do the surprising. Can we have the party at your house? I think it should be like Halloween, and it always feels like Halloween here. We could all show up in costumes and watch lots of old episodes of *The Library* and eat ice cream."

"Sure," Jeremy said. And then: "This is terrible! What if there's a new episode of *The Library* while I'm gone? Who am I going to watch it with?"

And he'd said the perfect thing. Elizabeth felt so bad about Jeremy having to watch *The Library* all by himself that she kissed him again.

There has never been a giant spider in any episode of *The Library*, although once Fox got really small and Ptolemy Krill carried her around in his pocket. She had to rip up one of Krill's handkerchiefs and blindfold herself, just in case she accidentally read a draft of Krill's terrible poetry. And then it turned out that, as well as the poetry, Krill had also stashed a rare, horned Anubis earwig in his pocket which hadn't been properly preserved. Ptolemy Krill, it turned out, was careless with his kill jar. The earwig almost ate Fox, but instead it became her friend. It still sends her Christmas cards.

These are the two most important things that Jeremy and his friends have in common: a geographical location, and love of a television show about a library. Jeremy turns on the television as soon as he comes home from school. He flips through the channels, watching reruns of *Star Trek* and *Law & Order*. If there's a new episode of *The Library* before he and his mother leave for Las Vegas, then everything will be fine. Everything will work out. His mother says, "You watch too much television, Jeremy." But he goes on flipping through channels. Then he goes up to his room and makes phone calls.

"The new episode needs to be soon, because we're getting ready to leave. Tonight would be good. You'd tell me if there was going to be a new episode tonight, right?"

Silence.

"Can I take that as a yes? It would be easier if I had a brother," Jeremy tells his telephone booth. "Hello? Are you there? Or a sister. I'm tired of being good all the time. If I had a sibling, then we could take turns being good. If I had an older brother, I might be better at being bad, better at being angry. Karl is really good at being angry. He learned how from his brothers. I wouldn't want brothers like Karl's brothers, of course, but it sucks having to figure out everything all by myself. And the more normal I try to be, the more my parents think that I'm acting out. They think it's a phase that I'll grow out of. They think it isn't normal to be normal. Because there's no such thing as normal.

"And this whole book thing. The whole shoplifting thing, how my dad steals things, it figures that he went and stole my life. It isn't just me being melodramatic, to say that. That's exactly what he did! Did I tell you that once he stole a ferret from a pet store because he felt bad for it, and then he let it loose in our house and it turned out that it was pregnant? There was this woman who came to interview Dad and she sat down on one of the—"

Someone knocks on his bedroom door. "Jeremy," his mother says. "Is Karl here? Am I interrupting?"

"No," Jeremy says, and hangs up the phone. He's gotten into the habit of calling his phone booth every day. When he calls, it rings and rings and then it stops ringing, as if someone has picked up. There's just silence on the other end, no squeaky pretend-Fox voice, but it's a peaceful, interested silence. Jeremy complains about all the things there are to complain about, and the silent person on the other end listens and listens. Maybe it is Fox standing there in his phone booth and listening patiently. He wonders what incarnation of Fox is listening. One thing about Fox: she's never sorry for herself. She's always too busy. If it were really Fox, she'd hang up on him.

Jeremy opens his door. "I was on the phone," he says. His mother comes in and sits down on his bed. She's wearing one of his father's old flannel shirts. "So have you packed?"

Jeremy shrugs. "I guess," he says. "Why did you cry when you saw what Dad did to the van? Don't you like it?"

"It's that damn painting," his mother says. "It was the first nice thing he ever gave me. We should have spent the money on health insurance and a new roof and groceries and instead he bought a painting. So I got angry. I left him. I took the painting and I moved into a hotel and I stayed there for a few days. I was going to sell the painting, but instead I fell in love with it, so I came home and apologized for running away. I got pregnant with you and I used to get hungry and dream that someone was going to give me a beautiful apple, like the one she's holding. When I told your father, he said he didn't trust her, that she was holding out the apple like that as a trick and if you went to take it from her, she'd stab you with the peeling knife. He says that she's a tough old broad and she'll take care of us while we're on the road."

"Do we really have to go?" Jeremy says. "If we go to Las Vegas I might get into trouble. I might start using drugs or gambling or something."

"Oh, Germ. You try so hard to be a good kid," his mother says. "You try so hard to be normal. Sometimes I'd like to be normal, too. Maybe Vegas will be good for us. Are these the books that you're bringing?"

Jeremy shrugs. "Not all of them. I can't decide which ones I should take and which ones I can leave. It feels like whatever I leave behind, I'm leaving behind for good."

"That's silly," his mother says. "We're coming back. I promise. Your father and I will work things out. If you leave something behind that you need, he can mail it to you. Do you think there are slot machines in the libraries in Las Vegas? I talked to a woman at the Hell's Bells chapel and there's something called The Arts and Lovecraft Library where they keep Cleo's special collection of horror novels and gothic romances and fake copies of *The Necronomicon*. You go in and out through a secret, swinging-bookcase door. People get married in it. There's a Dr. Frankenstein's LoveLab, the Masque of the Red Death Ballroom and also something just called The Crypt. Oh yeah, and there's also The Vampire's Patio and The Black Lagoon Grotto, where you can get married by moonlight."

"You hate all this stuff," Jeremy says.

"It's not my cup of tea," his mother admits. Then she says, "When does everyone show up tonight?"

"Around eight," Jeremy says. "Are you going to get dressed up?"

"I don't have to dress up," his mother says. "I'm a librarian, remember?"

CR

Jeremy's father's office is above the garage. In theory, no one is meant to interrupt him while he's working, but in practice Jeremy's father loves nothing better than to be interrupted, as long as the person who interrupts brings him something to eat. When Jeremy and his mother are gone, who will bring Jeremy's father food? Jeremy hardens his heart.

The floor is covered with books and bolts and samples of upholstering fabrics. Jeremy's father is lying facedown on the floor with his feet propped up on a bolt of fabric, which means that he is thinking and also that his back hurts. He claims to think best when he is on the verge of falling asleep.

"I brought you a bowl of Froot Loops," Jeremy says.

His father rolls over and looks up. "Thanks," he says. "What time is it? Is everyone here? Is that your costume? Is that my tuxedo jacket?"

"It's five-ish. Nobody's here yet. Do you like it?" Jeremy says. He's dressed as a Forbidden Book. His father's jacket is too big, but he still feels very elegant. Very sinister. His mother lent him the lipstick and the feathers and the platform heels.

"It's interesting," his father allows. "And a little frightening."

Jeremy feels obscurely pleased, even though he knows that his father is more amused than frightened. "Everyone else will probably come as Fox or Prince Wing. Except for Karl. He's coming as Ptolemy Krill. He even wrote some really bad poetry. I wanted to ask you something, before we leave tomorrow."

"Shoot," his father says.

"Did you really get rid of the novel with me in it?"

"No," his father says. "It felt unlucky. Unlucky to keep it, unlucky not to keep it. I don't know what to do with it."

Jeremy says, "I'm glad you didn't get rid of it."

"It's not any good, you know," his father says. "Which makes all this even worse. At first it was because I was bored with giant spiders. It was going to be something funny to show you. But then I wrote that you had a brain tumor and it wasn't funny any more. I figured I could save you—I'm the author, after all—but you got sicker and sicker. You were going through a rebellious phase. You were sneaking out of the house a lot and you hit your mother. You were a real jerk. But it turned out you had a brain tumor and that was making you behave strangely."

"Can I ask another question?" Jeremy says. "You know how you like to steal things? You know how you're really, really good at it?"

"Yeah," says his father.

"Could you not steal things for a while, if I asked you to?" Jeremy says. "Mom isn't going to be around to pay for the books and stuff that you steal. I don't want you to end up in jail because we went to Las Vegas."

His father closes his eyes as if he hopes Jeremy will forget that he asked a question, and go away.

Jeremy says nothing.

"All right," his father says finally. "I won't shoplift anything until you get home again."

Jeremy's mother runs around taking photos of everyone. Talis and Elizabeth have both showed up as Fox, although Talis is dead Fox. She carries her fake fur ears and tail around in a little see-through plastic purse and she also has a sword, which she leaves in the umbrella stand in the kitchen. Jeremy and Talis haven't talked much since she had a dream about him and since he told her that he's going to Las Vegas. She didn't say anything about that. Which is perfectly normal for Talis.

Karl makes an excellent Ptolemy Krill. Jeremy's Forbidden Book disguise is admired.

Amy's Faithful Margaret costume is almost as good as anything Faithful Margaret wears on TV. There are even special effects: Amy has rigged up her hair with red ribbons and wire and spray color and egg whites so that it looks as if it's on fire, and there are tiny papier-mâché golems in it, making horrible faces. She dances a polka with Jeremy's father. Faithful Margaret is mad for polka dancing.

No one has dressed up as Prince Wing.

They watch the episode with the possessed chicken and they watch the episode with the Salt Wife and they watch the episode where Prince Wing and Faithful Margaret fall under a spell and swap bodies and have sex for the first time. They watch the episode where Fox saves Prince Wing's life for the first time.

Jeremy's father makes chocolate/mango/espresso milk shakes for everyone. None of Jeremy's friends, except for Elizabeth, know about the novel. Everyone thinks Jeremy and his mother are just having an adventure. Everyone thinks Jeremy will be back at the end of the summer.

"I wonder how they find the actors," Elizabeth says. "They aren't real actors. They must be regular people. But you'd think that somewhere there would be someone who knows them. That somebody online would say, hey, that's my sister! Or that's the kid I went to school with who threw up in P.E. You know, sometimes someone says something like that or sometimes someone pretends that they know something about *The Library*, but it always turns out to be a hoax. Just somebody wanting to be somebody."

"What about the guy who's writing it?" Karl says.

Talis says, "Who says it's a guy?" and Amy says, "Yeah, Karl, why do you always assume it's a guy writing it?"

"Maybe nobody's writing it," Elizabeth says. "Maybe it's magic or it's broadcast from outer space. Maybe it's real. Wouldn't that be cool?"

"No," Jeremy says. "Because then Fox would really be dead. That would suck."

"I don't care," Elizabeth says. "I wish it were real, anyway. Maybe it all really happened somewhere, like King Arthur or Robin Hood, and this is just one version of how it happened. Like a magical After School Special."

"Even if it isn't real," Amy says, "parts of it could be real. Like maybe the World-Tree Library is real. Or maybe *The Library* is made up, but Fox is based on somebody that the writer knew. Writers do that all the time, right? Jeremy, I think your dad should write a book about me. I could be eaten by giant spiders. Or have sex with giant spiders and have spider babies. I think that would be so great."

So Amy does have psychic abilities, after all, although hopefully she will never know this. When Jeremy tests his own potential psychic abilities, he can almost sense his father, hovering somewhere just outside the living room, listening to this conversation and maybe even taking notes. Which is what writers do. But Jeremy isn't really psychic. It's just that lurking and hovering and appearing suddenly when you weren't expecting him are what his father does, just like shoplifting and cooking. Jeremy prays to all the dark gods that he never receives the gift of knowing what people are thinking. It's a dark road and it ends up with you trapped on late-night television in front of an invisible audience of depressed insomniacs wearing hats made out of tinfoil and they all want to pay you nine-ninety-nine per minute to hear you describe in minute, terrible detail what their deceased cat is thinking about, right now. What kind of future is that? He wants to go to Mars. And when will Elizabeth kiss him again? You can't just kiss someone twice and then never kiss them again. He tries not to think about Elizabeth and kissing, just in case Amy reads his mind. He realizes that he's been staring at Talis's breasts, glares instead at Elizabeth, who is watching TV. Meanwhile, Karl is glaring at him.

On television, Fox is dancing in the Invisible Nightclub with Faithful Margaret, whose hair is about to catch fire again. The Norns are playing their screechy cover of "Come On, Eileen." The Norns only know two songs: "Come On, Eileen," and "Everybody Wants to Rule the World." They don't play real instruments. They play squeaky dog toys and also a bathtub, which is enchanted, although nobody knows who by, or why, or what it was enchanted for.

"If you had to chose one," Jeremy says, "invisibility or the ability to fly, which would you choose?"

Everybody looks at him. "Only perverts would want to be invisible," Elizabeth says.

"You'd have to be naked if you were invisible," Karl says. "Because otherwise people would see your clothes."

"If you could fly, you'd have to wear thermal underwear because it's cold up there. So it just depends on whether you like to wear long underwear or no underwear at all," Amy says.

It's the kind of conversation that they have all the time. It makes Jeremy feel homesick even though he hasn't left yet.

"Maybe I'll go make brownies," Jeremy says. "Elizabeth, do you want to help me make brownies?"

"Shhh," Elizabeth says. "This is a good part."

On television, Fox and Faithful Margaret are making out. The Faithful part is kind of a joke.

Jeremy's parents go to bed at one. By three, Amy and Elizabeth are passed out on the couch and Karl has gone upstairs to check his email on Jeremy's iBook. On TV, wolves are roaming the tundra of The Free People's World-Tree Library's fortieth floor. Snow is falling heavily and librarians are burning books to keep warm, but only the most dull and improving works of literature.

Jeremy isn't sure where Talis has gone, so he goes to look for her. She hasn't gone far. She's on the landing, looking at the space on the wall where Alice Mars's painting should be hanging. Talis is carrying her sword with her, and her little plastic purse. In the bathroom off the landing, the singing toilet is still singing away in German. "We're taking the painting with us," Jeremy says. "My dad insisted, just in case he accidentally burns down the house while we're gone. Do you want to go see it? I was going to show everybody, but everybody's asleep right now."

"Sure," Talis says.

So Jeremy gets a flashlight and takes her out to the garage and shows her the van. She climbs right inside and sits down on one of the blue-fur couches. She looks around and he wonders what she's thinking. He wonders if the toilet song is stuck in her head.

"My dad did all of this," Jeremy says. He turns on the flashlight and shines it on the disco ball. Light spatters off in anxious, slippery orbits. Jeremy shows Talis how his father has hung up the painting. It looks truly wrong in the van, as if someone demented put it there. Especially with the light reflecting off the disco ball. The woman in the painting looks confused and embarrassed, as if Jeremy's father has accidentally canceled out her protective powers. Maybe the disco ball is her Kryptonite.

"So remember how you had a dream about me?" Jeremy says. Talis nods. "I think I had a dream about you, that you were Fox."

Talis opens up her arms, encompassing her costume, her sword, her plastic purse with poor Fox's ears and tail inside.

"There was something you wanted me to do," Jeremy says. "I was supposed to save you, somehow."

Talis just looks at him.

"How come you never talk?" Jeremy says. All of this is irritating. How he used to feel normal around Elizabeth, like friends, and now everything is peculiar and uncomfortable. How he used to enjoy feeling uncomfortable around Talis, and now, suddenly, he doesn't. This must be what sex is about. Stop thinking about sex, he thinks.

Talis opens her mouth and closes it again. Then she says, "I don't know. Amy talks so much. You all talk a lot. Somebody has to be the person who doesn't. The person who listens."

"Oh," Jeremy says. "I thought maybe you had a tragic secret. Like maybe you used to stutter." Except secrets can't have secrets, they just *are*.

"Nope," Talis says. "It's like being invisible, you know. Not talking. I like it."

"But you're not invisible," Jeremy says. "Not to me. Not to Karl. Karl really likes you. Did you hit him with a boa constrictor on purpose?"

But Talis says, "I wish you weren't leaving." The disco ball spins and spins. It makes Jeremy feel kind of carsick and also as if he has sparkly, disco leprosy. He doesn't say anything back to Talis, just to see how it feels. Except maybe that's rude. Or maybe it's rude the way everybody always talks and doesn't leave any space for Talis to say anything.

"At least you get to miss school," Talis says, at last.

"Yeah," he says. He leaves another space, but Talis doesn't say anything this time. "We're going to stop at all these museums and things on the way across the country. I'm supposed to keep a blog for school and describe stuff in it. I'm going to make a lot of stuff up. So it will be like Creative Writing and not so much like homework."

"You should make a list of all the towns with weird names you drive through," Talis says. "Town of Horseheads. That's a real place."

"Plantagenet," Jeremy says. "That's a real place too. I had something really weird to tell you."

Talis waits, like she always does.

Jeremy says, "I called my phone booth, the one that I inherited, and someone answered. She sounded just like Fox and she told me—she told me to call back later. So I've called a few more times, but I don't ever get her."

"Fox isn't a real person," Talis says. "*The Library* is just TV." But she sounds uncertain. That's the thing about *The Library*. Nobody knows for sure. Everyone who watches it wishes and hopes that it's not just acting. That it's magic, real magic.

"I know," Jeremy says.

"I wish Fox was real," Fox-Talis says.

They've been sitting in the van for a long time. If Karl looks for them and can't find them, he's going to think that they've been making out. He'll kill Jeremy. Once Karl tried to strangle another kid for accidentally peeing on his shoes. Jeremy might as well kiss Talis. So he does, even though she's still holding her sword. She doesn't hit him with it. It's dark and he has his eyes closed and he can almost imagine that he's kissing Elizabeth.

Karl has fallen asleep on Jeremy's bed. Talis is downstairs, fast-forwarding through the episode where some librarians drink too much Euphoria and decide to abolish Story Hour. Not just the practice of having a Story Hour, but the whole Hour. Amy and Elizabeth are still sacked out on the couch. It's weird to watch Amy sleep. She doesn't talk in her sleep.

Karl is snoring. Jeremy could go up on the roof and look at stars, except he's already packed up his telescope. He could try to wake up Elizabeth and they could go up on the roof, but Talis is down there. He and Talis could go sit on the roof, but he doesn't want to kiss Talis on the roof. He makes a solemn oath to only ever kiss Elizabeth on the roof.

He picks up his phone. Maybe he can call his phone booth and complain just a little and not wake Karl up. His dad is going to freak out about the phone bill. All these calls to Nevada. It's 4 A.M. Jeremy's plan is not to go to sleep at all. His friends are lame.

The phone rings and rings and rings and then someone picks up. Jeremy recognizes the silence on the other end. "Everybody came over and fell asleep," he whispers. "That's why I'm whispering. I don't even think they care that I'm leaving. And my feet hurt. Remember how I was going to dress up as a Forbidden Book? Platform shoes aren't comfortable. Karl thinks I did it on purpose, to be even taller than him than usual. And I forgot that I was wearing lipstick and I kissed Talis and got lipstick all over her face, so it's a good thing everyone was asleep because otherwise someone would have seen. And my dad says that he won't shoplift at all while Mom and I are gone, but you can't trust him. And that fake-fur upholstery sheds like—"

"Jeremy," that strangely familiar, sweet-and-rusty door-hinge voice says softly. "Shut up, Jeremy. I need your help."

"Wow!" Jeremy says, not in a whisper. "Wow, wow, wow! Is this Fox? Are you really Fox? Is this a joke? Are you real? Are you dead? What are you doing in my phone booth?"

"You know who I am," Fox says, and Jeremy knows with all his heart that it's really Fox. "I need you to do something for me."

"What?" Jeremy says. Karl, on the bed, laughs in his sleep as if the idea of Jeremy doing something is funny to him. "What could I do?"

"I need you to steal three books," Fox says. "From a library in a place called Iowa."

"I know Iowa," Jeremy says. "I mean, I've never been there, but it's a real place. I could go there."

"I'm going to tell you the books you need to steal," Fox says. "Author, title, and the jewelly festival number—"

"Dewey Decimal," Jeremy says. "It's actually called the Dewey Decimal number in real libraries."

"Real," Fox says, sounding amused. "You need to write this all down and also how to get to the library. You need to steal the three books and

225

bring them to me. It's very important."

"Is it dangerous?" Jeremy says. "Are the Forbidden Books up to something? Are the Forbidden Books real, too? What if I get caught stealing?"

"It's not dangerous to you," Fox says. "Just don't get caught. Remember the episode of *The Library* when I was the little old lady with the beehive and I stole the Bishop of Tweedle's false teeth while he was reading the banns for the wedding of Faithful Margaret and Sir Petronella the Younger? Remember how he didn't even notice?"

"I've never seen that episode," Jeremy says, although as far as he knows he's never missed a single episode of *The Library*. He's never even heard of Sir Petronella.

"Oh," Fox says. "Maybe that's a flashback in a later episode or something. That's a great episode. We're depending on you, Jeremy. You have got to steal these books. They contain dreadful secrets. I can't say the titles out loud. I'm going to spell them instead."

So Jeremy gets a pad of paper and Fox spells out the titles of each book twice. (They aren't titles that can be written down here. It's safer not to even think about some books.) "Can I ask you something?" Jeremy says. "Can I tell anybody about this? Not Amy. But could I tell Karl or Elizabeth? Or Talis? Can I tell my mom? If I woke up Karl right now, would you talk to him for a minute?"

"I don't have a lot of time," Fox says. "I have to go now. Please don't tell anyone, Jeremy. I'm sorry."

"Is it the Forbidden Books?" Jeremy says again. What would Fox think if she saw the costume he's still wearing, all except for the platform heels? "Do you think I shouldn't trust my friends? But I've known them my whole life!"

Fox makes a noise, a kind of pained whuff.

"What is it?" Jeremy says. "Are you okay?"

"I have to go," Fox says. "Nobody can know about this. Don't give anybody this number. Don't tell anyone about your phone booth. Or me. Promise, Germ?"

"Only if you promise you won't call me Germ," Jeremy says, feeling really stupid. "I hate when people call me that. Call me Mars instead."

"Mars," Fox says, and it sounds exotic and strange and brave, as if Jeremy has just become a new person, a person named after a whole planet, a person who kisses girls and talks to Foxes.

"I've never stolen anything," Jeremy says.

But Fox has hung up.

Maybe out there, somewhere, is someone who enjoys having to say good-bye, but it isn't anyone that Jeremy knows. All of his friends are grumpy and red-eyed, although not from crying. From lack of sleep. From too much television. There are still faint red stains around Talis's mouth and if every-one wasn't so tired, they would realize it's Jeremy's lipstick. Karl gives Jeremy a handful of quarters, dimes, nickels, and pennies. "For the slot machines," Karl says. "If you win anything, you can keep a third of what you win."

"Half," Jeremy says, automatically.

"Fine," Karl says. "It's all from your dad's sofas, anyway. Just one more thing. Stop getting taller. Don't get taller while you're gone. Okay." He hugs Jeremy hard: so hard that it's almost like getting punched again. No wonder Talis threw the boa constrictor at Karl.

Talis and Elizabeth both hug Jeremy good-bye. Talis looks even more mysterious now that he's sat with her under a disco ball and made out. Later on, Jeremy will discover that Talis has left her sword under the blue fur couch and he'll wonder if she left it on purpose.

Talis doesn't say anything and Amy, of course, doesn't shut up, not even when she kisses him. It feels weird to be kissed by someone who goes right on talking while they kiss you and yet it shouldn't be a surprise that Amy kisses him. He imagines that later Amy and Talis and Elizabeth will all compare notes.

Elizabeth says, "I promise I'll tape every episode of *The Library* while you're gone so we can all watch them together when you get back. I promise I'll call you in Vegas, no matter what time it is there, when there's a new episode."

Her hair is a mess and her breath is faintly sour. Jeremy wishes he could tell her how beautiful she looks. "I'll write bad poetry and send it to you," he says.

Jeremy's mother is looking hideously cheerful as she goes in and out of the house, making sure that she hasn't left anything behind. She loves long car trips. It doesn't bother her one bit that she and her son are abandoning their entire lives. She passes Jeremy a folder full of maps. "You're in charge of not getting lost," she says. "Put these somewhere safe."

Jeremy says, "I found a library online that I want to go visit. Out in Iowa. They have a corn mosaic on the façade of the building, with a lot of naked goddesses and gods dancing around in a field of corn. Someone wants to take it down. Can we go see it first?"

"Sure," his mother says.

Jeremy's father has filled a whole grocery bag with sandwiches. His hair is drooping and he looks even more like an ax murderer than usual. If this were a movie, you'd think that Jeremy and his mother were escaping in the nick of time. "You take care of your mother," he says to Jeremy.

"Sure," Jeremy says. "You take care of yourself."

His dad sags. "You take care of yourself, too." So it's settled. They're all supposed to take care of themselves. Why can't they stay home and take care of each other, until Jeremy is good and ready to go off to college? "I've got another bag of sandwiches in the kitchen," his dad says. "I should go get them."

"Wait," Jeremy says. "I have to ask you something before we take off. Suppose I had to steal something. I mean, I don't have to steal anything, of course, and I know stealing is wrong, even when *you* do it, and I would never steal anything. But what if I did? How do you do it? How do you do it and not get caught?"

His father shrugs. He's probably wondering if Jeremy is really his son. Gordon Mars inherited his mutant, long-fingered, ambidextrous hands from a long line of shoplifters and money launderers and petty criminals. They're all deeply ashamed of Jeremy's father. Gordon Mars had a gift and he threw it away to become a writer. "I don't know," he says. He picks up Jeremy's hand and looks at it as if he's never noticed before that Jeremy had something hanging off the end of his wrist. "You just do it. You do it like you're not really doing anything at all. You do it while you're thinking about something else and you forget that you're doing it."

"Oh, Jeremy says, taking his hand back. "I'm not planning on stealing anything. I was just curious."

His father looks at him. "Take care of yourself," he says again, as if he really means it, and hugs Jeremy hard.

Then he goes and gets the sandwiches (so many sandwiches that Jeremy and his mother will eat sandwiches for the first three days, and still have to throw half of them away). Everyone waves. Jeremy and his mother climb in the van. Jeremy's mother turns on the CD player. Bob Dylan is singing about monkeys. His mother loves Bob Dylan. They drive away.

Do you know how, sometimes, during a commercial break in your favorite television shows, your best friend calls and wants to talk about one of her boyfriends, and when you try to hang up, she starts crying and you try to cheer her up and end up missing about half of the episode? And so when you go to work the next day, you have to get the guy who sits next to you to explain what happened? That's the good thing about a book. You can mark your place in a book. But this isn't really a book. It's a television show.

In one episode of *The Library*, an adolescent boy drives across the country with his mother. They have to change a tire. The boy practices taking things out of his mother's purse and putting them back again. He steals a sixteen-ounce bottle of Coke from one convenience market and leaves it at another convenience market. The boy and his mother stop at a lot of libraries, and the boy keeps a blog, but he skips the bit about the library in Iowa. He writes in his blog about what he's reading, but he doesn't read the books he stole in Iowa, because Fox told him not to, and because he has to hide them from his mother. Well, he reads just a few pages. Skims, really. He hides them under the blue-fur sofa. They go camping in Utah, and the boy sets up his telescope. He sees three shooting stars and a coyote. He never sees anyone who looks like a Forbidden Book, although he sees a transvestite go into the women's restroom at a rest stop in Indiana. He calls a phone booth just outside Las Vegas twice, but no one ever answers. He has short conversations with his father. He wonders what his father is up to. He wishes he could tell his father about Fox and the books. Once the boy's mother finds a giant spider the size of an Oreo in their tent. She starts laughing hysterically. She takes a picture of it with her digital camera, and the boy puts the picture on his blog. Sometimes the boy asks questions and his mother talks about her parents. Once she cries. The boy doesn't know what to say. They talk about their favorite episodes of *The Library* and the episodes that they really hated, and the mother asks if the boy thinks Fox is really dead. He says he doesn't think so.

Once a man tries to break into the van while they are sleeping in it. But then he goes away. Maybe the painting of the woman with the peeling knife is protecting them.

But you've seen this episode before.

It's Cinco de Mayo. It's almost seven o'clock at night, and the sun is beginning to go down. Jeremy and his mother are in the desert and Las Vegas is somewhere in front of them. Every time they pass a driver coming the other way, Jeremy tries to figure out if that person has just won or lost a lot of money. Everything is flat and sort of tilted here, except off in the distance, where the land goes up abruptly, as if someone has started to fold up a map. Somewhere around here is the Grand Canyon, which must have been a surprise when people first saw it.

Jeremy's mother says, "Are you sure we have to do this first? Couldn't we go find your phone booth later?"

"Can we do it now?" Jeremy says. "I said I was going to do it on my blog. It's like a quest that I have to complete."

"Okay," his mother says. "It should be around here somewhere. It's supposed to be 4.5 miles after the turn-off, and here's the turn-off."

It isn't hard to find the phone booth. There isn't much else around. Jeremy should feel excited when he sees it, but it's a disappointment, really. He's seen phone booths before. He was expecting something to be different.

Mostly he just feels tired of road trips and tired of roads and just tired, tired, tired. He looks around to see if Fox is somewhere nearby, but there's just a hiker off in the distance. Some kid.

"Okay, Germ," his mother says. "Make this quick."

"I need to get my backpack out of the back," Jeremy says.

"Do you want me to come, too?" his mother says.

"No," Jeremy says. "This is kind of personal."

His mother looks like she's trying not to laugh. "Just hurry up. I have to pee."

When Jeremy gets to the phone booth, he turns around. His mother has the light on in the van. It looks like she's singing along to the radio. His mother has a terrible voice.

When he steps inside the phone booth, it isn't magical. The phone booth smells rank, as if an animal has been living in it. The windows are smudgy. He takes the stolen books out of his backpack and puts them in the little shelf where someone has stolen a phone book. Then he waits. Maybe Fox is going to call him. Maybe he's supposed to wait until she calls. But she doesn't call. He feels lonely. There's no one he can tell about this. He feels like an idiot and he also feels kind of proud. Because he did it. He drove cross-country with his mother and saved an imaginary person.

"So how's your phone booth?" his mother says.

"Great!" he says, and they're both silent again. Las Vegas is in front of them and then all around them and everything is lit up like they're inside a pinball game. All of the trees look fake. Like someone read too much Dr. Seuss and got ideas. People are walking up and down the sidewalks. Some of them look normal. Others look like they just escaped from a fancy-dress ball at a lunatic asylum. Jeremy hopes they've just won lots of money and that's why they look so startled, so strange. Or maybe they're all vampires.

"Left," he tells his mother. "Go left here. Look out for the vampires on the crosswalk. And then it's an immediate right." Four times his mother let him drive the van: once in Utah, twice in South Dakota, once in Pennsylvania.

The van smells like old burger wrappers and fake fur, and it doesn't help that Jeremy's gotten used to the smell. The woman in the painting has had a pained expression on her face for the last few nights, and the disco ball has lost some of its pieces of mirror because Jeremy kept knocking his head on it in the morning. Jeremy and his mother haven't showered in three days.

Here is the wedding chapel, in front of them, at the end of a long driveway. Electric purple light shines on a sign that spells out HELL'S BELLS. There's a wrought-iron fence and a yard full of trees dripping Spanish moss. Under the trees, tombstones and miniature mausoleums.

"Do you think those are real?" his mother says. She sounds slightly worried.

"'Harry East, Recently Deceased,'" Jeremy says. "No, I don't."

There's a hearse in the driveway with a little plaque on the back. RECENTLY ~~BURIED~~ MARRIED. The chapel is a Victorian house with a bell tower. Perhaps it's full of bats. Or giant spiders. Jeremy's father would love this place. His mother is going to hate it.

Someone stands at the threshold of the chapel, door open, looking out at them. But as Jeremy and his mother get out of the van, he turns and goes inside and shuts the door. "Look out," his mother says. "They've probably gone to put the boiling oil in the microwave."

She rings the doorbell determinedly. Instead of ringing, there's a recording of a crow. *Caw, caw, caw.* All the lights in the Victorian house go out. Then they turn on again. The door swings open and Jeremy tightens his grip on his backpack, just in case. "Good evening, Madam. Young man," a man says and Jeremy looks up and up and up. The man at the door has to lower his head to look out. His hands are large as toaster ovens. He looks like he's wearing Chihuahua coffins on his feet. Two realistic-looking bolts stick out on either side of his head. He wears green pancake makeup, glittery green eye shadow, and his lashes are as long and thick and green as AstroTurf. "We weren't expecting you so soon."

"We should have called ahead," Jeremy's mother says. "I'm real sorry."

"Great costume," Jeremy says.

The Frankenstein curls his lip in a somber way. "Thank you," he says.

"Call me Miss Thing, please."

"I'm Jeremy," Jeremy says. "This is my mother."

"Oh please," Miss Thing says. Even his wink is somber. "You tease me. She isn't old enough to be your mother."

"Oh please, yourself," Jeremy's mother says.

"Quick, the two of you," someone yells from somewhere inside Hell's Bells. "While you zthtand there gabbing, the devil ithz prowling around like a lion, looking for a way to get in. Are you juthzt going to zthtand there and hold the door wide open for him?"

So they all step inside. "Iz that Jeremy Marthz at lathzt?" the voice says. "Earth to Marthz, Earth to Marthz. Marthzzz, Jeremy Marthzzz, there'thz zthomeone on the phone for Jeremy Marthz. She'thz called three timethz in the lathzt ten minutethz, Jeremy Marthzzzz."

It's Fox, Jeremy knows. Of course, it's Fox! She's in the phone booth. She's got the books and she's going to tell me that I saved whatever it is that I was saving. He walks toward the buzzing voice while Miss Thing and his mother go back out to the van.

He walks past a room full of artfully draped spider webs and candelabras drooping with drippy candles. Someone is playing the organ behind a wooden screen. He goes down the hall and up a long staircase. The banisters are carved with little faces. Owls and foxes and ugly children. The voice goes on talking. "Yoohoo, Jeremy, up the stairthz, that'thz right. Now, come along, come right in! Not in there, in here, in here! Don't mind the dark, we *like* the dark, just watch your step." Jeremy puts his hand out. He touches something and there's a click and the bookcase in front of him slowly slides back. Now the room is three times as large and there are more bookshelves and there's a young woman wearing dark sunglasses, sitting on a couch. She has a megaphone in one hand and a phone in the other. "For you, Jeremy Marth," she says. She's the palest person Jeremy has ever seen and her two canine teeth are so pointed that she lisps a little when she talks. On the megaphone the lisp was sinister, but now it just makes her sound irritable.

She hands him the phone. "Hello?" he says. He keeps an eye on the vampire.

"Jeremy!" Elizabeth says. "It's on, it's on, it's on! It's just started! We're all just sitting here. Everybody's here. What happened to your cell phone? We kept calling."

"Mom left it in the visitor's center at Zion," Jeremy says.

"Well, you're there. We figured out from your blog that you must be near Vegas. Amy says she had a feeling that you were going to get there in time. She made us keep calling. Stay on the phone, Jeremy. We can all watch it together, okay? Hold on."

Karl grabs the phone. "Hey, Germ, I didn't get any postcards," he says. "You forget how to write or something? Wait a minute. Somebody wants to say something to you." Then he laughs and laughs and passes the phone on to someone else who doesn't say anything at all.

"Talis?" Jeremy says.

Maybe it isn't Talis. Maybe it's Elizabeth again. He thinks about how his mouth is right next to Elizabeth's ear. Or maybe it's Talis's ear.

The vampire on the couch is already flipping through the channels. Jeremy would like to grab the remote away from her, but it's not a good idea to try to take things away from a vampire. His mother and Miss Thing come up the stairs and into the room and suddenly the room seems absolutely full of people, as if Karl and Amy and Elizabeth and Talis have come into the room, too. His hand is getting sweaty around the phone. Miss Thing has a firm hold on Jeremy's mother's painting, as if it might try to escape. Jeremy's mother looks tired. For the past three days her hair has been braided into pigtails. She looks younger to Jeremy, as if they've been traveling backwards in time instead of just across the country. She smiles at Jeremy, a giddy, exhausted smile. Jeremy smiles back.

"Is it *The Library?*" Miss Thing says. "Is a new episode on?"

Jeremy sits down on the couch beside the vampire, still holding the phone to his ear. His arm is getting tired.

"I'm here," he says to Talis or Elizabeth or whoever it is on the other end of the phone. "I'm here." And then he sits and doesn't say anything and waits with everyone else for the vampire to find the right channel so they can all find out if he's saved Fox, if Fox is alive, if Fox is still alive.

The Devil's got a flashlight with two dead batteries.

Lull

THERE WAS A LULL IN THE CONVERSATION. We were down in the basement, sitting around the green felt table. We were holding bottles of warm beer in one hand, and our cards in the other. Our cards weren't great. Looking at each others' faces, we could see that clearly.

We were tired. It made us more tired to look at each other when we saw we weren't getting away with anything at all. We didn't have any secrets.

We hadn't seen each other for a while and it was clear that we hadn't changed for the better. We were between jobs, or stuck in jobs that we hated. We were having affairs and our wives knew and didn't care. Some of us were sleeping with each others' wives. There were things that had gone wrong, and we weren't sure who to blame.

We had been talking about things that went backwards instead of forwards. Things that managed to do both at the same time. Time travelers. People who weren't stuck like us. There was that new movie that went backwards, and then Jeff put this music on the stereo where all the lyrics were palindromes. It was something his kid had picked up. His kid Stan was a lot cooler than we had ever been. He was always bringing things home, Jeff said, saying, You have got to listen to this. Here, try this. These guys are good.

Stan was the kid who got drugs for the other kids when there was going to be a party. We had tried not to be bothered by this. We trusted our kids and we hoped that they trusted us, that they weren't too embarrassed by us. We weren't cool. We were willing to be liked. That would have been enough.

Stan was so very cool that he hadn't even minded taking care of some of us, the parents of his friends (the friends of his parents), although sometimes we just went through our kids' drawers, looked under the mattresses. It wasn't that different from taking Halloween candy out of their Halloween bags, which was something we had also done, when they were younger and went to bed before we did.

Stan wasn't into that stuff now, though. None of the kids were. They were into music instead.

You couldn't get this music on CD. That was part of the conceit. It came only on cassette. You played one side, and then on the other side the songs all played backwards and the lyrics went forwards and backwards all over again in one long endless loop. La allah ha llal. Do, oh, oh, do you, oh do, oh, wanna?

Bones was really digging it. "Do you, do you wanna dance, you do, you do," he said, and laughed and tipped his chair back. "Snakey canes. Hula boolah."

Someone mentioned the restaurant downtown where you were supposed to order your dessert and then you got your dinner.

"I fold," Ed said. He threw his cards down on the table.

Ed liked to make up games. People paid him to make up games. Back when we had a regular poker night, he was always teaching us a new game and this game would be based on a TV show or some dream he'd had.

"Let's try something new. I'm going to deal out everything, the whole deck, and then we'll have to put it all back. We'll see each other's hands as we put them down. We're going for low. And we'll swap. Yeah, that might work. Something else, like a wild card, but we won't know what the wild card was, until the very end. We'll need to play fast—no stopping to think about it—just do what I tell you to do."

"What'll we call it?" he said, not a question, but as if we'd asked him, although we hadn't. He was shuffling the deck, holding the cards close like we might try to take them away. "DNA Hand. Got it?"

"That's a shitty idea," Jeff said. It was his basement, his poker table, his beer. So he got to say things like that. You could tell that he thought Ed looked happier than he ought to. He was thinking Ed ought to remember his place in the world, or maybe Ed needed to be reminded what his place was. His new place. Most of us were relieved to see that Ed looked okay. If he didn't look okay, that was okay too. We understood. Bad things had happened to all of us.

We were contemplating these things and then the tape flips over and starts again.

It's catchy stuff. We could listen to it all night.

"Now we chant along and summon the Devil," Bones says. "Always wanted to do that."

Bones has been drunk for a while now. His hair is standing up and his face is shiny and red. He has a fat stupid smile on his face. We ignore him, which is what he wants. Bones's wife is just the same, loud and useless. The thing that makes the rest of us sick is that their kids are the nicest, smartest, funniest, best kids. We can't figure it out. They don't deserve kids like that.

Brenner asks Ed if he's found a new place to live. He has.

"Off the highway, down by that Texaco, in the orchards. This guy built a road and built the house right on top of the road. Just, plop, right in the middle of the road. Kind of like he came walking up the road with the house on his back, got tired, and just dropped it."

"Not very good feng shui," Pete says.

Pete has read a book. He's got a theory about picking up women, which he's always sharing with us. He goes to Barnes & Noble on his lunch hour and hangs around in front of displays of books about houses and decorating, skimming through architecture books. He says it makes you look smart and just domesticated enough. A man looking at pictures of houses is sexy to women.

We've never asked if it works for him.

Meanwhile, we know, Pete's wife is always after him to go up on the roof and gut the drains, reshingle and patch, paint. Pete isn't really into this. Imaginary houses are sexy. Real ones are work.

He did go buy a mirror at Pottery Barn and hang it up, just inside the front door, because otherwise, he said, evil spirits go rushing up the staircase and into the bedrooms. Getting them out again is tricky.

The way the mirror works is that they start to come in, look in the mirror, and think a devil is already living in the house. So they take off. Devils can look like anyone—salespeople, Latter-day Saints, the people who mow your lawns—even members of your own family. So you have to have a mirror.

Ed says, "Where the house is, is the first weird thing. The second thing is the house. It's like this team of architects went crazy and sawed two different houses in half and then stitched them back together. Casa Del Guggenstein. The front half is really old—a hundred years old—the other half is aluminum siding."

"Must have brought down the asking price," Jeff says.

"Yeah," Ed says. "And the other thing is there are all these doors. One at the front and one at the back and two more on either side, right smack where the aluminum siding starts, these weird, tall, skinny doors, like they're built for basketball players. Or aliens."

"Or palm trees," Bones says.

"Yeah," Ed says. "Sure. Palm trees. And then one last door, this vestigial door, up in the master bedroom. Not like a door that you walk through, for a closet, or a bathroom. It opens and there's nothing there. No staircase, no balcony, no point to it. It's a Tarzan door. Up in the trees. You open it and an owl might fly in. Or a bat. The previous tenant left that door locked—apparently he was afraid of sleepwalking."

"Fantastic," Brenner says. "Wake up in the middle of the night and go to the bathroom, you could just pee out the side of your house."

He opens up the last beer and shakes some pepper in it. Brenner has a thing about pepper. He even puts it on ice cream. Pete swears that one time at a party he wandered into Brenner's bedroom and looked in a drawer in a table beside the bed. He says he found a box of condoms and a pepper mill. When we asked what he was doing in Brenner's bedroom, he winked and then put his finger to his mouth and zipped his lip.

Brenner has a little pointed goatee. It might look silly on some people, but not on Brenner. The pepper thing sounds silly, maybe, but not even Jeff teases Brenner about it.

"I remember that house," Alibi says.

We call him Alibi because his wife is always calling to check up on him. She'll say, So was Alec out shooting pool with you the other night, and we'll say, Sure he was, Gloria. The problem is that sometimes Alibi has told her some completely different story and she's just testing us. But that's not our problem and that's not our fault. She never holds it against us and neither does he.

"We used to go up in the orchards at night and have wars. Knock each other down with rotten apples. There were these peacocks. You bought the orchard house?"

"Yeah," Ed says. "I need to do something about the orchard. All the apples are falling off the trees and then they just rot on the ground. The peacocks eat them and get drunk. There are drunk wasps, too. If you go down there you can see the wasps hurtling around in these loopy lines and the peacocks grab them right out of the air. Little pickled wasp hors d'oeuvres. Everything smells like rotting apples. All night long, I'm dreaming about eating wormy apples."

For a second, we're afraid Ed might tell us his dreams. Nothing is worse than someone telling you their dreams.

"So what's the deal with the peacocks?" Bones says.

"Long story," Ed says.

So you know how the road to the house is a private road, you turn off the highway onto it, and it meanders up some until you run into the house. Some day I'll drive home and park the car in the living room.

There's a big sign that says PRIVATE. But people still drive up the turnoff, lost, or maybe looking for a picnic spot, or a place to pull off the road and fuck. Before you hear the car coming, you hear the peacocks. Which was the plan because this guy who built it was a real hermit, a recluse.

People in town said all kinds of stuff about him. Nobody knew. He didn't want anybody to know.

The peacocks were so he would know when anyone was coming up to the house. They start screaming before you ever see a car. So remember, out the back door, the road goes on down through the orchards, there's a gate and then you're back on the main highway again. And this guy, the hermit, he kept two cars. Back then, nobody had two cars. But he kept one car parked in front of the house and one parked at the back so that whichever way someone was coming, he could go out the other way real fast and drive off before his visitor got up to the house.

He had an arrangement with a grocer. The grocer sent a boy up to the house once every two weeks, and the boy brought the mail too, but there wasn't ever any mail.

The hermit had painted in the windows of his cars, black, except for these little circles that he could see out of. You couldn't see in. But apparently he used to drive around at night. People said they saw him. Or they didn't see him. That was the point.

The real estate agent said she heard that once this guy had to go to the doctor. He had a growth or something. He showed up in the doctor's office wearing a woman's hat with a long black veil that hung down from the crown, so you couldn't see his face. He took off his clothes in the doctor's office and kept the hat on.

One night half of the house fell down. People all over the town saw lights, like fireworks or lightning, up over the orchard. Some people swore they saw something big, all lit up, go up into the sky, like an explosion, but quiet. Just lights. The next day, people went up to the orchard. The hermit was waiting for them—he had his veil on. From the front, the house looked fine. But you could tell something had caught fire. You could smell it, like ozone.

The hermit said it had been lightning. He rebuilt the house himself. Had lumber and everything delivered. Apparently kids used to go sneak up in the trees in the orchard and watch him while he was working, but he did all the work wearing the hat and the veil.

He died a long time ago. The grocer's boy figured out something was wrong because the peacocks were coming in and out of the windows of the house and screaming.

So now they're still down in the orchards and under the porch, and they still came in the windows and made a mess if Ed forgot and left the windows open too wide. Last week a fox came in after a peacock. You wouldn't think a fox would go after something so big and mean. Peacocks are mean.

Ed had been downstairs watching TV.

"I heard the bird come in," he says, "and then I heard a thump and a slap like a chair going over and when I went to look, there was a streak of blood going up the floor to the window. A fox was going out the window and the peacock was in its mouth, all the feathers dragging across the sill. Like one of Susan's paintings."

Ed's wife, Susan, took an art class for a while. Her teacher said she had a lot of talent. Brenner modeled for her, and so did some of our kids, but most of Susan's paintings were portraits of her brother, Andrew. He'd been living with Susan and Ed for about two years. This was hard on Ed, although he'd never complained about it. He knew Susan loved her brother. He knew her brother had problems.

Andrew couldn't hold down a job. He went in and out of rehab, and when he was out, he hung out with our kids. Our kids thought Andrew was cool. The less we liked him, the more time our kids spent with Andrew. Maybe we were just a little jealous of him.

Jeff's kid, Stan, he and Andrew were thick as thieves. Stan was the one who found Andrew and called the hospital. Susan never said anything, but maybe she blamed Stan. Everybody knew Stan had been getting stuff for Andrew.

Another thing that nobody said: what happened to Andrew, it was probably good for the kids in the long run.

Those paintings—Susan's paintings—were weird. None of the people in her paintings ever looked very comfortable, and she couldn't do hands.

And there were always these animals in the paintings, looking as if they'd been shot, or gutted, or if they didn't look dead, they were definitely supposed to be rabid. You worried about the people.

She hung them up in their house for a while, but they weren't comfortable paintings. You couldn't watch TV in the same room with them. And Andrew had this habit, he'd sit on the sofa just under one portrait, and there was another one too, above the TV. Three Andrews was too many.

Once Ed brought Andrew to poker night. Andrew sat awhile and didn't say anything, and then he said he was going upstairs to get more beer and he never came back. Three days later, the highway patrol found Ed's car parked under a bridge. Stan and Andrew came home two days after that, and Andrew went back into rehab. Susan used to go visit him and take Stan with her—she'd take her sketchbook. Stan said Andrew would sit there and Susan would draw him and nobody ever said a word.

After the class was over, while Andrew was still in rehab, Susan invited all of us to go to this party at her teacher's studio. What we remember is that Pete got drunk and made a pass at the instructor, this sharp-looking woman with big dangly earrings. We were kind of surprised, not just because he did it in front of his wife, but because we'd all just been looking at her paintings. All these deer and birds and cows draped over dinner tables, and sofas, guts hanging out, eyeballs all shiny and fixed—so that explained Susan's portraits, at least.

We wonder what Susan did with the paintings of Andrew.

"I've been thinking about getting a dog," Ed says.

"Fuck," we say. "A dog's a big responsibility." Which is what we've spent years telling our kids.

The music on the tape loops and looped. It was going round for a second time. We sat and listened to it. We'll be sitting and listening to it for a while longer.

"This guy," Ed says, "the guy who was renting this place before me, he was into some crazy thing. There's all these mandalas and pentagrams painted on the floors and walls. Which is also why I got it so cheap. They didn't want to bother stripping the walls and repainting; this guy just took off one day, took a lot of the furniture too. Loaded up his truck with as much as he could take."

"So no furniture?" Pete says. "Susan get the dining room table and chairs? The bed? You sleeping in a sleeping bag? Eating beanie weenies out of a can?"

"I got a futon," Ed says. "And I've got my work table set up, the TV and stuff. I've been going down to the orchard, grilling on the hibachi. You guys should come over. I'm working on a new video game—it'll be a haunted house—those are really big right now. That's why this place is so great for me. I can use everything. Next weekend? I'll fix hamburgers and you guys can sit up in the house, keep cool, drink beer, test the game for me. Find the bugs."

"There are always bugs," Jeff says. He's smiling in a mean way. He isn't so nice when he's been drinking. "That's life. So should we bring the kids? The wives? Is this a family thing? Ellie's been asking about you. You know that retreat she's on, she called from the woods the other day. She went on and on about this past life. Apparently she was a used-car salesman. She says that this life is karmic payback, being married to me, right? She gets home day after tomorrow. We get together, maybe Ellie can set you up with someone. Now that you're a free man, you need to take some advantage."

"Sure," Ed says, and shrugs. We can see him wishing that Jeff would shut up, but Jeff doesn't shut up.

Jeff says, "I saw Susan in the grocery store the other day. She looked fantastic. It wasn't that she wasn't sad anymore, she wasn't just getting by, she was radiant, you know? That special glow. Like Joan of Arc. Like she knew something. Like she'd won the lottery."

"Well, yeah," Ed says. "That's Susan. She doesn't live in the past. She's got this new job, this research project. They're trying to contact aliens. They're using household appliances: satellite dishes, cell phones, car radios, even refrigerators. I'm not sure how. I'm not sure what they're planning to say. But they've got a lot of grant money. Even hired a speechwriter."

"Wonder what you say to aliens," Brenner says. "Hi, honey, I'm home. What's for dinner?"

"Your place or mine?" Pete says. "What's a nice alien like you doing in a galaxy like this?"

"Where you been? I've been worried sick," Alibi says.

Jeff picks up a card, props it sideways against the green felt. Picks up another one, leans it against the first. He says, "You and Susan always looked so good together. Perfect marriage, perfect life. Now look at you: she's talking to aliens, and you're living in a haunted house. You're an example to all of us, Ed. Nice guy like you, bad things happen to you, Susan leaves a swell guy like you, what's the lesson here? I've been thinking about this all year. You and Ellie must have worked at the same car dealership, in that past life."

Nobody says anything. Ed doesn't say anything, but the way we see him look at Jeff, we know that this haunted house game is going to have a character in it who walks and talks a lot like Jeff. This Jeff character is going to panic and run around on the screen of people's TVs and get lost.

It will stumble into booby traps and fall onto knives. Its innards will sloop out. Zombies are going to crack open the bones of its legs and suck on the marrow. Little devils with monkey faces are going to stitch its eyes open with tiny stitches and then they are going to piss ribbons of acid into its eyes.

Beautiful women are going to fuck this cartoon Jeff in the ass with garden shears. And when this character screams, it's going to sound a lot like Jeff screaming. Ed's good at the little details. The kids who buy Ed's games love the details. They buy his games for things like this.

Jeff will probably be flattered.

Jeff starts complaining about Stan's phone bill, this four-hundred-dollar cell phone charge that Stan ran up. When he asked about it, Stan handed him a stack of twenties just like that. That kid always has money to spare.

Stan also gave Jeff this phone number. He told Jeff that it's like this phone sex line, but with a twist. You call up and ask for this girl named

Starlight, and she tells you sexy stories, only, if you want, they don't have to be sexy. They can be any kind of story you want. You tell her what kind of story you want, and she makes it up. Stan says it's Stephen King and sci-fi and the *Arabian Nights* and *Penthouse Letters* all at once.

Ed interrupts Jeff. "You got the number?"

"What?" Jeff says.

"I just got paid for the last game," Ed says. "The one with the baby heads and the octopus girlies, the Martian combat hockey. Let's call that number. I'll pay. You put her on speaker and we'll all listen, and it's my treat, okay, because I'm such a swell guy."

Bones says that it sounds like a shit idea to him, which is probably why Jeff went and got the phone bill and another six-pack of beer. We all take another beer.

Jeff turns the stereo down—

Madam I'm Adam

Oh Madam my Adam

—and puts the phone in the middle of the table. It sits there, in the middle of all that green, like an island or something. Marooned. Jeff switches it on speaker. "Four bucks a minute," he says, and shrugs, and dials the number.

"Here," Ed says. "Pass it over."

The phone rings and we listen to it ring and then a woman's voice, very pleasant, says hello and asks if Ed is over eighteen. He says he is. He gives her his credit card number. She asks if he was calling for anyone in particular.

"Starlight," Ed says.

"One moment," the woman says. We hear a click and then Starlight is on the line. We know this because she says so. She says, "Hi, my name is Starlight. I'm going to tell you a sexy story. Do you want to know what I'm wearing?"

Ed grunts. He shrugs. He grimaces at us. He needs a haircut. Susan used to cut his hair, which we used to think was cute. He and Andrew had these identical lopsided haircuts. It was pretty goofy.

"Can I call you Susan?" Ed says.

Which we think is strange.

Starlight says, "If you really want to, but my name's really Starlight. Don't you think that's sexy?"

She sounds like a kid. A little girl—not even like a girl. Like a kid. She doesn't sound like Susan at all. Since the divorce, we haven't seen much of Susan, although she calls our houses sometimes, to talk to our wives. We're a little worried about what she's been saying to them.

Ed says, "I guess so." We can tell he's only saying that to be polite, but Starlight laughs as if he's told her a joke. It's weird hearing that little-kid laugh down here.

Ed says, "So are you going to tell me a story?"

Starlight says, "That's what I'm here for. But usually the guy wants to know what I'm wearing."

Ed says, "I want to hear a story about a cheerleader and the Devil."

Bones says, "So what's she wearing?"

Pete says, "Make it a story that goes backwards."

Jeff says, "Put something scary in it."

Alibi says, "Sexy."

Brenner says, "I want it to be about good and evil and true love, and it should also be funny. No talking animals. Not too much fooling around with the narrative structure. The ending should be happy but still realistic, believable, you know, and there shouldn't be a moral although we should be able to think back later and have some sort of revelation. No *and suddenly they woke up and discovered that it was all a dream.* Got that?"

Starlight says, "Okay. The Devil and a cheerleader. Got it. Okay."

The Devil and the Cheerleader

So the Devil is at a party at the cheerleader's house. They've been playing spin the bottle. The cheerleader's boyfriend just came out of the closet with her best friend. Earlier the cheerleader felt like slapping him, and now she knows why. The bottle pointed at her best friend who had just shrugged and smiled at her. Then the bottle was spinning and when the bottle stopped spinning, it was in her boyfriend's hand.

Then all of a sudden an egg timer was going off. Everyone was giggling and they were all standing up to go over by the closet, like they were all going to try to squeeze inside. But the Devil stood up and took the cheerleader's hand and pulled her backwards-forwards.

So she knew what exactly had happened, and was going to happen, and some other things besides.

This is the thing she likes about backwards. You start out with all the answers, and after a while, someone comes along and gives you the questions, but you don't have to answer them. You're already past that part. That was what was so nice about being married. Things got better and better until you hardly even knew each other anymore. And then you said good night and went out on a date, and after that you were just friends. It was easier that way—that's the dear, sweet, backwards way of the world.

Just a second, let's go back for a second.

Something happened. Something has happened. But nobody ever talked about it, at least not at these parties. Not anymore.

Everyone's been drinking all night long, except the Devil, who's a teetotaler. He's been pretending to drink vodka out of a hip flask. Everybody at the party is drunk right now and they think he's okay. Later they'll sober up. They'll think he's pretentious, an asshole, drinking air out of a flask like that.

There are a lot of empty bottles of beer, some empty bottles of whiskey. There's a lot of work still to be done, by the look of it. They're using one of the beer bottles, that's what they're spinning. Later on it will be full and they won't have to play this stupid game.

The cheerleader guesses that she didn't invite the Devil to the party. He isn't the kind of guy that you have to invite. He'll probably show up by himself. But now they're in the closet together for five minutes. The cheerleader's boyfriend isn't too happy about this, but what can he do? It's that kind of party. She's that kind of cheerleader.

They're a lot younger than they used to be. At parties like this, they used to be older, especially the Devil. He remembers all the way back to the end of the world. The cheerleader wasn't a cheerleader then. She was married and had kids and a husband.

Something's going to happen, or maybe it's already happened. Nobody ever talks about it. If they could, what would they say?

But those end-of-the-world parties were crazy. People would drink too much and they wouldn't have any clothes on. There'd be these sad little piles of clothes in the living room, as if something had happened, and the people had disappeared, disappeared right out of their clothes. Meanwhile, the people who belonged to the clothes would be out in the backyard, waiting until it was time to go home. They'd get up on the trampoline and bounce around and cry.

There would be a bottle of extra-virgin olive oil and sooner or later someone was going to have to refill it and go put it back on the pantry shelf. You'd have had these slippery naked middle-aged people sliding around on the trampoline and the oily grass, and then in the end all you'd have would be a bottle of olive oil, some olives on a tree, a tree, an orchard, an empty field.

The Devil would stand around feeling awkward, hoping that it would turn out he'd come late.

The kids would be up in their bedrooms, out of the beds, looking out the windows, remembering when they used to be older. Not that they ever got that much older.

But the world is younger now. Things are simpler. Now the cheerleader has parents of her own, and all she has to do is wait for them to get home, and then this party can be over.

Two days ago was the funeral. It was just how everyone said it would be.

Then there were errands, people to talk to. She was busy.

She hugged her aunt and uncle good-bye and moved into the house where she would live for the rest of her life. She unpacked all her boxes, and the Salvation Army brought her parents' clothes and furniture and pots and pans, and other people, her parents' friends, helped her hang her mother's clothes in her mother's closet. (Not this closet.) She bunched her mother's clothes up in her hand and sniffed, curious and hungry and afraid.

She suspects, remembering the smell of her mother's monogrammed sweaters, that they'll have fights about things. Boys, music, clothes. The cheerleader will learn to let all of these things go.

If her kids were still around, they would say I told you so. What they did say was, Just wait until you have parents of your own. You'll see.

The cheerleader rubs her stomach. Are you in there?

She moved the unfamiliar, worn-down furniture around so that it matched up old grooves in the floor. Here was the shape of someone's buttocks, printed onto a seat cushion. Maybe it would be her father's favorite chair.

She looked through her father's records. There was a record playing on the phonograph, it wasn't anything she had ever heard before, and she took it off, laid it back in its empty white sleeve. She studied the death certificates. She tried to think what to tell her parents about their grandchildren, what they'd want to know.

Her favorite song had just been on the radio for the very last time. Years and years ago, she'd danced to that song at her wedding. Now it was gone, except for the feeling she'd had when she listened to it. Sometimes she still felt that way, but there wasn't a word for it anymore.

Tonight, in a few hours, there will be a car wreck and then her parents will be coming home. By then, all her friends will have left, taking away six-packs and boyfriends and newly applied coats of hair spray and lipstick.

She thinks she looks a bit like her mother.

Before everyone showed up, while everything was still a wreck downstairs, before the police had arrived to say what they had to say, she was standing in her parents' bathroom. She was looking in the mirror.

She picked a lipstick out of the trash can, an orangey red that will be a favorite because there's just a little half-moon left. But when she looked at herself in the mirror, it didn't fit. It didn't belong to her. She put her hand on her breastbone, pressed hard, felt her heart beating faster and faster. She couldn't wear her mother's lipstick while her mother lay on a gurney somewhere in a morgue: waiting to be sewn up; to have her clothes sewn back on; to breathe; to wake up; to see the car on the other side of the median, sliding away; to see her husband, the man that she's going to marry someday; to come home to meet her daughter.

The recently dead are always exhausted. There's so much to absorb, so many things that need to be undone. They have their whole lives ahead of them.

The cheerleader's best friend winks at her. The Devil's got a flashlight with two dead batteries. Somebody closes the door after them.

Soon, very soon, already now, the batteries in the Devil's flashlight are old and tired and there's just a thin line of light under the closet door. It's cramped in the closet and it smells like shoes, paint, wool, cigarettes, tennis rackets, ghosts of perfume and sweat. Outside the closet, the world is getting younger, but in here is where they keep all the old things. The cheerleader put them all in here last week.

She's felt queasy for most of her life. She's a bad time traveler. She gets time-sick. It's as if she's always just a little bit pregnant, are you in there? and it's worse in here, with all these old things that don't belong to her, even worse because the Devil is always fooling around with time.

The Devil feels right at home. He and the cheerleader make a nest of coats and sit down on them, facing each other. The Devil turns the bright, constant beam of the flashlight on the cheerleader. She's wearing a little flippy skirt. Her knees are up, making a tent out of her skirt. The tent is full of shadows—so is the closet. The Devil conjures up another Devil, another cheerleader, mouse-sized, both of them, sitting under the cheerleader's skirt. The closet is full of Devils and cheerleaders.

"I just need to hold something," the cheerleader says. If she holds something, maybe she won't throw up.

"Please," the Devil says. "It tickles. I'm ticklish."

The cheerleader is leaning forward. She's got the Devil by the tail. Then she's touching the Devil's tail with her pompoms. He quivers.

"Please don't," he says. He giggles.

The Devil's tail is tucked up under his legs. It isn't hot, but the Devil is sweating. He feels sad. He's not good at being sad. He flicks the flashlight on and off. Here's a knee. Here's a mouth. Here's a sleeve hanging down, all empty. Someone knocks on the closet door.

"Go away," the cheerleader says. "It hasn't been five minutes yet. Not even."

The Devil can feel her smile at him, like they're old friends. "Your tail. Can I touch it?" the cheerleader says.

"Touch what?" the Devil says. He feels a little excited, a little nervous. Old enough to know better, brand-new enough, here in the closet, to be jumpy. He's taking a chance here. Girls—women—aren't really domestic animals at the moment, although they're getting tamer, more used to living in houses. Less likely to bite.

"Can I touch your tail now?" the cheerleader says.

"No!" the Devil says.

"I'm shy," he says. "Maybe you could stroke my tail with your pompom, in a little bit."

"We could make out," the cheerleader says. "That's what we're supposed to do, right? I need to be distracted because I think I'm about to have this thought. It's going to make me really sad. I'm getting younger, you know? I'm going to keep on getting younger. It isn't fair."

She puts her feet against the closet door. She kicks once, like a mule.

She says, "I mean, you're the Devil. You don't have to worry about this stuff. In a few thousand years, you'll be back at the beginning again and you'll be in good with God again, right?"

The Devil shrugs. Everybody knows the end of that story.

The cheerleader says, "Everyone knows that old story. You're famous.

You're like John Wilkes Booth. You're historical—you're going to be really important. You'll be Mr. Bringer-of-Light and you'll get good tables at all the trendy restaurants, choruses of angels and maître d's, et cetera, la, la, la, they'll all be singing hallelujahs forever, please pass the vichyssoise, and then God unmakes the world and he'll put all the bits away in a closet like this."

The Devil smirks. He shrugs. It isn't a bad life, hanging around in closets with cheerleaders. And it gets better.

The cheerleader says, "It isn't fair. I'd tell him so, if he were here. He'll unhang the stars and pull Leviathan right back out of the deep end of the vasty bathwater, and you'll be having Leviathan tartare for dinner. Where will I be, then? You'll be around. You're always around. But me, I'll get younger and younger and in a handful of years I won't be me at all, and my parents will get younger and so on and so on, whoosh! We'll be gone like a flash of light, and you won't even remember me. Nobody will remember me! Everything that I was, that I did, all the funny things that I said, and the things that my friends said back to me, that will all be gone. But you go all the way backwards. You go backwards and forwards. It isn't fair. You could always remember me. What could I do so that you would remember me?"

"As long as we're in this closet," the Devil says, he's magnanimous, "I'll remember you."

"But in a few minutes," the cheerleader says, "we'll go back out of the closet and the bottle will spin, and then the party will be over, and my parents will come home, and nobody will ever remember me."

"Then tell me a story," the Devil says. He puts his sharp, furry paw on her leg. "Tell me a story so that I'll remember you."

"What kind of story?" says the cheerleader.

"Tell me a scary story," the Devil says. "A funny, scary, sad, happy story. I want everything." He can feel his tail wagging as he says this.

"You can't have everything," the cheerleader says, and she picks up his paw and puts it back on the floor of the closet. "Not even in a story. You can't have all the stories you want."

"I know," the Devil says. He whines. "But I still want it. I want things. That's my job. I even want the things that I already have. I want everything you have. I want the things that don't exist. That's why I'm the Devil." He leers and it's a shame because she can't see him in the dark. He feels silly.

"Well, what's the scariest thing?" says the cheerleader. "You're the expert, right? Give me a little help here."

"The scariest thing," the Devil says. "Okay, I'll give you two things. Three things. No, just two. The third one is a secret."

The Devil's voice changes. Later on, one day the cheerleader will be listening to a preschool teacher say back the alphabet, with the sun moving across the window, nothing ever stays still, and she'll be reminded of the Devil and the closet and the line of light under the door, the peaceful little circle of light the flashlight makes against the closet door.

The Devil says, "I'm not complaining," (but he is) "but here's the way things used to work. They don't work this way anymore. I don't know if you remember. Your parents are dead and they're coming home in just a few hours. Used to be, that was scary. Not anymore. But try to imagine: finding something that shouldn't be there."

"Like what?" the cheerleader says.

The Devil shrugs. "A child's toy. A ball, or a night-light. Some cheap bit of trash, but it's heavier than it looks, or else light. It shines with a greasy sort of light or else it eats light. When you touch it, it yields unpleasantly. You feel as if you might fall into it. You feel light-headed. It might be inscribed in a language which no one can decipher."

"Okay," the cheerleader says. She seems somewhat cheered up. "So what's the next thing?"

The Devil shines the flashlight in her eyes, flicks it on and off. "Someone disappears. Gone, just like that. They're standing behind you in a line at an amusement park—or they wander away during the intermission of a play—perhaps they go downstairs to get the mail—or to make tea—"

"That's scary?" the cheerleader says.

"Used to be," the Devil says. "It used to be that the worst thing that could happen was, if you had kids, and one of them died or disappeared. Disappeared was the worst. Anything might have happened to them."

"Things are better now," the cheerleader says.

"Yes, well." The Devil says, "Things just get better and better nowadays. But—try to remember how it was. The person who disappeared, only they didn't. You'd see them from time to time, peeking in at you through windows, or down low through the mail slot in your front door. Keyholes. You might see them in the grocery store. Sitting in the backseat of your car, down low, slouching in your rearview mirror. They might pinch your leg or pull your hair when you're asleep. When you talk on the phone, they listen in, you hear them listening.

The cheerleader says, "Like, with my parents—"

"Exactly," says the Devil. "You've had nightmares about them, right?"

"Not really," the cheerleader says. "Everyone says they were probably nice people. I mean, look at this house! But, sometimes, I have this dream that I'm at the mall, and I see my husband. And he's just the same, he's a grown-up, and he doesn't recognize me. It turns out that I'm the only one who's going backwards. And then he does recognize me and he wants to know what I've done with the kids."

The last time she'd seen her husband, he was trying to grow a beard. He couldn't even do that right. He hadn't had much to say, but they'd looked at each other for a long time.

"What about your children?" the Devil says. "Do you wonder where they went when the doctor pushed them back up inside you? Do you have dreams about them?"

"Yes," the cheerleader says. "Everything gets smaller. I'm afraid of that."

"Think how men feel!" the Devil says. "It's no wonder men are afraid of women. No wonder sex is so hard on them."

The cheerleader misses sex, that feeling afterwards, that blissful, unsatisfied itch.

"The first time around, things were better," the Devil says. "I don't know if you remember. People died, and no one was sure what happened next. There were all sorts of possibilities. Now everyone knows everything. What's the fun in that?"

Someone is trying to push open the closet door, but the cheerleader puts her feet against it, leaning against the back of the closet. "Oh, I remember!" she says, "I remember when I was dead! There was so much I was looking forward to. I had no idea!"

The Devil shivers. He's never liked dead people much.

"So, okay, what about monsters?" the cheerleader says. "Vampires? Serial killers? People from outer space? Those old movies?"

The Devil shrugs. "Yeah, sure. Boogeymen. Formaldehyde babies in Mason jars. Someday someone is going to have to take them out of the jar, unpickle them. Women with teeth down there. Zombies. Killer robots, killer bees, serial killers, cold spots, werewolves. The dream where you know that you're asleep but you can't wake up. You can hear someone walking around the bedroom picking up your things and putting them down again and you still can't wake up. The end of the world. Spiders. *No one was with her when she died.* Carnivorous plants."

"Oh goody," the cheerleader says. Her eyes shine at him out of the dark. Her pompoms slide across the floor of the closet. He moves his flashlight so he can see her hands.

"So here's your story," the cheerleader says. She's a girl who can think on her feet. "It's not really a scary story. I don't really get scary."

"Weren't you listening?" the Devil says. He taps the flashlight against his big front teeth. "Never mind, it's okay, never mind. Go on."

"This probably isn't a true story," the cheerleader says, "and it doesn't go backwards like we do. I probably won't get all the way to the end, and I'm not going to start at the beginning, either. There isn't enough time."

"That's fine," the Devil says. "I'm all ears." (He is.)

The cheerleader says, "So who's going to tell this story, anyway? Be quiet and listen. We're running out of time."

She says, "A man comes home from a sales conference. He and his wife have been separated for a while, but they've decided to try living together again. They've sold the house that they used to live in. Now they live just outside of town, in an old house in an orchard.

The man comes home from this business conference, and his wife is sitting in the kitchen and she's talking to another woman, an older woman. They're sitting on the chairs that used to go around the kitchen table, but the table is gone. So is the microwave, and the rack where Susan's copper-bottomed pots hang. The pots are gone, too.

The husband doesn't notice any of this. He's busy looking at the other woman. Her skin has a greenish tinge. He has this feeling that he knows her. She and the wife both look at the husband, and he suddenly knows what it is. It's his wife. It's his wife, two of her, only one is maybe twenty years older. Otherwise, except that this one's green, they're identical: same eyes, same mouth, same little mole at the corner of her mouth.

"How am I doing so far?"

"So-so," the Devil says. The truth (the truth makes the Devil itchy) is, he only likes stories about himself. Like the story about the Devil's wedding cake. Now that's a story.

The cheerleader says, "It gets better."

It Gets Better

The man's name is Ed. It isn't his real name. I made it up. Ed and Susan have been married for ten years, separated for five months, back together again for three months. They've been sleeping in the same bed for three months, but they don't have sex. Susan cries whenever Ed kisses her. They don't have any kids. Susan used to have a younger brother. Ed is thinking about getting a dog.

While Ed's been at his conference, Susan has been doing some housework. She's done some work up in the attic which we won't talk about. Not yet. Down in the spare bathroom in the basement, she's set up this machine, which we get around to later, and this machine makes Susans. What Susan was hoping for was a machine that would bring back Andrew. (Her brother. But you knew that.) Only it turns out that getting Andrew back requires a different machine, a bigger machine. Susan needs help making that machine, and so the new Susans are going to come in handy after all. Over the course of the next few days, the Susans explain all this to Ed.

Susan doesn't expect Ed will be very helpful.

"Hi, Ed," the older, greenish Susan says. She gets up from her chair and gives him a big hug. Her skin is warm, tacky. She smells yeasty. The original Susan—the Susan Ed thinks is original, and I have no idea if he's right about this, and, later on, he isn't so sure, either—sits in her chair and watches them.

Big green Susan: am I making her sound like Godzilla? She doesn't look like Godzilla, and yet there's something about her that reminds Ed of Godzilla, the way she stomps across the kitchen floor—leads Ed over to a chair and makes him sit down. Now he realizes that the kitchen table is gone. He still hasn't managed to say a word. Susan, both of them, is used to this.

"First of all," Susan says, "the attic is off-limits. There are some people working up there. (I don't mean Susans. I'll explain Susans in a minute.) Some visitors. They're helping me with a project. About the other Susans, there are five of me at the moment—you'll meet the other three later. They're down in the basement. You're allowed in the basement. You can help down there, if you want."

Godzilla Susan says, "You don't have to worry about who is who, although none of us are exactly alike. You can call us all Susan. We're discovering that some of us may be more temporary than others, or fatter, or younger, or greener. It seems to depend on the batch."

"Are you Susan?" Ed says. He corrects himself. "I mean, are you my wife? The real Susan?"

"We're all your wife," the younger Susan says. She puts her hand on his leg and pats him like a dog.

"Where did the kitchen table go?" Ed says.

"I put it in the attic," Susan says. "You really don't have to worry about that now. How was your conference?"

Another Susan comes into the kitchen. She's young and the color of green apples or new grass. Even the whites of her eyes are grassy. She's maybe nineteen, and the color of her skin makes Ed think of a snake. "Ed!" she says, "How was the conference?"

"They're keen on the new game," Ed says. "It tests real well."

"Want a beer?" Susan says. (It doesn't matter which Susan says this.) She picks up a pitcher of green foamy stuff, and pours it into a glass.

"This is beer?" Ed says.

"It's Susan beer," Susan says, and all the Susans laugh.

The beautiful, snake-colored nineteen-year-old Susan takes Ed on a tour of the house. Mostly Ed just looks at Susan, but he sees that the television is gone, and so are all of his games. All his notebooks. The living room sofa is still there, but all the seat cushions are missing. Later on, Susan will disassemble the sofa with an ax.

Susan has covered up all the downstairs windows with what looks like sheets of aluminum foil. She shows him the bathtub downstairs where one of the Susans is brewing the Susan beer. Other Susans are hanging long, mossy clots of the Susan beer on laundry racks. Dry, these clots can be shaped into bedding, nests for the new Susans. They are also edible.

Ed is still holding the glass of Susan beer. "Go on," Susan says. "You like beer."

"I don't like green beer," Ed says.

"You like Susan, though," Susan says. She's wearing one of his T-shirts, and a pair of Susan's underwear. No bra. She puts Ed's hand on her breast.

Susan stops stirring the beer. She's taller than Ed, and only a little bit green. "You know Susan loves you," she says.

"Who's up in the attic?" Ed says. "Is it Andrew?"

His hand is still on Susan's breast. He can feel her heart beating. Susan says, "You can't tell Susan I told you. She doesn't think you're ready. It's the aliens."

They both stare at him. "She finally got them on the phone. This is going to be huge, Ed. This is going to change the world."

ଔ

Ed could leave the house. He could leave Susan. He could refuse to drink the beer.

The Susan beer doesn't make him drunk. It isn't really beer. You knew that, right?

There are Susans everywhere. Some of them want to talk to Ed about their marriage, or about the aliens, or sometimes they want to talk about Andrew. Some of them are busy working. The Susans are always dragging Ed off to empty rooms, to talk or kiss or make love or gossip about the other Susans. Or they're ignoring him. There's one very young Susan. She looks like she might be six or seven years old. She goes up and down the upstairs hallway, drawing on the walls with a marker. Ed isn't sure whether this is childish vandalism or important Susan work. He feels awkward asking.

Every once in a while, he thinks he sees the real Susan. He wishes he could sit down and talk with her, but she always looks so busy.

By the end of the week, there aren't any mirrors left in the house, and the windows are all covered up. The Susans have hung sheets of the Susan beer over all the light fixtures, so everything is green. Ed isn't sure, but he thinks he might be turning green.

Susan tastes green. She always does.

Once Ed hears someone knocking on the front door. "Ignore that," Susan says as she walks past him. She's carrying the stacked blades of an old ceiling fan, and a string of Christmas lights. "It isn't important."

Ed pulls the plug of aluminum foil out of the eyehole, and peeks out. Stan is standing there, looking patient. They stand there, Ed on one side of the door, and Stan on the other. Ed doesn't open the door, and eventually Stan goes away. All the peacocks are kicking up a fuss.

Ed tries teaching some of the Susans to play poker. It doesn't work so well, because it turns out that Susan always knows what cards the other Susans are holding. So Ed makes up a game where that doesn't matter so much, but in the end, it makes him feel too lonely. There aren't any other Eds.

They decide to play spin the bottle instead. Instead of a bottle, they use a hammer, and it never ends up pointing at Ed. After a while, it gets too strange watching Susan kiss Susans, and he wanders off to look for a Susan who will kiss him.

Up in the second-story bedroom, there are always lots of Susans. This is where they go to wait when they start to get ripe. The Susans loll, curled in their nests, getting riper, arguing about the end of some old story. None of them remember it the same way. Some of them don't seem to know anything about it, but they all have opinions.

Ed climbs into a nest and leans back. Susan swings her legs over to make room for him. This Susan is small and round. She tickles the soft part of his arm, and then tucks her face into his side.

Susan passes him a glass of Susan beer.

"That's not it," Susan says, "It turns out that he overdosed. Maybe even did it on purpose. We couldn't talk about it. There weren't enough of us. We were trying to carry all that sadness all by ourself. You can't do something like that! And then the wife tries to kill him. I tried to kill him. She kicks the fuck out of him. He can't leave the house for a week, won't even come to the door when his friends come over."

"If you can call them friends," Susan says.

"No, there was a gun," Susan says. "And she has an affair. Because she can't get over it. Neither of them can."

"She humiliates him at a dinner party," Susan says. "They both drink too much. Everybody goes home, and she breaks all the dishes instead of washing them. There are plate shards all over the kitchen floor. Someone's going to get hurt; they don't have a time machine. They can't go back and unbreak those plates. We know that they still loved each other, but that doesn't matter anymore. Then the police showed up."

"Well, that's not the way I remember it," Susan says. "But I guess it could have happened that way."

Ed and Susan used to buy books all the time. They had so many books they used to joke about wanting to be quarantined, or snowed in. Maybe then they'd manage to read all the books. But the books have all gone up to the attic, along with the lamps and the coffee tables, and their bicycles, and all Susan's paintings. Ed has watched the Susans carry up paperback books, silverware, old board games, and holey underwear. Even a kazoo. The Encyclopædia Britannica. The goldfish and the goldfish bowl and the little canister of goldfish food.

The Susans have gone through the house, taken everything they could. After all the books were gone, they dismantled the bookshelves. Now they're tearing off the wallpaper in long strips. The aliens seem to like books. They like everything, especially Susan. Eventually when the Susans are ripe, they go up in the attic too.

The aliens swap things, the books and the Susans and the coffee mugs for other things: machines that the Susans are assembling. Ed would like to get his hand on one of those devices, but Susan says no. He isn't even allowed to help, except with the Susan beer.

The thing the Susans are building takes up most of the living room, Ed's office, the kitchen, the laundry room—

The Susans don't bother with laundry. The washer and the dryer are both gone and the Susans have given up wearing clothes altogether. Ed has managed to keep a pair of shorts and a pair of jeans. He's wearing the shorts right now, and he folds the jeans up into a pillow, and rests his head on top of them so that Susan can't steal them. All his other clothes have been carried up to the attic

—and it's creeping up the stairs, spilling over into the second story. The house is shiny with alien machines.

Teams of naked Susans are hard at work, all day long, testing instruments, hammering and stitching their machine together, polishing and dusting and stacking alien things on top of each other. If you're wondering what the machine looks like, picture a science fair project involving a lot of aluminum foil, improvised, homely, makeshift, and just a little dangerous-looking. None of the Susans is quite sure what the machine will eventually do. Right now it grows Susan beer.

When the beer is stirred, left alone, stirred some more, it clots and makes more Susans. Ed likes watching this part. The house is more and more full of shy, loud, quiet, talkative, angry, happy, greenish Susans of all sizes, all ages, who work at disassembling the house, piece by piece, and, piece by piece, assembling the machine.

It might be a time machine, or a machine to raise the dead, or maybe the house is becoming a spaceship, slowly, one room at a time. Susan says the aliens don't make these kinds of distinctions. It may be an invasion factory, Ed says, or a doomsday machine. Susan says that they aren't that kind of aliens.

Ed's job: stirring the Susan beer with a long, flat plank—a floorboard Susan pried up—and skimming the foam, which has a stringy and unpleasantly cheeselike consistency, into buckets. He carries the buckets downstairs and makes Susan beer soufflé and Susan beer casserole. Susan beer surprise. Upside-down Susan cake. It all tastes the same, and he grows to like the taste.

The beer doesn't make him drunk. That isn't what it's for. I can't tell you what it's for. But when he's drinking it, he isn't sad. He has the beer, and the work in the kitchen, and the ripe, green fuckery. Everything tastes like Susan.

The only thing he misses is poker nights.

Up in the spare bedroom, Ed falls asleep listening to the Susans talk, and when he wakes up, his jeans are gone, and he's naked. The room is empty. All the ripe Susans have gone up to the attic.

When he steps out into the hall, the little Susan is out there, drawing on the walls. She puts her marker down and hands him a pitcher of Susan beer. She pinches his leg and says, "You're getting nice and ripe."

Then she winks at Ed and runs down the hall.

He looks at what she's been drawing: Andrew, scribbly crayon portraits of Andrew, all up and down the walls. He follows the pictures of Andrew down the hall, all the way to the master bedroom where he and the original

Susan used to sleep. Now he sleeps anywhere, with any Susan. He hasn't been in their room in a while, although he's noticed the Susans going in and out with boxes full of things. The Susans are always shooing at him when he gets in their way.

The bedroom is full of Andrew. There are Susan's portraits of Andrew on the walls, the ones from her art class. Ed had forgotten how unpleasant and peculiar these paintings are. In one, the largest one, Andrew, life-sized, has his hands around a small animal, maybe a ferret. He seems to be strangling it. The ferret's mouth is cocked open, showing all its teeth. A picture like that, Ed thinks, you ought to turn it towards the wall at night.

Susan's put Andrew's bed in here, and Andrew's books, and Andrew's desk. Andrew's clothes have been hung up in the closet. There isn't an alien machine in the room, or for that matter, anything that ever belonged to Ed.

Ed puts a pair of Andrew's pants on, and lies down on Andrew's bed, just for a minute, and he closes his eyes.

When he wakes up, Susan is sitting on the bed. He can smell her, that ripe green scent. He can smell that smell on himself. Susan says, "If you're ready, I thought we could go up to the attic together."

"What's going on here?" Ed says. "I thought you needed everything. Shouldn't all this stuff go up to the attic?"

"This is Andrew's room, for when he comes back," Susan says. "We thought it would make him feel comfortable, having his own bed to sleep in. He might need his stuff."

"What if the aliens need his stuff?" Ed says. "What if they can't make you a new Andrew yet because they don't know enough about him?"

"That's not how it works," Susan says. "We're getting close now. Can't you feel it?"

"I feel weird," Ed says. "Something's happening to me."

"You're ripe, Ed," Susan says. "Isn't that fantastic? We weren't sure you'd ever get ripe enough."

She takes his hand and pulls him up. Sometimes he forgets how strong she is.

"So what happens now?" Ed says. "Am I going to die? I don't feel sick. I feel good. What happens when we get ripe?"

The afternoon light makes Susan look older, or maybe she just is older. He likes this part: seeing what Susan looked like as a kid, what she'll look like as an old lady. It's as if they got to spend their whole lives together. "I never know," she says. "Let's go find out. Take off Andrew's pants, and I'll hang them back up in the closet."

They leave the bedroom and walk down the hall. The Andrew drawings, the knobs and dials and stacked, shiny machinery watch them go. There aren't any other Susans around at the moment. They're all busy downstairs. He can hear them hammering away. For a minute, it's the way it used to be, only better. Just Ed and Susan in their own house.

Ed holds on tight to Susan's hand.

When Susan opens the attic door, the attic is full of stars. Stars and stars and stars. Ed has never seen so many stars. Susan has taken the roof off. Off in the distance, they can smell the apple trees, way down in the orchard.

Susan sits down cross-legged on the floor and Ed sits down beside her. She says, "I wish you'd tell me a story."

Ed says, "What kind of story?"

Susan says, "A bedtime story? When Andrew was a kid, we used to read this book. I remember this one story about people who go under a hill. They spend one night down there, eating and drinking and dancing, but when they come out, a hundred years have gone by. Do you know how long it's been since Andrew died? I've lost track."

"I don't know stories like that," Ed says. He picks at his flaky green skin and wonders what he tastes like. "What do you think the aliens look like? Do you think they look like giraffes? Like marbles? Like Andrew? Do you think they have mouths?"

"Don't be silly," Susan says. "They look like us."

"How do you know?" Ed says. "Have you been up here before?"

"No," Susan says. "But Susan has."

"We could play a card game," Ed says. "Or I Spy."

"You could tell me about the first time I met you," Susan says.

"I don't want to talk about that," Ed says. "That's all gone."

"Okay, fine." Susan sits up straight, arches her back, runs her green tongue across her green lips. She winks at Ed and says, "Tell me how beautiful I am."

"You're beautiful," Ed says. "I've always thought you were beautiful. All of you. How about me? Am I beautiful?"

"Don't be that way," Susan says. She slouches back against him. Her skin is warm and greasy. "The aliens are going to get here soon. I don't know what happens after that, but I hate this part. I always hate this part. I don't like waiting. Do you think this is what it was like for Andrew, when he was in rehab?"

"When you get him back, ask him. Why ask me?"

Susan doesn't say anything for a bit. Then she says, "We think we'll be able to make you, too. We're starting to figure out how it works. Eventually it will be you and me and him, just the way it was before. Only we'll fix him the way we've fixed me. He won't be so sad. Have you noticed how I'm not sad anymore? Don't you want that, not to be sad? And maybe after that we'll try making some more people. We'll start all over again. We'll do everything right this time."

Ed says, "So why are they helping you?"

"I don't know," Susan says. "Either they think we're funny, or else they think we're pathetic, the way we get stuck. We can ask them when they get here."

She stands up, stretches, yawns, sits back down on Ed's lap, reaches down, stuffs his penis, half-erect, inside of her. Just like that. Ed groans.

He says, "Susan."

Susan says, "Tell me a story." She squirms. "Any story. I don't care what."

"I can't tell you a story," Ed says. "I don't know any stories when you're doing this."

"I'll stop," Susan says. She stops.

Ed says, "Don't stop. Okay." He puts his hands around her waist and moves her, as if he's stirring the Susan beer.

He says, "Once upon a time." He's speaking very fast. They're running out of time.

Once, while they were making love, Andrew came into the bedroom. He didn't even knock. He didn't seem to be embarrassed at all. Ed doesn't want to be fucking Susan when the aliens show up. On the other hand, Ed wants to be fucking Susan forever. He doesn't want to stop, not for Andrew, or the aliens, or even for the end of the world.

Ed says, "There was a man and a woman and they fell in love. They were both nice people. They made a good couple. Everyone liked them. This story is about the woman."

This story is about a woman who is in love with somebody who invents a time machine. He's planning to go so far into the future that he'll end up right back at the very beginning. He asks her to come along, but she doesn't want to go. What's back at the beginning of the world? Little blobs of life swimming around in a big blob? Adam and Eve in the Garden of Eden? She doesn't want to play Adam and Eve; she has other things to do. She works for a research company. She calls people on the telephone and asks them all sorts of questions. Back at the beginning, there aren't going to be phones. She doesn't like the sound of it. So her husband says, Fine, then here's what we'll do. I'll build you another machine, and if you ever decide that you miss me, or you're tired and you can't go on, climb inside this machine—this box right here—and push this button and go to sleep. And you'll sleep all the way forwards and backwards to me, where I'm waiting for you. I'll keep on waiting for you. I love you. And so they make love and they make love a few more times and then he climbs into his time machine and whoosh, he's gone like that. So fast, it's hard to believe that he was ever there at all. Meanwhile she lives her life forward, slow, the way he didn't want to. She gets married again and makes love some more and has kids and they have kids and when she's an old woman, she's finally ready: she climbs into the dusty box down in the secret room under the orchard and she pushes the button and falls asleep. And she sleeps all the way back, just like Sleeping Beauty, down in the orchard for years and years, which fly by like seconds, she goes flying back, past the men sitting around the green felt table, now you can see them and now they're gone again, and all the peacocks are screaming, and the Satanist drives up to the house and unloads the truckload of furniture, he unpaints the pentagrams, soon the old shy man will unbuild his house, carry his secret away on his back, and the apples are back on the orchard trees again, and then the trees are all blooming, and now the woman is getting younger, just a little, the lines around her mouth are smoothing out. She dreams that someone has come down into that underground room and is looking down at her in her time machine. He stands there for a long time. She can't open her eyes, her eyelids are so heavy, she doesn't want to wake up just yet. She dreams she's on a train going down the tracks backwards and behind the train, someone is picking up the beams and the nails and the girders to put in a box and then they'll put the box away. The trees are whizzing past, getting smaller and smaller and then they're all gone too. Now she's a kid again, now she's a baby, now she's much smaller and then she's even smaller than that. She gets her gills back. She doesn't want to wake up just yet, she wants to get right back to the very beginning where it's all new and clean and everything is still and green and flat and sleepy and everybody has crawled back into the sea and they're waiting for her to get back there too and then the party can start. She goes backwards and backwards and backwards and backwards and backwards and backwards and backwards and backwards and backwards and backwards and backwards—

The cheerleader says to the Devil, "We're out of time. We're holding things up. Don't you hear them banging on the door?"

The Devil says, "You didn't finish the story."

The cheerleader says, "And you never let me touch your tail. Besides, there isn't any ending. I could make up something, but it wouldn't ever satisfy you. You said that yourself! You're never satisfied. And I have to get on with my life. My parents are going to be home soon."

She stands up and slips out of the closet and slams the door shut again, so fast the Devil can hardly believe it. A key turns in a lock.

The Devil tries the doorknob, and someone standing outside the closet giggles.

"Shush," says the cheerleader. "Be quiet."

"What's going on?" the Devil says. "Open the door and let me out—this isn't funny."

"Okay, I'll let you out," the cheerleader says. "Eventually. Not just yet. You have to give me something first."

"You want me to give you something?" the Devil says. "Okay, what?" He rattles the knob, testing.

"I want a happy beginning," the cheerleader says. "I want my friends to be happy too. I want to get along with my parents. I want a happy childhood. I want things to get better. I want them to keep getting better. I want you to be nice to me. I want to be famous, I don't know, maybe I could be a child actor, or win state-level spelling bees, or even just cheer for winning teams. I want world peace. Second chances. When I'm winning at poker, I don't want to have to put all that money back in the pot, I don't want to have to put my good cards back on top of the deck, one by one by—

Starlight says, "Sorry about that. My voice is getting scratchy. It's late. You should call back tomorrow night."

Ed says, "When can I call you?"

Stan and Andrew were friends. Good friends. It was like they were the same species. Ed hadn't seen Stan for a while, not for a long while, but Stan stopped him, on the way down to the basement. This was earlier. Stan grabbed his arm and said, "I miss him. I keep thinking, if I'd gotten there sooner. If I'd said something. He liked you a lot, you know, he was sorry about what happened to your car—"

Stan stops talking and just stands there looking at Ed. He looks like he's about to cry.

"It's not your fault," Ed said, but then he wondered why he'd said it. Whose fault was it?

α

Susan says, "You've got to stop calling me, Ed. Okay? It's three in the morning. I was asleep, Ed, I was having the best dream. You're always waking me up in the middle of things. Please just stop, okay?"

Ed doesn't say anything. He could stay there all night and just listen to Susan talk.

What she's saying now is, "But that's never going to happen, and you know it. Something bad happened, and it wasn't anyone's fault, but we're just never going to get past it. It killed us. We can't even talk about it."

Ed says, "I love you."

Susan says, "I love you, but it's not about love, Ed, it's about timing. It's too late, and it's always going to be too late. Maybe if we could go back and do everything differently—and I think about that all the time—but we can't. We don't know anybody with a time machine. How about this, Ed—maybe you and your poker buddies can build one down in Pete's basement. All those stupid games, Ed! Why can't you build a time machine instead? Call me back when you've figured out how we can work this out, because I'm really stuck. Or don't call me back. Good-bye, Ed. Go get some sleep. I'm hanging up the phone now."

Susan hangs up the phone.

Ed imagines her, going down to the kitchen to microwave a glass of milk. She'll sit in the kitchen and drink her milk and wait for him to call her back. He lies in bed, up in the orchard house. He's got both bedroom doors open, and a night breeze comes in through that door that doesn't go anywhere. He wishes he could get Susan to come see that door. The breeze smells like apples, which is what time must smell like, Ed thinks.

There's an alarm clock on the floor beside his bed. The hands and numbers glow green in the dark, and he'll wait five minutes and then he'll call Susan. Five minutes. Then he'll call her back. The hands aren't moving, but he can wait.

Publication History

These stories were previously published as follows:

The Faery Handbag, *The Faery Reel*, 2004
The Hortlak, *The Dark*, 2003
The Cannon, *Say . . . What Time is It?*, 2003
Stone Animals, *Conjunctions 43*, 2004
Catskin, *McSweeney's Mammoth Treasury of Thrilling Tales*, 2003
Lull, *Conjunctions 39*, 2002

Acknowledgements

First, thanks to my family: Annabel Jones Link, Bill and Linda, Holly, Ben, and Edwin and Lou Jones. Thanks to my agent, Renée Zuckerbrot, for her care and patience. Thanks also to Richard Butner, Barb Gilly, Gwenda Bond, Christopher Rowe, John Kessel, the Sycamore Hill Workshop, Jonathan Lethem, Jeffrey Ford, Maureen F. McHugh, Walter Jon Williams, the workshop at Rio Hondo, Sarah Smith and CSFW, Kim Stanley Robinson, Sean Stewart, China Miéville, Jim Cambias and Diane Kelly, Jedediah Berry, Vincent McCaffrey and Thais Coburn, Yoshio Kobayashi, Jack Cheng and Julie Crosson, Ada Vassilovski and Peter Cramer, Fleur Penman, Julide Aker and Andrew Cohen, Batu Erman for the loan of his name; *Lonely Planet Turkish Phrasebook* for help with the phrases; Hugh Fowler, Jim Baker, Charles Brown, Veronica Schanoes, Eileen Gunn and John Berry, Eliani Torres, Holly Black, Joshua Lewis, Cassandra Claire, Haymarket and JavaNet. Thanks to Paul Ingram, Micha Hershman, and Deb Tomaselli, and all the booksellers for their enthusiasm and support for *Stranger Things Happen*. Thanks to The Magnetic Fields and Future Bible Heroes—Claudia Gonson, Chris Ewen, Stephin Merritt—for letting me open for them; thanks to editors Ellen Datlow, Terri Windling, Sharyn November, Jim Frenkel, Peter Straub, Michael Chabon, Bradford Morrow, Ted Thompson. Thanks to my students at the Clarion workshops, and the writers of the Online Writing Workshop. Thanks to: Christopher Barzak for sending me CDs from Japan; Karen Joy Fowler for the wedding chapel; William Smith for the zombie movies; Shelley Jackson for lots of stuff; Gavin J. Grant for everything.